The Stuff of Heroes

Chris Oswald

NEWMORE PUBLISHING

First edition published in 2018 by Newmore Publishing.

ISBN 978-1-9997868-4-7

Cover design by Book Beaver.

Book design and layout by Heddon Publishing.

Chris Oswald has lived in America, Scotland and England and is now living in Dorset with his wife, Suzanne, and six children. For many years he was in international business but now has a little more time to follow his love of writing. His books have been described as dystopian but they are more about individual choice, human frailty and how our history influences the decisions we make, also about how quickly things can go so wrong.

For Jack,
without whom there would be no books by me.

The Stuff of Heroes

The Party

The footman checked his appearance in the full-length mirror then turned the door handle, the tray wobbling slightly so that a little of the schnapps – just a drop or two – escaped and spread across the shiny surface.

If he had not been wearing his tight white gloves, he would have been tempted to scoop up the spilled alcohol and lick his fingers, sending the warmth down into his shallow belly. Hunger gnawed at him. Frau Nullgeben liked her servants trim and lithe as well as smart.

And what Frau Nullgeben wanted, she generally received.

Thomas, the footman, had to impress today; another reason not to go for the beads of schnapps that glided over the shiny silver tray, each orb reflecting the beautifully decorated room and the beautifully decorated inhabitants. Instead, noticing Bunce, the butler, standing by the huge bay window nearest him and looking directly at him, expecting him to fail, he spun the tray with a flourish and presented the glasses to the various guests. There were no more spills.

Everybody at the party drank schnapps. Schnapps and coffee, not gin and tea. Downstairs, much later, duties complete and guests gone, it would be gin and tea for them, making him want the schnapps all the more.

"Coarse gin is cheap," he had once heard Herr Nullgeben state. "It is a fitting drink for the *unterschichts*."

Thomas was an *unterschicht*, although Thomas was not his real name. It was his *Benannten Namen*, or BN. Most *schichts* had BNs if they worked in domestic service. His real name was Trevor Case, or Clever Case as his schoolteachers had christened him. He was unquestionably bright.

So bright that when he had left school last year they had sent him to the commander's home. So bright that the much duller butler felt threatened; did not like the intelligent new boy; sought to get rid of him.

But the head cook was on his side. That was a blessing. Head cooks by convention were always Mrs, although none were married. For their surname they were given a name of great historical significance. Mrs Britain, just like the other head cooks, had no first name. To everyone, friend or foe, commander's wife or boot boy, she was just Mrs Britain.

Just as Thomas had no surname, Mrs Britain had no forename.

"Domestics need only one name," Frau Carla Heidi Georgia Rhona Brammigen Nullgeben had explained on Thomas' arrival into the household ten long months ago. "More than one would be confusing."

"Thomas, stand at the back of the room and hold your tray steady!" The craggy butler spoke with venom like the shots of spit hissing between his gappy teeth.

"Yes, Mr Bunce," Thomas whispered, turning and positioning himself in the correct spot.

His view from the side of the room was perfect. He could see all the guests in the ballroom. It was a sight for sore eyes.

The most striking was Frau Nullgeben. She always was. Tonight she was dressed in blue silk, the colour of a late July sky just before the sunset sent rays of invading pinks and oranges across the dome that hemmed them in. The power of the sun is seen in the type of blue it creates: deep, consistent and rich, just the faintest hint of the explosion of colour to come seen in her jewellery, her blonde hair, her make-up.

The dress rustled as she moved, laughing, eyes dancing as her body would later, jewels glistening like extra-large drops of schnapps, catching colours as she moved around the room. Thomas followed her with his eyes, as did many of the guests. She joked frequently, leaning on men's arms, holding court briefly like a beautiful summer insect, before moving on to the next group. They all turned to see her as she approached, dropping their previous conversations to hang on her words. Thomas felt sorry for one young man, dressed in the *ReichsUberseeDiplomatischerDienst* dress uniform of navy blue, the letters RUDD in gold thread on his epaulettes. The man, quite junior, was approaching the climax of his prepared story when his audience deserted him. Unsure whether to continue, he briefly raised his voice, then faltered, progressing to an embarrassed silence.

"Herr von Scholtz," Thomas heard Frau Nullgeben say in her aristocratic tones, "you must forgive me but I have a message from your aunt, the Countess. She asks me to tell you to be sure to keep away from the gambling tables."

"Madam, I never gamble. It is…" His face reddened rapidly; perhaps his face was the setting sun aiming to send its shafts across the deep blue sky of Carla Nullgeben's dress. But we never heard what von Scholtz thought of gambling for Frau Nullgeben, the hostess of this glorious party, had moved on under cover of the false laughter her comments invoked.

The commander, Herr Werner Nullgeben, moved in opposing circles. To Thomas it was like a set piece dance where partners step away and then come back around to each other from different angles. He was resplendent in his RUDD uniform, wearing the boots that Thomas had polished that very morning; high boots that had to be heaved into place, clacking solidly on the hardwood floor. Thomas watched him make conversation. He was far more earnest, much less at ease, than his wife; pumping hands as he spoke, left hand on his listener's elbow. He tended to speak to one person at a time and for much longer than his wife did, hence his circles were slower and wider. Thomas imagined his wife as his dance partner, telling him in her loud, confident voice to step on it and keep to the routine.

"Thomas, this way, quickly. Put your tray on the sideboard." Bunce directed him to the large double doors which led from the dining room to the ballroom. He took one side, motioning impatiently for Thomas to take the other. "When they knock, open the door at the same speed as me. Can you do that, Thomas?"

"Yes, Mr Bunce." There was no point in taking offence at the condescension. After eighteen years of life, the last ten months in this establishment, he was used to it, knew how to cope with it, but it burned all the same. "Who's coming through the door?" he asked, but Bunce did not answer. Thomas had not expected to be told.

The knock was light; a child's hand, he deduced. Bunce made no movement, he clearly had not heard.

"Mr Bunce, the door," he whispered, moving to take hold of the door handle.

"Be quiet, keep still," the butler spoke back, a little too loudly.

Then came the voice, through the door. It was a young female, speaking in English in order to be understood by the servants.

"Will some oaf open the door before our arms drop off!"

Incredibly, to Thomas, there was still no movement from the old butler.

"Mr Bunce, they are calling now."

"Thomas, shut up before I have you disciplined." Again, too loud for discretion.

"You are the fellow who will be disciplined," came the aristocratic voice from the other side. "Now open the stupid door."

This time Bunce did hear, sprang to the door, bumped into the much larger Thomas, who was also moving inwards. He fell back onto the floor with a thump that was heard across the now hushed room. Thomas, acting quickly, opened both doors, the right jamming against Bunce's legs. Thomas hauled the butler up and freed the door, pushing it fully open with his foot, then dragged Bunce out of the way to a pantry just off the ballroom.

Thus Thomas missed the first sight of Georgia and Edmund carrying the huge birthday cake.

By the time he returned, they had placed the cake on a table, sweeping off the plates and cutlery to make room. Edmund was shaking his arms, as if to free them of cramp.

"You oaf!" Georgia spat at Thomas. "Did you not hear us through the door?"

"Yes Fraulein, but..." but Georgia was not listening, had gone to place herself in front of the commander.

"Happy Birthday, Father." She curtsied, while Edmund bowed. Then the two children led the guests in *Zum Geburtstag viel Glück*. Both had excellent singing voices, clear and in tune.

Edmund's voice was not yet broken but held a hint of what was to come, while Georgia's voice took Thomas to another world.

She looked delightful too, in a mid-blue ball gown, like a lighter version of her mother's, only more modest with a high neckline and full sleeves. It set her pale skin off beautifully, like a postcard of the sea with tropical beaches all around. Her long blonde hair was tied in two tresses then wound in a delicate pattern around her head, displaying a long, slender neck that Thomas' eyes kept coming back to. She seemed shimmering to Thomas, who was more used to seeing her in everyday clothes. The only problem was her nose, inherited from her father's side, but watered down from his eagle beak; it nevertheless was a little too large, making her look a little too like a bird of prey. If one could overlook the nose, concentrate instead on the large, blue eyes, the exact same colour as her dress, then she would be declared a beauty.

That was Thomas' opinion: not quite as beautiful as her mother, but almost there.

Then it was champagne time. Thomas reflected that it was not all schnapps and coffee; often champagne was served on special occasions. He had once drained a recently discarded bottle, loving the bubbles and the instant lift.

"Don't get a taste for that, kiddo," Mrs Britain had caught him with the bottle in full tilt. "You know a bottle will set you back a month's wages." She had tweaked his cheek with her long fingers, liking the honest intelligence that was so evident. He had replied, "Never will, Mrs Britain," but the grin gave him away.

Now he took tray after tray of bubbling glasses and walked, as trained, sedately around the room.

"You forgot me, oaf." Thomas turned to see Georgia. She seemed to be smiling, or amused; one could never tell with Georgia.

"Forgive me, Fraulein, can I offer you a glass or two of the finest champagne?" Thomas was a risk-taker.

"Stand over there." She pointed to the other side of her. When he did as instructed, she took a glass in either hand and gulped them down quickly, taking two more as replacements.

Thomas looked around to see whether anyone had noticed and saw that he had been perfectly positioned to block sight of her by her parents, standing together by the cake.

"Georgia, come over here and meet the new American ambassador, just arrived this morning."

"Dratted Americans! Got to go, oaf." She hiccupped and tried to appear sober as she crossed the room to be with her parents, curtseying a little unsteadily to the ambassador.

Thomas watched her go then realised his tray was empty. She had cleaned him out of champagne.

Bunce made it back towards the end of the evening, anxious to assert his authority and hedge against any criticism. He sent Thomas downstairs with threats of dismissal. But for Thomas it worked out well for Mrs Britain was alone in the kitchen and gave Thomas a left-over partridge with heaps of potato stew, followed by a huge slice of birthday cake, sent down for the senior staff.

"No one will know," she said, tracing her fingers through his short dark hair.

"You spoil me," he replied.

"You're special," she said, like a mother would.

"What do you mean?"

"You'll see." Then she paused, pressed her fingers on his lips, leant over and kissed him on the forehead. "Doubly special. Now, clean yourself up before Mr Bunce gets down here. We have enough trouble from him as it is!"

"Bunce has to go, dearest." Carla was sitting at the breakfast table, a delicate piece of toast and a half-grapefruit in contrast to the cold sausage and scrambled eggs piled on her husband's plate.

"He tells me it was Thomas who…"

"Rubbish, Werner, I saw it all. The idiot was asleep at his station, or else he is deaf as a doorpost! I want a new butler, darling."

"Well, Thomas is far too young."

"Good God, I was not thinking of Thomas. He can't be much

more than seventeen, Georgia's age. No, I want the best. We are the first family of this sector. We deserve the best. Bunce can be pensioned off. He once told me he has an unmarried sister in Eastbourne. Let him go there with, say, fifty marks a month. That is adequate for someone of his station; generous, in fact."

"OK, darling. We will do this. Now I have to be away for a few days."

"I have your permission to retire Bunce and get a new butler?" She knew she did not need his permission but her tactics were impeccable.

"You have my permission. I'll get Freda to do the forms for the pension."

The first part was done immediately after Werner left. Bunce was summoned, thanked, and told to pack his bags almost before the commander's staff car was down the long drive.

"I am pleased to inform you that with your years of duty you qualify for a pension of forty marks a month."

"Forty marks, Madam? I was expecting a bit more."

"I believe it is sufficient. You will be living with your sister and will not need much for a comfortable life."

"Thank you, Madam." There was no point in arguing. Forty was not so bad if he led a quiet life. Ale was twenty pennies a litre; a quarter-kilo of pipe tobacco just under a mark. He would have to give his sister fifteen marks a month. Maybe he could suggest twelve? "Would you cover my train fare to Eastbourne, Madam?" Train fares were expensive.

"I will do that, now run along and pack and let me make plans for the future."

"Yes, Madam. Can I just say it has been a pleas..."

"Run along, Bunce."

Thomas heard first, bumping into Bunce on the back stairs leading down to the kitchen.

"Mr Bunce, are you alright?" The man was holding back tears; not succeeding; all hostility vanished in his greater distress.

Thomas disregarded his duties and turned to the task in hand. Knowing he could do nothing to reverse Frau

Nullgeben's decision, he did the next best thing he could think of, requiring the young footman to visit every member of staff, every estate worker he could find, and as quickly as possible.

It was a doubly tearful Mr Bunce who said goodbye to his staff in the kitchen ninety minutes later, two suitcases his total possessions. One set of tears for the position he had lost; the responsibility and the power. The other was for the kindness, led by the boy he had despised more than any in the household.

"Mr Bunce, we organised a collection for you." Thomas should have said 'I organised', for he had been both instigator and functionary. "It is not much but we had so little time." He handed over an egg box stuffed with notes and some change.

"Thank you, Thomas, it is very kind of you all. I shall miss you all." Said and meant.

Later, on the train, Mr Bunce opened the egg box and counted the money, amazed at the generosity when he got past the hundred-mark barrier and still had some notes and all the coins to count. "Goodness!" he said to himself a few minutes later. "One hundred and ninety-six marks and forty pennies." He resolved at that moment to pay his sister twenty marks a month, half his pension, and to cut down on his tobacco to make ends meet. He would survive. And he was looking forward to seeing his sister again.

Thomas was not the only one to become active on hearing of Mr Bunce's departure. Mrs Britain requested an interview with Frau Nullgeben that same morning and was granted one for after lunch. She closed the drawing-room door completely and was in there for forty minutes, smiling broadly on coming out.

"I'll know more at teatime," she said, when the staff clamoured to hear. But it was settled already. She just enjoyed the suspense.

Tea was the second main meal of the day, usually vegetable soup and white bread with butter. Each member of staff also had two biscuits and a piece of fruit. They could choose from the selection offered. There was as much tea as you could drink and a glass of gin for each staff member over the age of fourteen. Trading was forbidden; otherwise, some of the girls would have given their biscuits for another piece of fruit or a glass of gin. But nobody had thought to ban gifts and Mrs Britain regularly gave both her biscuits and her gin allowance to the younger ones, saying, "They need it more than I." She was always fair in her giving, even though Thomas was clearly dear to her, thus Thomas knew that every seventh day he would get a biscuit and, once a fortnight, the gin.

When everyone was settled, the head place vacant, Mrs Britain stood up. She was so unlike a cook: stick-thin and tall, her grey-brown hair in a ponytail and glasses giving her an administrative rather than domestic air, compounded by the fact she only wore her overalls when actually cooking. She was poised, with an elegance that spoke of upstairs rather than the kitchens. Yet she was the head cook and the best of her kind.

"Folks, as you know, Mr Bunce has been retired with immediate effect and he left this morning. He is going to his sister's in Eastbourne and has given his address to me, if anyone cares to write to him." She knew that was unlikely. Postage was expensive and he had not been particularly loved. But you never knew. There were a few kind souls in their team. She looked at Thomas and felt a wave of affection. "Now, I have had discussions with Frau Nullgeben this morning and the long and short of it is that we have settled on a new butler. Frau Nullgeben telephoned during our discussions and made all the arrangements. He will be starting on Monday."

"Mrs Britain, how come he is available at such short notice?" Millie asked. She was the maid to Frau Nullgeben; a post nobody envied.

"That's a good question, Millie. The reason he is available is that he has just finished working for another establishment and, because that termination was quite unexpected, he has not yet found a new position. Not until this morning, that is. We were very lucky to get him."

Now she paused for effect, looking over her glasses at her "family". There were twenty-seven, including both chauffeurs and the absent butler; twenty-six presently around the table. Several people called out "Who is he?" and "What is his name?" She knew she would need to give up her secret now.

"Folks, our new butler as of Monday morning is none other than Mr Fairway."

"But he is at the American embassy!"

"*The* Mr Fairway, coming to us?"

"How is this possible?"

Mrs Britain explained that the old American ambassador had retired due to ill health and the new ambassador, just arrived and at the party last night, had brought his own staff with him.

"As you know, Mr Fairway is renowned across the world for the skills of his trade. I know we are the first household of this sector but I think it nevertheless a remarkable coup to secure his services in this house."

Mrs Britain had another reason to be delighted but that, like her fondness for Thomas, had to be kept under wraps for the present.

All things in their own time. She was playing the long game.

In a Town Nearby

The colours did not match but nobody cared. Green-and-brown walls, grey concrete floors and bright orange suits; it made an out-of-tune symphony; a harsh discord on the eyes.

But nobody cared, least of all Mark Smith.

Mark cared only about survival.

He had an avenue of sight onto the real world. This levelled him, kept the emotions under control.

It was not easy. It involved contortions most thirty-plus adults would not consider sensible. He had found it by accident, this tiny excerpt of the outside come in.

The robin visited every day, just after the cell door slammed following recreation; that grim daily walk around the brick-and-dirt enclosure. Fifty-foot walls telescoped the sun so they could see it dancing on the upper levels but could feel none of it. Mark used his recreation wisely, stretching and pumping muscles, making no sudden actions to excite the guards; everything in a measured way. Sometimes he felt like talking them through it. "In a moment I am going to stretch my arms up above my head and then circle them slowly down, finally squatting on my haunches to exercise my calves and thighs. OK, I am about to start so no panic, especially you ones there with the machine guns trained down fifty feet, passing over us and lining us up, one by one."

Recreation was also trading time. It was the only hour they could guarantee to be together. Biff governed all trading, setting the prices, arbitrating in disputes, and exacting a surprisingly small tax as compensation. One cigarette in twenty was his typical rate. Once, early on, Biff had walked four circuits of the yard with Mark, explaining how it worked as Mark tried to match the gait of this giant of a man.

"I don't push it; no, man. I am the glue that keeps this whole place working. You see, man? I take a little tiny bit each time."

"You're not greedy, then?" Mark asked but this caused offence.

"Of course I'm greedy, you big white dumbo. I'm clever and

I'm greedy. I reckon it's better to get a tiny bit often so as to encourage the trade, man." As he spoke, the teeth he still had shone against his jet-black face. "Stick by me, Smith. I like the way you have with the guys."

"I'll stick by you, Biff," Mark had said but he'd felt at the time he had no choice. Biff was the big man in their enclosure. The big man was bigger than the screws; bigger than the warden, for he made the rules.

But Mark soon came to like Biff and admire his quick and rough justice. Because there were no secrets inside, it quickly became known that Mark was a near-genius. He became Biff's encyclopaedia and, after a year or two, was consulted in matters of justice, raising his status and underwriting his safety.

But Mark had little interest in exchange. His parents sent chocolate, toothpaste, writing-paper and stamps; all he needed. Occasionally, he traded chocolate for cigarettes, just to partake, not to be above it, but always gave the cigarettes to another prisoner, usually whoever seemed to have least. He discussed with himself that this was a type of trade, gaining an intangible in return for the cigarettes that were of no use to him.

The hour went too quickly; often causing Mark to wonder why one hour out of twenty-four would shoot by when all the others dragged. Was not time supposed to be above this world, an even measure of the passing of the present into the past? And as that happened, was not the future slotting into the queue to become the present and then, inevitably, shuffle on into the past with a never-changing tempo? Was that not the very nature of prison? That routine could only be established if time behaved with perfect exactitude? But here they had a rogue hour that set its expiry by its own standards, rushing headlong towards its end as if it had no regard for its creator or its higher duty.

The whistle blew, the guards thinking they, not Biff, were in charge, shouted the same orders every day. And the ninety-six prisoners of Biff's Brigade lined up and tramped back to where the doors slammed. Always slamming. Leaving Mark and the other ninety-five prisoners quite alone in their one-man cells.

Except that Mark had found his robin. It came every day between ten and a quarter past, just after the cell door slammed.

He had heard it first, chirping on the cell's high window ledge. To see it, he had to balance his stool on his toilet and climb the stack. By leaning over, sometimes too far and falling, he could see the brown, and then the bright patch of red breast.

It filled his heart with intense joy. Here was not only sound from Heaven, but natural colours that matched so incredibly beautifully.

Mark worked out who else would be able to see the robin from their cells and who could hear it too and passed the information on. It caused a great stir, this splash of colour and song. Soon, they were encouraging it with tiny particles of precious bread.

Around that time, Mark lost his real name and everyone, including Biff, calling him by his new nickname of Robin Redbreast. It further guaranteed his safety, giving almost cult status, fellow prisoners not wanting to risk losing the robin by hurting the man who had brought it to them.

In this way, Mark got to his sixth anniversary without a scratch or a broken bone; a remarkable achievement.

Recreation was not the only time they left their cells, at least for those with some hope. Three times a week, Mark and a handful of others were taken down several corridors and flights of metal stairs, into a basement, deep below ground.

This was clearly not like recreation. No free talking was allowed; just listening and answering to check understanding. There were no distractions, six low stools in a square room with whitewashed brick walls and a smooth grey concrete floor. At the front was a raised concrete podium for the lecturer so he could look down on them from a height.

The first time Mark was taken down there, he sat next to a hard-looking man in his late forties, livid scars crisscrossing his face, neck and arms like tyre tracks at a crime scene. His nose looked very broken; in fact, it had been several times over the years, and never set properly. He knew the man to be Symes, but had never spoken to him or his gang in the enclosure. The man gave him a nod, then closed his eyes a moment. Mark assumed that was it as far as becoming acquainted was concerned but then, just as the lecturer heaved his bulk onto the platform and started in a monotone, Symes shifted sideways on his tiny stool, put his hand to his mouth, and whispered through a fake cough.

"Don't listen to a word. I want to know how many bricks there are in this room and you'll be in big trouble if you can't tell me the exact number by the time we're finished."

"What?" Mark whispered back, hand over mouth.

"Count the goddamn bricks!" Symes coughed louder the second time. "For your bleedin' sanity."

Mark counted the bricks and kept counting them every session he had. He counted them along, then up and down and diagonally. In subsequent sessions he made imaginary patterns like wallpaper and counted the patterns, allowing for half shapes at each edge. He counted the whole bricks. He counted the half bricks. He counted those that were chipped and those that were whole, discoloured, freshly painted. Then he estimated the proportion of the wall that was cement. If there had been a skirting board, he would have worked that area out, too. Moving on, he checked alignment of the row of stools. They were usually adjacent to the twelfth and thirteenth bricks from the back of the room, seldom varying.

Once, he noticed they were set right back at the ninth brick, looked around the room and saw a different orderly on duty. That made sense. Next session, they were back at the twelfth brick.

Symes opened up slowly during recreation periods. Much of the time, he walked with Mark in silence, but gradually his story came out. He was forty-eight years old and was, like Mark, in for an indeterminable period for activities against the state.

"But I was really active. I don't expect to be out any time soon, if at all," Symes said one morning after they had walked several times around the enclosure.

"I was not told my sentence," Mark replied.

"That's standard procedure for 'crimes against the state', exactly the same for me. They'll just summon you one day and you will be free on licence. I've been here the longest of the state crimmies, close to fifteen years now."

Mark remembered shuddering at that point. He had been inside for just over six months, wondering every day about release, but here was someone who had been fifteen years waiting, with no knowledge of whether he would be released tomorrow or never.

"Did you go to university?" Mark asked, after two more circuits and an estimated six minutes until the bell.

"Yes, I went to Durham before the occupation. Then I joined up, got de-mobbed when they moved in, and got the option to go into teaching. I have a Masters in physics but was teaching history – their version of history. The propaganda made me sick to the gills so I joined the resistance."

Symes had been taught the same brick-counting trick by an old-timer when he had first been assigned to rehabilitation.

Fourteen long years ago.

Fourteen years of withstanding rehabilitation. Of counting bricks every way they could be counted. But it had worked. And it worked for Mark, too.

They had taken Symes away in the autumn of Mark's third year. They did that sometimes, just moved people to prevent too-strong friendships. Mark knew he was unlikely to see him again. He was saddened because as Symes had opened up there had been so much they talked about – literature, politics, science, and what they would do if they ever got out.

Now Mark just had memories of their conversations. He returned time and time again to them in the long hours between recreation and rehabilitation classes, during cell time.

Into those memories early one morning, the cell buzzer rang, harsh, loud and persistent. It had rung only twice before in six years. He did not know what it was at first, panicked at the thought of fire or riot, then heard the duty guard's cold voice.

"Smith, XX1Z2495, stand by your bed, back to the door, arms out to the side, hands open."

He did so.

He dared not look around as the locks turned and the bolts slid back.

"Walk out backwards, slowly."

He did so, very slowly.

"Faster, you idiot."

He walked faster, dropped his arms to get through the door, then immediately, but slowly, raised them again.

He was an old-timer now. He knew the drill.

"Hands behind your back." He felt the handcuffs click into place.

"Walk to your right." Mark hesitated; normally, everything was to the left. He was rewarded with a kick and an oath, told to get a move on.

Through the door at the end of the corridor was a long room with people in it. They were prisoners like him. He counted eight of them against a long refectory table. His first thought was food. But then he saw they were stripping and the table contained piles of grey, black and white clothes.

"Come." A young guard spoke to Mark, smiling at him. "I won't bite. We need to sort out some clothes for you." The guard leant over the table, turned Mark sideways, and took off his handcuffs.

She was the first woman Mark had seen in six years.

"Don't stare," she laughed. "You're making me embarrassed."

"I'm sorry, it's just that…"

"I know. I am the first girl you've seen since … well, since when?"

"21st March 1959."

"Six years, give or take a day. Well, do I pass muster? For your first sighting, I mean?"

"You certainly do."

"Jolly good. My name is Linda, by the way, and you are Smith, but you must have a first name?"

"Mark." It was first names now. Mark glanced at the other prisoners getting changed. There was one guard to each prisoner but nobody else quite like Linda. Most were male, gruff as ever. There was no smiling, no cheeriness.

"Well, what have we got here?" She indicated the pile of clothes on the narrow table between them. "Let's see if we can't smarten you up a bit, Mark." Her accent was not from around here; more northern, but despite its strength Mark could not place it. But every word rang in his ears like bells, like the fresh spring day he evidently was going out in.

For Linda unfolded a new white shirt, a checked tie, underwear of good quality, although old-fashioned, then pulled a smart suit from the rail behind her.

These were not prison clothes. Far from it.

"We're dressing you up to the nines," she laughed. Everything seemed funny to her. "But you don't want to be late so get undressed quickly. I'll turn my back, I promise!"

And she did, although her disciplined training could not prevent her from taking a peep or two.

Mark felt subconscious in his suit and tie; even more so after a haircut and fitted into a pair of shoes that shone with polish and newness. They creaked when he walked, causing more laughter from Linda.

"Lord, they've bottled you up so long you're creaking and groaning like old machinery!"

"Why am I so much smarter than the others?" he asked, wishing he could spend the rest of the day with her. But also, perversely, fearing the separation from his fellow prisoners, the safety of the pack.

"Because you're going somewhere else. I'll tell you about it in the car," she whispered. "I'm not supposed to let you know until we get there."

She led him into the prison reception area, through the metal detectors and search stations, signing him out, then, after showing her pass, through the big automatic doors.

"This is our car." It was a Mercedes, long and black, with a government number plate and tinted glass. She drove and he sat in the front next to her, with no other guards, not restrained in any way.

"Can I wind down the window?"

"Of course you can, my dearie." But the late March sunshine, lacking warmth but holding promise of hot days to come, was too much for him. She noticed him squinting and handed over her sunglasses.

"They may be too small but will protect your eyes a bit. I should have thought about that."

But Mark had had enough.

"Why me? Why this sudden special treatment? Why the smart clothes when everyone else going on work release is in overalls? Where are you taking me?"

"Lord, such a lot of questions!" Her laugh was like someone in love. Then she got more serious. "Mark, you're highly educated. Your PhD was in bio-engineering."

"I didn't finish it. A little matter of a long prison sentence got in the way." They were driving out of the town into beautiful countryside, still largely bare trees but with that beaten winter feeling. Mark saw a robin when they slowed down at a junction. It sat on a branch, ignored the car, and flew away suddenly, as if called to another job; perhaps to an appointment with a high-up window ledge on a grim cell block in town.

"I know, but you got five A star-grade A-levels at the age of fifteen and a double first from Cambridge when only eighteen. You know your science, but also one A-level was History; another, Philosophy. You're a linguist and a natural artist. You have a lot of all-round talent."

"Not used it much over the last six years."

"Well, that is about to change. You have heard of the Nullgebens?" Mark had because of rehabilitation classes but because he had determinedly not listened, he could not place them.

"Yes and no."

"He is the sector commander. The most senior official in what used to be our country." The last five words of Linda's sentence stayed with Mark long after the day's activities were concluded: *Used to be our country.* Did that imply sympathy for the resistance or was it just careless language? Linda Burton was a prison official. Surely she could not be a sympathiser?

"I still don't know what I am doing."

They want you to tutor the Nullgeben brat." Again, the lack of respect registered with Mark. "I mean the older one, the girl. They're hoping to get her into the *Statenthrump* next year and she needs to do the best she can for the entry exam next month. They've taken her out of school and want you to teach her what she needs to know."

"Talk about pressure," Mark said. "I don't think I can do this." For half a second, the familiarity of his cell welcomed him back. But he fought it off, closed the door behind him.

"Well, it's not as if you had anything else to do," Linda joked then added, "Seriously, if you do this and she gets in to the academy you'll get your freedom, I'm sure of it. But if you refuse, or she fails to get in, you can count on spending the rest of your life inside."

"The beauty of the indeterminable sentence, such flexibility."

"Wow, so you have got a sense of humour after all!" Linda replied, looking over to her passenger with a grin. The car swerved to the right as a result and rose onto the verge. There was a viscous noise of metal scraping along something hard. He imagined sparks flying.

"Shit, I'll be in trouble if the car is damaged." After she had straightened up and driven quietly for three minutes she added, "I really don't need to bring any attention to myself right now."

Who, he wondered, was she?

But there was no time to consider, for Linda turned the car left through two large pillars, gates opening when she pressed a device hooked onto the sun visor, then up a long, straight drive with cameras on poles like sentries along the way.

"The back way," she explained, just as they came out to a semi-courtyard with numerous doors leading off three sides and people bustling about, clearly all with tasks to do. It reminded Mark of the model of a medieval manor and village his class had made out of egg boxes, papier-mâché, and other assorted articles. His responsibility had been the stables. He had made them out of cereal packets, cutting up the inner bag to represent straw.

He could see the commander's stable yard now, beyond the oak trees that screened the kitchen yard from the rest of the grounds. Their model had not included trees acting as screens. It had been open, almost classless, in a homely way, despite there being a rigid social structure 800 years ago. Perhaps that was the benefit of youth? You created as you saw in a guileless way.

"Let's get you straightened out," Linda said, her cheeky grin returning. She leant across to Mark, straightening his tie, using her fingers to comb his hair. "That's better. It's important to make a good impression." She smiled again, her eyes matching her mouth: warm and generous. They got out of the car.

"That's my first time in a car for six years," he told her as she bent down to inspect the damage along the rear doorsill. "Here, let me look at that." He rubbed at it then pushed a little dirt where the undercoat was showing through. "I think that will do it."

"Thanks, Mark." As she spoke she placed her right hand lightly on his sleeve. "I'm going to be taking you every day so I'm sure we're going to be great friends."

"What the bloody hell are you doing down there?" The voice sounded like one of the machine guns looking down on the enclosure. Linda straightened up, blushed crimson-red.

"I'm Linda Burton, bringing Mark Smith, the new tutor. This is Mr Smith." She turned to Mark, moving her hands like a sales lady introducing the latest article.

"You're English?" the machine gun said in reply. "But you work in the prison?"

"Yes and yes! They've started taking English people now. It's a good job. Who are you?"

"My name is Harry Bootle. I'm Head of Security. I thought prison work was a reserved occupation." Bootle sounded half-way between suspicious and interested but his plain, block-type face gave nothing away. Mark noticed a dullness in his eyes. He had seen this everywhere in prison, expected that he himself had developed the same placidity after six years. But did not expect it in the world outside.

"No, Mr Bootle, it's all changed as of last year. They couldn't get enough manpower as things were. I started at the prison in September and finished my training in December. I've been on general duties for three months now. So, if you get bored here, you can always join me at the prison!"

"Follow me." He turned back towards the kitchen door, her joke either unappreciated or missed altogether. Linda gave a shrug behind his back, whispered something to Mark. He could not catch it but expected it was a joke about how chatty Mr Bootle was. Linda then made a point of stepping in Bootle's exact footsteps.

"What are you doing?" he turned to see her larking about.

"Just following you, Mr Bootle, doing what you told me to do."

"I'll take you to Frau Nullgeben," he said, again lifeless, dull, perfunctory. "She'll want to meet you."

"Take me alone first," Linda replied, showing another side to her. "I'll explain and then introduce Mr Smith."

"You mean she doesn't know?" It was an incomplete question but both Linda and Mark knew exactly what the big security man meant.

"The directive came down for the best tutor. It didn't say no crims, just the best tutor."

"I see. Thomas, look after Smith while I go and see Frau Nullgeben. See he gets a cup of tea and a piece of bread. He looks half starving."

"Yes, Mr Bootle. Mr Smith, please come this way."

An hour and a half later, Mark was summoned to the drawing room, led there by Thomas.

"Enter." Thomas opened the door.

"Smith, is it?" She barely gave him a glance. "This is most unusual. I would never expect to employ a felon; particularly one that has been convicted of crimes against the state. However, I understand you have a certain aptitude and that you are willing to dedicate your time to my daughter by way of partial recompense for your terrible crimes."

"Yes, Frau…"

"Don't talk unless you are asked a direct question. You are to be here for 7.30 each morning, Monday to Saturday. You will leave at 7.30 in the evening when we dine. You will do any marking or preparation outside these hours. Burton has a letter from me to the prison authorities, requiring them to support you in your efforts. On Sunday we have assembly in the morning and you are required from 2pm to 7.30. Is that understood?"

"Yes, Frau Nullgeben."

"The examinations are four weeks away. You are required to succeed. Bootle will take you to Fraulein Nullgeben. You will receive my thanks when my daughter is accepted by the *Statenthrump*." He was dismissed. Bootle ushered him out and closed the drawing room door.

Frau Nullgeben sat back in her chair and looked out of the window. Spring was starting, another dreadful winter in this rain-soaked country behind her. She longed for the weather at home. When it was winter at home it was cold. When it was summer at home it was hot. In between it was in between, but reliably so. She mused a moment that the English character was from their weather: chop and change, switching back and forth, nobody ever knowing where they stood.

She hated this country. Once, when particularly angry at the start of their tour to this sector, she had made a list of what annoyed her. She had forgotten all about it but now she was in the same frame of mind. She crossed the room to her ornate desk and rummaged around. It was filed with correspondence from her mother. Why she had thought to place the list there, she did not know. Perhaps she had hoped to discuss it with her mother when she got a chance. She would have understood exactly, she reflected bitterly, only she had died nine months ago; the same terrorist attack that had crippled her father, the count. She opened it up and read it out loud, imagining for a moment that it was a petition to God, only there was no god. It was entitled *Meine Irritierenden Dinge* and consisted of four neat points in her large but elegant handwriting:

> 1. *We are in the English sector with a five-year tour.*

She skipped over the rest of that point, it being all about the weather, the oafish behaviour, the lack of society. She knew all this only too well. But they were well over half-way through the tour now, so the point lost a little impact with every passing day. She moved on.

2. *My husband is in the RUDD.*

This was very irritating. If she had married into an OD family, none of these foreign tours would have happened. The *Offentlicher Dienst* never sent their people abroad. They had no need to as they had a monopoly of good positions at home. She reflected that this complaint was an extension of the first point. But then she thought about the intense rivalry between the OD and the RUDD. They had hated each other with absolute passion, ever since RUDD came about in 1941 to administer the overseas territories. And the more senior your husband got, the greater the hatred.

Then she thought of the advice her mother had given her before she had married. "Carla, my dear, think carefully. If you marry into the RUDD, you will be always sent away to foreign places. All our friends, all the people we know, are of OD stock. We won't even be able to help your husband in his career." But she had been briefly in love and had gone ahead regardless.

Well, I've made my own bed. Now I just have to keep making the best of it. It took a lot of effort, she had discovered, to make a career in the RUDD.

3. *My husband is not an aristocrat.*

This may not have mattered. Some people could carry their common blood with a false bearing that disguised their origins. But not Werner Nullgeben. He fell into another distinct category, one that made her shudder to think of it, for he was a fawner. To see him pay particular attention to anyone of aristocratic origin was so unsettling, especially when they were minor nobility. And there was worse, for the Counts of Brammigen were an ancient family and sometimes she detected others painting her with the same brush they used for him. It was unbearable to think about so she moved on.

4. *My husband is unfaithful.*

She did not reflect that this was only number four on her list. It irked her still. It was not silly things like love or loyalty. It was what people would say about his infidelity behind her back.

If it had been casual affairs, I could have overlooked it. But it is that damn woman. He had kept one woman for almost ten years now. Carla had seen her once in the stalls at the opera while they were in a box high up. The striking abundance of red hair was offset by a shimmering green dress. Carla had to admit that the woman was exceedingly attractive. Through her opera glasses, she could see the classical face with a hint of cheekiness, an upturned nose and a number of pretty freckles. But most of all she looked warm; inviting; everything Carla was not.

She had confronted him. He had promised to give her up. She was not going to cheapen herself by asking whether he had kept his promise. Instead, she had sent faithful Bootle to discover the situation, declaring to Werner that Bootle had a sick aunt he had to care for. He had returned two weeks later with the address of the apartment paid for by Werner and a copy of the deeds, in that woman's name. She had raised hell, threatening divorce, exposure, ridicule, the end of his career. He had, this time, stopped seeing the woman, signed papers placed in the safe, swearing legally to this effect. It was enough for her to believe it. Werner would not risk his career for any woman. It was in the past now.

Or so she assumed, for no sensible person would go that far against the tide.

Only one thing still intensely annoyed her about the whole affair between her husband and the redhead Barbara Leyland.

The damn woman was an English.

"I don't need you, oaf."

"Your mother thinks otherwise," Mark replied, then thought more. "But if you don't need me I am happy to leave immediately. Goodbye, Fraulein."

"Wait, stay." Georgia rose from her chair, seemed a bit flustered. Was she scared of her mother? "I may as well interview you to see if you are suitable, although I highly doubt it."

Over the course of the next thirty minutes it was clear that Mark Smith had the knowledge and also a knack for imparting it to others. Complex issues that had been beyond her grasp were explained patiently several times, trying a slightly different angle each time until her understanding was firm.

As the interview turned to a standard physics lesson, covering the basics that had eluded her before, Linda sat and fidgeted in the corner. Finally, Mark turned around and suggested that she remove herself from the room.

"I think it would be for the best. We have a lot to cover and it is essential that the Fraulein is able to concentrate."

"I'm in charge, oaf, don't you tell anyone what to do. You're the broom that sweeps the dirt … I mean, the dirt that sweeps the…" She faltered, aware that she had the metaphor mixed up. Linda came to the rescue.

"Fraulein, Smith only meant to advise. Of course, it is your decision. Would you like me to leave in order to aid your concentration?"

"Get out, oaf, you are both oafs. Now, tell me again about acceleration and try and do it so it makes sense."

The morning wound on. They were on the top floor of the family mansion. Georgia was fuming to be installed in the old nursery, with a desk and bench seat attached like a young schoolgirl, further exacerbated by the blackboard and larger teacher's desk. Mark had seen her school reports and was appalled. Her teachers had clearly given up on her. As he talked, his eyes roamed over the subject reports, desperately wondering how to build a plan.

He had four weeks.

Four weeks that could earn him his freedom or condemn him to Life.

"What time do you go to bed?" he asked her suddenly. His mind was working on several planes at once. One of those planes was totally outside his body, looking down on him in the old nursery and urging him on.

"Don't be impertinent. How dare you ask me that?"

"Fraulein, I only meant that I need to set you homework each day and, rather than piling on an unmanageable amount, I wanted to find out how much time you have."

"You should have explained that, oaf-face. I go to bed at half past nine." This said in a much quieter voice, embarrassed at the early bedtime for a seventeen-year-old.

"That does not leave much time. I'll have to adjust my plan accordingly." *What plan?* he asked himself. He had been thrown into this four hours ago. He had no plan.

But he would get one.

And that plan would get him his freedom.

Underground and Overground

M ark fell straight into the trap. He just did not see it coming. It was Linda, with her easy-going, fun-loving ways, that got him.

And it happened without him even realising. Suddenly he was in with them.

Perhaps his excuse could be the six years without a social life; indeed, without sight of a woman, concentrated on survival. Perhaps it was the way she seemed so warm, so inviting.

She was flirting with him, but it was an easy flirting; nothing pretentious, just natural. It was how she was, why she was so good at it.

Linda had two half-hour periods a day with Mark alone while she drove him to and from the Nullgeben residence.

Day two continued the easy chat and banter. But from day three it moved on. It was inevitable that the conversations would go deeper; into backgrounds, family history. What had brought them to this point, why they were both driving along quiet Berkshire lanes at a quarter to seven in the morning and a quarter to eight in the evening.

Her story was believable because it was true.

"I am an orphan," she explained. "My parents were both killed when I was thirteen."

"I'm so sorry to hear that. Do you mind me asking how it happened?" They were gliding through the countryside on the morning of day four. When they passed the spot where she had risen up on the verge, it had become his habit now to make some reference to it. Usually it was something like: "There's your favourite spot, Linda," or, "Are you going to stick to the road this time?"

Linda's parents had died together during the Clampdown of 1959, the same grand exercise that had seen Mark put behind bars. It had been the commander before the Nullgebens and it had been vicious and intense.

"They were suspected of harbouring state enemies. They were taken away in a large lorry. The soldiers kicked off the bags of belongings the people tried to throw on there before climbing up. I was in the crowd. I remember one big brutish man saying that they wouldn't need luggage where they were going. I remember screaming for them but my neighbour held me back, refused to let me go to them. Then they saw me and blew kisses my way. I blew some back but they were wet with tears. The lorry trundled slowly down the high street like it was daring me to run and jump on. But my neighbour held me firmly and I couldn't follow. I never saw them again."

"Do you know what happened?" Mark was also working out the dates. If she had been thirteen at the time of the Clampdown, she was just nineteen now. So young to be alone. He thought briefly of his own timid parents who never broke the law but had always been there for him, whatever happened.

"I got a letter saying my status was changed to orphan. It didn't say they were dead, just that my status was altered. It gave me thirty days to declare in front of a JP the name of an adult who was prepared to take responsibility, otherwise I would be placed in the state orphanage until the age of eighteen."

"My god! Did you go to the orphanage?"

"No way, José!" Laughter was always an inch away with her. Yet she had a weighted pack of sorrow on her back. "My neighbour took me in. She was not well and she was old but she just scraped the adoption criteria. I think it was because they didn't want to take in more of us, with the orphanage already overflowing. But I lived with Mrs Bassington, used to call her Aunt Jessie, until the poor dear died last summer. That was when I applied to the prison service and joined in September."

"How do you feel about the authorities after what they did to your parents?" That was Mark's first big mistake and Linda recognised it.

"I hate them, Mark, I really hate them."

"But you're working for them."

"Still hate them." She sounded briefly like a little girl,

skipped back over adolescence to be a child again. "Hate them with all my guts."

She did not talk again that journey. Mark felt the silence greatly but did not want to break it.

But that evening when Mark was tired, still with an essay and a trial exam to go over once back in the prison, she spoke again. It was still serious, reflective, choosing words like a poet.

"Mark, tell me how you feel about the authorities."

"How do you imagine I feel?" It was a good answer. He was not ready to declare his hatred, his disgust, his fear. "They came for me in a nightclub. It was a raid but it was my first time in that place. I was persuaded to go by some undergraduates at Cambridge. I was so close to finishing my PhD. I haven't seen my parents since. They send me chocolate and toothpaste but I am not allowed visits."

"I know, I had to learn all the rules for my training." She stopped talking a moment, as if referencing something in her mind, then continued again. "Category XX prisoners are not permitted visits, phone calls, letters or access to the news or the outside world. They are not permitted legal representation as there is no appeal against treason. They are permitted one package a month from a relative, provided the total retail value is less than or equal to five marks. This privilege is to be revoked on first occurrence of contraband in the package. Revoked privileges cannot be reinstated for XX prisoners. Permitted package articles include... But I won't list them all!"

She smiled, frowned, stopped the car in a layby.

"Mark, you have not said it but I think it is safe to assume you hate the authorities at least as much as I do." When he did not answer, she continued. "It would be an enormous help to us 'haters of the authorities' if you were able to find out a little information here and there."

"What information?"

"Anything about the movements of the Nullgeben family or anything you hear that you think might be of interest. You can pass it on to me on our journeys, if you like."

"You better start the car or we'll be late back to prison."

He had not said yes but he had not said no either. Both of

them thought about nothing else for the remainder of the journey.

They were early the next morning. Mark was delivered to the nursery by Harry Bootle who, try as Mark did to make conversation, would do no more than the absolute necessary. It seemed to Mark that Bootle only used speech in order to carry out his duties: specifically, questioning potential suspects and issuing orders.

They arrived at 7.23am but before opening the door they heard a furious argument from inside the nursery. It was Georgia, shouting at someone; a young male, who answered back defensively.

"Not again," Harry Bootle groaned.

"Who's the other person?"

"Edmund Nullgeben, her younger brother. We better go away and come back in ten minutes."

"We'll be late."

"Better late with a mild blasting from the Fraulein than a tongue lashing for breaking in on their privacy. Come on, Smith." But Mark was not coming, instead listening to the argument through the door.

"They're arguing about a summer camp – *Jahrliches Sommerlager*." Mark said.

"You speak their language?" Bootle stopped his retreat and came back to Mark's side.

"Enough to understand. The Fraulein doesn't want to go and the other one is saying it is her duty to go. She says she is too old for camp, almost an adult."

There was a loud bang at that point and Bootle, forgetting his worries but not his duty, heaved the door open to see Edmund Nullgeben on the floor, holding the fingers of his left hand under his right armpit, howling in pain.

"What happened?" Bootle grabbed the Fraulein by both upper arms and shook her slightly.

"Get off me you hairy beetle," she cried, suddenly laughing, pleased at the mocking corruption of the bodyguard's name. Mark had to admit it was appropriate: he had hair protruding from his ears, his nose and his neck, creeping up over his shirt collar like pervasive undergrowth. From the floor came a strange noise, a mixture of laughing and crying, but increasingly of laughter.

"Hairy beetle, hairy beetle," Edmund cried, now on his feet and hopping from foot to foot, not in pain but in mirth.

Harry Bootle let go of Georgia Nullgeben and stood awkwardly in the room, not sure what to do with himself, arms in front, hands wringing together.

"Fraulein, it is time to start our studies. May I suggest you ask your brother to depart so we many concentrate on the task at hand?" Mark instinctively took charge but knew he could not give them a direct order. "Mr Bootle, would you mind leaving us so that we may study?"

"Hairy Beetle, Hairy Beetle, you're to come with me." Edmund was beside himself with laughing. Mark noticed that Bootle did not respond but as he passed Mark on his way out, he whispered.

"Sticks and stones."

"Will break my bones," Mark whispered back instinctively. He was rewarded with the tiniest grin from this massive slab of a face. Then he was alone and prepared for Fraulein Nullgeben to let rip.

Only she did not.

"My little brother is a pig. He wants me to go on stupid camp with him. He doesn't understand that I am an adult now … well, almost one."

"Where do you go on camp? When is it, Fraulein?"

"They always go to some never-heard-of place in Sussex but I won't go with them. It is at the beginning of May. I've been every year since we came over here in 1961. It's called Harcourt Castle and it is in the middle of nowhere."

"It's right after your examination, then? Do you not think that maybe you might like to go to relax after all your hard work leading up to the examination?"

"No! No! No! Stop talking to me like you are my equal. You are just another oaf, an imbecile. I don't have to listen to an English."

"I apologise for talking out of turn, Fraulein. Shall we start our studies now? I have an interesting set of questions I worked out last night for maths. Perhaps we should start with them."

It was a long day with the Fraulein starting in fractious mood. Mark was fired twice, thankfully rehired each time. He was *oafed* and *imbeciled* all morning; berated, scolded, accused.

But something happened that afternoon of day five. In fact, two things happened, both giving hope to Mark.

The first was tangible. Georgia got full marks in both tests he set her. She seemed to funnel her anger into concentration, cutting swathes through the textbooks. For the first time, he saw her intellect at work, naked of all clothing, whether that clothing was arrogance or the ignorance of youth. It did not matter. Despite her terrible school reports, young Fraulein Georgia Nullgeben had an intellect that was well above that of most other people he had met.

The second was intangible, but just as rewarding. It happened steadily throughout the afternoon, starting before he became aware of it, so not really knowing when it started. No doubt she would have dismissed it had it been brought to her attention. But she seemed as unaware of it as he was.

It was only around 4.30pm that Mark realised he had not been called an oaf for quite a while. In fact, looking back afterwards, he could not remember being insulted all afternoon.

"How was it today with the brat?" Linda asked when they were safely in the car, heading back to prison.

"Rocky start but actually I started to enjoy myself. She has quite a brain and once she starts to use it she is pretty formidable." He told her all about the morning with Georgia and Edmund.

"Yes, I heard from Thomas," she replied.

"You know Thomas?" Mark had only seen him fleetingly since the first day.

"Well, actually he is my boyfriend. That is how I found out about the tutor vacancy."

"I see." Mark was relieved in a strange way. He was too purposeful for a relationship right now, concentrated on gaining his freedom.

"Mind you, if we fall out I'll be straight after my dishy crim!"
She leant over and gave him a big kiss on the cheek.

"Careful, you'll be back in the hedge soon! So, how did you find out about me?"

"I read all the notes on each prisoner when I started, thinking that with a cohort of political prisoners there was bound to be something interesting, something useful. Then I came across your academic record, made a few phone calls to Cambridge, and hey presto, I had a plan."

"You're really into this underground resistance, aren't you?"

"Too right, they killed my parents. Aren't you too, especially with your history?"

Now it was time to confess. Six years earlier, Mark had been right on the periphery of the resistance, not really involved at all. He was caught up in a moment of fantasy and very unlucky that the club was raided the only night he had ever visited it.

But instead he just said, "Sure."

"What did you find out today?"

He told her about the camp and the fact that Georgia most definitely did not want to go.

"I think she is more into make-up and talking about boys than building rafts and cooking by the fire."

"Can you find out more for me? When it is? How long for? Where exactly it is? Who goes on it?"

"I'll try." Should he, he wondered, break confidences for a cause he had nothing to do with; had never been truly involved with, but which had given him six years of grinding tedium in return for a casual acquaintance?

"Thanks," she replied, taking her eyes off the road again to give him a thoughtful look.

The next morning, Harry Bootle met Mark and Linda by the car. It seemed he had been waiting for them.

"I'll take him from here, miss. Cook has tea in the pot and she made buns yesterday, delicious they are, too." He tried to lick his lips but it came across more like a lizard flicking its tongue to catch insects.

"Sure thing, Mr Bootle. See you later, Smith. Be a good boy

now!"

She skipped off, flicking at the rhododendrons with her arms, so incongruous in her sombre prison guard uniform.

"Quite a character." Bootle was trying to be friendly but his eyes were two washed-out pebbles on the seashore; all colour, all life, bleached out and run dry. His mouth barely moved as he talked, as if he had never opened his lungs and yelled at the top of his voice. Perhaps he never had? Mark knew nothing about him.

Other than he worked for the authorities.

"But she is not what I wanted to talk to you about. I wanted to talk about yesterday morning."

"I've forgotten it already," Mark lied. It was easy lying to authority, far harder with your own.

"You will see it from time to time when those two get together. They fight like mad."

"Like a lot of kids," Mark reassured. But did not know. He had been an only child, his best friend the same.

"But I lost it a bit and I wouldn't want that to get to other people's ears, if you get my meaning." Mark only partially got it. He meant his boss, the commander, but how had he lost it?

"Lost it?"

"Sticks and stones."

"Oh, that! That was nothing."

"It showed disrespect. It should not have happened."

Mark felt like shaking this great slab of a man. Perhaps if he did shake him vigorously enough he would crack open and the shell would peel off, revealing a real person inside.

"Do they always argue about the same things?" Where had that question come from? He thought about Linda, always darting about yet seeming to have some purpose amongst the jumble.

"No, generally speaking Edmund winds up his sister with inflammatory comments and she explodes. It will be whatever he suspects will get to her."

"But this time it was about a summer camp?"

"I don't speak their language so I wouldn't know." Wooden tones had taken over again. He clearly knew a lot about the strained relationship between brother and sister, regardless of the language barrier excuse.

"Mr Bootle, you are not the only one with responsibilities. I have to get the Fraulein through this very important exam. I need to know the pressures she is under. If this summer camp is upsetting her, I need to know."

So, while they walked up the back stairs to the top floor and the old nursery where Georgia waited at her desk, flicking her pigtails with thumb and finger, trying to get them to land on her nose, Harry Bootle told Mark all about the summer camp; never once, bless him, imagining that Mark would be passing it straight on to the resistance.

"My god, Mark, this is Treasure Island!"

"Watch where you're going, Linda. You have to be the worst driver I've ever come across."

"So, let me get this straight. Young Nullgeben is taking her exam on Friday 30th April, then going that afternoon to the summer camp. She will be going alone as Edmund will have gone with the others earlier that day. She is going alone because of her exam. And Harry Bootle, her bodyguard, is going with her, along with a section of soldiers from Reading Barracks, so not entirely alone. But now we get to the interesting part for when she gets to Harcourt Castle in Sussex the soldiers will depart, mission accomplished. Her guard during the two-week camp will be just Bootle and the other instructors, mostly retired army specialists." This time, in her excitement, she crossed right over to the other side of the road, honked automatically at a slow truck approaching them, looked at a headlong collision, then swerved back at the last minute, horns blaring all around, the car slugging on through this latest panic, like a horse in wartime.

She glanced sideways at Mark, just a flick of the eyes to check his reaction, then back to the road, shocked at her lack of control. She saw his eyes firmly closed, expecting the screeching of metal on metal, the deep thumps, the blackness like the night around them. Only with this night there would be no dawn.

"Linda, when did you pass your test?" He asked, not yet

opening his eyes, but hearing the horns die away in the rear-view mirror, echoing up the road back towards them.

"What test?"

"The SF, the *Strasse Fahrprufung* for your *Einheimische Fuhrerschein.*"

"Oh, the EF. I didn't bother with that. I just faked one for my job application. I didn't have the time to mess around with those courses."

School's Out

"As a treat for the last day of term, we are going to study today…" There was a groan across the classroom: they had all hoped to be allowed to the gym or the football field. "As I was saying, we are going to study today one aspect of why we are leaders in the world." The elderly schoolmaster paused, looking around his charges. There were a dozen in this one class, covering thirteen- to fifteen-year-olds. There were only eighty in the whole school. He was terribly proud to be a part of this school, this home from home across the water, this little bit of the homeland come to England. He told himself this every day, sometimes several times.

"We are going to look at precisely why we won the Battle of Britain and what were the decisive factors in that victory. Any ideas, anybody?" He knew he would get the normal chorus of "Because we are better," and, "Because they are imbeciles." He was not disappointed in this expectation. It showed a certain pride in the home country. That was important.

But today he hoped, after the rush of puerile remarks, to go a little deeper, to explore and display his own pride a little more. For Senior Schoolmaster Edgar Strifer had not always been a schoolmaster. Far from it. He had joined the Luftwaffe in 1935, flown Stukas in Spain, then transferred to his beloved 109s. How he had loved that plane, now sadly retired. As Major Strifer he led a wing of 109s during the brief but decisive Battle of Britain. He had retired an *oberstleutnant* in 1956, gone into teaching because he had never saved from his pay.

All he wanted to do now was talk about his glory days.

"Boys and girls, quiet now. I want to introduce a subject to you that is dear to my heart. Why is it that the British had no capability of withstanding the 109 onslaught we sent over in the summer of 1940?"

Hands shot up. He selected some at random. The answers were all wrong. How was it that these youngsters did not know their basic history?

"Think hard now. Yes, Nullgeben, your turn."

"Because the English are oafs, sir," Edmund said smugly, causing a tide of laughter, until Strifer spoke again. Strifer knew someone would come up with a well-worn attempt to raise a laugh. But this was the commander's son so there was no place for sarcasm.

"Quite right, Nullgeben, well done. But why did they prove to be oafs? What did they do or not do that makes this a fair summary of their collective state of mind?"

More hands, more wrong answers. This was looking like it was going to be a struggle. He had done the same subject, with far better results, in his class last year, but of course that had been in Paris.

It was Edmund who came up trumps again. This time he was not seeking a laugh; rather the opposite. He had thought about the matter and suddenly he knew.

"Sir, sir, I know the answer!" If his hand stretched up much further it would become detached from his body and float like a zeppelin with its bombs ready.

"Yes, Nullgeben."

"Sir, it was because they did not have a weapon to fight our 109s. They had no suitable aircraft, nothing that could fight back. They failed to develop anything, thinking war would never come."

"Good, well done. You see, boys and girls, the answer can be obtained through analysis, exercising those brain cells. You, as future leaders, should not need to be spoon-fed like the locals. You need to develop your ability to use your minds to work out solutions to problems. Now, Nullgeben will come to the front of the class and explain the thought process that led to his right answer."

But the next half an hour was devoted not to a display of Edmund Nullgeben's immature logic, but to tale after tale of Strifer's glorious escapades.

"Sir?" A thin boy, seated at the back of the class, put up his hand, thoughtlessly interrupting Strifer in mid flow.

"Yes, Reckine, what is it?" He had little time for this boy from an unimportant family but had been kind to him since his father died unexpectedly, shot coming out of assembly one

Sunday. The resistance had obviously been aiming for a more important official but had missed. Herr Strifer would not have missed.

"Sir, I was reading about this in the library." That caused a new tide of laughter coursing through the classroom. Reckine was always in the library.

"Silence, class. Let Reckine continue."

"Sir, they almost developed a suitable plane. It was going to be called the Spitfire. There was an English designer called Mitchell and he was very good." That brought back memories for Strifer. There had been rumours in 1938 of just such a plane.

"So why did it not go into production?"

"Because the government couldn't get Parliament to approve the funding, sir."

"You make my point perfectly, Reckine. Sit down now. It is clear that the English do not have the moral fibre to pursue matters to their necessary conclusions. Now, Reckine's comments also illustrate the next point I intended to make, so it seems we are indebted to Reckine today." This caused more laughter at Reckine's expense.

"Quiet, now. Listen to my final point of the year. At one level it was their lack of moral fibre, quite evidently the case. However, at another level it is the weakness of democracy that caused this complete failure to arm and protect those dear to them. The will of the mob took precedence over common-sense planning. This is something that would never happen at home. For your holiday work, I want an essay on the Problems of Democracies in the Modern World. And try to be a bit thoughtful. If I suspect anyone has copied from the encyclopaedia they will be straight before the headmaster at the start of next term."

This workload, right at the end of term, dashed their collective hopes and produced a groan, then anger directed at Reckine, only partly diffused when Herr Strifer called "Dismissed!" and school was over.

"It was hard work with class three today." Strifer threw himself down into an easy chair in the common room. He lit a cigarette from a silver case, very much the fashion in 1940, puffing the smoke out in circles, thinking *That's another enemy plane smoking and crashing down.* "At least young Nullgeben can think for himself a bit. I'd still be there going through the basics if it wasn't for him."

"Nasty piece of work, though," Eric von Schnappmann said mildly, as if commenting on the condition of an old bicycle.

"At least he has a brain on his shoulders," Strifer snapped back, angry that one of the aristocrats had challenged him.

"He may have one solitary brain cell, I'll agree on that, but not a penny's worth of common sense to guide it," Von Schnappmann replied, taking up his newspaper again, angering Strifer further with his nonchalance.

"Where's Nullgeben's sister?" someone asked.

"I told you, Teazer, she's been taken out of school to take the *Statenthrump* entrance exam in a few weeks' time."

"Fat chance of her succeeding," the chemistry teacher said.

"Second that," the biology teacher added.

"Hear, hear!" came the literature teacher's response. Then followed the chorus; hard to depict individual voices but the volume told the story.

"She shouldn't have been allowed to leave during the school year," Strifer said when the birdsong had died down. "It's typical of the RUDD to think they can do anything they choose."

"They're so damn superior. They make the rules and they break them with impunity."

"Well, when she fails miserably, as she will, perhaps it will put the RUDD in their place for once," Strifer replied to general approval. But looking round at the chuckling faces, he felt he had been careless. Talk like that got a laugh from second-rate no-hope teachers but could equally land one a prison sentence. He noticed that von Schnappmann was no longer there. Strifer had not seen him leave. Had the infuriating aristocratic teacher heard his words about RUDD and then left to report him? Had he overstepped the mark? Surely a little gentle rivalry between government arms was permissible? If he were in charge, he would encourage such in order to build up team spirit and competitiveness.

But he was not in charge. He was just another aging war hero, not quite remembered, despite the reminders he gave out with regularity; planted now in some forgotten corner of the empire, educating the middle managers of the future. He had no family, no interests save the past; his past. He had no friends, only acquaintances and colleagues. To him, the only thing that was bright was the now distant long ago. Well, let von Schnappmann make trouble if he wanted to, Oberstleutnant Strifer (retd.) would be ready for him. Stubbing out his second cigarette, he rose from his chair, which was instantly taken by an ancient Latin teacher who could move more quickly than anyone where his comfort was concerned. Strifer, idea in mind, left the room.

He caught Edmund at the school gates, football boots slung over one shoulder, hanging down his front like kills from the hunt, loaded satchel over the other shoulder. Today was the last day of the school term; everything had to be cleared out. That was the rule.

"Ah, Nullgeben."

"Yes, sir?" Damn his luck for being caught by old Strife.

"I wanted a word with you. I will walk a while with you, my house is part-way home for you." He did not add that it was not his home, but that of a bulky, obnoxious and crude widow who rented out rooms for twenty marks a week, breakfast and supper included.

"Yes, sir." But the boy's body language spoke of invasion.

"Nullgeben," the teacher started as they crossed the road outside the gates and went down the bridle path that led to the village, "I think your father is doing a wonderful job as sector commander."

"Thank you, sir." Surely he had not been hailed by this old man to listen to meaningless compliments about his father?

"I hope you will remember him to me. I met him at a school inspection a few years ago."

"Of course, sir." *He wouldn't remember you in a month of Sundays,* Edmund thought.

"But there is something else I am concerned about and I think he should know about. I hope you will keep in strict confidence what I am about to say and repeat it just to your father. It comes from one senior professional to another."

"Yes, sir." If it sounded juicy enough he would tell all his friends, maybe even start with Georgia that evening. Not that he counted Georgia as a friend.

"Good, good. Now tell me, youngster, whether you have Herr von Schnappmann for any of your classes."

"Yes sir, I have him for advanced mathematics."

"Quite so, of course you are taking advanced mathematics, I should have known because of your intellect. Well, I am somewhat concerned about him. In fact, I overheard him saying something not at all pleasant about one of the Nullgebens. And no, before you ask, I will not divulge which Nullgeben family member he was not complimentary towards as that will only cause divisiveness. Suffice it to say it was the most important in the family to my unworthy eyes." Strifer looked at his pupil. He seemed to be buying it. "Will you tell your father this information quietly? I would not want it to cause upset in your family."

"I'll do that, sir! The villain should be arrested right away."

After they had parted, Strifer to his tedious lodgings, Edmund branching off across the village playing fields and towards the mansion, Strifer wondered whether he had overdone it. Edmund Nullgeben was a remarkably stupid boy; von Schnappmann was right about that at least. He would, in all likelihood, overact completely and make a whole drama out of a little story. But what was done was done. Being too reflective got you shot down.

And Strifer had survived 243 missions. He was not going to be shot down now.

Edmund walked on out of the trees that lined the path, his head full of plots and the resistance he had always heard about as some distant threat but which loomed large now after the murder of Reckine's father. Now Edmund was right in the middle of the action. He was a lead player. His mind whirled with possibilities, with him centre-stage in all scenarios: hero, saviour, spy, counter-terrorist.

He did not see the football. It thrust through the air, as if deliberately sent his way. It hit him squarely on the side of the head; ninety-degree angle to the temple, with a little downward motion for it had peaked in its trajectory and was curving down. It knocked him over.

When he opened his eyes, he was surrounded by a dozen local boys, staring at him. He put his hand up to feel his throbbing head.

"You ain't no good at heading the ball, mate." It took him a moment to understand the language.

"Call me sir, damn you, you, you … oaf." He tried to stand up but was dizzy and fell back, legs rising automatically in the air.

"Lordy, 'sir' is in a big state, all because of a little football." The boy started heading the ball repeatedly with great control and quite a lot of bounce, making Edmund incensed.

"Look, 'sir' has some boots, maybe he wants a game of footie."

"No, he's not up to it," said the bouncer, still doing neat headers as he talked. "Those are pansy boots. I think he's a ballet dancer with them boots."

"I'm better than the lot of you. You're just a bunch of imbeciles." Now they had to arrange a match. They hauled him to his feet, checked there was no bleeding. They argued over teams while he put on his boots. They were still arguing when he had the boots on and had done his warm ups.

"Listen, oafs, you need someone making the decisions. I'll be one captain, you be the other." He pointed to the bouncer. "Now there's eleven of you and then there's me so twelve in total. You select five."

The bouncer fell for it straight away, chose the best five.

"Thanks for choosing my team," Edmund said before the five could line up with the bouncer. "You get the others."

"What? You said for me to select my team."

"No, I said for you to select five players, that's all I said."

"He's got you, Eddie!" A couple of the players shouted. "Fair's fair. He never said you were selecting your own team."

Eddie the Bouncer gave way with bad grace, expecting to

lose badly now. They agreed on twenty minutes each way. Edmund had to provide the coin to toss for kick-off. He positioned himself in centre, quickly allocating places to the others, not knowing them but picking the fastest-looking for attack.

Forty minutes later, a breathless Edmund called a halt to the game. His team had won 7-1, Eddie the Bouncer scoring the only goal for the opposing side.

"You played well." Eddie said to Edmund through ragged breath.

But Edmund was incensed by the fact that he had not scored. He had been close eight times. He had set up goals for the other team members, all of whom, save the goalkeeper, had scored at least once.

But not Edmund.

"Go to hell, oaf-face. You're… you're… an English." He strode off, boot studs clicking on the concrete path like a noisy and ancient timepiece.

He did not look back, much as he wanted to. He wanted to see the shock on their faces but feared there would be derision instead.

He was still breathless, dirty and ragged, when he clattered across the hall of the mansion ten minutes later. He hadn't thought to change out of his football boots.

"Lordy me, Master Edmund. Whatever's happened to you?" An English voice, female, came floating across the hall, a little Welsh singsong to it, not that Edmund could discern.

"Don't call me Master, Nanny, I don't like it."

"Well, it doesn't seem that you can be so grown up, young sir. I remember when I first set eyes on…"

"Don't go on, Nanny. Run me a bath. I daren't go in looking like this."

Scrubbed and changed, clean suit carefully laid out on his bed for him while he washed, he reported to his parents in the drawing room forty-five minutes later. All thoughts of his talk with Herr Strifer dispelled by the twin angsts of the football match and presenting himself to his parents.

"Well, young Edmund." Both parents could do patronising speeches to a tee. This time it was his father's turn. "What are you planning to do that is constructive this holiday period?"

"I have the camp, sir."

"Yes, the last two weeks of the holiday, I believe. Before that, what do you plan?"

Edmund thought hard but came up with nothing. He mumbled about football, fishing, reading, although he never read if he could help it.

"Well, I have something I want you to do. This is important and I need someone who is up to the task."

"That's me, sir!"

"The camp committee is short staffed since Reckine died so suddenly last year. I have volunteered your services. You are to report to the camp leader at 0800 hours tomorrow and thereafter at her discretion."

This promised to be a tedious task, stretching out for three long weeks, but his father's use of 0800 hours rather than civilian time gave it an edge of excitement.

"Yes, sir, I hope I can be useful."

"I am sure you will be. Now, where is Georgia? We need to hear how her lessons went today. Please run and fetch her."

"Yes, Father."

Werner Nullgeben watched his only son leave the room and turned to look out of the window, away from his wife who sat at the piano, repeating scales then singing a few words from an old folk song she was working out how to play.

"The spirits wander through the land… no, that is not right." She sang it again and again, creating a backdrop, a rhythm that allowed Werner's thoughts to wander like the spirits.

But Werner's spirits had one home; they were not the wandering type. Whenever his mind was at rest he thought of his Barbara. He could feel her long, soft red hair; hear her breathing against his chest; laugh at her jokes and wait for her to laugh at his. It had been 102 days since he had resolved to give her up. He had seen her seldom since then, only spent a handful of nights with her. She had been enquiring as to why the frequency of visits had reduced so suddenly. He evaded answering, grew angry when she persisted.

"Werner, my dear, I am a part of your life. I am your lover, have been for over nine years now. You need to tell me what is going on in that funny mind of yours." She had kissed him on the forehead as she said that. When he closed his eyes, as now, he could feel her lips brushing and lingering.

He knew he had to do this. He needed resolve. He looked back at his wife.

His career was on the line.

"The spirits wander through the land. I wander with them hand in hand." She had the song now, was working on the accompaniment, long thin fingers ranging over the keys, testing chords.

"What are you thinking about?" she asked, half-singing the question.

"Georgia," he lied.

She probably knew it was a lie.

It had been the hardest thing he had ever tried to do and he had failed. The relationship was almost a decade old. They had met while she was at a translators' conference in Paris, right at the beginning of his posting there, before the family had moved to be with him. She had stood out a mile from the multitude of mainly bespectacled girls as he addressed the conference as guest speaker. His eyes kept coming back to her. He tried to follow his public speaking training and range across the audience but, like a puppet controlled by strings unseen, he came home each time to her. Her red hair had been tamed but not well enough. It broke out of its restraints and became a flood, an overflow, of vivid brightness amongst the neat grey and pastel dresses and jackets the ladies wore.

Later that night, after they had made love, she told a little of her story, arching her naked body on the bed, stretching like a wild animal.

"They selected me for the Ballshore Academy," she had said, "on account of my ability with languages." She spoke with a gentility that was delightful, so strange in an English, so inviting. "I was living with foster parents, my sister too, when they sent me to the Ballshore in Scotland. I was eleven years old." Her hair, now loosened completely, had a natural position like a huge stage curtain, her face the stage. She brushed the hair away often, illuminating the beauty behind as equally as the best stage lights could manage.

"Foster parents?"

"Yes, my father died in the Battle of France. Well, actually it was just before the battle proper started." The whole story came out then. He was an English intellectual, living with his wife and six children in a tall town house in Notting Hill.

"I shared a bedroom with my sister in the attic. We had a communal garden that we went to every day, rain or shine. Daddy made a living writing reviews for newspapers. He wrote novels too but they never sold well."

He had joined up the day war was declared; had always sought a cause, now had one. He was sent to France after initial training but never saw any action.

"How, then, did he die?" he had asked, looking in wonder at this red delight.

"He was run over."

"Truly?"

"Truly! He was put in charge of entertainment and organised a drop of film reels to put on a cinema show. The lorry delivering the films reversed into him. It broke his legs and pierced his lungs. He died in the new field hospital six days later. He was the only patient at the time."

"How sad." He kissed her, then asked her more about her past. He had met a few English before, but never one like this. She seemed cultured, certainly well educated. But then the authorities had set up Ballshore Academy for the brightest English.

"And your mother? Did she die also?"

"I don't know. We were separated during the Battle of Britain. We two girls were sent to a hops farm in Hampshire to get away from the bombs. Then came the invasion and we never heard from her again. But the farmer fostered us all the way through to 1946 when I was selected for Ballshore and my sister, she was fifteen by then, she went to that huge aircraft factory. But in my hols we sometimes stayed back on the farm together."

When they met after the conference the next day he gave her a diamond necklace. He had slipped out of his office and chosen it for her. He observed with pleasure how the diamonds reflected her beautiful red hair that fell everywhere around her.

"Father."

When he closed his eyes, he could still see that hair.

"Father."

It matched her smile in every way.

"Father!"

He had bought her many gifts over the years, a lot of jewellery, some paintings, and set up an apartment for her back in her native Notting Hill. It had a communal garden, just like the one she had played in as a child. He had promoted her several times, way beyond her experience.

"Father!"

"What? Oh, sorry. I was thinking about some work problems."

They both knew he was lying. But Georgia just said she was come at the end of the day to report on her study progress.

"Good," said Werner, trying to shunt Barbara out of his mind.

Networking

Mr Fairway and Mrs Britain sat together in the tiny cook's study under the back stairs, rather than the more spacious butler's pantry. It seemed appropriate to be tucked away. The room had only two comfortable chairs so Linda Burton sat on the window seat that looked out onto the side of the back yard. It had been explained to Mrs Britain when she had joined the household that this was the genteel side of the yard. Her neighbours were the butler's pantry to one side and the Senior Servants' Hall to the other.

But she did not care for such things. In truth, she had only pretended to give an impression of slight reluctance in taking the position. She had not wanted to appear too keen. In fact, she had made a great play of adding up the pros and cons compared to the Hoffmann household at the other end of the valley.

She had always intended to come to the commander's residence. It was a part of the plan, as was the arrival of Mr Fairway.

"So, you think we have Mark Smith on board?" Mr Fairway asked.

"It's hard to tell," Linda replied. "Talk about diffidence! But to be fair, he has not made a decision of his own for six years. Even a tiny bit of freedom can be a huge thing to cope with. He has given me some great information but I'm not sure yet that he is fully on board."

They had not known Linda long but both were impressed by her maturity. And it was so cleverly hidden behind a guise of playfulness and silliness. She was nineteen years old and had perfected her cover. Many would take years of coaching to achieve what she had done in four months.

"He's related to Jo Macclesfield, isn't he?" Mrs Britain asked.

"He's her nephew, Jo is his mother's younger sister," Linda answered.

"So, who else can we depend on?" Mr Fairway asked. He was new to the area.

Both Mrs Britain and Linda spoke at the same time in

answer, both laughing as they realised they had given the same name: Thomas.

"I'm dating him," Linda said. "He's bright, creative and brave. He's also lovely!"

"Amen to that," said Mrs Britain, eyes glassy, then losing herself in her cup of tea.

"But not quite yet," Linda continued, explaining and further impressing the older pair with her maturity of reasoning. "He's a year younger than me, living away from home for the first time, and boys can be much more careless than girls. I think he just needs a little more time."

It was agreed. Thomas would be approached at a future date. And because they worked on the principle of need to know, not one word would be breathed to him before the due time.

"What about Harry Bootle?" Mr Fairway asked.

"What?"

"You must be mad!"

"Why is that such a crazy idea?"

Linda told him.

"I think Mrs Britain will agree that he is totally loyal to the Nullgebens. If we approached him, he would go running straight to them. There is nobody less likely to join the resistance other than the Fraulein herself!"

"Agreed," said Mrs Britain.

"Well, you know he has a past. A really interesting past, in fact." Mr Fairway looked at his watch and sighed. "That will have to be for the next meeting. I'll summarise where we are. We have a similar set-up now in most of the principle households," puffing on his pipe, he paused for a long intake of smoke, despite time moving on. "The objective remains as always. We need to infiltrate every major household as part of each section's local organisation. Hence, for our section we have the Nullgebens as the principal family of the land, plus the Hoffmanns, the Steiners, and several more. I'd say we're about a third of the way through the set-up phase. So now we need to start feeding back information to the local HQ and on up the chain to regional and national level. The more quality information we can secure, the better. But we all need to be very careful. It only takes one accident to bring the whole structure tumbling down."

"Well, I'm hopeful that Mark Smith will get us some gems over the next few weeks. He may not have declared his hand but he has already got me some choice bits of info. Now, we better get back to work or I'll be late and all hell will break out."

"Not that there is a hell," Mrs Britain and Mr Fairway said together, smiling, clinking their teacups together.

"Linda, just be careful. You're a godsend to the resistance but don't let your enthusiasm cloud your judgment."

"Roger and out." Linda stood to mock-attention and saluted the pair of them, then saluted again with her left hand, followed in quickening succession with right and left and recurring.

"Lordy me!" Mrs Britain called, "Be away with you before I die of laughing!"

Linda closed the door behind her, straightened her cap in the hall mirror, and rushed upstairs to take charge of Mark Smith again.

That left the two older resistance members, cook and butler, alone in the tiny but cosy study. For a few minutes neither spoke, both deep in reflection, but those thoughts very different. Mr Fairway was full of practical matters, getting to grips with the new responsibility he faced, making half-plans and shooting them down like fighter pilots in the sky.

Mrs Britain was thinking of her son.

Her only son. And what he would be like now.

If he were alive.

Almost to the day, he would be Thomas' age. Almost to the inch, he would be Thomas' height. Build, temperament and humour were all remarkably similar.

Sometimes, she thought that Thomas had been sent to haunt her.

At other times, in fact most times, she wanted to hug him, to squeeze him so tightly he would yell out and wonder what on earth was going on.

She was a lady; only an English could not be a lady, really.

But let's say, for now, she was a lady. She was a lady torn in two.

"A penny," said Mr Fairway.

"Oh, I was just thinking of Linda." Then she decided to be truthful. "Actually, I was thinking how similar Thomas is to my son, my Steve."

With gentle probing, the whole story came out. Steve had been twelve and a natural rebel, every sinew like his dead father.

"Who was his father?" Mr Fairway asked.

"We were not married," she replied quietly.

"Mrs Britain, I'm not about to judge you. I just want to listen if you want to talk. If you don't then that is quite alright."

There followed several minutes of slow time. He sucked on his pipe and regarded her. She looked constantly at the back of her hands, such that he imagined that if the palms held secrets of the future, perhaps the backs held secrets of the past. Eventually she talked, each sentence starting with a sigh, dragging the painful past into the present, re-opening old wounds.

"His father was the love of my life." That told Mr Fairway nothing but he had survived twenty-five years in the resistance. He knew how to be patient. "His father was Mike Jazz."

"What?"

"Mike Jazz."

Mr Fairway was on his feet now, pipe forgotten, everything else forgotten.

"You knew Mike Jazz?" The real but unspoken question was, *You were intimate with him?*

"We were lovers from '44 until his death."

"What ... I mean how ... what is your real name?"

Of course, he knew; everybody knew, Mike Jazz's girlfriend was Penny Race. There was no need to answer, nor to break the Benannten Names Regulations. Instead, she could still observe the back of her hands, like looking for a mole or other blemish.

Mr Fairway's mind was racing. He tried to recall everything he knew about Mike Jazz. He had been born into a Jewish family in the East End in 1921. He had worked as a timesheet clerk in the dockyards both before and after the occupation, collecting the attendance records and calculating the hours to be paid to each individual. He might have still been there and lived out the remainder of his life in obscurity, but for the invasion. Mr Fairway remembered now some of the incongruity. Mike Jazz was a Londoner but his parents had come from eastern Europe, so he was a second-generation immigrant. Yet he displayed more patriotism and was more nobly carried than most English. He had stayed working in the docks yet also led the early resistance. He had been the inspiration behind so much of the early movement that had picked itself up after the shock of the invasion.

Had that blasted RUDD officer not stopped that day, all would have gone on as before; routine days followed by clandestine nights. The authorities had never suspected that a bookish clerk with thick glasses and a shuffling walk could be anything to do with the resistance. He had been free to organise and build up the initial network across the country.

But it was not to be. It was such a simple mistake and Mr Fairway had never believed that the RUDD officer was malicious; maybe incompetent, but not malicious.

He had drawn his pistol when there was a commotion at the dockyard gates. But with his right hand committed to a handshake with Mike Jazz, he had tried to use his left hand to manage his weapon, drawing it across his body. Then the gate guards had given the shrill whistle for stand-down. The officer fumbled his pistol back towards his holster, trying to do it with his left hand across his body, his right still shaking the hand of Mike Jazz.

Mr Fairway could imagine the clatter as the pistol dropped to the ground and hit the cobbled stones. Mike had squatted to pick it up. The officer had read his actions incorrectly; had panicked, reached the gun first, and blown Jazz's brains out.

"It was Friday 21st April 1959, was it not?" he asked, having exhausted his knowledge of the incident.

"Yes, Steve and I had gone to the dockyard to meet him. It was a beautiful spring day, the type only Britain can offer. We… we saw him being shot. I hid Steve's face in my skirt but he saw his father's brains spreading along the cobbles, sliding into the crevices."

"It was the start of the Clampdown," Mr Fairway said, but as if narrating a play, disconnected from the actors who took part.

"I still see my love's brains every time I close my eyes."

"How did Steve die?" Mr Fairway asked.

"He took it badly. He went into such a rage. He was twelve years old. His father was his life." Short, stubby sentences, clearly a hard tale to tell. "He had the fire of his father. But not the tact. They shot him in the street outside the police station. He died, like his father." She stopped a while, then added, "On the ground, spilling his blood onto the street."

Further delicate questioning brought out the rest of the story. Steve had been beyond himself with anger. He had pulled away from his mother's grip, run back home, taken the sharpest knife he could find, and gone directly to the police station. What he had hoped to achieve, they would never know, for three minutes after arriving at the steps under the bright red police sign, he was coughing blood and the world was closing in on him.

"I never saw him alive again," Mrs Britain said. "I had to deal with two bodies and my whole life torn apart."

Mr Fairway went over to her chair and hugged her tightly. After a long time, they heard voices outside, questioning where the butler and the cook were. They were needed.

"We better go," he said. "One final question." He pulled out his handkerchief and wiped tears from her eyes. "What happened to the RUDD officer?" It was as much to close the incident in his mind as to further the discussion, but he had an inkling that the officer had not suffered for the killing.

"They deemed it an accident, no charges were filed. That is when I decided to join the resistance and to take over where Mike left off. Not that I've achieved anything like he had done."

"That's not fair. The Clampdown changed everything. We had to start all over again and you have been a big part of the organisation in this region." He squeezed her arm. "You've kept this all secret for six years now. There is so much about our pasts that brings us to our current resolve. But right now, like Mike, we have to do our day jobs or we'll have everything tumbling down again!"

They left her study then, Mr Fairway issuing instructions as he strode along the passageways; Mrs Britain much more quietly going back to the kitchen and her duties. It took all sorts to build a resistance and these were two of the best.

The Pupil-Teacher Relationship

"April Fool!" Edmund yelled. "It's dead easy doing an April Fool on a real fool!"

Mark was wet through. The pail of water had been balanced perfectly on the doorframe, the door slightly ajar. It was the oldest joke in the world, one straight from the comic books he remembered as a child. Did they still make those comics?

"You're the fool," Georgia said acidly. "To count, a trick has to be performed before midday." She made a big thing out of checking the time on the nursery clock and her own watch; bending down to look at Edmund's too, so that he pulled his wrist away behind his back.

"Who says?"

"It's the rules, everyone knows that."

"It was funny, sir," Mark said, wanting to diffuse the developing row, anxious to get on with the studies that might just lead to his freedom. "But now I think we..."

"Who asked you?" Edmund interrupted. "You're not even a servant. You're way beneath servant. You're a ... you're a ... criminal and you're an English. You just don't count for anything."

"Shut up!" Georgia flew at her brother, caught his arm as he tried to leave the room, pulling him back and slapping his face repeatedly. Mark watched the rapid movements, palm against left cheek, back of the hand against right cheek, keeping rhythm like a metronome. She kept shouting, "He's my tutor, all mine. You just leave us alone."

Finally, she let her brother go and slumped into her seat, exhausted from her anger. Edmund, shocked at his sister's outburst, moved to the door, stepping across the pool of water in the doorway.

"Anyway, you're going on the camp. I saw your name on the list while I was helping them." It was the best way to get her back. He dared not add that he had suggested to the camp leader that she should be added.

"I know my sister will be very disappointed if she is left off," he had said.

"But she is too old, Nullgeben. No other seventeen-year-olds go on camp."

"I tell you, Miss, she begged. She was in tears about it."

She was added to the list.

"I'm sorry about my stupid brother's behaviour," Georgia said when Edmund had gone from the room, slamming the offending door as he left. "He is such an idiot."

"That's okay, Fraulein, now shall we get on with the chemical equations we have to learn today?"

They worked for an hour, the Fraulein clearly shaken by what had gone on and unable to concentrate fully.

"I'm not going on the camp, am I? It's against the rules for seventeen-year-olds. And I'm going to be eighteen in October."

"Is it against the rules, Fraulein? I don't know those rules."

"It must be, it has to be." She got up from her desk and walked across to the window. "I hope it is." That last in a much quieter voice, drenched in uncertainty.

"Fraulein, if you like I could try and talk to your parents. I'll say after all your work you'll be too exhausted. Only if you want me to, of course."

"Thank you, Smith, do that and I'll be grateful." She came over to his desk, leant down and made to give him a peck on the cheek, but diverted at the last moment to straightening her socks.

"On second thoughts, you will not get an audience with my parents easily. Instead, I want you to talk with Hairy Beetle. He will have my father's ear and I am sure he will involve Mother too."

"Yes, Fraulein, I will do that."

The rest of the afternoon, she applied herself diligently to her studies.

Mark was summoned to the drawing room on his way out that evening. Harry Bootle led him and Linda through the corridors and down the stairs. Linda signalled her enquiry as to why they were being called. Mark just mouthed the word 'Fraulein' and shrugged his shoulders.

Both parents were in the drawing room. Herr Nullgeben was standing at the large fireplace, left hand on the mantelpiece, right hand fingering the perpetual cigarette, playing the squire perfectly. Frau Nullgeben, however, was pacing back and forth from grand piano to bay window, arms swinging from side to front as she walked, as if willing her onwards and measuring her pace at the same time.

"Smith, what is this I hear about the Fraulein?" She was clearly agitated, and did not wait for Mark to answer. "I heard the most ridiculous story this evening, something about the Fraulein not wanting to go to camp. What nonsense have you been putting in her young head?" At that moment, Mark's hopes turned in on themselves. He heard a door bang at the back of the house. It could be his cell door slamming. Life suddenly took on a wholly different meaning.

"Frau…"

"Don't talk when I am talking. Don't you know I am the patron of the *Jugendlagerorganisation*? It is imperative that my children are active in it and are seen to be enthusiastic at all times. Do you understand this? It is really not that complex."

"Yes, Frau Nullgeben."

"Good. I understand from the Fraulein that the studies are going well. Don't blow it on manufacturing in her mind some stupid sentimental feeling when her duty is clear. You have a lot riding on this examination. I am sure you understand completely what I mean when I say that."

"Yes, Frau Nullgeben."

"Right, go back to your prison and think long and hard concerning what I have been saying to you. I expect total loyalty down to the tiniest degree. Now get out. I will be speaking to the Fraulein about this, too. I don't expect her to bleat on about things like this to the likes of you."

"Yes, Frau Nullgeben."

Bootle was shocked into speech as soon as they were out of the room, the door firmly closed.

"I don't know what to say. You involved me in your silly

games. Why did you do it? I don't understand how you gain from this interference. I have a position to keep. I can't be associated with things like this, not as Head of Security."

"I'm sorry, Mr Bootle. I said I would talk directly to her parents but she said I wouldn't get a chance and to use you as an intermediary. It was poor judgment on my behalf. I should have thought that it would end like this." He reflected that it was more the poor judgment of Harry Bootle, who knew the Nullgebens so much better. But he did not speak of his thoughts.

"Keep me out of it in future. I don't want to compromise my position in this household. Is that understood?"

"Yes, Mr Bootle." But Mark was left with the impression that there was much more to the situation than concern over a severe telling off.

Linda's only comments were, "Hey-ho, I think you've upset everyone there, my lovely." When back in the car she added, "Well, at least you got old Hairy to open up. That's the most I've ever heard him say in one go!"

The days settled back into the routine of grinding work. Even preparing for his finals or the height of his PhD thesis, Mark had not been so hard pressed. He was up at 5.30 every morning, with a shower every day ('the only problem with my tutor is he stinks of prison'); a cold shower because the hot water only came on an hour later. Linda met him at 6.05am to change his clothes and begin the process of checking him out. They usually pulled out of the prison gates at 6.42 and pulled into the mansion courtyard at 7.09. Once, when held up by a security alarm in the prison, Linda had done the twenty-seven-minute journey in eighteen minutes. It was not a pleasant memory for Mark.

Linda and he aimed to be in place in the nursery at 7.15, escorted up most days by Bootle and once or twice by Thomas. On Thomas' days, that inevitably meant whispering, giggling and scampering up the back stairs, Thomas in pursuit of Linda, who enjoyed being caught in the narrow corridors at the top of the house; the watch over their charge momentarily forgotten.

But on most days, it was a steady and sober walk up the four flights from basement to attic. Bootle would unlock the door, say something gruff and meaningless and then depart, leaving Mark and Linda in the empty nursery. Mark tried repeatedly to engage Bootle in conversation but his slab of a face and twisted mouth seemed capable of issuing only one syllable at a time.

The game Linda liked to play then was to sit at Georgia's desk and pretend to be at school, raising her hand and asking ridiculous questions. One time she said, "Sir is it true that the English don't have proper brains?" Another, "Sir, how many English does it take to change a light bulb?"

"How many?" Mark would say to play along.

"Six."

"Why so many?"

"One to change the bulb and five to remind him what his job is." It was a joke they made in kindergarten. But Linda found it funny, more so for the fake accent she put on; a virtual likeness of the Fraulein with an added dose of whining for good measure.

Then Mark would say for her to get out of the Fraulein's seat now, increasingly urgently as the clock moved on, but she always left it to the last minute, slipping out of the desk-chair combination and standing behind Mark seconds before Georgia entered the room.

"Good morning."

"Good morning, Fraulein," they would say in unison.

"You may go, Burton. Come back at noon to escort the prisoner to lunch." She said the same every day, as if she relied on the routine to bolster herself. After the first couple of dismissals, Linda started to do an exaggerated salute, before marching out of the door, leaving it wide open. Mark had to close it every day. Linda, he reflected, liked her routine as well, although she seemed to be poking fun at it as she bent to the schedule.

Mark was always the 'prisoner' until exactly half past seven, when he was promoted to 'my tutor'. At lunchtime and the end of the day he reverted to prisoner status. Thus, he was promoted and demoted twice every day; enough to make most men dizzy.

But not Mark. For Mark had single-minded purpose. This was his route out of jail.

Lunch was a highlight. He ate in the Junior Servants Hall, incongruously apart from Linda who as a prison guard had more status, but with Thomas when he was not on duty. Most days, he had soup, crusty bread, fresh water and an apple withered by storage but still with a speck of the taste he remembered. He had only twenty minutes because he had to be back in place before Georgia arrived back from her lunch at 12.30.

The afternoon stretched longer than the morning, partly because there were more hours, but also tiredness was breaking in and settling upon both of them. But this was the time when, if there were to be any divergence from the strict routine, it would happen. The mornings had the steel-like discipline of productive machinery and the afternoons were more explorative, stripping down the machine to learn how it worked and explore its limitations.

Georgia was much more restless in the afternoons. She managed the mornings but by noon there was excess energy waiting to burst out. Mark expected that she got no chance to let off steam during a serious lunch with her family. So, at reconvening, there was the extra from the morning bundling up with the afternoon's excesses. Sometimes she managed it, sometimes not. Then she would get out of her seat (not permitted), pace up and down and peer out of the window (proscribed as a distraction). Mark had learned not to attempt to correct her and actually saw value in the ability to roam, to stamp in knowledge and understanding through some muscle exercise.

And they were left entirely alone. Once, Edmund had broken in and caused a moment of mayhem, but his telling off had been severe.

The routine established itself and continued.

Until day twenty-three, six days before the entrance exam. They had made good progress all day. It was 5.20pm, the height of temptation for distraction. After this time, they could think of only two hours to go and it got easier.

Georgia was out of her desk-seat, walking up and down. They were discussing Einstein; a subject Mark knew intimately.

"I met him once," he said suddenly, breaking rule number one, never mix in personal information.

"Met who?"

"Einstein. He came to Cambridge when I was there."

"Before he went to America?"

"In fact, it turns out he was on his way there. He absconded just after his Cambridge visit and turned up in New York a month later."

"Why?"

"Because it is the free world."

"But it is capitalist!" Georgia replied, shuddering at the thought. "That would never do."

She was now standing at the window. The afternoon sunlight speckled in, as if it had been broken up by some giant machine between earth and sun, broken into tiny shards of intense light. Those shards sat on her like jewels, turning her tight braids into beautiful shimmering chains.

"Do you ever let your hair down?"

"What?"

'I'm sorry, Fraulein, I forgot myself. I'm really sorry, please forgive me." His world was closing in.

She crossed the room towards his desk, an expression on her face he could not read. She walked slowly, as if part of a funeral procession. That was it. Her face was solemn, properly solemn, like a professional mourner. Intensity no longer in the light beads, for they had remained dancing at the window, but in the subtle shadows her profile created.

Her eyes were so blue he almost expected miniature fighter aeroplanes to zoom across them, doing their own crazy but deadly dance, weaving patterns as they flew.

He wanted her then. He wanted to loosen the stiff braids. He wanted to bury his face in her liberated hair. He wanted to touch her skin, trace his fingers along the curves, dawdle on the teenage blemishes. He wanted to speculate what she would be like as a woman.

But if he touched her he would spend the rest of his life in prison.

It took forever for Georgia to cover the distance from window to teacher's desk. It was time enough for sense to prevail. All he needed to do was cough, stand up, shuffle some papers, break the vision that came steadily his way. Maybe he could still explain it away. Maybe he could buy her silence, if he had anything, anything that she might want.

He was breathless. He was hot, sweating. If he reached out now he would be able to touch her. *Move, Mark, move, before it is too late,* his mind screeched out. But he stayed completely still.

He could see her more clearly now. There was such colour in her cheeks. He had never noticed this before. He could hear her, too. Her breath was deep but shallow, long but short. It was belaboured. It was heavy.

"Smith."

"Fraulein."

They made love on the old nursery rug on the floor.

Afterwards, he was her world. She clung to him. She traced her fingers over his bare skin. She propped herself up on one elbow and smiled at him. She smiled with her ice-blue eyes. It was youth. It was hope. It was happiness. It was all these come together in a sensual moment. They spoke for a while, talking of gentle things, funny things, quaint things.

And then Edmund opened the door and walked into the nursery.

"Sis, you'll never guess what I just did." He stopped. There was nobody in the room, only he had heard their voices from the corridor.

Then he saw them, still on the floor, still together, although both frantically getting up.

"Edmund," said Georgia.

"Sir," said Mark.

"What are you … no, that is a stupid question. I know what you've been doing."

"Please don't tell."

"Why shouldn't I?"

"Because we'll come to some arrangement. I'll give you something, anything."

A deal was done that afternoon. It gave Mark and Georgia the security they wanted. Edmund was sworn to silence. He crossed his heart and hoped to die if he broke the bond they sealed together.

In return, Georgia had to pay a price. Edmund's mind whirled as he considered what to ask for. Her stamp collection? The wet weather gear he had always coveted? Maybe some period of servitude? That would be fun.

But in the end, he asked for something completely different.

"Sis, I want you to come on the camp with me."

"I have to come anyway. Mother laid down the law. I shall attend and go through the motions, although I am really an adult now and none of my friends are going."

"Yes, I know. But I want you to be wholehearted about it. I want you to be enthusiastic about every single part of it."

"Why do you care so?" Georgia wanted to know.

"Because, well because I want to get into the *Statenthrump* too." There, it was out now. He had said it.

"But you've always ridiculed my aspirations before."

"Yes, I know, but I want to be like Father, powerful and famous. I want to be a sector commander one day and to do that I have to go to the *Statenthrump*."

"Sir, could I ask a question?" Mark asked.

"Of course," Georgia replied before Edmund could deny the request, which he looked about to do.

"I just wondered why the camp was so important for your *Statenthrump* hopes, sir. If you don't mind me asking."

"Because I've spent half the holidays organising it! And I have managed a major coup. I wrote to Herr Heffernott, the head of RUDD. He has only replied and said he fully intends to visit during the camp."

"Well, that changes everything," Georgia replied. "If Herr Heffernott is coming then I will definitely be there. I really want to impress him. I'll need a new uniform, Edmund, mine was quite tatty after last year."

"I'll order it now," he replied, pleased at her reaction. "It will go down on my *lebenslauf* as a major achievement. I've put so much effort into it. It won't get me into the *Statenthrump* on its own but it will be a big part of my application. I want it to be the most successful camp ever. I don't suppose you can understand that, being an English." That last comment was made to Mark but again Georgia replied first, visibly excited now.

"You've got a deal, Edmund. I'll make it the camp of a lifetime for everyone involved. I promise." Georgia would have given anything to keep this afternoon's lovemaking secret. But this was no price to pay at all – to have the chance of meeting Herr Heffernott!

"Thanks, Georgia. In return, I'll never let on about what I saw. I promise, too."

The deal was done.

"We still have some work to do, Fraulein," Mark said, hugely relieved that there was a deal made but aware that the day of reckoning was almost upon them. He would fail if she failed the entrance exam.

"Oh, I almost forgot," Edmund said, strangely not wanting to leave, happy in the warmth their arrangement gave, not used to experiencing comradeship of any kind. "The reason why I came here. I've arranged a football match; us against the local oafs. It's tomorrow morning, Sunday. Father has given permission to miss assembly this one time. He says it will be good for relations with the locals. He wants you to come, sis."

"Certainly, I'll come, it will make a change." She would agree to anything right then, her relief mixed with joy at the opportunity opening up for her, created by her little brother. "Can my tutor come, too?"

"Well, we would be stuck without him because he is going to be the referee! God knows why they thought an English could do it, but Father said not to get one of us because when they lose they will just complain about unfair refereeing. That is their nature. They make a half-hearted effort and then bleat on about the results." Edmund sounded like he was quoting from his father. "So, I guess we are stuck with him. It was

Father's idea, to give Smith a break after all his hard work. But it seems he's been taking breaks anyway!"

"Edmund, that is not in the spirit of our agreement and is careless talk, too." The chiding was gentle, a slight sharing smile. They did now share a secret and an opportunity. Sharing was a new experience to both of them. Georgia almost liked her brother.

"Sorry, sis, but do you approve of Smith being referee?"

"Yes, of course."

Great, thought Mark, *now as well as the marking and study preparation tonight, I also need to brush up on the rules of football.*

But out loud he just said, "Thank you, sir. It will be my privilege."

The Inside Man Inside Out

"This is brilliant news, Mark." Linda was ecstatic, so much so that Mark felt it safer to keep his eyes focused on the road. "So, let me get this right; they are both going on Friday. The brat is going with the main body of happy campers, while the bratess is going later in the day, after her exams. And old Heffernott will be there at some point. Now, we need to know who exactly is going, where exactly, which adults and so on. Are they sleeping in tents? What are they going to be doing? Is there any routine they follow regularly? Everything and anything you can find out will be helpful. But most importantly we need to know when Heffernott will be there and what contingent he will bring with him. Your work has just started, Marky love! But you have done so well."

Mark felt dishonest, uneasy, depressed, the more so for the praise from her. In fact, he felt dishonest in several distinct ways. It took the edge off his news, even the edge off the deal with Edmund that had seemed to solve the problems arising from their passion that afternoon.

Firstly, he had not mentioned this passion to Linda. Should he? He contemplated further as the car sped down darkening lanes, their vision of the world around them drawing in like prison walls going up into the sky. Was it her business to know how he had got his information? He persuaded himself not, but it took nine minutes of the twenty-seven-minute route to get to that conclusion. Now they were approaching the town, lit up with street activity as if emerging from a dark tunnel into a different landscape.

Secondly, he knew that he did not care deeply for Georgia. She was too selfish, too tied up in her own importance and arrogance. She had caught the moment superbly, but that was it. Her excitement at meeting the head of RUDD just told him what she really was. She was her father's daughter. She was part of the authority that had put him where he was now.

But she was also tender in his arms, loving and warm. Her ice-cold manner had melted as she crossed the room. If he closed his eyes, he could almost see the melted puddles of ice coldness pooling on the nursery floorboards. Without her icy exterior she had become so warm, so inviting, so much something to be held.

He was very lucky that Edmund had not gone squealing straight to their parents. He had been reckless and stupid, right at the closing stages of his one chance at freedom.

There was another way he felt dishonest but this one he would not admit to. The journey was not long enough to dig and delve this one out; to give it substance. They were turning into the prison gates now. In a moment the numbing routine, numbers not names, waiting in line, locks clanking and doors slamming, would take over. He had been a tutor, pretty Georgia's tutor and lover, but right now he was a prisoner, sucked back into his prison.

The debate he refused to have centred on Georgia. Was it fair to pass on this information and to obtain more? He was not a natural resistance fighter, the irony of his current sentence notwithstanding. What were they planning to do with the information?

He realised as the gates closed behind him and Linda's car came to a halt that he would never ask. If he asked, they might tell him. That was far more involvement, more responsibility, than he wanted.

Here was a highly educated, brilliantly intelligent man choosing ignorance over knowledge. Such was the perversity of the world they lived in.

"Gosh, you have been thoughtful today. If you want to mention anything else to me, it is last chance saloon right now!" There was a beauty about Linda that he appreciated. She was always close to a joke. Everything went through her humour machine and came out better and brighter. He wanted to kiss her but knew he never could; not in the prison yard, not with machine guns watching them like vultures waiting.

"No, Linda, nothing. I'm just tired." It was surprisingly easy to lie to her. She was, after all, a part of the authority, albeit twisted and shaped for different purposes.

"Well, get some rest. You have a big day tomorrow

refereeing! I'll be meeting you about eight. I'll borrow some kit for you and bring it with me." She placed her hand on the side of his chair, not touching. They looked at each other and Mark knew then that she would like to kiss him too, but there was too much at stake. She was restrained, self-disciplined, despite her often frivolous behaviour. Her eyes were firmly on the purpose of resistance. Mark, by contrast, had given in to passion with Georgia, forgotten any other or higher purpose. Indeed, he had no other possible purpose than his freedom and he had been reckless with that.

He was tired and he was depressed as he was led back, handcuffed, to his cell like a monk, busy with tasks all day but expecting the solitude at the end; always the aloneness, nothing changing, nothing improving. But whereas a monk welcomed it, he despised it.

Just as he had come to despise himself. Everything bad he saw in the world seemed a reflection of him. Anything with an ounce of nobility seemed in the pockets of others.

The match was a hard-fought, no-score draw. Mark had not had time or resources to check the rules so had gone on common sense. As a result, both teams were thoroughly disillusioned with the quality of refereeing.

"Let's play extra time," one of Edmund's team suggested.

They did so, for nobody could deny them their wants. Mark forgot to change ends, such that there was a slight downhill advantage remaining with Edmund's team.

Edmund scored within 90 seconds of restarting play. He dribbled frantically along the left wing, right under his parents' gaze, refused to pass, almost lost the ball to Eddie the English, regained control and shot at goal. It soared past the goalkeeper and went straight into the back of the net, plumb centre.

That was enough for everybody. Honour had been satisfied. Edmund was hoisted up on his teammates' shoulders and carried around the field.

Afterwards, they hosted the English for a meal back at the mansion using one of the servants halls. They had fresh milk, buns, bread and butter and homemade biscuits. To cap off the feast, every boy was served a doughnut straight from the oven. Melted jam and sugar abounded.

"Well done, Edmund," was heard more than once. Mark, helping to serve the English contingent, thought that Edmund should have passed the ball to someone in a better position. He had risked all in his rush for glory.

This time he had been lucky.

It was hard to settle down after the fresh air of the morning. Mark was allowed to use a bathroom and ran a bath; his first for six years. He settled back in the water and thought about what information he had to obtain. It was obvious that the resistance was planning something. But, no, he was not going to go down that route. He was just a funnel of information. What they did with that information was not his worry.

"Hurry up, Mark. I hope you haven't escaped out of the window?"

"I'm coming, Linda. I thought about the window but then I got an image of you cutting the rope I've made out of the towels and plunging to the ground." The bathroom was on the ground floor, looking over a rose border.

"Ha ha, you're better off trying to bore me to death with your jokes. Seriously, I don't think you should be late for the Fraulein."

When Mark did come out a few minutes later, Linda pretended not to recognise the cleaned-up version of her charge. Then she talked about the football match.

"They gave you a hard time, both sides. But for a non-football-player I think you did a really good job."

"How do you know I'm not a footballer?" he asked, still drying his hair as he walked along the corridor.

"You forget, I've studied your files. I know everything about you; every weakness, every foible!" She ran ahead to the corner of the corridor and said, "It takes two flights for Thomas to catch me, let's see what you can do."

Georgia was quite different that afternoon. She was already waiting for Mark, sitting on her desk rather than on the seat, swinging her legs back and forth.

"I'm sorry, Fraulein," Linda said, suddenly less sure of herself. "We didn't realise you were waiting for us."

"No matter, Burton, you can leave us now."

The moment Linda left, Georgia was on her feet.

"Mark." She leant up on tiptoes and kissed him on the lips.

"Fraulein, we've got to be careful." To put meaning to his words he looked back at the door. But Georgia had a plan for that. She closed it then picked up his chair and placed it under the doorknob, rattling the handle to check it was secure. She turned back to him. She was grinning; something Mark had not seen before in all the weeks of intense study.

"I've been complaining about that door sticking for a while but the English never sort things out." She was forgetting that she was talking to one of the English. "Now it works to our advantage."

Her laughter was a joy. It started with a quaint smirk, as if she was willing her mouth not to form into laughter mode, fighting the instinct. But her resistance was overwhelmed as giggles rose up like bubbles of fizz from somewhere deep inside. Her pale face turned shade after shade darker, like degrees of a red-hot oven. Her body shook, first the shoulders, then the whole of it. Her feet, weighed down by sensible heavy shoes, seemed to lose all sense of properness. Mark saw as her body shook so her feet danced a private clumping jig.

Then came the actual laughter.

Her laughter was beautifully clear, ringing out like bells made in Heaven.

And it did not stop.

Mark had arrived at 2.11pm. Linda had left at 2.12pm. The chair had gone in place a minute later, followed directly by the laughter. She was still laughing when the big nursery rhyme clock on the wall chimed out for three.

Gradually, Mark was able to calm her. But they did no work that day. Instead, between the bouts of laughter, finding the silliest things to giggle at, they made love three times.

Mark chose his time quite well. Between the first and second, as she began to get playful again, he started his questions.

"Fraulein, tell me about the camp. Why do you dislike it so?" She gave the normal stuff about growing up, not wanting to build rafts and sit around campfires.

"Did you go last year?"

"Yes."

"To the same place?"

"Yes."

"Tell me about it, then."

"Why do you want to know?" She looked at him curiously. Had he gone too far too quickly?

"I want to imagine you there." It was the perfect answer. She loved it. "I want to know where you sleep, what you get up to, who's there with you. I want to know everything so I can picture you while you're doing it."

He heard everything, then, from her lips, lying on the rug, facing him, looking him over from end to end, marvelling in him.

"Everything except the movements of Heffernott," Linda slid the Mercedes into drive.

"I can't ask her that. It would give the whole game away."

Mark was exhausted, not sure of anything anymore. Logically, he should not like Georgia Nullgeben, yet a part of him did, very much. He was not a fighter yet was aiding a cause that could get him shot. He had a chance at freedom after six years' imprisonment yet he was risking it all.

"Let's work out a way to ask her as we drive."

"She doesn't know anyway."

"How do you know?"

"Because she opened up to me completely. I could tell. If she knew anything about it, she would have relayed it to me. Anyway, why should she know?"

At that moment, the car came to a screeching stop, brakes jammed on.

"My God, Linda, what have you…"

"It's okay, Mark." This time she did put her hand on his leg, then leant over and kissed him warmly. "I've wanted to do that for a while, never had the chance," she said in the dark but outside there were lights flashing, people moving up ahead, two barriers being placed across the road. "You understand it was a kiss for a very good and dear friend, nothing more?" He nodded. Things were moving too fast. He took hold of her hand, squeezed it, started to say something but then both rear doors opened and two figures in heavy coats got in, one on the left and one on the right. Two doors closed again.

"Detour 17," said Mr Left.

"Right-oh," said Linda.

"What's going on?" said Mark.

"All in good time," said Ms Right, in a voice that made Mark swing around.

"Auntie Jo! What are you doing here?"

"Aren't you pleased to see me, Mark?"

"Of course, of course," Mark replied. "There is just so much going on." Six years of never ending tedium was the backdrop to this rapid series of events. "It's been so long. I thought you were captured. I don't know what to think."

"I was captured but I escaped. But there is no time for explanations. You have to listen to us, both of you." She leant forward and tapped Linda on the shoulder. "Detour 17 means we have seventeen minutes to brief you both. That requires concentration and focus. There will be another time for catch up. Do you understand?"

"Yes," said Mark, numbed by change.

"Yes," said Linda, fingers drumming on the steering wheel in excitement.

Mark thought he would not sleep that night, might never sleep again. There was so much to take in, so much to think about. They had arrived back at the prison exactly seventeen minutes late.

"There was an accident on the Durrington road, ma'am," Linda explained to the duty supervisor who, having been taught never to believe the English, went straight to the phone and called Traffic Control. After several minutes of frustrated waiting, boots tapping on the concrete floor, she wrote down the details of an accident and replaced the receiver.

"Where did it happen?"

"On the Durrington Road, like I said."

"The Durrington Road goes all the way from Durrington to Market Castle. Where on the Durrington Road did your accident happen?" The way she gave possession of the accident to Linda said it all – she was determined to catch the English out.

"At the junction with the B352. I think a lorry pulled out but I can't be sure. I was about six cars back and we were detoured around Framble and then the back road to here."

The Duty Supervisor checked her notes, sighed and called for the incoming prisoner processors. They took over. Linda saluted the duty supervisor and vanished back into the night, the free world.

The guard who led him back to his cell was a gentle soul, nearing retirement. He was a fish out of water. He always chatted, usually about his wife's health and how they planned, when retired, to go back home to live with their daughter and the grandchildren.

"You look tired, Smithy."

"I am, sir. I think the football took it out of me. I was only refereeing but I am not used to exercise."

"Well, I wish you a very good night. Rumour is you won't be here much longer."

"What have you heard, sir?"

"Well, I'm not sure I should be telling you. I mean, spreading rumours is not the done thing for a guard."

"Please."

"Well, the word on the street is that you have done exceedingly well at teaching young Fraulein Nullgeben and that the commander, her father, is delighted. Furthermore, I understand, although please don't take this as certain, that the commander has signed release papers for you, subject only to his daughter passing the entrance examination for which you have been coaching her."

"She'll pass alright," Mark said, then remembered, "sir,

sorry sir."

"Don't worry about that, Smithy. There is enough of 'sirs' in here as it is. It makes me feel like I'm back in the army."

"Thanks."

"How come you're so sure she'll pass?"

Mark thought to say because he had never met anyone as bright as her, saving himself.

"Because she is super bright, sir. I mean…"

"That's alright. When no one is around you can call me Ernst, that's my name." His name badge said 'Horer' so Mark assumed Ernst was his first name. "I've only got three weeks to retirement so what does it matter?"

Mark thought he would never sleep. But after he had brushed his teeth in the tiny plastic sink, flipped off his soft prison shoes and laid down on his familiar bed, he fell instantly into a dreamless sleep, only awakened by an irritated guard on the buzzer.

"Smith, XX1Z2495, stand by your bed, back to the door, arms out to the side, hands open."

It was Monday morning and he was going to see Georgia.

Friends and Relations

Jo Macclesfield let the water run through her fingers. It was intensely cold, such that temperature seemed set on a circular scale, there being no difference between very cold and very hot. Ice could burn as well as a furnace. She liked to let it pour through her fingers, bending them back with its force, lodging a twig between thumb and forefinger or up against the palm.

But nothing would wash away her past.

The stream by their campsite was pure. It only served one purpose, to rush the water down the hillside from the pines at the top to the oaks at the bottom. How she wished she could simplify things so, like the stream, concentrate on one task, be satisfied with one objective.

For things were horribly complicated for Jo Macclesfield now. Once they had been simple. Once, when she was young, she had been a stream.

But not now.

Her very name was complicated. She was born an O'Donnell, not English but Irish living in England. She and her sister, Mark's mother, had grown up in the beautiful Peak District, 'a home from home' as her father, the ranger, had said. There had been plenty of boys in the village. It was expected that they both would marry and settle down as farmer's or ranger's wives. Both were very pretty and tall, with classical features topped with an abundance of wavy brown hair. It made the boys turn and look. It was expected that the two sisters would have the pick of all of them.

But both girls had taken different paths. Jenny, Mark's mother, had married the schoolteacher, recently transferred on a cultural exchange trip from Toronto. After three years he was due to be transferred back but they had decided to remain, Jenny not wanting to leave the country of her birth. Instead, they had moved to a new position and a semi in Blackheath, then on again to a village, Fontby Green, outside Tonbridge. They moved this last time for the education for Mark. For by the age of eight it was apparent that he had a powerful intellect.

Jo, the younger of the two, did not marry for a while so there was a twelve-year gap between the two wedding dates.

In fact, there was a huge gap in everything else surrounding the two weddings.

For Jo married a young RUDD officer.

His name was Bertrand Fischer and he came to her village to do a study on the fish population of the area. He was an avid fisherman, following countless generations of sea fishers, presumably giving rise to the surname.

They met when her father, the ranger, was tasked with showing him around. Nobody among the English, their adopted home, liked the authorities. And the O'Donnells were no exception. O'Donnell showed him only a few spots, not the best, then left him to fend for himself.

Only his daughter felt sorry for the handsome fishing inspector and undertook to show him around.

They were married six weeks later. They were married in London, quite suddenly on a Friday afternoon, a day after he proposed to her.

At first, she had refused him.

"It will damage your career," she had said. But he insisted that nothing mattered other than that they were together. She relented and they married the next day. There was no family from either side other than Jenny, who had been forbidden to have anything to do with them but slipped into the back of the registry office and slipped out again after catching her sister's eye and blowing a kiss.

For their honeymoon they went fishing in Devon. They had wanted to go to Ireland or Scotland but she could not get a permit.

Their world was already closing in on them.

The marriage lasted until his family heard about it.

They sent over a delegation of brothers and cousins, led by his spinster sister who Jo disliked immediately. He was bundled back to his North Sea home. She was taken to work in a steelworks, producing knives and triggers for guns. When it was clear that she was pregnant they transferred her to a hospice. They took the baby after three days and she had never seen him again, although she had received a 16mm film spool from Bertrand's sister ten years ago; an act of intense spite. Her boy, now called Rudolf (not the name she had given him), was seven years old. The film showed him in his school, looking for all the world like he belonged there and nowhere else.

She had not been able to watch it again but cycled down to the river and threw it in.

Always water rushing along but not cleansing with its path.

She had later on gone to the authorities about her name. O'Donnell was no longer available. Once married, it was lost. Fischer would not be appropriate. She had to come up with another name. They did not care what name she chose provided it was fitting. She had lodgings and a job at a paper mill in Macclesfield so named herself after the town.

The paperwork was done quickly. They were good at paperwork. She sometimes wondered if she had helped to make the paper that her new name came on. It was, in itself, nothing special; a plain piece of A4, but her new identity card, new residence permit and new control document, with 'single' marked under marital status, bulked out the package.

Sometimes she wondered about Bertrand, her husband of such short duration. It had been a marriage that lasted for the honeymoon only. Two glorious weeks in Devon, fishing and camping by streams – always water rushing by her. When they had returned to his London flat his sister and half-a-dozen male relations had been waiting for them.

"You can't marry an English," the sister had said. She was undoubtedly the leader.

"She's not an English."

"She looks it, look at her," sneered Cousin Albert.

"It is pleasure now but think of the future, think of when the novelty wears off. Think then, my dear brother, how you will be held back."

"We're happy," Bertrand had said lamely. "Surely that counts for something?" Jo remembered thinking, why is he reasoning with them? She had withstood the intense anger of her family so why couldn't he do the same?

"You can get your pleasure anywhere, any time. Keep her as a toy if you will, but keep yourself free for a good marriage, for goodness' sake." That was another brother; younger but apparently wiser.

He had retaliated a little longer. Jo, on reflection, preferred 'retaliate' to 'fight' because it seemed more on the back foot, more descriptive of how he had been.

They had led him away to the hotel they were staying in. Then the sister had returned with one brother. They told Jo to get out immediately. They gave her 100 marks; a lot of money, but she threw it back at them. The brother picked it up and stacked the notes, counting them to be sure.

She left then, with one bag for her belongings. She left and she never went back, never saw her husband again.

The paperwork flowed, of course. The annulment arrived at her parents' house six days later. She had gone there and thrown herself in her misery on their mercy and, like most parents, they had welcomed her in, never saying 'I told you so'.

A week after the annulment, a large white package arrived for her. It was a ZA; a *Zuordnung Auftrag*. They were sufficiently rare to cause her family to gather around when she opened it.

"Old Fred got one some years back," her father had commented. "After he got in the dog house about his son refusing national service. They were packed up in two days and gone someplace..." He petered out as he contemplated that his daughter, maybe all of them, might share a similar fate.

But the authorities were kind, in fact had not even considered the wider family. Jo was to report within three days to the Great Moresby Steelworks for training in steel production. The package included everything she would need: a travel permit, a third-class train ticket, and a residence allocation. She was to bring only one bag for space in the residence was limited. She would be provided with work clothes and essentials. She was to come ready to work, conditions as enclosed.

Her mother picked up the package and tipped it up. There was one other piece of paper in it. It was entitled *Haircut*

Anleitung. Nobody in their community had seen one of these before. It explained in simple words that long hair was a safety risk in the steelworks and required all workers to have suitable hairstyles. She was to report to the local police station so that they could take care of it.

When Jo arrived at Great Moresby two days later with her beautiful hair cropped to collar-length, the first thing her landlady said to her was that nobody bothered with those requirements anymore.

"Everyone gets a hat to wear that keeps long hair away from the machinery."

She had defied the authorities. What else could she expect?

That had been almost twenty years ago. At first, she had strictly conformed, in the hope of seeing her son again. But after Fraulein Fischer sent the film she knew it would never happen. She changed fundamentally as she watched the film reel bobbing in the water and being carried downstream. She vowed revenge. She joined the resistance. She worked her way up: first section leader, then section head, now divisional commander.

"Let's move out," she ordered, taking her hand out of the stream, drying it on her coat, facing her section heads as they gathered. "We're off to sunny Sussex. I'll brief you more when we get there but, suffice to say, this is a critical mission."

They were an army, but you would never know it. There were no uniforms, no standard equipment. Jo called it the 'Peasants' Revolt' because they seemed put together by accident. When they moved, they did not travel in convoy; rather haphazardly, splintering into tiny groups, sometimes on foot, hitching rides in lorries or borrowing cars where they could. Jo had a beaten-up Volkswagen van, bald tyres and a leaking radiator that limited journeys to thirty minutes before a top-up. But it worked, for the authorities did not care what the English drove. In fact, they secretly preferred them driving scrappy cars as it separated them distinctly. Thus, to drive a government car, any English had to pass the SF and go through security checks to gain their *Einheimische Fuhrerschein.*

But if you drove a private car they could not care less, provided you pulled over when a government car passed and you did not leave your *Heimatgebeit* or home area.

Jo was not even in her *Heimatgebeit* in the first place. She would be sure to pull over at the very hint of a government car, avoiding risk of discovery.

She had a plan and now was the time to put it into operation. Over the last forty-eight hours she had visited resistance headquarters to sell it to them.

"It was our idea, our sources and our information. We should be allowed to put it into execution." She had stood before her bosses and argued her case, even though it meant crossing into another division and most divisions were jealous of their territories.

"We think the plan might work," the chief marshal said, "but want you to share with Sussex. You can't send everyone over to Harcourt Castle. You need to keep some in reserve in the locality. Plus, of course, you need to protect your source if he is threatened."

"Of course, Chief Marshal, that makes complete sense." She had not thought of the need to protect her nephew.

She worked on the plan, chopped it and changed it, improvements and nuances. By midnight on Tuesday it was as good as it was going to get.

Half her force would go early to Harcourt Castle, meeting up with a similarly sized force from Sussex. Crucially, Jo would have command. Two small contingents would shadow the two groups going to attend the camp – Edmund's group including the rest of the campers and then, later in the day, Georgia, Bootle and the detachment of soldiers to guard her on route. A sizeable force would remain in Berkshire to maintain a presence and protect the chain of informers should that prove necessary.

For the plan, if it worked, would cause a great deal of upset.

As she was leaving HQ, pre-dawn on Wednesday, the chief marshal summoned her back. Jo was annoyed, anxious to be on her way, but tempered with the knowledge that he would surely not keep her from her duty for any frivolous reason.

The chief marshal was a big, bald man with a peculiar habit of suddenly touching his cheek with his hand, rubbing it back and forth furiously, then seeming to become aware and forcing his hand down to his side, left hand taking the right one down. A moment later, he was doing it again. He was worried about her initiative. He sought reassurances and tried to place caveats on their actions. If the guards were too many, they were to pull the operation. If there were too many patrols in the area, likewise. If the head of the Kent and Sussex resistance had objections, they should not go ahead. He shook his head, shifting his weight, hand back to his cheek.

Jo responded by exaggerating her confidence, dismissing his arguments with passion, wondering at the back of her mind how this timid man had come to be the chief marshal of their organisation. The more nerves he displayed, the more bombastic her courage became. Finally, he agreed once more: "If you really think it will work, go ahead, but…"

"No 'buts', sir. It is well planned and will be well executed. It will work, sir."

"Jo, I would very much appreciate it if you could take someone back to Berkshire with you." He waited for a response, his vast frame jigging from side to side. Nerves were terrible things.

"Who?"

"His name is Pete Morris."

"Mark's friend?" Mark's best friend from childhood days had been imprisoned in the 1959 Clampdown, the same net that had caught Mark, Jo and many others. She had escaped before trial but others had not been so lucky.

"Precisely. He has had a rough time since '59. He escaped in '63. He has a lot of promise, I mean divisional commander-level like you, but he needs guidance from someone who has seen pretty well everything." He was flattering her and she knew it but liked it all the same. "Plus, I am convinced that Mark is going to be exposed and I think he will need all the friends he can get. Jo, I don't mind telling you we are nervous about this plan of yours and really only doing it because of respect for you. If it goes wrong, we are not in a strong enough position to recover. This could be a calamity of the first order. It could be the undoing of us all." He was almost wringing his hands in angst.

"Sir, it can't go wrong. It is a perfect opportunity to capture the head of RUDD. We need a strike like this to make a difference." There was far too much pessimism around HQ. Maybe this mission would turn them for once and all.

Jo had little doubt about her plans, for Mark had done wonders; creating, without knowing it, this wonderful chance to hit back. He reported to Linda on the Monday before camp started that Heffernott planned to be there on the second Wednesday.

"How did you find this out?" Linda had asked.

"I have my ways," he replied then, thinking his response too flippant, "I asked her and she came out with it. I think she is excited because she is so looking forward to meeting him. She has gone through 180 degrees from hating the thought of camp to being super excited about it."

But he was not being totally honest. She had reacted badly when he had asked.

"Why do you want to know that, Marky love?" This time propping herself up on an elbow was insufficient. She sat up, drew her long legs in from beside him, retreating within herself.

"Because I want to know everything about you, Fraulein." She had never said to call her by anything else. Now 'Fraulein' had almost become a term of endearment. It was how he thought of her.

"Really? I mean..." She did not finish because Mark sat up and kissed her slowly, passionately.

He cared about her. That was certain. So why was he using her? And risking his own freedom as well?

"What will happen to me?" Mark had to get her off the subject. "I mean, when you go and my work here is done."

"I don't know. How long is your sentence?"

"It is indeterminate."

"Oh, then I suppose you will go back to prison." She had not thought about it, had a wonderful naivety that came out as directness; no concern for the impact.

But his tactic worked for, rather than discuss it more, she turned to him and kissed him back.

Being kissed under these circumstances did nothing for his self-respect.

But it did give the resistance everything they needed

In not-so-distant Wiltshire, in the small town of Puttering, on the edge of Salisbury Plain, a package arrived by special delivery. It was Wednesday morning.

"It's for Mark," said Mark's mother, handing it to her husband.

"We'll need to open it," said Mark's father, handing it back to his wife.

They set it on the mantelpiece, propped behind the carriage clock he had received in recognition of thirty years of teaching dedication.

"They engraved his clock with a special message," Jenny used to say when visitors very occasionally came by. "No, don't handle it or the letters will wear away. I can tell you what it says."

Once Jo had visited, on the run, only she dared not let her sister know that. For Jenny and Gerry, her husband, had never broken the law; would never break the law. Instead, Jo made up a story about living as an itinerant.

"It's the only life I can happily lead now."

Afterwards, when Jo had gone, with a change of clothes and a full belly, they had said how awful it was.

"All because she married above herself."

There the package stayed, on the mantelpiece, behind the carriage clock, until the next day when the postman knocked on their door.

"Mr Smith, no packages today. I was just wondering if you had a special delivery response to the special delivery you received yesterday." Everyone knew of the Smiths' son's incarceration, although nobody in Puttering had met him. "My betting is it's government papers and with it being addressed to your son, like, we wondered if some change might be in the wind." Said so cheerily that Gerry Smith could not take offence, indeed asked him in for a cup of tea.

And for the grand opening of the package.

It was a *Zuordnung Auftrag*, a ZA.

"Does this mean...?" Jenny asked, not able to put the full question.

"I think it does, it must do. Look, there are instructions to report on Monday May 10th to the Sector Laboratories in Westhaven. It says more here. He is to be employed as a Laboratory Runner; that means fetching and carrying for the scientists. He is to report at 8am on the tenth. That has to mean he is going to be released!"

The nosy postman was then treated to an unusual sight. This staid, law-abiding couple threw caution aside and danced a jig together in their small front room, holding hands, their eyes shining.

"And our boy has got himself a proper job as well."

"I think this calls for a sherry."

The nosy postman did not object.

Day of Departure

Georgia was nervous; nervous all over her young body, feeling it like an itch and burning combined. She was early, waiting for Mark who was being trusted to invigilate the examination.

"I've never heard of an English invigilating before," Edmund had said at breakfast. "What is this world coming to?"

"Quiet, Edmund," said Frau Nullgeben. "Prisoner Smith has earned a modicum of respect through his diligence. He is intelligent, far more than the average English, and has proved a perfectly acceptable tutor."

"If only you knew."

"What was that, Edmund?" his father asked sharply, senses alert.

"Sir, I was about to say if only you knew how confident Georgia has become through this extra tuition. I hope she wins a scholarship and paves the way for me to follow at the *Statenthrump*." Then with an innate knowledge of how to please, he added, "I hope this is the start of a great tradition of the Nullgebens attending *Statenthrump*. It was not around in Father's time so he could not go. We are the first generation to have a chance to establish ourselves as *Statenthrumpers*."

"That's my boy," his mother said, ruffling his hair, approving his declaration of conventionalism. "Now, off you go to get ready. You'll be leaving for camp inside the hour."

"Yes, Mother, goodbye." He kissed his mother and raced out of the room.

"Such youth, such enthusiasm."

But now Georgia had to wait. It was 6.56. Mark, her tutor, her lover, her invigilator, would be here at 7.15. The exam would start at 8am. That gave them forty-five minutes from when she dismissed Burton. But she knew she was far too nervous.

Mark arrived late, held up with extra security checks due to the camp convoy heading off that morning. He and Linda and Thomas were breathless when they barged through the nursery door at 7.27.

"My apologies, Fraulein. We were held up…"

"Just go, Burton."

"Yes, Fraulein." She and Thomas backed out quickly, this time Linda closing the door behind her.

Mark was staring at Georgia.

"What's the matter?" she asked in a small voice, sort of knowing the answer.

"It's just … well, you look so different; I mean, still lovely."

"It's my camp uniform." She stated the obvious. Mark looked again at her. In her tan socks, brown ankle boots, brown skirt and tan shirt covered in badges from prior conquests, she looked more like thirteen than going-on eighteen. Her hair was tightly braided and then pinned around the side of her face, topped with a small brown and round hat that sat perched on the back of her head. "I now have to go straight after the examination. There will be no time to change afterwards."

"You look lovely, Fraulein." He meant it, but so young. Then he thought, something is not right. "But why do you have to go right after the exam? I thought we might have some time together."

"Oh, didn't I tell you yesterday? Herr Heffernott is coming early. He's coming this afternoon. I have to rush straight off to make sure I catch him."

"What? Early? Coming this afternoon? Oh no."

"What does it matter to you?" she replied, some enquiry on her young face.

"It's just that I had built up a whole scenario in my mind of you over the next two weeks of camp." He was thinking fast. But was also confused. She was so desirable but so undesirable at the same time.

"Oh Marky, never mind! This is such an opportunity for me. Father is coming, too. We are doing some field exercises tomorrow, big games through the grounds. I really want to impress him." She came over to him, stretched up and kissed him on the mouth. "I am so happy," she said, eyes closed, half there in the nursery with her lover, half in the fields around Harcourt Castle, commanding a troop of brave young things with Herr Heffernott looking on.

They kissed for a few more minutes then Mark said they should settle down for the exam. The papers were in his desk drawer, in a sealed envelope. He placed the papers face-down then kissed her again. She settled at her desk, he at his. They watched the clock. At 8am exactly he told her to turn over the papers for the exam had begun.

"Good luck," he said, but she was already working on the first question; an island of calm in a stormy sea.

Mark was anything but calm. He could not leave the room until Linda and Thomas came back at noon. He would have to tell her the news about Heffernott's altered schedule as soon as they were alone in the car.

Then he remembered that the Nullgebens had wanted to see him at noon; Harry Bootle had said it was to thank him for his hard work. That would mean more delay until he could get the message to Linda. Would she be able to relay the news in time to make a difference?

Time dragged, just as it rushed in the enclosure yard, with no respect for accurate measurement. Mark wondered if this was the payback for all those speedy hours in the yard. He fidgeted, could not get comfortable. At one point Georgia looked up, slight questioning on her perfect pale face, framed by her hair tied in neat braids with tan ribbons. He looked into her eyes, smiled. She returned to her work, head bent.

Time dragged as he agonised over the slowly ticking clock. He tried not to look at it until he had judged thirty minutes had passed but each time his judgment fell short. His mind was split into a hundred different parts, each one with a conflicting thought, bombarding the others. If he helped Linda he hurt Georgia, hurt her chances of impressing her father's boss. If he did not help Linda he was standing aside, effectively assisting those who had imprisoned him. And what of all the others who had been imprisoned along with him in the Great Clampdown? What of his Auntie Jo? But what of his own chances of freedom? He had impressed the Nullgeben parents but threatened to blow it all with his support of the resistance. And then there were his feelings for Georgia.

What do you do when your mind is going in every direction at once?

You take a deep breath, count to some high number and then breathe out. You become calm and you decide your priorities.

He knew he had to get the schedule revisions to Linda and she could get them on to Auntie Jo.

Now that his decision was made, time stepped up its pace. Seconds turned to minutes and minutes flashed by. He settled back in his chair, put his hands behind his head as the clock hand headed north, then east, south, west and north again.

"Time, Fraulein."

"I finished ten minutes ago," she laughed. "I've been watching you stare at the ceiling! What is up there? A trapdoor to your freedom?" Well, it was, sort of. "Marky, I'm going to miss you. I'm so excited by the camp, but actually it will be boring after Herr Heffernott is gone. Maybe I can visit you in prison when I get back? Maybe Mother and Father would allow it?"

They kissed again, then a detached hug, aware that at any moment Linda could walk into the room to take Mark away.

There was a knock at the door. They separated, one last cling of the hands, then some distance between them.

"Enter," called the Fraulein.

The door opened. It was Thomas, but not Linda. The guard this time, this last time, was not Linda Burton with all her fun and laughter hiding a serious dedication. It was gentle Ernst Horer.

"I've to take you to Herr and Frau Nullgeben," he said with a smile. "Then back to you-know-where."

Mark had to wait fifty-five minutes for the Nullgebens to arrive, then stand for ten more minutes while they praised the way he had brought out the best in the Fraulein. Then, when he thought it was coming to an end, Frau Nullgeben had a gift.

"Smith, I know you don't get much food in prison; not the best quality, I am led to understand. As a mark of our appreciation I have arranged for a last lunch downstairs with a little surprise for you as well. Horer, take him down to the Junior Servants' Hall and put him in the care of Thomas. You can then go and have some lunch in the Senior Servants' Hall."

"Thank you, Frau, thank you, sir."

"Thomas, where's Linda?" Mark whispered as soon as he could.

"I've no idea. She said she would be back before noon. She got a radio call while we were … well, never mind where we were. She had to leave straight away."

"Tell her all change on dates. Next week is today."

"What?"

"She'll know what it means. Just tell her."

"Silence for grace. Thomas, you cannot eat now. You are to serve next door."

Mark watched his one hope walk smartly towards the Senior Servants' Hall.

His surprise after lunch was a big bar of chocolate. He broke it open there and then, knowing it would be confiscated at the prison. He shared it with the others, the young maids in particular taking great pleasure in two squares each of sugary chocolate.

"Good luck," they cried as his guard led him out, looking at his heavy watch, concerned about time drifting. "We'll miss you." Some of the bolder girls gave him a peck on the cheek; two hall boys shook his hands; a junior chauffeur clapped him on the back and said, "Keep your spirits up mate, you never know what the future holds."

And they left. His tutoring over, assignment complete. He had done his best. It was all in the hands of others now.

Ernst Horer chatted all the way back in the car, then through processing, into handcuffs and back towards the cells. Horer's world was so light, so lacking in responsibility. *If only,* thought Mark, *if only.*

"Not that way, Smithy," Horer called. "You're to be in separation for a while." Horer led the way past the normal cellblock, on to an area Mark had never visited before. "Here's your home from home."

The cell was windowless and very small, one dull bulb high up gave a semblance of light. He could make out a narrow board bed, a thin mattress, one rug and a bucket.

"Food and water is once a day through this little hatch. Don't eat and drink it all at once now."

"Thanks, Ernst."

"Goodbye, Smithy." A pat on the back and he was alone in his narrow, tall box.

Alone, totally alone. Just the walls to echo back his thoughts. He sat on the bed, head in hands. Despair swept over him like waves at the seaside. Why was he here, in this prison within a prison? Where was Linda?

After a long while, survival kicked in. He paced his tiny cell, estimated it to be six feet by five. He worked out the cubic capacity by estimating the ceiling height. Then counted the bricks in all the walls.

It was back to the old days.

Change of Plans

Georgia ran from tree to tree, signalling frantically to her troop, who followed behind in a ragged line. It was England showing its best, just for this special occasion. The sun edged through the new leaves, making patterns on the ground that swayed with the breeze. Bluebells had come early this year, looking across at their fellows in a race to be the tallest, touching the world Georgia ran through with a hint of purple, a hint of blue, like an artist, like God, only there was no god. Everything seemed so new, so sprung-up overnight, like a puppy growing daily with gangly legs and huge clumsy paws.

Edmund came into sight, also in charge of a squad, waving the youngsters this way and that as they descended the hill in some semblance of immature order.

"Ah, Nullgeben, you say your son Edmund did most of the organisation for this event?" Heffernott had a heavy patrician accent and an enormous ability to condescend.

"Yes, sir. Unfortunately, we lost our camp leader last year to a vicious terrorist attack. Some English stepped in but it lacked direction, decisiveness."

"Provided by your son?"

"Precisely, sir." The commander found his voice moving up the patrician scale. It often happened when he came face-to-face with an aristocrat. "I am enormously pleased with the lad's efforts."

"And your daughter, she is the opposing leader?"

"Yes, sir, that is her over there, just behind the grove of trees. Their objective is to capture each other's flags."

They watched the manoeuvres for several minutes. It was clear that they were both naturals in command. Werner suspected that Georgia was getting a slight edge over Edmund. He glanced at his boss, wondering what the old man was thinking about.

"You've done a decent job of bringing them up, Nullgeben."

"Thank you, sir."

"Now let's see what they are capable of in the field."

Heffernott blew a whistle that hung about his neck on a leather strap. "The Battle of Britain," he said, flourishing it with pride. As early as 1940, they had switched from medals, which served no useful purpose, to tools of the trade; something of great use in the field. Nullgeben had a compass from his earlier days on campaign. It had a secret compartment for codes hidden in the lid.

A moment later, a cohort of armed soldiers moved out of hiding on the opposite hill behind Edmund's position. Edmund glanced around quizzically, was about to say something to them, seeking an explanation, when they fired at him.

Of course, they were blanks, but the shock factor was there. Edmund froze then shouted, "Down, down, get down." The undulating land saved them, made natural pockets that boys and girls could hide in. But it was the next action that really made the day. Edmund crawled backwards to meet with half a dozen of his followers, whispered for a minute, and then he and three others stood up, arms in the air.

"They've surrendered!" Heffernott exclaimed, trying to sound neutral but not doing it well.

But Werner Nullgeben saw movement on the hillside. Three figures crawling back to the trees where Georgia was watching events. Then a huddle of conversation, arms pointing back to the soldiers just below the crest of the hill. Then a blur of rapid movement and nothing: no sound, no motion.

"It appears your forces are no match for the real thing." Heffernott was tactful enough not to mention the leadership of those forces, then added, "Of course, we're talking about youngsters against professionals." Nullgeben did not reply for he had an idea as to what was about to happen.

"Hands up. Drop your weapons." The cry rang across the field like an order across a parade ground. They looked up to the ridge to see Georgia's contingent with some of Edmund's also, holding sticks as weapons, forming a circle so they could not be encircled themselves.

"Excellent!" said Heffernott. "I've seen nothing today but the very best!"

He clapped his hands. Edmund stood up and matched

Georgia's grin. Herr Nullgeben, however, had the broadest smile.

"I don't know what to do." Jo's senior section head was deeply frustrated, shaking his head as he walked across the campsite to sit on one of a series of stones that, years before, had been placed in a semi-circle around a fire. Who and why was lost to history, but they served their purpose all over again.

"Let's recap." Jo tried to sound positive. Whatever the frustrations, her belief was that there were always some positives. You just had to seek them out. "Our main force was in place on Thursday evening, hidden in the woods no more than three miles from Harcourt Castle, with scouts out at strategic places. The party under Sandy shadowed the campers down on Friday morning, supposedly to meet up with us. Only the campers did not stop at Harcourt Castle. Well, they stopped briefly, ate packed lunches on the lawn and then moved on to a place called Betherington Manor, about sixteen miles away, in Kent."

"Which is where we are now," Jake, the senior section head, replied. "Then the Fraulein, her father and a larger contingent of soldiers than we expected, flew by several helicopters straight to Betherington Manor, arriving slightly before the main body of campers, who had stopped at Harcourt Castle and travelled by lorry."

"But all the kit was waiting at Harcourt Castle. While the kids had lunch, extra lorries came to take it all to Betherington. That means that they had expected to come here but changed their minds at the last minute." Jake had a habit of shaking his head as he spoke, as if he disagreed with himself. He was a big man with a lot of muscle. Yet he moved in jagged motions, perpetually ill-at-ease with himself or perhaps questioning his decisions as they were made? Jo had overlooked him for promotion the first time but last year had remedied this, explaining to HQ that he was fanatically devoted to the cause, would not talk about his past. The self-questioning seemed to result in sound, well-thought-out plans. She assumed he had lost family to the authorities, probably in the Clampdown.

"Or, they planned all this because they knew about our intentions." Jo worked often on gut reaction but she was able to sit and analyse equally well. Now was a time for analysis. Later, in the heat of the moment, she would trust to her instincts.

"That would mean they have a mole amongst us."

"Or somebody has extracted or heard the information we thought we were passing along securely."

They worked together, division and section heads, playing off each other to progress their reasoning. By the time dishes of stew were brought to them they had the foundations laid down.

"Get a message back to Berkshire. We have to know that the chain of information flow is secure."

"I'll do that straight away, Jo." Jake stood up.

"No, five minutes to eat your stew will not make a difference."

It was dusk on Saturday night; soldierly games complete, campfires lit and huddles made. There was singing; a little too much schnapps for the adults. They had cause to celebrate. Heffernott had decided, on impulse, to stay an extra night. Instead of leaving that afternoon, he had postponed his departure until Sunday morning.

"You have to allow an old man the chance to brush shoulders with the new generation of leaders," he had said as offhandedly as he could. But everyone knew he was deeply impressed by what he had seen. "The Nullgebens are a fine family," he had dictated to his secretary. "He makes the best commander this sector has ever seen, while both children have enormous potential. I have no doubt that both will thrive at the *Statenthrump* and I intend to meet with the Secretary General of Admissions next week. Please call and make the arrangements, Ruffner."

"Yes, sir."

The Nullgebens were smiling. And the commander had thought of his aristocratic wife. He had arranged a helicopter to fly down that day, complete with a bodyguard of hard men who hit each other in the stomach for amusement and ground out their own-rolled cigarettes on the palms of their hands or pinched them between thumb and forefinger.

Just before a campfire supper was cooked and served by the youngsters, Herr Heffernott called the Nullgeben family together in the drawing room at the manor house where he was staying and where the Nullgeben parents had also taken rooms. The huge old house, with its panelled walls, uneven floors and low ceilings from another age, was empty, with a 'For Sale' sign up at the lodge by the road. The owner was long-gone, had only been too glad to take three hundred marks for two weeks' occupancy.

Heffernott gave a rambling speech. Nullgeben got the impression he was telling a life story, those flashing seconds before death, yet spun out over forty minutes. He glanced at his wife, bored and suffering. He glanced at his children, enraptured, in another world. Heffernott mentioned retirement and Nullgeben sat bolt upright.

Retirement meant opportunity.

He nudged his wife. She looked at him. She had not been listening.

"Retirement." That word made her perk up. Retirement meant promotion. Promotion meant a senior posting back in the homeland. Perhaps even Heffernott's position could be theirs. There was a precedent, back in '54.

"It was first-class planning to (a) change my arrival date and (b) change location right at the last minute. That is the sort of planning and foresight that the RUDD needs. I commend you for it, Werner."

"Thank you, sir."

"Earlier, I mentioned my retirement. I will be seventy in December this year. I just wanted to let the Nullgeben family know that I have been asked to recommend my successor. I am going to be meeting with the Senior Appointments Committee on my return. You see, I had a reason for coming here. I wanted to see first-hand…"

Carla was thinking *Just spit it out, man* but Heffernott continued to waffle. He had wanted to see the sector operations first-hand, culminating in this marvellous idea of attending the camp in order to see the next generation of leaders proving themselves.

"I can move towards my retirement now knowing that there are excellent young leaders in the system moving up to take over eventually. Of course, they won't be ready by the end of this year!" This produced obligatory laughter. But he was eventually getting to his point. "Werner, when I see the Senior Appointments Committee next week I will have no difficulty in making a strong recommendation that my successor be you. And, furthermore, provided there is no hint of scandal, the Senior Appointments Executive have indicated that there will be no divergence from my recommendation."

There, it was said.

"Thank you, sir," Werner said, thinking of Barbara, how it really had to end now.

"Thank you, Herr Heffernott," Carla said, thinking the same.

Much later that night, Werner Nullgeben, Sector Commander, sat at a borrowed desk in the anteroom to the bedroom he and his wife were occupying. She was asleep next door, having retired earlier saying she was exhausted.

"I just have a few things to attend to," Werner had said, "some official documents." He had not needed to mention officialdom but by saying it had underlined his intentions. He kissed Carla on the cheek.

"Very well, Werner. I know you will always carry out your duty. Goodnight, my dear." Could her words be any more pointed?

He opened a well-folded letter. It was from Barbara. Enclosed in the folds was his draft reply. He read it again, tore it up and wrote:

Dear Barbara, much as I would relish the idea of meeting you again, it would be unwise under the circumstances. My position within RUDD is at a critical juncture. It makes me very unhappy to ask you to please consider our relationship ended and not to contact me again.

You wrote in your letter about your financial difficulties. As you are aware, I have no money of my own; everything is with my wife. I have managed, however, to squirrel away a little and enclose a cheque made payable to cash with this letter. The bank account upon which the cheque is drawn has funded the many presents I have given you over the years. This final cheque exhausts the account and I will today write to the bank asking them to close it.

Although it pains me enormously to write these words, our relationship is now at an end and I cannot afford the risk of scandal. As you love me you will do as I ask and cease all contact.
Yours ever in affection
W.
XXX

He did not read it again, for fear it would break his resolve. Instead, he sealed it quickly and pulled the bell for his secretary.

"Ah, Frau Katzenartig, please be so kind as to send this confidential letter securely. You will understand that it is personally confidential? I would not want anyone else to know of its existence."

"Yes sir, of course." She took it. The deed was done. "Sir, did you sign the papers I left for you in your study at home?"

"What papers?" He had forgotten with the excitement of Heffernott's visit. "Was there anything important?"

"No sir, nothing of any consequence. The main one I recall was the release documentation for Prisoner Smith. There were a few diary entries for some summer events and there was a draft report to review on gin consumption by the English."

"Ah, so nothing critical. No matter, I will take care of these next week on my return. Goodnight, Frau Katzenartig."

"Goodnight, sir."

He sat a long time after Frau Katzenartig left while the night plodded on, broken only by foxes and owls calling out as if arranging their social calendar. He could recall the letter still now, but he did not. He could not, because of what Carla had threatened to do.

He tried to move his thoughts to more positive matters. If he took old Heffernott's place as the headman of RUDD, he would have undoubtedly made it. Carla would no longer be able to look at him as she did, with that cold stare wringing with condescension. As the chief of RUDD he would be in the top echelon of leadership, the pinnacle of an astounding career, yet still only forty. He would, at long last, be her equal.

Well, almost.

That Bitter Taste of Freedom

Mark could not see to the top of his cell. He estimated it was eighteen feet tall but with the dim light behind a reflective shield high up, the line between wall and ceiling was distorted. It looked higher where the light shone directly, lower where the shadows reigned.

He went with his estimate of eighteen feet. The bricks were a metric measurement so he first had to do a conversion. He could imagine the wheels turning in his brain, clicking past counters, pausing on key numbers, holding half-done calculations until another part was complete, then pulling everything together.

"There are 2016 bricks," he said to himself. "But I can only count to 1432 because of the poor visibility." Later on, he had calculated that the door took 4.6% of the available wall space, while the bed covered exactly half of the floor, actually very slightly over because one leg was bent outwards, extending into his walking area by almost an inch.

He knew he had been there over a week, because he had counted to eight meals being slotted through the door, learning to slot back both the tray from the previous day and his bucket, quickly emptied and thrust back. But now he was not sure whether he had been fed ten times or eleven.

He sang every song he knew, recited whatever poetry he could remember, then the whole of his PhD thesis, still there after six long years. He made some late amendments, had wondered about the relevance of a whole paragraph. So out it went, replaced with what he had wanted to write but his adviser had not liked.

Now he was estimating the depth of the wall and calculating the weight of material encapsulating him, wondering if he would ever break out of this cocoon.

He was fighting madness, fighting with every ounce of his brain. He could not reflect on how close he had been to freedom, how he had seen real people, eaten real meals, worn real clothes. How he had made love to Georgia. Then this.

"Smith, XX1Z2495, stand by your bed, back to the door, arms out to the side, hands open."

He was dreaming, dreaming of release.

Only this man calling him was persistent. Why didn't the dream move on?

"Smith, XX1Z2495, stand by your bed, back to the door, arms out to the side, hands open."

The Tannoy! It was up by the light fixture. The harsh voice bounced and funnelled down to him.

He stood up by the bed, back to the door, arms out to the side, hands open.

And the door opened, flooding the cell with borrowed light from the passage outside.

"You'll need to shade your eyes, Smithy." It was Horer. "The light will hurt. I don't need you to hold your hands out. I trust you."

Mark needed help with the step out of the cell, then help coping with the space in the passage outside. Horer guided him.

"Good news! The governor is supposed to tell you but I'm going to anyway. You're a free man. You're being released. Now, I just need to put on the cuffs so you can go to the governor's office. You can lean on me, that's fine."

Ernst Horer chatted about his retirement, now just ten days away.

"What day is it today?" Mark managed to ask.

"It's Thursday, 13th May. Surely you kept count in there?" The old guard replied incredulously.

It was fascinating how speedy bureaucracy could be. Mark was summoned from his cell at 10.14am and was out on the street at 10.56am. In the intervening forty-two minutes he had been led up to the governor's office, experienced an embarrassing pat-on-the-back type lecture about how the prison service had once again succeeded in bringing about rehabilitation for one of its 'members', with only a passing reference to the long hours of tutoring Mark had given Georgia.

"Additionally, your service to Fraulein Nullgeben did not go unnoticed."

Then he was led by Horer back down the stairs to the processing centre and passed his belongings – the suit of clothes he had worn to court six years ago, his watch, his wallet and five marks in shiny new coins.

"The bus stop is at the corner. This is a ticket to the bus station in town. Then this one, you can tell the difference because it is larger, is to your parents' hometown of Puttering. The bus leaves the station at 12.32 and arrives at 14.56. Your parents are expecting you."

"Thank you, sir," Mark remembered to say.

"There is one other thing," the processing office said. "Horer will take you down to the bus station but first here is a revised *Zuordnung Auftrag*. You will see the original at your parents' house. It seems your release was delayed unavoidably and without this revision you would be deemed a no-show at your new posting. Now you don't start until Tuesday 18th so you have a long weekend ahead of you."

"Thank you, sir."

There followed the usual stuff about not wanting to see Smith back again 'in these four walls'. Mark did not respond with the cubic volume and weight of the entire prison walls; the calculation he had finished just that morning.

But it was a touching goodbye with Horer.

"Smithy, good luck, keep out of trouble."

"Same to you, Ernst. Enjoy your retirement and the grandkids." They hugged very briefly at the bus stop. It was the type of hug that could be explained away as a pat on the back.

"Where's Linda Burton?" Mark dared to ask. "Have you seen her?"

"Yes, she was on my shift the day before yesterday. Were you friends?"

"Yes, we were. Can you tell her I tried to get word to her? She will know what I mean."

"Of course. Now, here's your bus coming around the corner." This time, with others around, they shook hands, nothing more familiar, and Horer turned around and made smartly off.

Mark was alone but free.

It had happened on Bootle's watch. He had known it would, but desperately hoped otherwise.

He had been daydreaming; thinking back to the old days, to his youth as an excited engineer in thrilling times. He had worked with Reginald Mitchell right up to his death in 1937. It had been as sickening to see his work wasted as it had been exhilarating to see the developments in action. To witness the still-young Mitchell racked by cancer attending the trials of his beloved Spitfire, although hating the name, preferring and using instead the term 'type 300'. It had been a time of wonder, of rapid progress, of teamwork and togetherness and brilliance in so many forms. Every time his mind went to rest it returned him to the glorious 1930s and the flight trials near the old railway town of Eastleigh outside Southampton.

"It's your greatest weakness, Bootle, this daydreaming," the commander had often said.

"I'm sorry, sir." But he felt like adding, *Would you not daydream if you had been part of something so brilliant? I was a trainee engineer under Mitchell, now I am head of security. Would you not live in the past if that were you?*

But, of course, he kept his words to the minimum, terrified that he would say too much, terrified to draw attention, determined to stay faceless. Sometimes he thought he was the only one left who recognised how everything could have been, if only they had not cancelled this project on Mitchell's death. He knew the emerging plane they had worked on would have smashed the ME 109s out of the sky.

"We could have won the Battle of Britain," he told himself and his younger son every night.

"I know, Dad, and you worked on it! Do you think I could have made a good pilot?"

"The best." Harry was not inclined to lie. His sixteen-year-old son had excellent reactions and his party piece was riding a bicycle in circles while juggling seven balls in the air. He chuckled to think of it now.

"Something amusing you, Bootle?" the policeman asked.

"No sir, not at all," he lied, but the police inspector had moved on.

It had happened on his watch, as he had suspected it might. It had happened late afternoon on the second Thursday of the camp, 13th May. Heffernott had long gone, as had the commander and his wife. The camp had settled down to a numbing routine, as Georgia had expected it would, with pointless field games interspersed with swimming races and canoeing excursions. Every night there was the same type of supper cooked on open fires before they sang the same old campfire shanties.

The resistance came out of the woods at the very point when Bootle was emerging from a cloud at the controls of his Spitfire. He was chasing two 109s, rattled off the machine gun and saw a thin tail of smoke from the body of one. The other was more of a challenge. It soared up into the sun and disappeared.

"Hands up! Now lie face-down, hands out to the side."

He took a dozen bullets in his fuselage but thankfully no real damage done.

"Where's Heffernott?" Jo Macclesfield asked, with the contempt the resistance had for any English working for the authorities.

He had to move quickly. He pushed the stick straight down and tumbled out of the sky, sacrificing height but gaining an element of surprise. For a moment the 109 pilot thought the spitfire was going down.

"I said where the hell is Heffernott?" Jo repeated, prodding Bootle with her stolen machine gun.

"He's not here, he left ten days ago." Now he jerked the controls back up, the Spitfire lifted its nose, decelerated with the climb and there in its sights he found the 109, flown ahead of him. A moment later it followed its colleague into the sea, black smoke trailing.

"Who's in charge?"

"I am."

"Get up, keep your hands out to the side. Now, what do you mean Heffernott has left the camp?"

The resistance scouts had not noticed the party of senior officers leaving eleven days earlier because they had not gone in state with a parcel of outriders as convoy but in the back of a supply lorry with just six of the hard-faced soldiers to guard them. They had lumbered along, bodies swaying as the lorry swung around corners, all the way to Croydon Aerodrome where Heffernott and his reduced contingent had taken off for the homeland, while the commander and his wife got into an armoured car to go home. It had been Edmund's idea.

'Just in case, sir," he had said. "Just in case."

Jo Macclesfield's instinct kicked in about 6pm. She called a meeting of section heads on the lawn outside Betherington Manor. The Jacobean house looked down on them, seeming to listen in to their plans, as it must have heard many such over the generations.

"OK, I need ideas. This is a potential disaster. Our major initiative for the summer knocked out by some clever dick's extra planning. We need to recoup something from this and … I know, the very thing!" The idea came to her mid-sentence. She did not need any other ideas now. "I've got it!" She stood up, hopping from foot to foot. "There's no Heffernott for sure but there is a brace of young Nullgebens!"

They discussed it a few moments, decided to let the other campers go. "They have little worth to us. They are the kids of minor officials. We'll go for the big prize."

"We'll take one lorry, tie them up in the back. Jake, you take charge of that. We'll need four guards in the back with them. Ben and Francis, you search everyone here for any information, weapons, radios, codes, etc. Then drive them blindfolded out to the middle of nowhere and we'll meet back at location C. Understood, everyone? Good, I want to move out within the hour."

The police came the next morning. Mark's mother had just treated him to his first eggs in six years. He had chosen them fried so he could see the bright richness of the yolk as he cut into them with his knife. She plied him with toast and tea until he felt bloated.

They knocked on the front door. There was a brick porch with clematis working its way up, hiding the view from the kitchen so they could not see who knocked. But it was a firm knock, not cheery like the postman's.

Mark's father showed them into the tiny sitting room.

"Mark Smith?" they said when Mark entered. "We need to talk to you." They were English, these two; a man and a tall, willowy woman. They introduced themselves as constables and said the detective inspector wanted to interview him down at the station.

"What's it about?" Mark's father's Canadian roots came out a little stronger when he was stressed. But the policeman ignored the father, turned to the son.

"Sir, if you'll just come with us, everything will become clearer later on."

But in the car, the tall, willowy constable could not maintain her silence. While her colleague drove, she spoke. "Mr Smith, have you not heard the news?"

"What news? What's happened?"

"There's been another resistance strike. Over in Kent, they only gone and kidnapped…"

"Georgia!" said Mark without thinking.

"Who?" The male constable asked. "Who is Georgia?"

"Fraulein Georgia Nullgeben, the commander's daughter. She was going to camp in Sussex. It must be her. Is she okay?"

But they knew nothing more. They were just English constables.

Mark was not interviewed by a detective inspector at the police station. Instead, a superintendent was driven down from London and took over the inspector's office.

"Smith, I'll cut straight to the point. I have taken over this investigation from the English. Some things are too important. I need you to tell me about the time you spent tutoring the Fraulein." He was a large man, in a double-breasted, well-worn jacket with a yellow handkerchief, matching his tie, in the breast pocket. He did not sit down but walked about the small room, right hand clasping the left arm behind his back. His hands were huge. Mark could imagine them around his neck, tightening with quiet, ferocious purpose. He seemed like a special operative from the army, posing as a detective.

"What do you want to know, sir?"

"Everything!" Said like a bullet from a gun.

He interrupted constantly, barking new questions, making growling comments, striding across the office, turning aggressively to stare directly in Mark's face. Everything about him was aggression: thin lips; short grey hair; cold eyes; trim waist; big heavy shoes; muscles that rippled below his jacket.

And he kept coming back to Ernst Horer. *What had Horer said to you at that stage and at this time? Why did he say that? What did he say about his retirement? Did he talk about money? Did he boast? Did he have plans?*

"Sir, I simply don't understand why you are concentrating on Herr Horer." In answer, the superintendent suddenly sat down in the inspector's chair. It was far too small for the muscle and sinew that made up this man.

"I don't have to tell you anything," he said, sneering, revealing broken teeth capped in gold, a wire brace holding one section in place. "But I will. You are clearly intelligent for an English. So, I will tell you what I don't need to tell you and then you will help me. Understood?"

"Yes, sir."

"Two things have happened. Number one is Fraulein Nullgeben, your ex-pupil, has been abducted, along with her kid brother. It happened yesterday evening when you were probably washing your filthy self in gin at your parents' place. I've just been to the scene and interviewed some nincompoop in security who let the bastards walk in and take over."

"Bootle?"

"That's the one. He's an English," said by way of explanation. "Number two is that Horer was overheard passing a message to another guard. It sounds suspicious and he was the guard that released you. We think that message came from you." He leant across the desk and jabbed his finger in Mark's chest, causing Mark to jerk backwards. He continued jabbing as he slowly gave the next sentence. "And we're going to find out exactly what the purpose of that message was and then we're going to find the Fraulein and I'm going to get a grateful handshake from the commander and an early promotion to boot." Then he sat back, hands behind his short grey hair as if restraining further aggression. "You just need to tell me everything right now, English!" The superintendent's fist slammed down from behind his head onto the desk top, breaking a plastic paper tray and sending a paperclip container over the edge of the desk. Instinctively, Mark rose from his seat to pick them up.

"Sit down!" his questioner roared. "Don't fart about with that. I want answers."

Mark pretended for as long as he could that his words to Ernst Horer were just an innocent message to pass on to someone who had helped him and he would not see again.

The questioning moved on to Linda Burton, fear spreading across Mark's face.

"Sir, Burton helped me a lot with planning lessons for the Fraulein. I used her as a sounding board on the journeys to and from the prison. It helped to talk about what I was trying to achieve."

But it did not wash. The superintendent needed a result. So, they went over it again and again.

Then, suddenly, as if tired of it all, the superintendent left the room, leaving the door to the small office wide open. Mark thought of walking out, stood up. Could he just walk out of a police station? Would they stop him? Was he under arrest? Nobody had used the right words, but did that matter?

"What the hell are you doing?"

"Sir, I just thought, I, well, I need to go to the men's room."

"You'll pee when I want you to pee. Get back inside."

Two constables, different to the ones who had brought him in, followed the superintendent into the room. They set up a projector and left after fiddling with the focus as the screen on the wall was less than eight feet away.

"Cin-e-ma time." The superintendent said, sticking his face directly in Mark's, careless as to the spit that escaped from his broken teeth. "Don't expect an ice cream, English!" He laughed at his little joke, still face-to-face, still not controlling his fluids.

The film was short. It showed Ernst Horer close-up. He was

crying, blubbering in terror. His nose was bloodied, broken. He was shivering, recoiling from movement. The film came to an end.

"I did that," the superintendent said. "He talked and now he's being looked after. I'm not interested in you, small fry. I'm after the big shots. I want the truth from you and then you can piss off back to your hole. Do you get my meaning?"

"Yes, sir." And Mark started talking.

The Cavern

It looked like an ordinary office block. It was just such. There was a paper importer on the ground floor. Upstairs was a conveyancing office over two floors. The top floor often changed hands. It had been a photographic studio for a while, then empty, and most recently a fruit importer, but the 'For Let' signs were up again. It was a modern office building, built of concrete pre-fabricated slabs trucked in on the back of extra-wide lorries with little buzzer cars ahead and behind, lights flashing.

The owner was a gentleman by the name of Horace Stoakes. He was a successful butcher, operating a chain, and had for many years now supplied all the meat to the RUDD kitchens. Stoakes did not own a single cow, lamb or pig. He bought and sold on, made a killing more times than he could remember, hardly ever had a deal that went sour.

"I have the bovine touch," he used to laugh. "Every time I buy a cow it turns to gold!" He laughed a lot, was popular all around, especially with the authorities.

But this was not reciprocated. For Horace Stoakes had a secret and a past.

Now sixty-two years old, he had been too young for the First World War, but both his brothers had died at the Somme; one on the first day blasted to pieces by a shell, the other not until December 1916, after a festering wound to his leg had laid him up since the previous August. He had been shipped back to England, to a hospice in Bexhill. There he had lingered on through his final autumn, giving up on life on Christmas Eve, the night his saviour had been born, except there was no god and, therefore, no saviour.

Horace had visited his brother frequently in those last days, staying with a distant cousin who had moved out of the East End. He had been with him when he died.

He had also been with his son almost a quarter-century later, when he had died. Bernie Stoakes had been full of life, doted on by his parents and grandparents. He was the only Stoakes in his generation, both Horace's brothers having died without children.

"You're the one to take the Stoakes name forward, my lad," Horace's father used to say. "We're all depending on you."

But that had not happened for Bernie had joined the Royal Air Force in 1938, quickly becoming a pilot. The burns he incurred during the Battle of Britain were awful. It was almost a relief when this bright young thing closed his eyes a final time and died quietly in his sleep. The invasion was over. He would not have wanted to live anyway so in many ways it was for the best.

In fact, on reflection, Horace Stoakes and his wife, Betty, had two secrets. The first was they were Catholics, the most forbidden of all religions. They practised at the dead of night with priest holes, and clandestine masses open air in the woods, deep in the Kent countryside. Betty considered their faith all-important. For Horace, it was a very close second to revenge.

The other secret was that they were beat parents, despite not being parents any longer at all. And this is where the office block he had purchased in '58 came in.

The key was the cellar, now used as a boiler room, with a large caretaker's cupboard in one corner. Open the cupboard door, carefully remove the mops, brushes and drainage rods, and fumble for a minute or two with the panels at the back. Eventually, the upper right panel will move three inches to the left. Place your hand in and turn the lever one half-turn to the right. Without a sound, the entire back of the cupboard swings out to the side, leaving a pitch-black interior. Hopefully you have remembered your torch; otherwise, for safety purposes, you need to replace the panel and retrieve it. To go on without some form of light would be foolhardy for the pitch-blackness covers a steep, winding staircase that goes down 112 stone steps, deep underground. When you eventually level off you are deep under Chislehurst, deep in a little-known adjunct of the Chislehurst Caves.

Horace and Betty had done the journey many times. They could do it without light but would not recommend you try it.

This was the home base for the beat kids. And Horace and

Betty Stoakes were their principal sponsors.

"Can't stand the music myself," Horace would laugh. "But it's the principle that counts."

More importantly right now, it was the perfect place to hide Georgia and Edmund.

And being a Catholic beat parent put you very close to the resistance. It was inevitable that Jo would think of location C as a hiding place for her captured pair.

The funny thing about Helmut Brandt was he was not English at all, but from the homeland. His father, also Helmut, was a senior engineer attached to RUDD in this sector. His job was to ensure consistency of engineering production, whether aircraft or teaspoons. He was enormously important and knew it.

But his son was different. He was a beat kid.

Helmut, being from the homeland, was assigned to look after Georgia and Edmund. He immediately demanded that they be untied and allowed some freedom of movement.

"But we don't want them to escape," Jake had argued.

"If we untie you and allow you some freedom of movement do you undertake not to try and escape?" Helmut had asked.

"No," said Georgia.

"No," said Edmund, following his sister's lead.

They reached a compromise. Hands tied when outside the one room they used for sleep, but so long as hands were secured they could roam through the immediate tunnels and caverns, provided they were accompanied also.

"Why do you speak English?" Georgia demanded of Helmut as he led the two of them into their room.

"Because it is a superior language."

"What?" Both Nullgebens were incredulous.

"Well, what I mean is that it is more poetic, more expressive. It's like … more artistic."

"Stuff and nonsense," said Edmund.

But Georgia was more interested in practical matters. She asked who he was and where they were.

"I can't tell you where we are but my name is Helmut Somebody. I am a beat kid." Said with pride; immense pride.

Georgia had heard something of the beat kids, Edmund nothing. What Georgia had heard was not flattering. They were indulgent layabouts, wanted to wear American clothes and listen to dreadful music. Helmut was actually wearing a pair of blue jeans, carefully torn on one knee. Georgia had never seen blue jeans before. He had a rounded-neck shirt on top with no collar and short sleeves, a little like a vest. It was multi-coloured with no obvious pattern, more like a toddler's proud painting.

"It's a 'T-shirt'," he explained. "They're all the rage in America. See - the shape of a 'T'!" Helmut traced the shape of a 'T' across his chest.

Georgia thought his shirt; awful, both colours and style.

But her eyes kept coming back to the blue jeans.

At that moment, someone in a room nearby put a record on a turntable and strange sounds filled the room. There seemed some structure to the music, but the melody was coarse and the backing simplistic, loud and repetitive.

"That's Bill Haley's *Rock around the Clock*," said Helmut.

"More like *Rock around the Bog*," replied Edmund.

"But I prefer the later music. Have you heard of Jefferson Airplane?"

Of course, they had not.

"Most of it is American, but there are some English too, a few brave souls."

"Can you turn the volume down?" Georgia asked. To her ears, the bass was a relentless thump, reverberating deep down into her ears, hurting her brain, preventing clear thought. Helmut walked to the door and made a request. The volume halved with a new song.

"The Doors," he said. He knew them all. "But wait until you hear the live music. Tomorrow, Friday night, there will be plenty."

"Heaven save us," Edmund replied. "Only there is no heaven."

But Georgia liked this song much better. It had a way of winding around her mind, opening doors to rooms never visited before.

They had no choice but to settle in. The rules were enforced. If they wanted to leave their room they had their hands tied. Edmund refused to leave, other than to use the bathroom, which he did as seldom as he could manage. But Georgia was far more restless, hated being cooped up underground in one small room, no more than twenty feet square. She accepted Helmut's offer of a guided tour when he came in after school on Friday. It seemed strange to see him still in his school uniform, so familiar to them, but he quickly changed into his jeans.

There was a whole world underground. Helmut led Georgia through the dance floor and into the bar, then through to the kitchens. He showed her several sitting rooms opening off the main cave, all lit with subdued lamps, casting shadows on the cave walls. There was a band setting up on the long, low stage that stretched from the bar all the way along the length of the dance floor. They had large amounts of amplifiers, drums and guitars. Wires were trotted out all over the place.

"Quite a hazard," Helmut commented. "Last month someone tripped and broke their arm when they fell."

"Gosh, what happened to him?"

"It was a girl," Helmut replied. Then, rather than explain, he took her along a dark stone passageway with doors built into openings on either side. "Dorms," he said as they passed.

"You mean people sleep down here?"

"Of course, some all the time because they are orphans and some stay over on Fridays and Saturdays when the music goes on long after curfew."

"But you don't have to worry about the curfew, you're not an English. Do you not go home after the music stops?"

"No, I stay." The way he said it made Georgia realise that here was a fellow citizen of hers, albeit nowhere near an aristocrat, but one that wanted above all else to be an English. It was an incredible thought.

"The English smell," she said. "How can you sleep in the same dorm with them?" Then wished she had not said what she had said.

"Don't be foolish," he replied. "Everybody smells of something or other. Now, here is the sick bay. This is where we bring anybody who is hurt. This is where the girl with the broken arm came. I helped her get here. And this is our matron. Actually, she is a doctor, well sort of."

He made the introductions. Janet Fisher had been a doctor many years ago, but was struck off in 1943 when the *Zentrale Medizinische Autoritat* realised that J. Fisher MD was a female.

"I got my degree from Southampton University under the auspices of the old GMC. That was good enough for me."

"What do you do here, Fisher?"

"I look after the kids."

"The beat kids?"

"Yes, the beat kids. Some of them live down here. I am doctor, teacher and mother combined to forty-eight of them."

To the obvious question of where their parents were and why were they not looking after their children, Janet just sighed crossly and moved away from all possible conversation, pretending to attend to a vague medical situation at the other end of the sick bay.

"What did I say?" Georgia asked Helmut when they were back in the passageway.

"Have you never heard of the Clampdown?"

"Yes, but that was for adults who broke the law. I studied it last year in 'Empire and Politics'. There were no children involved."

He stopped his rapid walk quite suddenly, turned to face her in the dark, stone-chiselled passage. He was much taller than her, looked down. "Did you never think that some of those adults who 'broke the law' may have had children?"

"Goodness, no. You mean these children..?"

"Exactly."

The first band started a little after 8pm. Helmut took Georgia, wrists tied securely, into the dance area. Edmund refused to leave their room, complained of the noise as soon as the band started and was ignored, kicking his boots against the rock floor, shouting insults against the tide of music sweeping through. Georgia took a half position, going into the main cave but refusing absolutely to change from her camp uniform into jeans.

"There's no way I'll dress like an American," she said, wondering what it felt like to wear them.

The music hit her immediately. It was like diving into a very warm pool. The rumbling, bubbling bass seemed to get into her bones, seemed to be of her very self. The dark-haired singer had collar-length greasy hair and a sneer as he sang. The words were too slurred for her to make out all the English but she understood it to be about his baby, his girl, and dancing all night long.

Then the guitar started, gently at first, echoing the singer in a haunting way. Georgia closed her eyes and saw slaves in America bussing out to the cotton fields. She had seen a film at school when she was younger.

"Are these slave songs?" she asked Helmut.

"Yes, originally, but now they are everybody's," he replied, foot tapping and body swaying.

"I like the rhythm, it sort of..."

"Yes, go on."

"Well, it sort of talks to you."

"Yeah, right on," said Helmut, eyes closed and body moving. Everyone around Georgia was dancing but she did not know how to do it. She had had no lessons. The steps were confusing. They almost looked improvised.

"Improvisation has no place in music. Precision is what counts." Her mother's clear voice rang out in her mind, above the thump of the bass. But even if she made up the steps she could not move her arms with her hands secured in front of her. Instead, her toes wriggled inside her camp boots, could not keep still.

"Can I go back now?" she asked quietly, then louder, but Helmet was nowhere to be seen.

Much later, she saw him on a sofa in the corner. He was with a girl, an English. The girl had long straight brown hair but was not as pretty as Georgia. They were kissing; long, slow kisses, not like the ferocious, urgent ones she had shared with Mark. These ones, to an observer, seemed to tease the senses, inviting the partner in and then shutting them out. Georgia raised both hands to her face and wiped the tears away.

Much later still he came to find her. She half-lied when he asked her whether she was having a good time.

"No."

She loved the music. It spoke to something deep inside her. She loved the casualness of everyone, never thought she would. But she was totally alone, lost and friendless, acutely conscious of the differences between her and the beat kids.

Moreover, if she gave in to these new pleasures, what would remain of her and what she was?

Three weeks later, having gone through her spare camp outfits, Georgia tried on her first pair of blue jeans. She and Elisa and Sarah were alone together in a small sitting room.

"Go on!" They had been urging her for over an hour.

"I don't know. It's so disrespectful, I mean for someone of my status."

"Just try 'em, Georgie." It was still a shock to be called by her first name, let alone a derivative of it. "No one need know. If you don't like 'em you can pull 'em straight off."

Sarah was all cockney, Elisa the genteel daughter of a wealthy landowner. Both had lived underground since the Clampdown. Both were beat kids and orphans. Not that they did not see the light of day. They sneaked up in twos and threes to visit parts of London; the museums, the art galleries, the window-shopping. Then there was the Grove, where a long passage from the caves suddenly broke the surface and they were in a glorious secret valley no more than twenty acres in size. It belonged to a farmer, a sympathiser, who left it strictly alone, farmed instead his other acres and sold his beef to Stoakes and Co., getting the best prices.

Georgia allowed her new friends to take off her skirt and pull up the tight blue jeans.

"You've got the legs for 'em" Sarah said, a tinge of envy circling her voice.

'Too true," said Elisa. "I'd give my right arm for legs like that!"

The jeans were wonderful.

She never wanted to wear anything else. In an instant she had become a beat kid. Elisa slipped a disc on the record player and Georgia felt the rumble of the bass, the rhythm in her bones, in her soul. She was on her feet now, could not remain sitting with that beat going, feet shuffling, body bending, arms ... but she could not move her arms, being tied at the wrists.

Georgia stopped suddenly, stood motionless despite the music urging her on, felt foolish being so still when all around was movement.

"It's too much you being trussed up like a chicken," said Sarah. "I'll be back in a jiffy." Sarah nipped out to the sick bay and returned with a pair of scissors, just as the disc finished.

"You shouldn't do this," Georgia said into the silence, instinct for order winning through.

"Live dangerously!" Elisa cried, holding both Georgia's hands up high.

"Don't fret, Georgie, I'll square it with the 'guvnor'! Now let's dance." She put a new record on, by an underground British band called the Warm Bodies.

And Georgia danced to the music as if the pent-up emotion of her entire life was let loose at once.

She also secreted the scissors, large surgical ones, by breaking two buttons on her shirt and slipping them inside.

Her plan was quite simple. Nobody had really noticed Edmund since their arrival. Some had called him the Great Sulk since he scowled at anybody who spoke to him, but the novelty had worn off. They had forgotten about him. Other than three times a day to go to the bathroom, they left him alone in their room.

The bathroom was close to the steps. The steps led to the cellar of the office. The office led directly to the real world. And to rescue.

She gave the scissors to Edmund and told him her plan.

He executed it perfectly, escaping on Friday evening, when everyone was getting ready for the live music. He had several hours of darkness to get from Chislehurst to RUDD HQ at Westminster.

All Change

The estate agent was obsequious. She had been warned about him. But he was also good at his job.

"With a fair wind we should touch sight of 6000 marks for this bijou apartment." The way he said 'bijou apartment' you would think he had a French mother.

"I'll tell you what I'll do," Barbara said, tossing her long, wavy red hair as she spoke. It made her feel better. "Set the floor at 7000 marks and I'll share anything above that with you, one quarter to you and three quarters to me. Deal?"

The actual deal was not done for another fifteen minutes. It included a one-third share above 6500 marks. They shook on it.

What Barbara did not know was that he already had a buyer. An Iranian businessman was looking for a small flat in London; "No more than eight rooms," he had said. Including the kitchen and both bathrooms, Barbara's flat had exactly eight rooms. He needed it immediately and was prepared to pay a handsome finders' fee.

What the estate agent did not know was that Barbara would have settled for an even 6500. It was all she needed to buy the estate she wanted deep in the Kent countryside.

She knew she had reacted badly to Werner's dismissal of her. She loved the man dearly, knew that he loved her too. But she should have reminded herself, like she did in the early days, that it could not last. He was not of her sort, could never be. He had a career and a wife. His wife was a cold one, for sure, but one with excellent connections. He would be daft to give all that up for nights of passion with Barbara Leyland, an English. Plus, he was a father. She had seen pictures of his two beautiful children. Once, she had seen them in person, at a rally in Westminster during the visit of the Spanish emperor. She was working as an interpreter, shortly after Werner and his family had arrived. They looked about fifteen and twelve and were the sweetest things ever.

And now he was to be a father again, for Barbara had received confirmation earlier that week from the doctor.

Luckily, she was over thirty so the authorities did not care, would not even hear about it, for there were no reporting requirements for the over-thirties. She shuddered to think of what would have been in store if she had been under thirty and pregnant. To discourage childbirth outside marriage, the mother was typically taken to a nursing home for the birth, separated from the child immediately, and then given a ZA to work in some tedious, heavy occupation for an acceptable period; usually a few years. The authorities pointed to the dramatic decline in childbirth out of wedlock since Werner had imposed these rules as one of his first proclamations. It clearly worked.

Barbara's pregnancy did not need to be reported so would not be known. And she had decided that she would keep it from Werner also. Only trouble would come of his knowledge of another child. Instead, she would keep it as her 'Werner reborn'; a Werner, whether male or female, she could have forever without risk of losing.

She had known the relationship could not last, had often thought of what she would do when it ended. She had no career now. They would never promote an ex-mistress of a senior RUDD official. She had been promoted several times during the good years, probably way beyond her capabilities. Many would see reversal as her just reward. Now she just had to accept she would never see him again. She had to put the plans she had made long ago into action. These plans took her back to her wartime childhood, to the little bit of security she had once known. It was not much but it was something.

She had trawled around the antique shops and jewellery shops of central London. Just two weeks ago she had completed the last sale, which was sufficient, with what she had saved from her inflated salary, for a generous deposit on the estate. The purchase price, including costs and taxes, was 31,500 marks and she had 27,000 in the bank, including the generous cheque Werner had just sent her. If she kept back 2000 for emergencies and to survive until the first hops came in in September she needed just 6500 marks from the sale of the flat Werner had given her.

She had exchanged contracts and was due to move in as soon as the flat sold. She had handed in her notice to work, knowing that nobody there would be sorry to see her go. There is a hatred born of envy that cuts to the bone. She had to make a completely new life.

The phone call from the estate agent the next morning delighted her. There was a buyer willing to pay 8000 marks if she could move out immediately.

"He wants to move in when he is over in London early next week," the most obsequious estate agent in London; also the wealthiest, told her.

"I'll consider the offer and get back to you," she had said coolly.

She called her lawyer. She called her boss at work, briefly saying she would not work her notice. He did not care, would save the week's wages. She called her bank. Finally, when she had filled thirty minutes, she rang the estate agent and accepted the offer.

One phone call later and she was the new owner of Betherington Manor. Her mind then turned to her sister, Maggie, her only known family.

Pete Morris, Mark's childhood friend, was the inspiration behind the plan. Jo loved it and approved it within half an hour, calling Jake and Sandy to go over the details.

It was incredibly simple. Mark, they knew, was being held in Horsham police station. Create a massive diversion, move in to the police station in force, cut him out: maximum confusion, maximum speed.

The explosion was at 6.42pm on Saturday 5th June. Jake and his team had moved around the Homeland Centre earlier that day under the pretence of undergoing a survey of all government buildings, using a cleverly forged survey form and instructions, together with fake government ID cards.

"We've got so many properties to cover, we have to work Saturdays and Sundays too. It's like re-doing the bloody Doomsday Book!" he joked to the guards. They imagined, naturally, that the rush was probably why they had to use the

English for this vital task. They stepped aside, even gave helpful directions. Both guards received a complimentary fillet of best steak, courtesy of Stoakes and Co.

The explosion, they said afterwards, could be heard in Haywards Heath; twelve miles, as the crow flies. There were broken windows in Pease Pottage. Pete and a crew of five others were waiting at the corner of the road, thirty yards from the police station; earmuffs and dark glasses. They were in a gas utility van, next to an identical one containing six more resistance members. They removed their earmuffs as the police cars started streaming out and down the road towards the Homeland Centre two-and-a-half miles away.

They did not get out until Pete gave the signal. He almost gave it too early, as the last car disappeared down the road, lights and sirens going as if to speed the angry policemen on. But something made him linger a moment longer.

It was as well he did for, later than the rest, the two armoured cars rumbled out, down the ramp to the road, swung left and on their way to the incident; the heavy reinforcements, in case they were required.

"Go, go, go!" Pete shouted as they turned the corner.

Twelve men, like twelve disciples, only there had not been any disciples because there was no god, moved decisively. There was little resistance; a clutch of older police and civilian staff. Nobody to defy the automatic weapons that ranged the place, each held by a grim-faced member of the team.

They had rehearsed it to perfection, even building a model out of cereal packets and cardboard boxes. They had tapped local knowledge to get the ins and outs to the building, then learned their routes and roles until they could think of nothing else.

It went perfectly, just like in a child's war story comic strip. They surprised the diminished staff, blindfolded and tied them, laid them on the floor in rows, explaining that if one moved the machine gun would rake them all.

Nobody moved, except the old lady who was sent for the cell keys. She was ordered up and scampered off, two fighters following her.

For good measure, Pete ordered all the cells to be opened, all prisoners to be extracted, all led outside.

"It will confuse them. They won't be sure it was Mark we came after."

Within six-and-a-half minutes they were back in their vans, racing away.

When Pete reported back to Jo that night, he not only presented his old friend, Mark Smith, but also half a handful of released prisoners who were keen to join up, plus two racks of rifles and machine guns.

It had been a textbook operation.

They quizzed Edmund until he felt his ears would fall off. They wanted to know every inch of the underground caverns. Edmund could tell them little, for he had refused to be shown around. Regretting now his stubbornness, all he knew was the stone staircase winding down to the underground world.

"They play crazy music all day and half the night," he complained. "Electric music."

"The beat boys?" the superintendent asked, looking over at Edmund's father, the boss of his boss, the man he had to impress, irritatingly several years younger than him. He had long searched for these American-style degenerates with hair over their collars and straggly beards, and the revolting blue jeans. Now he could kill two birds with one stone. God was being good to him, only there was no god.

"Let me take the lead." He had decided to be bold, ask the commander directly. "I can guarantee if your daughter is there she will be rescued safely. The others, her captors, won't get the same guarantee."

"I should hope not. But we need to plan this carefully. If we rush in, we risk losing her to these animals. Edmund says Friday is the main live music night. I think we plan the rescue mission for next Friday."

It was agreed. Various police and military experts were called in and the planning began, the superintendent in charge, the commander at his elbow. It made for a long day and night and into the next day, as they went without stopping until they had a plan; coffee, sandwiches and schnapps were wheeled in by greedy-eyed constables who dreamed of taking part in the refreshments. It was late on Tuesday when they finally finished, the day Barbara moved into Betherington Manor with her entire remaining belongings packed into two suitcases in the back of her VW Beetle.

It was time to pack up. They had worked well and had a good plan. Then the commander, standing and stretching, suddenly remembered something.

"Oh, super."

"Yes, sir?" To the superintendent they had developed a strange familiarity over the last thirty-six hours. It would have surprised him enormously just then to have learned how much the commander detested him, for he cloaked it well for the sake of Georgia.

"I almost forgot. Have Horer and Burton executed."

"Yes, sir." The superintendent had not forgotten, had wanted to ask, but had not thought of a way to do so.

"But do it properly, I mean a trial, jury, verdict and sentence."

"Of course, sir." That would be an administrative headache, but nothing too bad. He could always make something of the publicity.

Mark had his second breakfast of eggs, not with his parents but with Jo, Jake, Sandy and Pete. He got no choice this time as to the method of cooking. They all had scrambled eggs on coarse brown bread toasted under an old grill in the corner, fed from a gas bottle. They washed it down with bottles of beer.

"I wouldn't trust the water," Jo said. There was no running water and the tank in the yard had stood there, dark and still, since the houses had been abandoned. "No one has lived here since '59."

"It looks it," said Sandy, looking up at the holes in the roof, through which the fine rain sent a mist of dampness, ganging up on corners and edges to produce real drops of water that splashed on their faces below or down the backs of their necks, aimed with precision.

"Why are these houses derelict?" Mark asked. "They don't look that old."

They were camped in the remains of New London. Stretching out over the flats of Essex, it looked like a ghost town. Mark, unable to sleep, had watched his surroundings emerge as the sun had risen onto a grey day. Each minute extended his view of another street, another deserted shopping parade.

"This is New London," Jo said in explanation. It was all Mark needed.

New London had been the authorities' great settlement attempt. 200,000 new homes in clusters of 1000. Each cluster was a self-contained unit for everyday purposes – shops, doctors, dentists, vets, primary schools, everything needed. Clusters were grouped into regions to provide secondary schools, technical colleges, hospitals and cinemas, swimming pools, theatres. It had been the brilliant idea of Dr Joseph Ergo. Rents were reasonable and one-tenth went into a fund for continued improvement.

Each cluster was a circle of housing, small garden back and front, roads running in between the concentric circles with a neat one-way system for those that had cars.

"But most people won't need cars," Dr Ergo had pronounced. "They can walk to their everyday needs and the buses go from cluster to cluster." Its crowning glory was the overhead rail system. This took the workers from each cluster to the vast factories of Essex and, across the river, to Kent. One large branch took almost 100,000 a day to Old London where they found employment in the restaurants and offices and government buildings. There was always a need for janitors, shop staff, deliverymen, nurses and waiters. It was neat. It was organised. It was almost perfect.

It only had one flaw. That flaw was the reason it was now a concrete desert.

It had quickly proved to be an ideal setting for the growing resistance movement. Within a year of completion, each cluster had a resistance cell. The underground mirrored the organisation gone into the site design so cells formed together into sections, just like the clusters formed regions.

It had developed from a brilliant idea on paper to a headache of incredible proportions.

They had solved it in '59, part of the Clampdown. They had quite simply emptied it. The same careful organisation that went into its construction saw to its closing. Loudspeakers had counted down the time to departure over twenty-four hours, booming into both day and night with its repetitive message.

"Take your belongings and leave. You have until 6am."

The trains were quickly overloaded; several broke down. Buses were commandeered by families, desperate to move their cheap wardrobes, bicycles, rabbit hutches. Prams pushed their way through the crowds, topped with suitcases, cardboard boxes of pots and pans, record players, cricket bats, blank-faced dolls with orange hair and soft bodies.

The clearance teams looked on from their various vantage points and smiled. This was the English moving.

But they missed one significant point. Not one crime was committed that night. For all the jostling, barging, scrumming, there was no looting, no attacks, no knives flashing. Instead, there was cheery banter, laughter bursting through the bustle, magically keeping crime at bay.

Then it was the clearance teams' turn to move in. They were efficient. They enjoyed their cleansing task. They did it well.

Now there were 200,000 empty houses looking at each other in their neat rows and asking what their purpose was.

Deep in the homeland, in the beautiful mountain house he had designed and built, Dr Joseph Ergo kept one step ahead of the authorities. They found his body swinging from a beam in his underground gym when they came to arrest him.

Now New London made a perfect hiding place for the resistance. No longer the breeding ground for recruitment, it had become somewhere to hide out and rebase. The vast extent of roads and housing estates made it impossible to find anyone who did not want to be found.

"We've got a major problem," Jo said, unlike her to place stress on it. "Edmund Bloody Nullgeben got away on Friday night or first thing Saturday morning. They didn't check him from Friday evening until the next morning so we don't know when he got out."

"So at least twenty-four hours?" Mark confirmed. "How did it happen?"

Jo recounted quickly what they knew. They had found Elisa Houndsworthy stabbed to death in one of the little used bathrooms mid-morning on Saturday. The ropes that presumably had tied Edmund's hands were scattered in pieces on the floor. There was no sign of a weapon. Jo expected Edmund had taken it with him. The bathroom door had been cleverly locked from the outside so the 'engaged' sign was on all the time.

"We think he got out the way he came in, through the office cellar. Then, if it was dark, there was no way he could be detected."

"If it was dark he might have got lost," Sandy said.

'No, not him. He's pretty switched-on." All eyes turned to Mark. They had forgotten that he knew both Edmund and Georgia. "He will have done two things for sure by now. First, he would have found his way to a government building. Even the most basic establishment would listen to him. He's obviously not an English. He will be identified by now and reunited with his parents."

"Agreed," Jo replied. "What was the second thing?"

"He will know exactly where to find Georgia."

"Nobody will have told him." Jake was being defensive. It was under his watch that Edmund had escaped.

"Edmund has his head screwed on. He will have found a way to locate it, probably referencing something as he walked, even in the dark. Don't fool yourselves, he will know exactly where Georgia is."

"OK, we need to move her."

"Here?"

"No." Jo's instinct was kicking in. "The one disadvantage of New London is there are only a few ways in. They can blockade us easily and they're probably watching the Cavern right now. No, we'll go to somewhere else. We need to move fast and confuse them, then get her safely out into the countryside. Sandy, you'll take over. I'll talk to you in a moment about where; not everyone needs to know. No, Jake, I am not making judgment on you, so calm down and stay focused on what matters. It is just that I need you for something else. We need to move the entire cavern population somewhere else. Not New London for the same reason. This place is only good if no one is actively chasing you. I need you to take them west, at least the western extremity of our region, maybe even into Wiltshire or Somerset. Their safety is paramount so I'm putting my best person on it, Jake. The slip-up of Edmund's escape happened under your command. Security was lax. I want no risks this time. What's happened has happened, concentrate on the present. I want every one of the beat kids safely out of the way."

"Yes, Jo. I'll get straight onto it."

"You better stick with us," Mark's aunt said, turning to him. "There's nowhere for you to go back to."

"My options are limited, but what could I do with you? I don't have any military experience. I'm a damn physicist!"

It was agreed as the sun worked its way up past the rows of houses, shrinking the shadows and banishing the grey drizzle that had welcomed the day in. The day had started grey and turned brighter, an exact reversal of the mood amongst these leaders of the resistance.

Pete, his old friend, wanted Mark with him. He had a vacancy as assistant section head.

"We'll see how you get on," Pete said. "Now we need to be getting out of here. It's Operation Normal for us. That means harrying the enemy at every turn!"

"Pete, you're spot on," said Jo. "On your way back to Berkshire, give them some things to keep them occupied, take their mind off Georgia's rescue. I'll square it away with the Kent and Sussex commander. With what happened to young Elisa they will back you every inch of the way." Jo left then, anxious to find her Kent and Sussex counterpart and brief them on what had happened. Sandy trailed out after her, equally anxious to tie down her new responsibilities.

Georgia did not dare leave her cave room, even if she had been allowed to. Ever since they discovered that Edmund was missing she had been bound hand and foot, trussed to her bed, dirty oily cloth gagging her mouth. Sarah, her new cockney friend, had been her only visitor so far that day.

"You bastard," she had said, turning her over, spitting in her face, then wrenching the jeans off her, before retying the knots even more securely around her legs. "To think we befriended you and gave you my spare jeans. You're scum … filth … pig shit." Between each insult she spat, crouching down to get her saliva right in Georgia's eyes, jerking her body like a medieval siege catapult to get maximum force. Georgia could not understand what had caused such hatred. Edmund had escaped, obviously, but that was to be expected. It was a fair return for the capture of the two of them in the first place.

Helmut worked out what had happened. He patiently quizzed Sarah, finding out about the scissors. Then he pulled the gag from Georgia's mouth, summoned two witnesses, and asked a series of questions about the previous evening.

"Georgia," he said. Her name was so familiar to him as a fellow national, yet now it seemed to jar in his throat. It wrung with complicity. "Georgia, did you secrete the scissors on return to your room after the dance last night?"

"Yes, I did, pig-face." Helmet jumped up to stop one of the witnesses from slapping her around the face.

"No, we'll do this properly."

"Why?" he asked Georgia.

"Because I had a plan for Edmund to escape and get help." There was little point in denying it. "Can you really imagine I would do anything else? You kidnapped us and held us against our will."

"What was your intention with the scissors?"

"Edmund was to cut his ropes when he went to the bathroom and then find a way to escape. We thought he would use the stairs we came down. You did not think to blindfold us when you brought us here! You are ignorant oafs, all of you!"

"Did you plan for Edmund to use the scissors against anyone during his escape?"

"No, of course not, pig-face. I told him to leave the scissors in the bathroom. Then pretend to be still bound on the way back and to give whoever was his escort the slip, probably where those three tunnels come together. The lighting is bad there. It was his best chance."

"Well, Fraulein." The word was said with disdain. "Your brother did not obey you. He used the scissors to stab Elisa…"

"Is she okay? My God, Elisa!"

"She was found dead in the bathroom this morning. Dr Fisher thinks she bled to death. She thinks she was stabbed around midnight and it took several hours in extreme pain to die. Georgia, she died all alone on a bathroom floor and in agony and your brother did this."

Georgia's world closed in. She could think of nothing to say. The last thing she remembered hearing was someone calling, "The bitch has fainted."

Maggie was five years older than Barbara. She was not a redhead; rather, a deep brunette, not as pretty, but with a quirky sense of humour and a deep love for her younger sister, the type of love that is forged stronger through being orphaned.

They camped out that first night. Barbara's purchase had included the furniture but they had no sheets or pillows and found the dark corridors and heavy short and fat creaking doors a little too scary. They camped out in the small dining room on the ground floor, using rugs Maggie brought from her digs, eating bread and cheese, for they could not get the oven to work.

"It's as well you kept a bit of cash back," Maggie said, pouring the remainder of the first bottle of wine into Barbara's glass. "You're going to need a chunk of it to get this place straight."

"Too right, I would have offered less if I realised about some of the problems."

"I've got some put by," Maggie replied, opening the second bottle.

"But that's yours. You don't live here. I couldn't take your money."

"You haven't asked me," Maggie said after a few moments of silence.

"Asked you what?"

"Whether I want to live here."

Barbara sat up, knowing her sister so well, taking her hands in her own. "Maggot, are you saying you want to?" Barbara's eyes were shining again, like they used to.

"All I'm saying, Baba, is you have not asked me."

Now Barbara raised herself on one knee, like an altar boy frozen in the act of genuflection. "Miss Maggot Leyland, will you do me the honour of becoming my house companion, for better and worse, for richer and poorer?" She did not want to add the bit about 'to death do us part'; there was too much about death these days.

"Yes Baba, I want to live here with you." For once Maggie was serious. "I have some money saved."

"Then we can be partners!"

"We'll be the best hops farmers in the country, just like the old days."

Werner was livid. He distinctly remembered telling the detective superintendent to go about the disposal of Horer and Burton with full attention to the correct procedures. Three days later, there he was bragging on the radio of the summary execution of a traitor to the homeland.

"Horer was a despicable traitor. Long will he burn in hell," said the Super on the radio interview, then remembered. "Figure of speech, of course there is no hell."

The commander dashed off a vitriolic memo, demanding no more executions without written approval from him. He considered further action against this renegade police officer, then forgot when his wife rang to demand an update on their daughter.

"So, I'll see her on Saturday?" Carla demanded.

"So long as she's still there. It might be very late before we get her," Werner replied.

"I'll be there..."

"I wouldn't advise..."

"Then don't advise." Carla twisted her husband's words. "I'll be in those damn caves and will be part of the rescue of my beloved daughter. I want to be the first to see her."

Or the first to see the carnage, Werner thought as he issued some calming words and replaced the receiver.

Action in the Field

Mark and Pete squirmed up the rise on their stomachs. Mark watched as his boyhood friend observed the valley and the road before them. First, Pete did a quick scan, noting the general layout, looking for anything unusual; maybe a patch of incongruous colour or a sudden movement. Satisfied that he had the time for a proper observation, he spoke quietly of what was next; the teacher at work.

"After the initial scan, I divide my field of vision into slightly overlapping segments. See, I start to the right and have eight segments." He indicated with his hand eight choppy movements across the 180 degrees before them. "Now I concentrate on each one in turn. I slow right down, even if there is great urgency. Rushing is never a good idea when observing. I study each section slowly. I ask myself constantly, is it reasonable to see what I see? Now, you do the next segment and talk me through it."

"Okay, boss." That got the slightest of grins, but no movement away from the visual Pete was locked on. "Okay, my segment starts two yards to the right of the tree by the road and it runs to the boulder on the far hill at one o'clock; no, one thirty, to our present position."

Mark went up and down. He could equally have looked right to left. But he reasoned that if there were anyone down there they would have moved down the hill into position. He wanted to see the trail they would have made. Shading his eyes against the early morning sun that looked set to burn its way across the land from left to right, east to west, he spoke of his findings in a whisper.

"I see the rotten tree trunk. Behind it, the grass is flattened slightly. It could be an animal or it could be one of them in hiding. But they are not there now. From this height I can see right behind the tree."

"What about inside the trunk? Maybe it's hollow?" Pete asked, impressed by how quickly Mark was picking up on things.

"No, it is not hollow. It still has leaves attached. See, on the left end. That means it is too recent a fall to be hollow. Also, there is a pheasant walking right behind it. There is no way a pheasant would do that if a human was present or had been recently."

The valley was clear. They had spent thirty minutes checking it out. That left them less than forty to get in position for the ambush.

"But you don't want people hanging around in concealment too long anyway," Pete explained. "They get restless, they move, they make noise. An observant enemy, even travelling at speed, will see or hear them. Now, remembering what I told you before, I'd like you to position our forces."

"Okay, boss!"

Mark thought about the problem. They knew at least six vehicles would be in the convoy; maybe more. First, though, he needed to be sure of his approaches.

"Stephens, take two men and scout to the west." He indicated to the right. "That is the direction we are expecting the convoy. I want four bleeps on the radio if it is the convoy, two long bleeps if anything else comes along. Now Carter, take two men eastwards Your signal is one long beep and two short."

"Good work," said Pete under his breath as Stephens and Carter strode away.

Mark then considered the length of the convoy. Its likely size was four lorries plus an armoured car back and front. But this could be added to. The problem was a physical one. If he set up his troops in the position for a six-vehicle ambush and there were actually twelve in the convoy then the lead troops would open fire before the rear vehicles were ensnared. They would be outside the field of fire and could reverse out of danger.

He thought for a moment of the variables, as if setting up an experiment in the physics lab. If the convoy length was unknown he had to find a way to lengthen the possible attack line, to make it flexible. And he had to be in a position to make the decision to open fire as late as possible. He checked his resources; thirty-four men, eight Bren guns, two armour-piercing rocket launchers. They looked like bazookas but fired rockets that could pierce a battle ship.

Then he had his plan. "Rocket Launcher One to the west of the valley, Number Two to the east. Two men per rocket launcher plus two to provide covering fire. You deal with the armoured vehicles. There will be one out front and one in the rear regardless of how many vehicles in the convoy."

That left twenty-six men, including himself and Pete. "The rest to split into six teams of four. Pete, I want you and me to be the runners." That got a laugh all around, especially when one fighter made a quip about Pete's stomach and whether he was the best person for that role. Mark let the humour trickle away, then continued.

"On each side of the road we have two teams at the front or eastern end and one team in the rear. One forward team is at the six-vehicle mark; the other is at the twelve-vehicle mark. Think of it as a train coming to rest at a station – there is a six-carriage stop point and a twelve-carriage stop point. I will come with you now to detail those positions. After positioning the teams, Pete and I will go back beyond the rear teams in order to see the approaching convoy and then run up here, using the ridge as cover. I will fire one shot with a flare gun to signal when to open fire. The rocket launchers take out the armoured vehicles. The other teams shoot down the valley to the west at the soldiers as they spill out of the lorries. Don't shoot eastwards and don't shoot at the lorries themselves, just at the soldiers. Any questions?" There were a few, mainly about the cargo, but Mark did not know what it was. Pete did but just reminded everyone to follow the instructions and not shoot at the lorries.

"Mark is in command for this exercise. I am an observer. Mark, remember to check everyone's understanding and then move them out." Was he right in taking a back seat on this one? The 'cargo' was all-important psychologically but of little practical use. Its capture would damage the reputation of the authorities and dramatically increase their anger, but it would not advance the position of the resistance materially. For that they needed weapons and vehicles and both were hard to come by. Pete reflected on their arsenal for this job. It seemed impressive but it was Jo's entire stock of heavy weaponry. It was typical of Jo, he was learning; put everything into one huge effort to humiliate the enemy. But it might have been better to split the arsenal and concentrate on obtaining more.

"That's everyone in position, Pete, just got to wait now."

"Good work, Mark, now it's fingers crossed." Then Pete told Mark of the human cargo travelling in this convoy.

Sandy was deeply concerned as she looked down at the body lying on the bed. She crouched, her drab green jacket brushing against the cave wall, then felt Georgia's forehead, cheeks and neck. They were burning hot. Georgia was deep in the throes of a fever, tossing, turning, sweating, muttering to herself all the time.

"Have we a doctor here?"

"Yes; Janet Fisher," replied Jake. "But she is scheduled to come with me to look after the beat kids."

"Has she seen the Fraulein?" She had not been summoned. There had been too much anger against Georgia amongst the underground community. Helmut had tried, seeing the fever in Georgia's eyes, feeling her temperature, but he had been shouted down, asked who cared if she died. Perhaps it was for the best.

"Call her immediately." Sandy rose from the bedside, angry now, too. "Get her here this minute."

Janet Fisher was found. She examined Georgia, shaking her head.

"Why was I not called before?"

Nobody answered. Nobody could now say they had wanted to punish this girl for her brother's crime.

"I am going to need Dr Fisher with me." Sandy was still angry. "The Fraulein needs constant medical attention."

"Sandy, Janet is a mother to these kids. They need her. I can't let her go with you."

Sandy, her anger now cold but solidifying into iron resolve, seemed to give way. "Okay then, so be it. I'll go and see whether she has any medicine for the Fraulein and can brief me on what to do. I need to get going soon."

"Right, well I'm going into a meeting now to work out how the hell to move all these kids to a safe place. Logistics is a nightmare. We don't have enough vehicles to begin to move them all." Jake seemed relieved by Sandy's change of heart; more friendly and open because of it.

"Can you use Stoakes' delivery vans?"

"No, we've ruled that option out. They could be checking the vans if they know of Mr Stoakes' involvement. His whole cover has been compromised by that boy's escape. Pete is busy trying to get me some lorries right now. If that works, I should be able to move out tomorrow."

Eight people left the caves thirty minutes later. The party consisted of five men; all tough fighters and well-armed, and three women. Georgia was one of the females, laid out on a stretcher then placed carefully in the back of Jo's camper van, loaned for the occasion. Sandy and Janet Fisher jumped in the back with her, along with three of the men.

"Location Y," Sandy ordered the driver. They left Chislehurst by the light of the moon, driving down silent streets and into the countryside through tiny lanes and tracks, constantly turning and turning again. They had the advantage that the driver had grown up in this area, had been picked for the task. They were spotted by the commander's watching vehicles as soon as they turned on the engine and followed for some of the way but shook off all pursuit long before the sun in the east sent its waking rays across the county of Kent.

"How far are we going?" Janet asked Sandy. "I'm concerned about the effects of all this bumping around on the Fraulein."

"It's not too far now," she replied. "We've got a safe house in Tenterden. It's outside the village, in a very quiet spot."

Only it was not so safe. As they turned off the road onto a dirt track that led to the oasthouse, its two bent funnel-type rooves sticking up into the deep blue sky and piercing the faint clouds that drifted by without purpose, the driver came to a sudden halt and then a panicked reverse, crunching gears and slipping tyres, mud and noise everywhere.

"The house!" cried the driver. "It's occupied."

"See the cars around the back?" shouted the upfront passenger, twisting around so that Sandy and the others could see his anguished face. "That means they've got my wife and the kids."

His cries made Georgia stir.

"What's going on?" She recognised no one around her, reached out but felt no cave walls. At least she was not bound anymore. "Where are we?" Then, as her senses started to kick in, "You've moved me! I won't be rescued now." She felt a gentle hand on her cheek, closed her eyes, and was asleep again, fighting in her dreams for her freedom.

"We've made it." Sandy breathed a long sigh of relief as they headed back into Tenterden. The occupiers of Frank Wetherby's old oasthouse had not seen them.

"Maybe they are preoccupied with torturing my family," Frank said, the bright, pretty day making not one dent in his gloom.

"No Frank, I can assure you they are not," Sandy replied, leaning over into the front bench seat from behind, arms drooped over the space between the driver and Frank.

"How can you be sure? How can you be so damn calm?"

"Because I know they are safe. I've just seen them. Over there." Several sets of eyes followed her hand gesture, the driver going up on the pavement and having to swerve to miss a post box. There in the Tenterden Arms' garden sat Emily and the three children, drinking orange squash and fighting over the remains of some crisps.

"Go to them, Frank. You've done your job here. Keep them safe."

"Are you sure? I'll be at my mother's if you need me. 14 Church Street, just over there." He scrambled out and the last Sandy saw of him he was hugging his wife, miniature Wetherbys dotted around their legs and clamouring for attention.

It would be nice to have a family, thought Sandy, not knowing that Janet was having an identical thought at that moment.

They drove back to Goudhurst, through several small villages, seeming to them unreal in their calmness: farm hands, butchers, a laundry van stopping frequently and holding up the light traffic, a primary school class going on a nature trail with magnifying glasses and jars for newts or tadpoles or some such thing. Nobody looked at the beaten-up camper van. If they had known, most would have helped. Kent was where the occupiers had first come. It was where the resistance was strongest.

They stopped at a pub in a hamlet outside Horsmonden called the Blunted Scythe. It seemed an odd name for a pub. It only had one bar. The garden had wobbly wooden tables and benches, with a mass of old farming equipment in the corner, long grass poking up through the rusting iron, slowly strangling the alien metal. The front door was crooked and low, the step worn in the middle almost to the dirt below. The pub should have been swept away, replaced with a modern and functional version, but somehow it had survived, probably because it was tiny and not to be noticed.

Georgia was awake again and Janet advised Sandy that the girl needed a break. They stopped at the pub and had beer and sandwiches in the garden. No restraints were needed for Georgia. She was too weak to run.

"Fisher, is that you?" she suddenly said, after Janet had been talking for several minutes.

"Yes, Fraulein."

"What are you … are you looking after me?"

"Yes, Fraulein."

"Where are we going?"

They did not reply for they did not know. A moment later she said, "I'm cold, just want to lie down and close my eyes."

When next she woke she was in a bed, albeit a hard one, with clean sheets and a bouncy pillow that her head made no impression on. There was another woman, someone she had never seen before, standing over her. She was tall and skeleton-thin, like something from a fantasy story. She had hairs growing on her chin and one eye half closed and squinting, like she was seeing another world with that eye. She did not smile as she straightened the bed sheets and moved the pillow. Her hard, calloused hands touched Georgia's cheeks and forehead. Georgia shuddered, tried to move away.

"Don't worry," she said matter-of-factly. "I just want to check your temperature." Her voice belied her appearance. It was silky-smooth and full, brim-full, of life. It was only a few moments later that Georgia realised that this old lady was talking in her language.

"Are you an English?" Georgia croaked, trying to rise up slightly but failing. She looked an English peasant but did not sound one at all.

"I am now, but I come from the homeland. I married an English and so now I am an English. Does that make sense to you?" Georgia tried to nod, it was too much effort. She managed a small smile. "Good," the old lady continued, "so I know what it is like to be hated."

"Do you?"

"Yes, but don't trouble your pretty self with that right now. I've brought some soup."

"Not hungry."

"Nevertheless, you will eat."

She ate two bowlfuls and fell back into a sleep, feeling the old lady's rough hands and gentle touch stroking her hair as she drifted off.

Pete split the force after the ambush. He and twelve men took six of the eight captured lorries straight up the A21 towards Chislehurst. It was exactly what Jake needed and Pete got a hug for saving the day. They loaded up, dozens of youngsters crammed into the lorries with supplies and bedding. Then they drove out, but not the usual way, so the waiting police saw nothing from their strategic points around the streets of Chislehurst.

The transports had gone to the Grove, driven the last half-mile over a series of bumpy fields, tyres stuck several times so the farmer with the contract with Stoakes and Co. dragged them out with his shire horses. The children had walked back and forth along the tunnels with bundles of bedding and food until everything they needed was stacked carefully in the open then loaded quickly onto the lorries.

Not many people even knew of the existence of the Grove.

As far as the authorities were concerned the beat kids were still in the caves, deep underground, half-way already to hell, only there was no hell.

They left on Friday late afternoon, appearing to be a military convoy. They were not stopped once on their long journey to Salisbury Plain. In fact, several times they noticed cars driven by English stopping to let them pass, as was the law.

They arrived at Salisbury Plain a little after midnight. No one thought it odd to see six army lorries drive up to an abandoned army camp, push open the barbed wire gate and disgorge a hundred scurrying figures, hard to make out in the dark. Soon, they were all settled, the lamps and torches turned off and the army camp, wakened from the oblivion of disuse, returned to sleep.

Jake was proud of his endeavour. It had gone well. The only problem was damn Sandy running off with the doctor. Now he would have to be mother to a hundred or more children, along with all his other responsibilities.

Mark had the remainder of the force. Together, they had rescued Linda Burton. She had been the human cargo, on route from her place of torture to her place of trial. They had thus achieved the objective Jo had set them when the news of Horer's execution hit the airwaves.

"Linda will be next," Jo had said. "We must rescue her." Mark and Pete had devised the ambush while Jo had ranged far and wide with her scouts to determine Linda's location and planned movements.

Pete had also discovered something else. Mark was a brilliant tactician, a natural.

"He'll have your job next week," he had joked to Jo.

"Whatever it takes!" she had replied, the cause coming first.

Mark did not recognise Linda when he helped the female shape down from the back of the fourth lorry. The scene was ugly; everywhere there were bodies, dozens of dead soldiers caught in the ambush, others wounded, groaning, crawling or lying looking at the sky.

But Linda was far more shocking. She was bald, just a few straggles of her glorious brown hair to tease her with what had once been; brutally shaved, jagged razor marks scouring her scalp.

All life was gone from her once dancing eyes, now rimmed with dark bruises and vicious cuts, still oozing blood as if designed to bleed her slowly to death. Her skin was pallid, scraped, torn. She was lame, had no footwear but swollen feet; toenails all gone in a bloody mess.

She would never skip again. Never know a carefree moment. Or so it seemed right then.

Mark had to force himself not to stare. Instead, he tried to be practical, to think of the essentials.

"We have to get away," he said to no one in particular. He was right. A patrol or another convoy could be along at any moment. They had two lorries remaining. He quickly delegated tasks and within minutes the two lorries moved out, a dozen of the worst wounded enemy soldiers in the back of one, Linda and he in the other; his fighters split between the two.

The wounded they left behind would survive with a wait of several hours for help. Mark wondered briefly whether the enemy rescuers, coming upon the wounded at the side of the road, bandaged and treated for comfort and pain, would make a comparison between their treatment of Linda and his team's care for the wounded soldiers. He hoped so but doubted it. Then his mind moved on to other things. Where should they go? They were driving south now, having turned right a few miles back. They had some disguise with the lorries. They would not be expected to stop at roadblocks for the moment. But when word got out of the ambush? That was a different matter.

They had to get somewhere safe. They had an hour, Mark thought. Pete had meant to brief him on safe locations but in the rush of battle it had not happened.

He did not know where he was. How far south was the coast? He could not keep driving aimlessly. He had to have a plan.

A crossroads came up. It was decision time. As they

approached, he saw a sign to Harcourt Castle to the left. They must have drifted over into Sussex then. There had been no signs announcing entry into Sussex because the authorities disapproved of regional names, preferring numbers. Kent was R1, because it was the first place they had come to. Greater London was R2. He did not know what number Sussex was for nobody in his world used the numbers.

Harcourt Castle. That was the place Georgia was going to go to for her camp. It was a busy place, a spa for senior officers in the old castle.

"Turn left for Harcourt Castle," he said, without thinking. In fact, he had to think harder, better, more effectively. Pressure mounted as the miles ticked on. He was heading for disaster because Harcourt Castle was the only place he had ever heard of. He felt like a fly being sucked into a web.

But there was another place he had heard of. What was the name of the place they moved the camp to?

"Driver, do you know Barrington Manor?"

"Never heard of it, guv." Damn it. He needed local knowledge.

Then the front passenger turned around. "You don't mean Betherington Manor, do you?"

"Yes, that's the one. Betherington, not Barrington."

"It's deserted, been empty for years. I grew up in the next village, Fripham."

"Perfect, is it close?"

"Five miles, maybe six."

"Right, give us directions. We're going to Betherington Manor as fast as we can."

Only, of course, it was not empty any longer.

Deep Underground

"Super's livid. I ain't exaggerating, Derek. Sooner you than me reporting to him." The round-faced policeman had a cheery grin, enjoyed promoting discomfort.

"What's up, Bert?"

"What do you think, Dumbo Derek? He's only gone and blown it all."

"Blown it all?" Derek's nickname had apparently been aptly given.

"The bleeding raid, of course. Don't tell me you ain't heard down in 'orsham. What the bloody 'ell is this telephone thing for, then?" Bert leaned across his ply-board desk and rattled the standard issue black phone with its brown curly cord spiralling off into the wall.

"Nobody told us. Besides, I've been driving for the last two hours. I had to get up from Horsham somehow, didn't I?" Dumbo Derek's logic was impeccable so Bert ignored it.

"Well, a good copper keeps 'is ears open, that's what I always says. But I'll take the time now to brief you, mind you millions wouldn't be arsed. But that's the sort of bloke I am. Put the kettle on, DD, and I'll fill you in. Got any of those cakes you normally bring?"

Dumbo Derek was not the brightest bobby on the beat but he had sense enough to realise that cakes from the bakery in his home village: sweet, fruity and soft, could buy a lot of friendship, could ease the way.

"Sure, got one with your name on it," he joked, thinking of the largest one in the bag.

The raid, Derek learned over large mugs of hot, sweet tea, had been a complete disaster.

"Imagine you's the Super," Bert had started. "You got 200 men, real soldiers as well as us bobbies. You watch the place carefully. You sees them going in and coming out. Now, down in them caves is a million of them little squitters going about their everyday business like they ain't got a care in the world. You anticipates a great big 'aul of the bastards. You ain't got enough fingers and toes to count the numbers you're gonna catch. You give the word. No, let me back up a bit. You've got teams watching day and night. You're planning to go in at 0100 on Saturday morning. You're all geared up. Then you give the word. The uniforms all move forward, seal the escape routes. You find the stairs down to this bleeding underground world. You send your crack squads down there. 'ere, make us another cuppa, won't you? Then I'll tell you what happened next."

Derek's mouth fell open, spilling cake crumbs on Bert's desk, when he heard the next instalment.

"You mean…?"

"Exactly, the whole bloody place was empty. As empty as you are up there!" Bert rose half out of his seat and slapped Derek playfully on the temple.

Dumbo Derek did not mind being the butt of such jokes. He had, after all, just heard the most amazingly good news.

Good, that is, if you sided with the resistance.

And doubly good if you were also bringing the disastrous news of the convoy capture and the resulting escape of Prisoner Burton.

The Super did not feel like having sex despite the prettiness of the young boy the desk sergeant had brought him. But he hated to dismiss such beauty, even if it was an English, so settled him in the corner of his office with a notepad and pencil.

"He's doing work experience," he told anyone who came in. But they all knew why he was there.

Only not today.

Today was Sunday 6th June. Outside his office window, summer broke into the suburban environment. It could not be denied its clinging, voracious grip on life, bursting from every nook, every cranny, sending new light shooting across sky, street, car park and office canteen. But not into the Super's office. Not one light or sound particle managed to penetrate there.

For today he had to report to the commander. He had managed to delay all day yesterday, claiming to be following up leads, clues, trails; anything that moved or did not move. But today there were no more excuses. The commander would be here at noon, with his wife, the dreadful Frau Nullgeben. She had enough contacts under any letter in her address book to ensure the superintendent never worked again.

And in four hours he had to face them both.

And there was more. For the idiot who had just left his office – PC Derek Sideley – had told him of the deeply embarrassing capture of Burton, the despicable traitor he should have executed alongside Horer.

At least the commander must now agree that the summary execution of Horer had been a sound move; a good judgment call.

It was not that the Nullgebens did not know of these things. Their communication systems were too efficient and, anyway, both had been present at the raid on those caves in Chislehurst, anxious to make sure their daughter was safe. It was more that today was the day he had to account for himself.

"Come over here," he said to the boy in the corner.

"What me, sir?" The boy looked up from his doodling.

"Who the hell else is in this room right now?" the superintendent snapped back. "I want you to rub the back of my neck and my shoulders. I want you to ease the damn tension so I can concentrate on what to do."

He meant who to blame.

The elite squad, 100 hand-picked men, had tumbled down the stairs, almost fighting to be the first to glory. They had neat, stubby machine guns strung across their shoulders and the latest night-vision glasses strapped across their faces, like skiers on a long, downward slope.

They had instructions to find the Fraulein and free her, then they were to create as much havoc as possible. Finally, when daylight broke, they were to lead those remaining alive out of the caves in a long line, roped together like slaves on their trip through Africa to the waiting ship. It was hoped to parade the captured beat kids through the suburbs of southeast London before taking them off to their new lives.

And the superintendent hoped to go on to a new life on the

back of theirs. He hoped for a promotion with a posting back home, some radio interviews, a great deal of recognition. Then, when he finally retired to his luxury flat with gilded wallpaper in the study, he would write his memoirs and become famous all over again.

At first, it had all gone so well. The crack troops had rattled down the stairs. Then silence. That was to be expected. But there was no gunfire. Surely gunfire would have started by now? Were they having a hard time locating the Fraulein? The superintendent directed his ears like a bat down the winding staircase, wondering what the darkness deep down below would bring for his future. But he heard nothing but a few muffled, distant shouts, like someone lost at sea, disappearing beneath the waves.

Then there was the sound of troops returning; not rushing, but taking each step deliberately, as if not wanting to make the journey. It was then he knew all was not right. But he hoped on, as people do, despite the evidence growing as each footstep sounded louder.

"Sir!" The voice was breathless, despite the steady plod up the stairs. "There is no one there."

"What do you mean?" His mind felt like it was already cast down into the deepest cavern, lost in the absolute darkness, nothing to hang on to.

It took the rest of the night to search the passages and caves. They found no people, just unwanted items or those too bulky for the beat kids to take. They did find amplifiers, guitars, and a drum set. The soldiers gleefully smashed them. The superintendent watched. Normally, it would give him some satisfaction but there was none this time, especially with the Nullgebens gone back to their London home, a mixture of disgust and concern on their faces.

In the early hours of the morning they found the Grove, then they saw more items left behind in the open air; evidence of a rushed departure. And then they found the tyre tracks. They left the Grove by foot, following the tracks, stopping only to arrest the farmer. Eventually, the tracks met the main road and were lost to them. Their trail was cold.

The farmer said only that there had been strange noises that night and he had been visited by three men who suggested he and his family stay indoors with the curtains closed.

"Why didn't you phone?"

"I don't have a phone."

There was little else the police could do but they locked him up anyway. Maybe a night or two in the cells would reveal something else.

Saturday afternoon was filled with phone calls, frantic ringing around to see if other police stations had reported any unusual movements.

It was only this morning, when PC Sideley stood nervously in front of his huge mahogany desk, fumbling with his helmet, twisting it endlessly between fingers and thumbs, that the superintendent made a leap of imagination and put the two disasters together.

"You say there was nothing but the burnt-out armoured cars?"

"Yes sir, and some dead and wounded bodies."

"Never mind about them. What of the lorries?"

"All gone, sir."

One arm of the resistance had stolen eight lorries, destroying two perfectly good armoured vehicles in the process. There were some dead and wounded too, in order for the other arm to ship out all the beat kids moments before his troops had arrived. It was sickening.

And they had liberated Burton as well.

It was easy, once the superintendent could concentrate. The boy had eased the tension and enabled him to think.

"Sir, the surveyors did not indicate there were other entrances. They did a sloppy job back in '61 despite your predecessor's orders." The superintendent slid a copy of the survey and the original order across the dark, stained table top. "If we had known there was another significant entrance we would have planned completely differently. We've issued arrest warrants for the surveyors, of course." What had inspired him to look for old surveys of the caves?

The truth was, it was his secretary's idea. He had been about to sack her for taking an early lunch without permission. But she had turned up with a briefcase and a smile on her pretty face, just as the Nullgeben fleet of cars pulled into the car park.

He would reward her after his time with the boy, when the Nullgebens had left.

"What matters is our child." Frau Nullgeben's words cut through his thoughts.

"We are tracing the movement of the lorries." That was only a half-lie. They were looking for the vehicles but had received no sightings of them so far. "But I need more men."

"All leave has been cancelled," the commander said. "You can have 20,000 troops if it helps." A vision shot across the Super's mind of him in a tank, a vast army behind him.

"Just get my child back," added Frau Nullgeben with a look on her face the superintendent would never forget.

They left then, their black cars pulling out of the police station and heading like the chinks of a chain back to Westminster, back to the seat of power; their power. That is where they would stay, all resources available, until they had more news of Georgia. Perhaps more loved in her absence, some would say, but then the English would say anything.

The superintendent waited for twenty minutes, watching the clock. He had to wait a short while in case they thought of something else and turned the big black chain around. But he would not wait longer than necessary for his pleasure. It had been a stressful day but he had pulled through. He deserved something.

There was a knock on his door. This would either be the English boy or a warning that the commander had turned back.

In fact, it was Bert's cheery face that poked around the door.

"Sir, a word if I might."

"Can it wait? I'm busy." That was rich, saying it to the man who had organised the boy, had then explained to the boy about the tension and the need to wait until after the meeting, fed him tea and biscuits and then summoned him back twenty minutes ago.

"I won't be 'alf a minute, sir. It's just that I heard a report of a strange sighting on Friday night." He told the superintendent about the camper van disappearing into the night, seeming to head east but turning this way and that.

"When I heard it was changing direction all the time, I grew suspicious, sir."

"Quite right. Well done, sergeant." *Will I ever get any peace?*

"Sir, if I could be so bold…"

"Yes, sergeant, spit it out. I'm a busy man." *Give the English an inch…*

"Of course, sir, I was just going to say I think they've gone into R1, sir. We have a list of suspected safe houses in R1 and the duty inspector ordered all of them to be checked out."

"Good initiative, sergeant. Keep me posted."

"Thank you, sir. Oh, and the work experience lad is here, sir. I think you wanted to go over a few things with him?"

"Show him in, sergeant. Tell my secretary to stay as well. I know it's Sunday but needs must when the chips are down.

Georgia loved those slim, bony fingers. They moved across her body and head with the confidence of age yet when she opened her eyes she saw the beauty of youth in them.

"Your fingers are so beautiful."

"Thank you."

Georgia knew her name now. It was Hilda Farringdon. Years ago, before she came to England, she had been Hilda Stein, but now it was Hilda Farringdon. Only Georgia did not know whether to call her Frau Farringdon as a fellow national or Farringdon as an English. She settled it by not using a name, until the one morning Hilda told her to use 'Mrs Farringdon'.

"For that is who I am now."

"I'm feeling much better today, Mrs Farringdon," she said in answer to the lady's enquiry on the twelfth day, seeming strange to use a title along with an English name but reassuring to know what to call her.

And it was the truth. Her fever had gone, her headaches and dizziness, too. All that remained was the exhaustion that hit every hour or so.

"You'll be moving on soon, I expect."

"Where to?"

"I have no idea, little one." Normally, Georgia would have angered at an endearment like this but somehow with Hilda Farringdon it seemed acceptable.

Several days later, Hilda took Georgia out into the pub garden. It was mid-afternoon and the pub was closed, the garden secluded. They sat next to a late-flowering rhododendron bush with its purple immature flowers daring to investigate their surroundings. The bush rambled across the front of the tiny garden, blocking any view from the road but also creating a sense of another world, where the primary colours were deep, shiny green and fresh, young purple. It seemed a safe world; a barricade against the roads and concrete and metal everywhere outside.

"Mrs Farringdon, is this your pub?"

"It is now," she replied, drawing up a stool to sit next to Georgia. On the table were a tray of fresh lemonade and a gingerbread man, just baked, giving another strain of other worldliness. Georgia almost expected the gingerbread man to jump up and run away. "Since my husband died."

"I'm sorry, I mean that he died."

"Thank you, little one." Her long, bony fingers touched Georgia's cheek; something her mother never did. It tingled. It burned. It felt wonderful.

"How did he die?" she asked, but something in Mrs Farringdon's eyes told the story already. "It was the Clampdown, wasn't it?"

"It was, *liebling*." She paused a moment and then decided to say more. "That's why your father was sent over here, because the Clampdown was such a disaster. They wanted someone younger to make changes."

Again, the story did not need elaborating, for Georgia knew deep down, only would never admit it, that nothing had changed. In fact, nothing ever could change in this strange country.

"I hate the English."

"Why? How?" Mrs Farringdon leaned over in earnest, then straightened herself. "I have been living here for forty-four years. To all intent and purpose, I am an English. But consider this…"

"But you are different, Mrs Farringdon. You are cultured and sensible and, well, like the rest of us." But then she thought of Helmut.

"But consider this." Hilda would not be put off. "This is their country and we came across and took it from them, saying we were cleverer than them, smarter, more able, more organised."

"Well, we are, otherwise we would not have been able to take the country over so easily." Georgia's logic was solid so Hilda tried something different.

"When the invasion happened, a few people here turned against me. There were one or two who wanted my husband to leave me, to send me back. But he would have none of it. The dear man stood by me. Do you know what he did?"

"No." But Georgia thought, it was bound to be something pathetic because he was an English at the end of the day.

"He banned from his pub anyone who spoke against me. It's called barring them. Anyone who said anything seriously disrespectful or hateful was barred for life, could never come into this pub again. He then taught me how to deal with hatred."

"How's that?" Georgia was interested, suddenly feeling there was a little hatred in her, wrapped up in uncontrollable anger.

The answer came in one word.

"Love." But she was good enough to expand on this for Georgia. "Love those that hate you. Seek ways to help them, don't get angry when they do mean things to you."

"You sound like a Christian," Georgia said. "And Christians are not allowed." But she was thinking how lovely and beautiful this old stick lady was.

That evening, Sunday 27th June, they had a conference in the tiny sitting room behind the bar. Georgia was not invited. Instead, she was confined to her room.

"They are trying to work out what to do next. There is great risk of discovery here." Hilda settled her down in her bed with hot chocolate and biscuits. "Already, the authorities seem to have guessed your location; at least, the general area anyway. They have turned Tunbridge Wells upside-down. I'll be locking you in, little one, not because I don't trust you but because I want to be able to say to them in the meeting that you are so."

"You should not trust me, Mrs Farringdon. It is my duty to try and escape."

But all Hilda did in response was lean over the bed, kiss her lightly, and run those bony fingers through her hair once again. "I've washed, mended and ironed all your clothes, just to be ready."

Georgia was wearing a borrowed nightie, ready for bed. She saw two sets of camp uniform laid out on the chair, her small backpack hanging next to the clothes. With her short boots sitting on the floor nearby this amounted to her total worldly possessions to hand.

"I'll miss you, Mrs Farringdon."

"There, there, now I must be going. I'll come and check on you later."

The sitting room directly below Georgia's bedroom was crowded when Hilda arrived. There were five occupants and she made up the sixth. She sat on her desk chair, turning it around to face the others.

"I'm sorry to be late. I was settling down the Fraulein."

This led, inevitably, to questions as to her health. Hilda replied that she was much improved.

"I'm so glad," Janet said. "I was quite worried about her. I'll give her an examination first thing in the morning and then, if she's okay, we'll need to be on our way."

"I agree, I think we all do," said one of the soldiers, turning to face Sandy. "It is high risk being here at all. We've all managed to stay undetected for almost four weeks by staying with local families. But even this meeting here tonight is a great risk."

"Let's move on to possible destinations," Sandy said, and they did.

But after two hours, fuelled by bread, cheese and beer, they were no closer to determining their next stop. Early on, they had ruled out New London, for the reasons given by Jo. They discussed crossing the river to Essex, strictly R6, but getting through the vast complex of factories on the northern banks of the river seemed impossible. Every factory had its own set of guards, plus there was the *Industrielle Polizei*, or IP, to get around.

"I really don't fancy a skirmish with those fun guys."

"Have we thought about getting across to Sussex?"

But the barrier here was the A21, the vast road that went straight to the tunnel. It was guarded incredibly closely under normal circumstances; much more so with the hunt for the Fraulein going on.

"I think that's why they are concentrating on Kent for their searches," said Sandy. "They realise that our options to leave are limited."

"Look, we can't be seen here after closing time," the senior soldier, a man called Charles Grey, said. 'It is far too risky. We need to break off and return to our various digs one at a time. Say ten to fifteen minutes apart? Then meet sometime tomorrow again, maybe the back of the old cricket pavilion."

"I'll go last," Janet said. "That way, I can examine the Fraulein now and don't have to risk coming back in the morning."

The three soldiers in their group left and went to the bar, agreeing who would leave first and second. Sandy stayed behind in the sitting room. She was going to go second-last, after she had heard from Janet as to Georgia's condition for travel. Hilda took Janet up the steep, panelled staircase and knocked on Georgia's door before turning the lock and entering.

"I was asleep," she said crossly when the light was turned on. "What's Fisher doing here?"

"I'm sorry, Fraulein. Dr Fisher wanted to examine you, just to check you are on the mend."

"I am getting better. Come back in the morning and examine all you like."

"She certainly sounds better," Janet muttered before saying out loud, "Unfortunately, Fraulein, that is not convenient. I apologise but I need to examine you now as we are planning to leave imminently."

"Where are we going?" Georgia was more interested now, sleep banished.

While Janet examined her and pronounced her fit to travel, Hilda told her something of the frustrating discussion down below.

"I know," Georgia interrupted her early on. "You don't have the slightest idea where to go." She seemed triumphant, explaining that the chimney worked as an excellent channel for their voices. "You were almost as loud as those beat kids!" she laughed, remembering them suddenly with a modicum of tenderness. "But I know exactly where you should go. Well, we should go, as no doubt you are not planning to free me."

"Where's that, Fraulein?" Janet stopped her examination momentarily.

"Why, you're all such oafs not to think of it!" she cried, delighted to have an audience. "Betherington Manor, of course!"

"What?"

"Are you deaf also? I said Betherington Manor, the last place they would ever think to look for us.

"Hilda, can you get Sandy right now?"

It was the perfect solution. But Sandy had to be convinced.

"How do we know you're not leading us into a trap?"

"Because I say I am not and I never lie, never ever."

"No, we can't do it," Sandy, just arrived with a hurried explanation from Hilda on the stairs, was thinking fast. "It is too much risk. Thank you, Fraulein, for the suggestion but we aren't going to do it. Now it's time for me to leave. Goodnight, Fraulein. Come, we must go."

They closed the bedroom door, Sandy indicating silently for them to descend the stairs and go directly into the garden.

"I've made my mind up," she said breathlessly when safely behind the rhododendron mass. "We're going to Betherington Manor. But don't breathe a word about our destination to anyone, particularly not the Fraulein. I'll talk to Charlie Grey tonight on my way back. Nobody else need know."

The next morning, Georgia was ready to go. She was dressed in her freshly laundered clothes, standing at the tiny window when Hilda unlocked the door and entered the room.

"Tell Fisher to come here," she ordered her host, in return for the morning greeting. Hilda left.

"You wanted to see me, Fraulein."

"Are you really a doctor, Fisher?"

"Yes, I trained at Cambridge. It was a long time…"

"Braid my hair while we talk." Georgia sat down on the bed, her back to Janet, tossed her long blonde hair backwards.

"Sorry, Fraulein?"

"Are you deaf, Dr Oaf? I said braid my hair. You must have done it a million times for those beat kids under your charge. I can't go out with my hair loose."

Janet wanted to state that the beat kids were not into platted hair. In that same moment, she wondered also why Hilda had not been instructed to do her hair, just like the other days.

But she did not make complaint. Instead, she went to the other side of the bed, perched on the side of it, and started the process of braiding Georgia's hair.

"Did you really train at Cambridge?"

"I really did," Janet replied with a slight laugh. "Really and truly."

"To be a proper doctor? Not a nurse?"

"To be a proper doctor." Then she realised the point of the questioning. In Georgia's world, you did not get female doctors. Men became doctors and women became nurses.

"What's it like? Did you save any lives? Did you do any operations? What was the hardest thing you ever did?" The questions came tumbling out.

"Hold on a mo, Fraulein! I can't answer any of your questions if you don't pause occasionally."

"I was pausing, of course I was. Did you ever disagree with the other doctors? Did you ever make the wrong diagnosis?"

Janet worked on the hair from behind, not in a position to

see the shine of Georgia's eyes. But something told her that shine was there.

There was one more question, different in tone to the others.

"Was it hard being a lady doctor? I mean a woman doctor." The English were not ladies.

They left early that morning, the bright colours of the camper van merging with the summer flowers as they swung down the little lanes of Kent. Georgia's face was deep pink, like the wild flowers along the roadside, for one of the younger resistance fighters had done a long whistle as she strode from pub to camper van.

"Cor, they caught a pretty one there," he had cried.

"Shut up, Jeff," Grey called to instant silence. "The Fraulein is a guest of ours and we will treat her with respect."

They were crowded in the van, eighteen people sharing ten seats. Georgia sat between the window and Janet. She did not frame any more questions about doctoring where she could be overheard. There was a quietness in the van after Grey's telling off, just occasional stilted remarks as they worked their way south on the smallest roads, stopping sometimes at lonely farm cottages to ask the way of mothers with brown hair, chequered aprons, grubby youngsters playing with sticks and stones. Each time, Sandy got out and spoke quietly so nobody in the back could hear the directions. Each time, Georgia was told to squirm down in her seat, then Janet leant across her as if fascinated by the hedge or chicken house outside.

But Georgia was no fool. They should have blindfolded her on capture but they did not. She recognised things by mid-morning. At first, it was the general lay of the land, the way the hills curved and leant over each other. But then her suspicions were confirmed by actual sightings. She dug her elbow into Janet. "I know where we are going." When the doctor looked blankly at her, she dug harder and whispered with her hands cupped between her mouth and Janet's ear, "We're going where I said we should go. We're going to Betherington Manor."

She only said one more thing that journey. It was as the camper van swung through the gates; one missing, the other half off its hinges, and started up the long drive.

"You need me for all the big…"

But the sentence was not finished, for the driver slammed on the brakes and the van shuddered and slid to a stop, a long, high-pitched squeal to announce their presence.

Then a long rifle barrel pointed through the side window, directly at Georgia, more poking through other windows. With a sickening feeling, Sandy realised they were caught. She had a premonition of long interrogation followed by the deadening solitude of prison.

But Georgia was not the slightest bit flustered. She moved the barrel away from her face and said, "Marky, what on earth are you doing here?"

Role Change

There was plenty of space in the panelled drawing room that stuck out like a giant nose on the face of the main house. Flanked by lawns on three sides, it had three almost identical window seats down each long side and a large stone bay window at the end; almost a grey pimple on the end of the nose. The furniture had come with the house. It was large, old, heavy, and generally uncomfortable. When Georgia sat in the drawing room she preferred window seat number three on the left-hand side, from where she could see the early sun powering its way across the estate. She would sit, like a child, with her legs off the floor, curled up underneath her. Sometimes she tried to line her bare knees up with the tapestry of the cushion that featured woodland scenes from long ago. She tried not to squash the woodman with his axe, lest she cut herself. And she kept well away from the elves, in case they had magic they might use against her.

But most of the time she told herself that these were childish games and that she was almost an adult now. When in this mood, she would plump herself down anywhere on the cushion, deliberately disregarding the figures she crumpled beneath her then checking quietly at intervals that no real damage was done.

As July turned to August, Georgia remained idle, excluded, unhappy.

But today she had not been allowed in the drawing room and that angered her, especially as she was bored. Nobody of the English would talk much to her. They were politely distant. Mark was different but he was often out leading the fighters. She did have some talk with the owner; a beautiful redhead English called Barbara Leyland, but she and her older sister seemed often too busy, running off to the fields like peasants, or upstairs helping Fisher with the ever-growing numbers of wounded as the fighting spread across several counties.

It seemed only she had nothing to do.

And now her favourite spot to sit and watch was being

denied her.

"Fraulein, I'm sure you will be perfectly happy in the morning room, or even the old nursery upstairs. I believe there are some good jigsaw puzzles…"

"I am not a child," Georgia shouted, stamping her foot like a child.

"Of course not, Fraulein." Barbara apologised, thinking, *This is surely not the daughter of my beloved Werner?* "I just meant for you to be occupied in some way."

"I'll choose my own occupation and certainly don't need advice from an English." Georgia thundered out, leaving the drawing room doors wide open.

She had already investigated the nursery and done a large jigsaw puzzle showing a race between two fine tea clippers out on the choppy waves. The helmsman's head of the lead ship was missing, as if lost overboard. But his body still performed its duty, hence his ship was ahead. Otherwise, the jigsaw was complete, lined up perfectly in the middle of the large tea table with an equal margin of shiny wood around the sides. She had, one day, tipped it to a slant, carefully moving the pieces as a whole so it did not break. But the slant had offended her so the next morning it was placed back in line.

She had not slept well the night the jigsaw was in its experimental position. Maybe she was just tired but she slept a lot better the following night.

She had counted the steps on all three staircases. She had counted the number of rooms, but this was just an estimate for there were many places that were out of bounds.

Now, she supposed, her principle spot denied her, she would investigate the attics. She hoped there were no spiders up there. She crossed the hall to the back stairs, uncarpeted and worn down by countless servants over the years. These stairs led to the top floor, where the servants had slept. Then there was a spiral staircase going up into the roof. Perhaps she would find a weapon up there.

Only she never made it.

On reaching the first floor she stopped suddenly, left foot still on the last stair, as she heard a cry. She had heard cries before, but always distant and vague. This was just through the brown leather studded door and there was such agony behind it. She had never been beyond that door. It was out of bounds.

On impulse, she opened the door, closed it rapidly and stood, hand on door handle, shaking with what she had seen.

Then she slowly opened the door again and walked ahead into the makeshift critical ward. She saw Dr Fisher's back, bent over a bed, then a patient. Instinctively, she knew it was he who had cried out. He was very young with blonder-than-blond hair and a fair complexion. But in place of his eyes was a thick bandage, blood edging through like an invasion of oil on canvas. She looked lower and saw his right arm had been blown away at the elbow. Barbara rushed up to attempt to stem the bleeding.

"Not now, Fraulein, go back the way you came. We're too busy." There was blood everywhere, contrasting with the white sheets, their white aprons. It was pooling on the pine floorboards, no doubt collecting in miniature reservoirs below the floor, collecting from bodies left and right in their suffering.

"Go back, Fraulein." Barbara tried again but Georgia could not move; would not move. She was struck motionless by the blood, her pretty mouth open at the hinges, her breathing ragged like she had won a race.

Then she crossed to the bed where the young soldier lay, took his remaining hand in hers and stroked his filthy blond hair with her other.

"What is your name?"

"Hans Spatzler," he spluttered, bringing up blood.

"You're with a countrywoman of yours now, Hans, my dearest. I'll look after you." Her mind was racing. She looked up to see she was alone. Dr Fisher and Barbara had both moved to an even more critical case lying on a stretcher by the window. They were totally absorbed. For a moment her mind was blank, sweat trickling down her shirt. She did not know what to do. Should she call Fisher over? She looked again at the doctor, hoping to catch her eye. Then she would come over and tell her what to do. But the doctor was trying to save the life of a sergeant with deep red blood churning like a fountain from his chest.

Georgia was on her own and could not rely on anyone else.

She tried to think of her first aid training. They had spent a day on it during the last camp. It had seemed a game then, playing doctors and nurses, larking about in the little meadow only three minutes' walk from where she now leant over this wounded body. If only she had paid more attention. She dredged her mind for what to do with gushing blood.

"Tourniquet!" she shouted, grabbing a sheet from the laundry cart nearby. Within a minute, she had it wrapped tightly around the upper arm, turning it to squeeze together the pulsing veins. "There, Hans, my champion, that should hold the worst at bay." She turned to the doctor. "Where's the morphine, Fisher?" Janet turned long enough to see a genuine need, nodded to the cupboard in the corner, said, "Twenty milligrams, don't spill any." That was because there was little left. But at least now Hans was sleeping, gently sleeping, the cares and agony slipping from his features. But Georgia's duty was not done. As she turned from Hans she saw an English lying on cushions on the floor. She held his hand while he slipped away, murmuring quiet words, trying to soothe and reassure. She imagined death bringing relief from the pain, but not a good ending. There was never a good ending with war.

Then there were others to turn to; some saved, some helped to die in a gentle way. She did not wait for instruction, just did what she thought was best: stem flowing blood, clean wounds, find makeshift splints for broken bones. She called Janet to help with resetting those bones, knowing her limitations. They worked all afternoon, not stopping for a moment.

"Thank you, Fraulein," Janet said at half past four. "But you need to get some rest."

"These patients don't have beds, Fisher."

"I know, there are no more beds available. We have to make do."

"There are two beds in my room alone. There are lots of beds. Here, whatever your name is," she turned and addressed Maggie, Barbara's sister. "Go downstairs and get six or ten men. Tell them to get every single bed not occupied by a patient down to the drawing room, then move the sofas in there up to the bedrooms. We can make do on sofas. Move, you oafish English, before I lose my temper."

"Yes, Fraulein." Maggie darted away, her calls for help fading down the stairs.

Georgia looked at the two remaining workers on the ward. Fisher looked exhausted, wiping her brow with the back of her hand and leaving a trail of someone's blood on her forehead. She was old, probably past retirement age.

"When did you start work today, Fisher?" The answer was that she had not stopped from the previous day. Yet there were more wounded coming in every day and she had seen how low the supplies were.

"And you, Leyland, are you a nurse?"

"No Fraulein, I am not a nurse," Barbara replied, propped against the edge of a bed, rubbing her back with one hand, trying to straighten her hair with the other. Georgia had never seen such striking red hair. For a moment she wanted to trade her blonde for this woman's red. She was a beauty. But there was something about her. Suddenly she knew.

"When is the baby due?"

"You could tell?" Barbara stood up, astonished. Dr Fisher, also.

"Yes," she said simply.

"It is due in early December, Fraulein." She was about five months.

"How will you bring the hops harvest in?" Why she thought about hops when they had people dying around them, she did not know.

"We'll manage, Fraulein."

"Perhaps some of the wounded will be better by then and able to help."

"Yes, perhaps they will," Dr Fisher answered for Barbara. "With a little luck, we will have an army of hop-pickers!"

The conference in the drawing room was still going on when the twelve men burst in like removers, one at each end of a bed. Mark jumped up, thinking they had been discovered.

"What in hell's name are you men doing?" Grey recognised some of his men in the party.

"Orders from the Fraulein. Beds from the bedrooms in here and we're to take the sofas upstairs."

"Are we supposed to all sleep down here?"

"No," Georgia's voice cut across the others as she entered the drawing room. "You stay in your bedrooms, only you lose your beds. This room is now an extension of the hospital. We've got patients lying on stretchers up there and it won't do. Move out now and make room. Now!" She turned to the bed men. "I want two rows of beds down each side. Leave space in the middle for passage and for the medicine trollies."

"There ain't no trollies, lady," said one cockney lad with coiffed hair and a brown leather jacket, a belt of bullets strapped over one shoulder. "This 'ere 'ospital don't run to no trollies." He had expected a laugh but she stared him down to silence from the others.

"What's your name?"

"Alf Turner, miss."

"My title is Fraulein. When you've finished here, Turner, you and your 'mates' will start in the kitchens and sculleries and then go to the outbuildings. I want you to find, steal or construct a dozen medicine trollies before the day is out. Do you understand, Turner?"

"Yes, Fraulein."

Later that day she inspected fourteen trollies and passed them fit for purpose.

The conference reconvened in the morning room fifteen minutes later, Sandy having the sense to go to the kitchen and grab a crate of beer.

"I'll recap where we are," she said, using a drawer handle to flick off the lid. "What started as a neat move to snatch the Nullgeben kids has become a fully-fledged local rebellion. The whole of Kent and much of Sussex and Surrey is up in arms. Also, over in Berkshire, Jo is raising merry hell. The big problem is, as always, how to gain traction. We've been here many times before and it's led to nothing. The question is, how do we not just keep it going but get it to spread?"

They had discussed it from every angle. Mark had wanted to send delegations directly to other regions, bypassing resistance headquarters who were clearly unable to make a decision either to support the uprising or to stop it. He had some support but, crucially, Grey and Sandy were against the idea.

"We can't bypass HQ. It would be anarchy and then everything would crash. The authorities would walk all over us then."

"But we have virtual anarchy right now," Mark replied. "HQ doesn't support us and it doesn't prevent us. We don't know where we stand."

In the end, they compromised. Grey would travel that night to HQ to try and impress the strategic vision centred in Kent, while Sandy and Mark would keep up the struggle from their home base.

"We need a really good strike," Grey said. "Preferably the day after tomorrow, while I am at HQ. It would go a long way to reinforcing my arguments."

They drank their beers, the meeting over. Grey made ready to move out, hugging Sandy and shaking Mark's hand vigorously.

The problems had not been solved but they had been aired extensively.

One thing that had irritated Georgia intensely during the first six weeks at Betherington Manor was that Mark had changed. He was still courteous but seemed in another place. In particular, each evening he was there he did not seek her out but visited Burton, the English prison guard who wrestled with death. Georgia tried to tell herself that it was natural for him to be concerned for Burton. She reasoned that there was nothing between them, just a determination on his part that she should live. But that did not explain the polite distance towards Georgia.

She had found him alone on the main stairs one afternoon in early August. She had been bored and brooding. Mark was clattering up the staircase, trailing equipment from his makeshift webbing, machine gun in hand.

"It's not loaded," he said, slapping the magazines clipped on his belt. "I've just got in."

"From where?" He would not say, but the blood on his jacket and smeared on his wrist said it had been a fight with her countrymen. There were always contingents of resistance fighters going out to make battle, Mark amongst them. They did not all come back but some came back wounded and brought others wounded with them, friend and foe, so that the makeshift hospital was bursting at the seams. At that point, Georgia had not seen where the wounded went; they seemed to disappear on the first and second floors. But she had heard the screams as she passed.

"Are you going to see Linda now?"

"I am."

"I could look after you." She did not mean to say those words but accompanied them by drawing close to him. They could hear each other breathing. There was something suddenly of the schoolroom on the top floor of the Berkshire mansion but it was like watered-down beer, weakened by dilution.

They stood together a moment, Georgia fixing her eyes on a statue on the landing of a goddess running, her cloak flying behind her; spear, now broken, in her right hand and held high. The goddess seemed to run to battle but what would she do when she faced the enemy with no weapon to hand? Then back to Mark, her one-time lover. He was tired, his senses stretched like a stressed spider's web. She could see that. He looked down at her upturned face and saw she was in need and so he turned back down the stairs, took her to the small dining room to be alone.

"Fraulein…"

"If you want you can call me Georgia, that's my name." He did not want to but did, for her.

"Georgia, I…" He did not know how to say it. It was too complicated. He did not want her. He did but he did not at the same time. But it was not because of Linda. He visited Linda religiously because he had given information about her to that vicious police officer. He had led them directly to her because he was weak. He hated himself for what they had done to her; what he was responsible for. It was too late for Ernst Horer. Mark was responsible for that kind man's death, just as he was looking at his retirement back home. What would his wife, arriving at the train station alone, say to their daughter? How would she explain his execution to his family? How would Mark ever know a day without anger again? It was hatred that woke him in the morning and hatred that lulled him to sleep at night. Hatred does not share with love. It can never be. If you are full of hatred you cannot love, just as you cannot fill a jug of vinegar with beer. Yet here was the Fraulein asking for love.

It was not the Fraulein's fault. Yet she was suffering for his weakness. Why can't the guilty suffer and the innocent know only joy? But was she innocent, the daughter of his oppressor? Perhaps it was guilt by association, by belonging to a race, an order of things? Perhaps her guilt was an innocent guilt, if there could be such a kind?

Making Linda better, monitoring any progress, willing her to heal, was something he had to do. He was fond of her. He was fond of Georgia, excessively so, but, well, it was too much. A month ago, he had been in prison, facing four walls that stared back at him as he watched them. He had known where he was then. Everything was hard and concrete. You could touch the boundaries. You knew the rules off by heart. Now it was so complicated.

Not that he wished to be back in prison, just that he prayed for simplicity.

Mark mumbled that he needed time, there had been so much change. Georgia nodded at his words but did not understand.

But the night after her discovery of the hospital and the role she could possibly play, lying on two sofa cushions on the floor of her vast bedroom, feet or head inevitably on the floor, her tired thoughts were for once not on Mark and his confused and offhand manner, as they had been every night since she had arrived at Betherington Manor. Instead, her head was filled to overflowing with what she needed to do the next day to get order amongst this rabble that called itself a hospital. She would start with … but her mind gave in to sleep and she thought no more until morning sent the sun to wake her.

Meanwhile, Linda opened her eyes for the first time since her assault and gave Mark a weak smile, smirking inwardly as if she had woken remembering a good joke.

Do Not Doubt Thomas

Thomas arrived at Betherington Manor three nights after Georgia's first experience in the hospital; twelve hours after he had heard from Mrs Britain that Linda was there. It was the first day of September but with no sign of autumn coming to that remote part of Kent.

"Be careful, Thomas." Mrs Britain sent him off. "I don't want you to get hurt. Also, Linda is in a bad way, there is no getting around that. Be prepared for a shock and," at this point she stood up and drew the young boy to her, hugging him tightly, "be prepared that she may not pull through."

Thomas had left immediately, only stopping to change out of his servant's livery into the one set of clothes he owned; a grey suit too small for his long arms and legs so he had the appearance of a rare species of unusual anthropoid as he stood at the roadside and waved down cars, ready to hide if a government vehicle approached. Mrs Britain gave him a note as he left. "Give this to Mark Smith when you get there."

"Mark Smith? The prisoner who was a tutor here?"

"Yes. He is now a leading resistance fighter. Be on your way, my darling boy and come back as soon as you can." She kissed him again, her agony of remembrance overwhelming her. Was her substitute son also marching to an early grave?

His peculiar appearance worked for he got lift after lift. The first took him to the outskirts of Reading, where he waited by the side of the road while the vast aeroplane factories and test sites frowned down on him. His next lift was going all the way to Southampton. It was a lorry bearing huge slip rings for satellites being launched into space on the continent. The driver dropped him at Winchester and trundled on, lights flashing orange to indicate a government load. Then there were a series of small, frustrating lifts down small roads so Thomas wondered whether he would be forever wandering around in rural Hampshire, perhaps going in ever smaller circles until he was turning in on himself. He took any lift that was going east and some that were going south and counted the villages in his mind – Twyford, Botley, Curdridge, Wickham. Finally, by early evening he made it to Portsmouth, saw the Napoleonic forts looking out over the harbour; remembered a story his father had told him about some diehards during the invasion. They had holed up in one fort with sufficient supplies for six months and a good number of weapons, too. The fort, now just a bare crater, had been turned nominally into a tourist attraction, actually a reminder that defiance would never be tolerated. Thomas passed it at speed but would not sacrifice his lift with the carpet salesman to stop and see. But it made him think again of Mark and the resistance. He had wondered about Linda being involved. She had never said, but there were some clues, some unexplained absences; some meetings with Mr Fairway that sat oddly with her role as a visiting prison official escorting Mark. It would explain why Linda was attacked and tortured by the police.

The carpet salesman was chatty, with an obvious wig on his bald head. He called it his 'carpet' but joked it was not for sale. He had a raucous laugh that interrupted his speech like a foghorn. Did Thomas think the owners of this place he was in such a hurry to get to would like some carpets? Would Thomas take his card and perhaps a few samples? Where was it, exactly?

Thomas lied and said it was in Tunbridge Wells.

"Well, I'm going close to there anyway. I have a call to make in Westerham. I'm running late so I tell you what I'll do, I'll take you to Westerham and then we can go on afterwards to Tunbridge Wells. I have some excellent samples in the back."

It took all Thomas' wit to get out of this arrangement and to persuade the carpet salesman to drop him first at Tunbridge Wells. Thomas threw the carpet book in a dumpster but kept the business card, felt better for keeping it.

He found a petrol station in the rundown and tired town and looked up a map. The main way south was the vast A21 leading to the tunnel. He could see Fripham on the map as a small village, but the hamlet of Betherington was not marked as such, just a collection of black blocks to represent houses, the largest one a half-inch further east. That must be Betherington Manor.

He could not risk the A21, especially not with so much

military traffic. Then he saw the train station; an enormous goods yard where the town centre had once been. On a hunch, he hoisted himself up onto a goods wagon attached to an engine that was puffing out steam.

He was in luck for twenty minutes later it pulled out of the station, heading south. It went the other side of Bewl Water with the enormous pharmaceutical plant perched on its western shore, then the train paralleled the A21. Thomas guessed the miles and jumped when it slowed down slightly, rolling down the bank, no damage done to his young body.

From here it was six miles to Fripham, then a mile to Betherington and another mile to the manor. He walked in the late twilight, jumping into a ditch or behind a hedge every time he heard movement. There were a lot of patrols, mostly the English, as far as he could tell. This reassured him. He was close to his destination.

Sandy was embarrassed and annoyed that this young lad had managed to penetrate her lookouts without detection. She cursed, put on her boots, went to re-organise and strengthen them. Mark was out with a skirmish patrol. Barbara had not wanted to let him in to see Linda at first but gave way at his polite insistence.

He was still sitting there at 6am when Georgia went around the makeshift hospital to conduct a survey of operations.

"Thomas! What on earth?"

"Fraulein." He stood up, hands clasped in front as taught.

"Why are you here?"

"For Linda, Fraulein. She's, she's my … girlfriend."

"Not Mark's?"

"No, of course not."

"That's okay then. Carry on, Thomas." She moved on to complete her inspection.

But there was a hammer in her heart. And it beat a sweet rhythm.

Georgia approached Janet Fisher on the fourteenth day of her hospital work. She had concentrated for two weeks on organisation, making a number of improvements to, at first, grudging acceptance. On the fourteenth day they had worked together, amputating a leg torn to pieces by a land mine. Janet took the lead but Georgia was right behind her in support, seeming to know what needed to be done next. The boy slept, having been given almost the last of the morphine, his stump well bandaged. They were tidying up the instruments, cleansing them of torn flesh and snippets of bone. Georgia paused in her work then looked at Janet and started laughing.

"What is it, Fraulein?"

"It's you, Fisher. You have a habit of wiping your face with your hands."

"So?"

"They are covered in blood. Look at your reflection in this bedpan. You look like a Red Indian with your war paint on!"

Janet looked at her reflection in the upturned bedpan. She giggled at the sight, then they laughed together long and hard, clasping each other's arms to steady themselves.

Afterwards, Georgia grew suddenly sober. "Fisher, will you teach me what you know?"

The doctor stopped laughing and looked at her young companion. At first, she saw function and purpose worn on her neat sleeves as if planted there by God, only there was no god. But as the second hand ticked a full revolution, she saw the certainty, some would call arrogance, disappear like mist on a summer morning. Underneath was a seventeen-year old girl who had found her calling.

"Do you really want to learn?"

"Yes, I do."

"Then I'll teach you everything I know…"

"Thank you, Fisher. When will we start? I thought…"

"You interrupted me. I will teach you everything I know on one condition."

"Fine, let me know what it is so we can start immediately."

"The condition is that you treat me and my staff with the respect you owe as a new student of medicine. I am Dr Fisher. Is that understood?"

"Yes, um … Dr Fisher."

"Barbara is Miss Barbara, while her sister is Miss Margaret."

"Yes, that is accepted … Dr Fisher."

"Come along then, Georgia. You have a lot to learn. Perhaps the most essential thing of all is how to make a bed so that it remains comfortable for an extended occupation." She could not resist using her first name, was slightly disappointed that Georgia did not object.

They had a meeting a few days later, including Mark and Sandy, both back from a fierce battle that had not gone well. They had travelled overnight to Worthing to join with the Sussex contingent and attack a massive fuel dump next to the home of a tank regiment. They had joked that they would make the night light up like the old Guy Fawkes night, banished as nonsense since the occupation; too much a reminder of the old constitution, religion and history.

They had been ambushed while setting up their positions and Mark had to lead a desperate group through woods, over downs lit by a million stars, to outflank the enemy who had pinned down Sandy in a broad valley on the approaches to Worthing. That part had been a success, at least. Sandy had hugged Mark afterwards, relief flowing like wine in the night. They had routed the ambushing party but there was no mighty lighting-up of the sky that night. Another defeat to register with resistance headquarters.

"But Mark, you were brilliant. Your quick thinking saved the day."

"The only thing that is going to save the day is a great victory. Grey is wasting his time up there without something to prompt HQ into action."

"I agree, but let's get to this meeting, then hit the sack and live to fight another day."

There were two items on the agenda. They addressed them in order of urgency. Janet Fisher spoke first.

"Colleagues, we are just about completely out of medical supplies. We need to get morphine, antibiotics, disinfectant and bandages; everything we can, and urgently."

"We need to raid a hospital," Sandy said.

"Rubbish," Georgia said from her chair. All eyes turned to her, most had not known she was present. She stood up quickly, her camp uniform now spotted with blood and torn in a dozen places; tie long volunteered for a tourniquet. "I mean, Miss Morris," her sudden deferential address to Sandy further surprised them; Mark more than most. "I mean, think of the poor publicity you would get by attacking a hospital. Think of the propaganda opportunities for the ... for the ... authorities."

It was an excellent point but did not solve their problem.

"I appreciate that point, Fraulein, but I don't have the foggiest what else to do," Sandy replied, into the type of silence you rarely hear in a room full of people.

"I do have an idea," Georgia replied. Now the silence was disturbed by the sounds of anticipation, thoughts breaking in such as *Can we trust her?* and *What can she know about medical supplies?*

"Go on," said Mark, knowing her better than the others.

"Well, correct me if I'm wrong but I do not believe that anyone has communicated my condition to my family. Am I right?" Was this to be about her, then?

"That is correct. Go on, Georgia, tell us what you are thinking." Now that he had used her first name in public the gates were wide open, all terms of respect blown away like the boy's leg. But Georgia just continued.

"I'm thinking of a trade," she said. "Or something between a trade and outright blackmail." She paused to see the reaction, nervous that it would be a bad one. Then she plunged on. "Make a film of me to show I am well and healthy and in that film, I will ask for a short truce. Also, I'll ask for medical supplies to be left in some remote place where we can collect them in our lorries during the truce and get back here safely."

It was an ingenious idea. It was the only idea presented. But she would not get away with a respectful response, for Maggie called out from the back, "The little miss wants to be a film star!"

Everybody laughed, Georgia the loudest, for mixed with humour was relief. It had gone down well.

They discussed the details. Georgia, seeming suddenly shy,

suggested delegation so a few minutes later there was a production team and a script team, plus a management team of Mark, Georgia and Maggie. Their job was to determine how to get the film to the authorities and where to arrange the drop of medical supplies.

"Sandy, you have one vital task," Mark said. "Get onto Grey and tell him maximum charm offensive with HQ. They are showing zilch leadership but, if this is going to work, it is important that they don't suddenly assert themselves and block it. It's a chance to save dozens of lives; no, hundreds. We've got to do it." Sandy was the closest to Grey and the two combined had the most influence with HQ.

"I'll get right on it, Mark, glad to do it."

Georgia asked to review the script before filming that afternoon and everybody agreed.

"It is important that it comes over as the genuine, Georgia," Barbara said, thinking of Georgia's father with an ache, then of Georgia's half-brother or half-sister waiting to enter this crazy world.

"Now, onto the other point," said Maggie, seeing how tired Mark and Sandy were. "What to do about Thomas."

The discussion was heated and polarised from the start. Thomas badly wanted to stay with Linda, who could now sit up for short periods of time and talk a little. But he had come with a note from Mr Fairway saying that he could excuse Thomas' absence for a short while, but he was needed back at the Nullgeben household as soon as possible. Not only to avoid suspicion but because he was needed for resistance work, especially now that Linda was no longer available.

"But he has seen the Fraulein and he found his way here so he knows exactly where we are," said Barbara, old habits on names slipping through. "If there is any suspicion at all, he will be questioned. He will talk; everyone does. Her presence here will be known." She was re-hashing the discussion of the last twenty minutes, seemingly unable to move it forwards.

"We can move Georgia," Sandy suggested.

"No!" Georgia was on her feet again. But this time logic deserted her. "I don't want to leave. I've... I've just got settled in." She sat down, impossible to hide the misery on her face.

"We can't afford to lose her assistance on the wards." That was Janet coming to her rescue. "It is out of the question." She had the firmness in her voice that Georgia had lacked. Age was standing in for youth.

"Then Thomas cannot leave," Mark said, bringing the discussion to a close. "He can join my division. I am short of people since we lost so many." It was a sombre note to break up the meeting. They all knew that without HQ support to spread the rebellion it was only a matter of time until they were overwhelmed.

Shooting for Hope

"It's amazing what a dozen people can do at short notice when they have focus," Barbara commented. It was late afternoon the next day. The September sun sat heavily upon the world, seeming to press the roof of Betherington Manor and threaten the foundations. Perhaps the foundations to their whole world were threatened, relying just on hope rather than sound engineering, stable structures.

Grey had arrived back, exhausted, that morning but bearing the news that HQ had blessed the initiative.

"They're an absolute mess up there," Grey reported. "They can't decide on anything, not even what to put in their sandwiches. There are more factions than senior staff, it seems to me. I'm glad to be away from it all!"

"At least they have backed the truce plan."

"More because they could not hold together any credible opposition so it ended up going through on default!"

"Well, never mind. Whatever the reason, it is going ahead."

"Next take," Barbara announced, enjoying her position as director. "We're almost there now. Georgia has made a few further suggestions for the script. Let's try and make this the last take. Come on, everyone, look lively!"

"Look lively, Leyland!" shouted someone from the back of the room to general laughter.

An hour later, they were finished shooting. The makeshift cameraman was Alf Turner, the cockney joker who had angered Georgia in the drawing room just days before. He had worked one summer in the studios where his father was assistant editor before the Clampdown. Now his father was a memory but it was sufficient connection for Alf to be given the dual roles of cameraman and editor-in-chief.

"I really don't know what I'm doing."

"It does not need to be too polished, Alf," Georgia said, thinking how strange to call an English by their given name.

They had a screening that night in the large dining room. As a joke, Alf set the chairs in rows like a cinema and sold tickets; squares cut from a newspaper.

"Film Premier! The new Georgia Nullgeben movie out now. Two fags for stalls, three for circle," he called to the tiny crowd outside. But he ended up giving the tickets away, going through the motions of accepting imaginary cigarettes before handing each one out.

Georgia was allocated a seat in the circle, rather liking the attention. "Only the best for the star!" Alf called, bowing as he presented her ticket. She thought Alf not such a bad fellow after all, for an English.

The film was short. The thing that struck Mark most was the simple humanity in Georgia's frame. She sat on the edge of a hospital bed occupied by a young officer with sandy hair. He was propped on a pillow so the viewers would have no doubt about his nationality. He smiled in a weak but appreciative way while Janet Fisher changed the bandage on his head, revealing a nasty shrapnel wound in the process.

Georgia had insisted on wearing her tired camp uniform. It was clean but tatty, with bloodstains she had scrubbed late each night. She did accept a Red Cross apron, pristine white with a large red cross like a crusader going into battle. This image was reinforced with the tight but practical way her blond hair was tied up away from her face, marking out the nobility of her countenance. Mark thought she looked wonderful.

But it was her words that made the film. She spoke to the whole world but addressed her parents.

"Father and Mother, you will see that I am well and talking to you voluntarily. This was my idea and nobody is forcing me to do or say anything that I do not want to do or say. I am in good health and they are caring for my needs. Please have no concern for my wellbeing for I have no complaints in that regard. I am tired but that is for a very good reason. I am tired because I am working very hard in the makeshift hospital we have here. You will see from my apron that I am a nurse. I am learning to be a nurse and, when I have learned this, I would like to train to be a doctor. This is my choosing.

"We treat both sides in this hospital. There is absolutely no discrimination. The soldier behind me is Carl Elderburg; an officer of yours, Father. He came here last week with a nasty gash in his side and shrapnel in his head. We operated last week. I assisted with that operation in a small way and we saved Elderburg's life. He has hope now because of the initiative we took. Please take a look at him. He says he knows you, Father. Perhaps you remember him?

"But our work here is threatened. It is threatened because we have a chronic shortage of medical supplies. I want to propose a solution to this, bearing in mind that we do not discriminate in any way as to who we treat.

"I propose a twelve-hour truce to start at midday on Friday. During this truce, you will deposit medicines and supplies as listed on the note accompanying this film at the old closed-down railway station at Borton in R1, or Kent as they call it here. The supplies will be placed on Platform One, directly opposite the double access gate, so that lorries may reverse up to the stores without hindrance. You will then leave and nobody will watch or approach the site until 8pm. I cannot stress enough that from noon to 8pm is our time to load the supplies. We will also deposit on the platform the walking wounded who are fit enough to travel. We estimate that there will be thirty-four people for you to pick up. These are all soldiers who have benefitted from our hospital and the care we give. Please question them with regard to that care as I am confident they will speak well of it. If you question them on the location of this hospital you will be disappointed because they do not know where it is and we have taken great pains to keep this knowledge from them.

"Please remember that I do not want to be rescued at present because of the job I feel I have to do. When that job is over there will be plenty of time for me to return to you and for us to be reunited.

"If this truce is successful we propose a similar twelve-hour truce on the 24th of each month. This will allow us to continue to treat wounded soldiers from both sides, saving lives and easing pain. I promise you that I am safe and well and here by

*my own free will. I will return to you, my family and my home,
the moment my work here is complete.*

*"You do not need to acknowledge acceptance of these terms.
All you need to do is deliver the medical supplies and we will
know that the truce is in operation. Remember we need the
medical supplies delivered at noon on Friday 24th September.*

*"I love you, Mother and Father, and I miss you dreadfully.
Give my love to Edmund. I hope to see you soon but first I have
to do this thing for the hospital. I feel compelled to do this but
it does not mean I am against you, my family. You are always
in my thoughts."*

The film had been placed in a captured diplomatic bag,
containing reports back to RUDD HQ dismissing the uprising
as trivial. Sandy had forwarded these reports to resistance
headquarters, out of loyalty, for they did not further their case.
The bag was driven to Berkshire and handed along a chain of
people, ending up with Mr Fairway. He had taken it later that
day to Herr Nullgeben, claiming that he did not know how it
was received.

"We were gathered in the Senior Servants' Hall for my
monthly address," he explained. "When we returned to the
kitchen, there it was. We did not open the bag, it being a
diplomatic one. I sent people out to scour the grounds but they
did not discover anything." He had sent most of the household
out, knowing it was a fruitless search, for appearances' sake
only. And, of course, Mr Fairway had been briefed exactly what
was in the bag. "Will that be all, sir?"

"Yes," said Werner, "no, get Bootle here."

"Yes, sir."

But Bootle could not be found. Mr Fairway diverted the staff
away from seeking intruders to finding the security manager.
Several of the younger ones treated the morning as a lark,
playing hide-and-seek until Mrs Britain called them to order.

"All this fooling around won't get the job done. Now, go and
look along the drive down to the lodge house and no messing
around. You'll be in full view of the Nullgebens in the front of
the house." She sounded severe but was passing out lemonade

and sugar-glazed buns to the hungry searchers.

Mr Fairway felt obliged to report back to Herr Nullgeben at intervals, noting his growing anger at each visit.

"We're just searching the grounds, sir. I'm sure we'll find him presently."

They did find him, just after Mr Fairway's third negative report to his employer. He had decided to look in the derelict workshops, now used for storage and occasional projects. Bootle was in a corner of a dusty room working a lathe, Eddie the English watching him intently. Mr Fairway stood and listened for a moment, fascinated by the conversation going on.

"You see, Eddie, no sooner had we got over the problem of the wing shape we found we had a new problem concerning how to mount the machine guns. Look at this mock-up and you'll start to get a feel for the issues we faced and how solving one problem created still more."

Eddie was clearly enraptured.

"Couldn't you mount them further back, Mr Bootle?" As he asked his question, he leant over the wooden model Harry had been working on and used a felt tip pen to mark a new position on the wings.

"Well, I never!" Harry replied. "That is exactly what we did do, well almost. Because, as you will see as we adapt the model..."

'There is no room for the wire controls running to the flaps."

"Excellent, you should by rights be an engineer, Eddie. You've got the knack for it. You're a natural."

"But engineering is a reserved occupation, as you well know." Mr Fairway stepped into the room. "Under present regulations, it is not something an English can do."

"Ah, Mr Fairway, I was just running through some of the principles of a project I worked on years ago, before the invasion. It was a revolutionary plane. I helped a designer called Mitchell before the invasion. I wasn't much older than Eddie here." Harry smiled fondly at his young and eager companion. Mr Fairway had to squint in the gloom of the dirty workshop, but thought he saw animation on Harry's face; the face that seemed bound to duty with no other emotion allowed to lodge there.

"The Spitfire," Mr Fairway replied.

"You've heard of it? It was undoubtedly going to be the most magnificent plane of its age. It was leagues ahead of its rivals. You know there are many who think it could have stopped the invasion."

"Tell me more, Harry." He knew that Herr Nullgeben was waiting impatiently but some things were more important than the authorities. Besides, he had an inkling where the interview between Harry and his boss may end up.

Mr Fairway remained in the room for the interview, fiddling with the schnapps decanter, polishing glasses, tidying books and magazines, remaining silent as he performed his duties.

"Bootle, what is the meaning of this?" Nullgeben waved the bag in front of the security manager's eyes. Harry had already received a blasting for the length of time it had taken to find him. "You are supposed to be my security manager!" Nullgeben had roared. "Fat good you will do skulking off somewhere." Mr Fairway had been warned of his employer's temper and had seen it rising all morning during the ineffectual search for Bootle. In contrast, Bootle now stood before the commander as emotionally shut down as ever.

"It's a diplomatic bag, sir." Harry did not think this was going to end well.

"Left on the kitchen table."

"I know nothing about it, sir."

"Precisely my point, Bootle. How can someone come over the wall, through the grounds and enter the house without detection? Furthermore, this same mystery person also left the house and grounds without detection. What sort of security system would allow that to happen?"

"I will investigate it, sir, immediately."

"You won't."

"Sir?"

"You lost my children, Bootle. By my son's initiative and no skill at your end, my son is safe. But extensive searches have not found my daughter. Now you let someone saunter in here and leave a package in broad daylight, while you're off on some blasted jaunt somewhere. There is only one thing you will do, Bootle. That is, pack your personal possessions and leave within the hour. You are dismissed with no reference." He noticed Mr Fairway still in the room, looked for a moment like he might dismiss him to, then said, turning his back to them, thinking was Barbara the only trustworthy English? "Fairway, see Bootle receives his last pay up until today, no longer, then see him off the premises."

"Yes, sir."

Mr Fairway consulted quickly and privately with Mrs Britain while Harry packed a few belongings into an old grip bag. He calculated the wages due exactly and gave the cash to Harry in a small brown envelope.

"Goodbye, Mr Bootle."

"Goodbye, Mr Fairway."

"It doesn't need to be this way," Mr Fairway said.

"What do you mean? I've been dismissed. There is nothing else to it."

"You could fight back."

"Me? Alone? What on earth…"

"You need not be alone. Harry, it is my afternoon off tomorrow. You know the Stray Dog pub in Chiselden? Meet me there at 1pm if you have any interest in striking back at this injustice. I often go to drink there on my afternoon off so it is no skin off my nose if you decide not to turn up." Mrs Britain had approved the approach. Mr Fairway hoped they were in business with a new recruit.

It was hours later that Werner, his anger cooling with the setting sun, remembered the package left in the morning room. They were entertaining the American ambassador and a host of government officials so it was late before he could return for the package. It was not to be found. He rang the bell.

"Fairway, where is the package?"

"I removed it, sir, for safe-keeping. It is in your study, sir. Shall I fetch it?"

Werner was about to say to do so when he stopped and

thought. What if it was an explosive?

"Open it, Fairway, and bring me the contents." Fairway was an excellent, but expendable, butler.

"Of course, sir. I'll bring it directly." The door closed without a sound. It opened again four minutes later.

"It appears to be a film, sir."

"Who sent it?"

"It does not say, sir. There is just the reel and a long list of medical supplies. It is addressed to both you and Frau Nullgeben. Shall I set up the projector in the dining room, sir? It should be cleared from supper now."

"Yes, go ahead, Fairway, and send somebody to ask my wife to attend."

"Certainly, sir."

Mr Fairway, watching silently in the corner of the dining room, agreed that Georgia played the part perfectly.

But he could not have predicted the response from the Nullgeben parents.

"I will arrange the truce and the supplies," Werner said on the second viewing of the four-minute film.

"Certainly not," came Carla's reply.

There followed a heated argument in the semi-dark, most of the lights off to allow the film to be seen. Mr Fairway remained motionless in the corner, lest he should be remembered and sent out of the room. The projector continued to whirr, the end of the reel flapping against the projector with each revolution. He dared not turn if off for risk of being dismissed so it continued to flap with a dull thud in a constant rhythm.

Carla was adamant; both were angry.

"What is this nonsense about becoming a doctor?" she raged. "It is ridiculous. She needs to go to the *Statenthrump* and then settle down with a nice husband."

"At least she is safe."

"Safe? *Safe?* She is lost to us, Werner. Her silly mind has been turned by the English. She is no good to anyone now."

It was close to midnight when Werner put his foot down.

"Carla, I am the man in this family. I am also the commander of this sector. I decide what to do. For both family reasons and sector security reasons, I have decided that the truce will go ahead. Now, that will be the end of it. Good night." He left the room. Mr Fairway shrank back to avoid being spotlighted by the shaft of light from the doorway. She followed without a glance back, muttering to herself about fools and idiots in charge of things they had no right to be in charge of.

Two hours later, in the dead of night, Mr Fairway made a short phone call.

"We're on," he said.

"Great. I'll pass it on."

Both parties replaced their receivers.

Mr Fairway considered the day a success as he trod the worn back steps to the servants' bedrooms. Tomorrow was going to be another challenge, bringing Harry Bootle on board with all his knowledge of how the house security worked.

"A challenge a day keeps the doctor away," he murmured to himself before letting himself in at Mrs Britain's door.

Mark crept silently from building to building down the stubby main street of Borton, watching out for Thomas, who was not as used to stealth as Mark had become. However, the soldiers did not seem to care as they unloaded their lorry onto the platform, slinging packages onto the broken concrete. There were several guards with machine guns but they seemed more interested in smoking and relieving themselves than keeping a lookout. Mark and Thomas accessed the old stationmaster's house overlooking the platform; now, like the whole station, deserted.

"I could pick off each one of them," Thomas whispered.

"But that would do no good at all," Mark replied in an equal whisper. He liked Thomas, saw his intelligence, thought he was a good match for Linda.

On the way over, as Mark drove the beat up Land Rover he had been using, Thomas had spoken of Linda's progress. It was looking hopeful.

"She's getting better every day," Thomas said. Mark did not tell him how she was when he had rescued her. Thomas was angry enough as it was, anger seen in the way he held his breath every time he passed an enemy wounded on the wards. He had almost been excluded from this mission because his anger sat awkwardly with the need for stealth. But Mark had brought him for his intelligence, thinking to control his temper if it flared up.

They watched the lorry being emptied, then saw it drive away. The truce was on. It was 1.45pm. They had allowed plenty of time. First, they would load the supplies into the back of the army lorries Mark had taken during his first ambush. They would use both in case the truce was broken: better the odds for one to get through. Then the camper van would need to make six trips to bring the thirty-six walking wounded to be delivered back to the authorities. They were being held at a staging post in the woods six miles away. The estimate was they would need every minute of their six hours and fifteen minutes left to do these tasks. He dialled into his radio and said, "Forward Post reporting. We're on, I repeat, we're on."

Start of Term

Edmund hated being walked to school by Harry Bootle. It was degrading to turn up with a minder or, as his classmates inevitably termed him, 'Edmund's nanny'.

"How did Baby Edmund do last night?" they asked. "Did Nanny put your nappy on in time?" And so it went on.

He had begged his mother to relent on the minder but she was adamant.

"My darling boy, you are the heir. The future looks very bright for you and for our family. These English oafs are such trouble. It is only sensible to protect someone as important and precious as you."

He liked being important but could do without the precious.

A further aspect to humiliate him was that, in a moment of pride, he had shared the 're-naming' of Harry Bootle as the Hairy Beetle with his class. It had seemed a splendid joke, at the time.

Now, as they tired of jokes about nappies and early bed times, the humour did not die naturally. Instead, it gyrated and evolved until Edmund had, himself, become a hairy and disgusting insect. Then some bright spark decided to swat him and before double maths was over he was enduring a flicking from countless textbooks.

He was delighted to hear of the Hairy Beetle's dismissal on the Tuesday of the third week of term. With luck, the memories and associated taunts would fade with the cause gone away. His friends would find someone else to tease mercilessly. It was someone else's turn to take the flak.

He was free of his burden on Wednesday. It felt like the end of a prison sentence. The jokes started as strong as usual but faded rapidly during the day. By lunchtime, they had discovered that Reckine wore a necklace under his shirt. It was something of his mother's. She had killed herself over the holidays, unable to face life without her husband, the unintended victim of an attack by the resistance the previous year. Edmund planted the seed when they changed for PE, then sat back and blessed the luck that had taken him from the limelight.

But at the beginning of Thursday, while walking across the football pitches, relishing day two of freedom, he was met by Old Strife.

"Good morning, Nullgeben."

"Good morning, sir."

"You might wonder why I'm waiting for you." There was a smirk of satisfaction about him. "Well, Nullgeben?"

"Yes, sir. I was just wondering why such an important master was waiting for lowly me." But sarcasm could not dent Strifer's smugness.

"I volunteered when I heard in the common room that you had lost your personal bodyguard. My house is just over there so it will be no problem to start twenty minutes earlier each day and walk up to your home to accompany you to school. And ditto in reverse on the way home."

"That really won't be necessary, sir." He tried several approaches, but all failed.

"Besides, I hear you too want to go to the *Statenthrump*. It will give us an excellent opportunity for me to drum into you some of the characteristics of that great institution. The better prepared you are, the more chance of entry; possibly even a scholarship may be within reach."

Scholarships were awarded for academic achievement and for general character. They were looking for future leaders.

They walked across the recreation ground, Strifer chatting easily, Edmund in deep depression about what his classmates would make of Old Strife escorting him into school each day.

There was a strong wind as they crossed the football pitches. Several English were kicking around a ball, seeming to argue more than putting in any serious practice. Did they ever go to school? He wished, for a moment, but just a moment, that he was transformed into an English, as free as the wind, worrying about the next goal, the next meal, not having to be a future leader.

A gust in the wind took his cap off and sent it dancing along the pitch. One of the English kicked it at goal. It caught the wind and sailed into the net.

"I scored! I scored!" he shouted. This led to a heated argument about whether a school cap counted as a ball. As far as Edmund was concerned, it did not, as there was a ball in play when his cap entered the field. But he did not join in the discussion.

Old Strife did, however.

"Hey, you boys, be so good as to retrieve Master Nullgeben's cap."

"What cap?" came the inevitable reply.

"The cap your fellow just kicked at goal." Old Strife made the mistake of taking their question seriously.

"Oh, that was a cap, was it? I thought it was a dead cat!" The boy who had been playing goalie picked it up, played a game of shaking it out and brushing it down. As he walked closer, Edmund recognised Eddie, his old adversary. Eddie tried the cap on. "Too small for my intellect," he said. "You better have it back, sir." He tossed it to Edmund, then added, "It's taken a bit of a beating, sir, may not pass muster at that posh school of yours."

"Right, I want names and addresses, all of you. Line up here." Old Strife fumbled in his briefcase for notebook and pencil, dropping some exercise books in the mud. Edmund went to assist his teacher. Old Strife looked up, prepared now to take down their names, but there were no English there. "Where did they go, the little devils?" But not said with any endearment. "Did you know any of them?"

"No, sir," lied Edmund, again wishing he could disappear on the wind like the fickle English.

"Never mind. I'll put in a full report. You won't get into trouble over the state of your cap."

But Edmund's mind was far away. Suddenly, he thought of the beat kids. Their music had sounded so unconventional, but one thumping riff came back to him on that windswept playing field in late September. The song had been something about casting your troubles to the wind. He had dismissed it as ridiculous at the time, but now had second thoughts. What was it like to be an English? Or a beat kid, even?

As they neared the school, the wind dropped and clouds gathered like a mustering army. Edmund's spirits sank with the weather. He felt the weight of his classmates' ridicule on him, heavier with each step.

And then came a lifeline.

"Nullgeben, did you happen to find time to mention my concerns to your father?" His obsequiousness told Edmund the enquiry meant much more to Old Strife than an everyday concern. Edmund reflected how sad it was to see a warrior declined to such a state that he begged small favours in unctuous tones. Better to go out in a blaze of glory as what you were than to die a slow death trying to be remembered.

"Goodness, sir, I quite forgot with the happenings of the summer." He had remembered from time to time but thought, on reflection, it was something of nothing.

"I understand, Nullgeben. Perhaps we can make an arrangement now, to further both our ends?"

Five minutes later, Edmund arrived alone at the school gates, swinging his satchel as if he did not have a care in the world. By agreement, Old Strife would meet him each morning at the mansion and leave him at the end of the playing fields, just before the wood that led up to the school. On the return journey, it would work in reverse. He would find the old pilot-turned-teacher at the end of the woods, safely away from his classmates, then would be accompanied home. In exchange, Edmund agreed to raise the matter of sedition in the school with his father at the earliest opportunity.

Edmund did not get that opportunity for a few days. When he returned home on Thursday, he found both parents were away suddenly.

"They had to leave because of the Fraulein," his old nanny greeted him at the front door. "They put me in charge and then there's Mr Fairway of course, for household matters."

"What news of my sister?"

"Lordy me, I don't know! Your father left this morning early, while your mother departed not long ago now. Dare I say, neither seemed in the mood to answer questions so I didn't ask.

All I know is that a parcel came mysteriously and I heard it was a ransom demand."

"Get Fairway here."

"Yes, Master Edmund. And then I thought a little supper in the…"

"Call me 'sir', like I've said before. And don't dare rabbit on about how I'm growing up."

"Yes, sir." Her Welsh inflexion, usually buoyant, was stilled by his rebuke.

"And run my bath and put out my clothes. I'll eat as normal in the dining room so tell Mrs Britain. I want it at 7.30 on the dot. And another thing, Nanny, my school cap got used as a soccer ball this morning. I want it as clean as new for the morning. See to it personally."

"Yes, sir." Nanny backed out as if he were royalty. Except there was no royalty now.

Mr Fairway, entering as silently as ever, was able to give a sensible update to Edmund.

"The Fraulein is safe and well, sir."

"I want to see the film. Set the projector up for me in the dining room. I'll see it at 7pm, then have my supper." There was only one way to deal with the English: command, command, and command again.

"Of course, sir."

A Round in the Pub

The Stray Dog pub in Chiselden was not its real name. That had varied wildly over time. There were rumours of names dating back to medieval times, names that would never get approval now. Chief amongst these was the Stinking Pot; a reference, some said, to the antiquated latrines. Others, less kindly, claimed it was due to the beer.

But in recent centuries it had been the Prince over the Water, reflecting a tiny pocket of die-hard Jacobins centred in the ancient village.

Then, between 1941 and 1943, every public house had been reviewed for suitability by the authorities. Those that were tired or lacked sufficient custom were refurbished or closed down. It was an early initiative to bring order and productivity, amongst the working population and their drinking establishments. The decision on each pub's future was made by the area committees of entertainment that reported through the regions to RUDD.

A small but powerful sub-committee was called the *Korrekter Namensausschuss*. It was headed by a fierce and ambitious young RUDD official named Albert Heffernott, later to rise to the very pinnacle of his organisation.

Herr Heffernott was not happy with the Prince over the Water; reference to royalty was frowned upon. Besides, it meant nothing now, almost 200 years after Bonnie Prince Charlie had fled to safety and ignominy in Rome. He thought Home from Home a far better option and that was what was registered in the town hall in Reading.

But nobody who drank there had ever called it so. The landlord under the new regime, Bert Grainger, had been a young itinerant worker with a scrappy dog at his heels wherever he went. He had settled in to pub life, his wandering days over, and somehow his dog had given his name to the pub; unofficially, of course.

The landlord was an old man now. But nothing had dimmed his enthusiasm for the resistance. He hid it well, seeming a loyal adherer; his gratitude for his position as landlord displayed in the private rooms he kept for local officials' entertainment. Little did these important officers know the plots and schemes being hatched in the public bar, directly beneath their private rooms. A raid on just about any day, lunch or evening, would net a sack full of senior resistance leaders.

But so far there had been no raid.

Mr Fairway stood at the bar as he did when he had a day off. He drank whisky. It was expensive so he sipped it with ice, appreciating how the first strong hit was gradually watered down as the ice melted, mellowing his mood and smoothing over any bumps in his day. Around him there was a controlled buzz. On entering the pub twenty minutes earlier he had looked around for anyone he did not know then checked with Bert behind the bar.

"All clear, Bert? I've got an update."

"All clear, Brian." Brian was his real name, not his BN, but he was with friends.

In a quiet voice, Mr Fairway had recounted his news about the film and Harry's firing.

"I asked him along here. I think he is ripe for membership of our club."

When Harry Bootle entered a few minutes later, it was inevitable that there would be a closing of the ranks. He was known and expected, but all talk of clandestine matters switched naturally to inane conversations about the weather or the Chiselden village cricket team's performance that summer.

Harry was English. He knew the conversations had slipped into automatic. He knew, also, why he had been invited. This big, loyal, usually immovable man was moved to a deep-rooted rage by his treatment the previous day. His was a slow fuse, but now that fuse was lit.

The conversation, nevertheless, had to dance to a tune. Nobody could say: 'You know what we want to talk about and we know that you know so let's just do it.' They had to seem to glide from one conversation to another, gradually stepping from bland to dangerous, from innocent to charged with purpose.

Mr Fairway took a table. The tables were in inglenooks made from stone half-walls covered in whitewash, making thick ledges for people leaning over with their pint pots. At the far end of each inglenook was a tiny leaded light window with a pewter vase and a few dried flowers, the late September sun highlighting the browns and reds of the petals and leaves.

At a push you could fit three down each side on the cushioned wooden benches. But Harry was a big man so he had the left-hand bench to himself. On the opposite side sat Mr Fairway, Jo Macclesfield and Pete Morris, Mark's childhood friend and now Jo's right hand man, with Sandy gone to Kent.

Still the talk skirted the main subject.

"You must be incensed at being fired," Jo said.

"It's a great worry. I won't get another job with any responsibility and," he lowered his voice, looking left and right, "I have a disabled child to look after." That was a significant step forward.

"No?" said Mr Fairway quite loudly, forgetting the need for discretion. Even in the Stray Dog it did not pay to mention disabilities amongst children.

"How wonderful," said Jo much more quietly. "How did you keep it from the authorities?"

"We lied. When he was four years old it became apparent that his mind was not right. He could not speak and he had regular fits. We knew if he was discovered he would be taken away and institutionalised so we faked his death."

"You mean you reported him as dead? But the doctor...?"

"He played along, wrote a totally fictitious report for the coroner. Apparently, Robbie died of chronic bronchitis at the age of four. We had a funeral, buried a coffin half-full of sand."

"And he's been living with you ever since? How old is he now?"

"That was 1948. Robbie is 21 next month."

This led naturally to a hushed conversation about the resistance. Mr Fairway led the charge. He outlined the possibilities, looking all the time for signs of rejection or acceptance in Harry's unreadable face, ready to switch back to safer ground at any moment.

But Harry felt his anger forge into something new. Loyalty can be so brittle, remaining unbreakable until the right pressure in just the right place, then *snap* and the broken shards on the floor bear no resemblance to the functioning article.

Bert, behind the bar, kept an eye on the door, where a couple of young farmhands were loitering, seeming to argue over whose round it was. They had no cause to signal back to Bert, for no one dangerous entered. Most of the RUDD officials were hard at work, keeping their drinking and other pleasures for the evenings.

"Great Scott!" said Harry at a pause. "I can see why I was fired."

"What do you mean?" asked Pete.

"I was head of security for the Nullgebens and, right in their family home, all this was going on. Jo, how many times have you been in the mansion over the last three months?"

"I don't know, maybe eight or nine times."

"Eleven times, including the drop yesterday morning," Mr Fairway corrected.

"So that was you?" He turned towards Jo and stared hard at her, an expression she could not read. "You caused me to lose my job." The same long stare, but this time she thought she could see the thought process. Harry had played for safety for so long because of his son. It was hard to move on, but he was doing just that.

"I did, but I'm offering you a much better one."

"I'll take it."

And Harry Bootle, the Hairy Beetle, joined the resistance.

And when he smiled, sitting with his new friends in the inglenook of the Stray Dog, it shook up those impenetrable features of his as if everything certain in their world had become gloriously and happily uncertain.

Now let's leave the Stray Dog for a walk. Take a right from the door of the pub, down through the haphazard village of Chiselden, fork right at the post office, where the signpost says Hennington. Then up the steep hill, the sunken lane still deeply shaded with oaks, chestnuts and field maples. You can reflect that in another few days; a week at most, their leaves will turn, clinging to their lofty world a little longer but then falling and exposing bare heads to the autumn sun.

It is a steep hill, but there is no need to go all the way. At the next crossroads you turn off the Hennington Road to your left. Your destination is the hamlet of Cheerwell, or 'Cheerful' as the locals call it, deep down in another sunken valley, the tiny houses like crustaceans in the bottom of a rock pool.

Your companion for this walk could be Harry, for he made his way there mid-afternoon on the day of the meeting in the pub. It was six miles, providing plenty of time to consider and reconsider what he had done.

When he let himself in at his home; a crooked, pebbledash cottage on the edge of the hamlet, he felt no different about the commitments he had made. In fact, he felt thirty years younger. He had a purpose he had not felt since the old Spitfire development days.

"Hello Ma," he called without seeing her. She was always in the kitchen in her wheelchair, trying to help.

"Hello, Harry." Her voice was wrung with love for her son.

"Where's Muriel?"

"She went to Upper Hill Farm." That was a long and steep walk, the other side of Hennington. "She heard they had a job going in the dairy." His mother had already filled the kettle, placed it on the range, put out a teapot and cups. "I'm getting tea ready for when she gets back."

"I've got a job. There's no need for her to go out to work. It pays the same as my old job." That had been the agreement that Jo Macclesfield had proposed, understanding as she heard his circumstances that he had commitments. "I'll just check Robbie."

"He's sleeping soundly. I checked a few minutes ago." For his mother to get upstairs Harry had rigged a sort of ski lift to the tiny staircase, operated by a hand pump located on the rig. It came down into the front hall so that it would not block the stairs. It was hard work to get it all the way up. It was a tribute to the old lady that she had gone up to check on her grandson.

But Harry, she knew, would check for himself. He stood at

the bedroom door a few minutes, watching the sandy red hair poking out of the blankets like a small mammal wanting to come out and play. He entered the room and drew down the blankets slightly to see his face, his smile. When he slept it looked like he was at peace.

If only he knew some peace in the waking periods.

He blew a kiss and returned to the kitchen, down the narrow stairs, his shoeless feet making no sound on the cheap pine boards. His mother had the tea ready, saw his massive, slab-like frame ducking through the door, but also sensed something else about the son she knew so well, admired so much; not only for what he had risked for Robbie, her oldest grandson. She had one other grandchild, quite different to Robbie. His brother, Nick, was sixteen; had been sent to the Ballshore Academy, his teachers reporting to the authorities of his remarkable mathematical skills. He came home twice a year in the school holidays, summer and winter; had just gone back to Scotland a few weeks ago. Harry and Muriel missed him dreadfully and had devised a code for the censored letters that went between them.

Harry told his mother about the new position as they sat at the kitchen table, wanted to tell her before Muriel, to gauge her reaction. She felt horror at first, but then looked up at the plastic crucifix hanging on the wall. It hung in the shade of the dresser where it could not be seen from any window, for the crucifixion had not happened.

"Jesus, bless my son's endeavours. Keep him and his family safe as he does your work."

For Harry Bootle's other secret was his whole family was Catholic.

And Catholics were forbidden.

For there was no god and never had been.

Mr Fairway sat with his almost-empty whisky glass long after Harry left; long after Jo and Pete left, too, kick-starting a motorcycle that, with both of them on, would struggle with Hennington Hill.

Bert offered him a refill on the house. He accepted it, moved back to the bar and talked in low voices with the landlord for the duration of his new glass.

"You've done wonders bringing Bootle on board," Bert said in between serving customers with their beer. "His knowledge of the house and grounds and the security system there is going to be invaluable."

"Thanks. The real bonus is that Herr Nullgeben will not suspect Bootle of disloyalty. He sees only a blind devotion to his family that survives even his sacking. The arrogance is incredible."

"You know what the problem is now?" Bert said with a smile, deliberately leaning back from the bar he had been crouched over and raising his voice so that others could hear him. "You're going to have to find some clever way to use all this knowledge. I sense fun times ahead!" This raised a quiet cheer, the customers aware that there was one RUDD official upstairs. But the heavy wooden radio was on in the corner, a football match commentary. It gave the perfect excuse for a bit of jovialness.

Just at the moment when Mr Fairway left the pub, heading for another meeting and other problems, Muriel arrived home from her long, job-seeking walk. She had not been offered the job and was in low spirits. She did not notice the wind had picked up, wrapped as she was against the autumn in her warm old mac, once her mother's. The wind slammed the door to the house, waking Robbie.

"I'm sorry, Harry," she cried as he rushed up the stairs. "I'll go to him." But Harry was up there in five steps, opening Robbie's door with the singsong greeting that soothed his tender nerves, Muriel just three steps behind him.

The Story of Linda and Thomas Part One

Linda was better by the day. As September closed and October opened, she was up and about the ward, unable to lie still. Her body was repairing itself rapidly. The mind, so troubled by torture, bounced back and led the way.

Her hair was her garden; 'soft fuzz', she called her lawn, straggles of longer growth at intervals.

"My herbaceous borders!" she said. She had a joke for every occasion.

Like a tenacious wildflower you just could not keep Linda down.

"When can I start some real work?" she asked Mark one morning, sitting on her bed because Dr Fisher had ordered her not to move.

"Real work?"

"Biffing of course!" She had read Evelyn Waugh's lovely fantasy about how Britain had actually won the war; a war that dragged on to 1945. She was, in her mind, a rebellious, controversial and somewhat odd, soldier.

Especially as, try as they might, they could not save her left eye. She wore a purple velvet patch made by Abby, a seamstress whose husband was a wounded resistance fighter. It was taken from a child's dress Abby found in the attic so it had limbs of white elves dancing across the purple background. Linda threatened to lift the patch and reveal what lay beneath but never did, for the eye had been totally destroyed.

And even Linda did not joke about that.

Mark did not want Linda to fight. He had seen her in her wretched state, still blamed himself.

The numbers of wounded were increasing, terrible to see; great flows of wrecked humanity. Sometimes when he closed his eyes, Mark saw red. Blood was so alive, so bubbling with oxygen and vitality. Yet, too many times he had seen it drain the life from a colleague.

He did not want Linda to follow those that were now in the makeshift cemetery beneath the spreading cedars, beyond the old kitchen garden.

But he had not counted on Linda's determination.

"I will fight," she declared.

And she did.

And when she fought, she had Thomas by her side. They made light of their hatred, this pair of youngsters that in another time would be dancing or taking exams or cycling with backpacks along the cliffs of Dorset. They joked about their hatred, these two of a kind. But that hatred was there and it brought out the best in them.

For Linda and Thomas turned themselves into formidable fighters, terrible in battle like berserks come again from a barely remembered age. And they had the instinct for it, these peaceful youngsters taken, hand-in-hand, along the road to hatred by the times they lived in.

They were tactical and practical. They were strategic and instinctive.

Linda took her appeal to fight to the top, never minding that Mark said no, that Janet Fisher thought she should recover a little longer. They called a meeting of the unofficial counsel in mid-October and won the day. They spent four days in training and then went out to battle.

On their first sortie they disobeyed orders. Instead of retreating when the armoured cars moved in, they circled behind them with a bazooka and disabled eight vehicles, rounding up two-dozen confused soldiers and herding them to where Sandy had banged her fists against a tree in frustration at their disobedience.

They broke every rule and almost turned the tide of battle.

One evening in October, Thomas took Linda down the drive to an old summerhouse, now green with mildew and ragged like they were with their ammo belts and camouflage still on them.

He knelt on one knee and asked her to marry him.

She asked him what his prospects were.
He said he planned a life of hopeless penury.
But he also planned to be happy.
She said yes, of course she would marry him.

They were married the next Saturday, 23rd October. The wind blew a gale, rain thrashed down, as if ordered to empty the tanks before they exploded later that day.

Barbara presided. They reasoned it was her house so she should have the honour. Dr Fisher signed the register. The walking wounded lined the staircase and cheered them. Grey, as best man, gave a speech. It was comic and heartfelt together, dwelling on the fun that emanated from them, but also touching on their devotion, their togetherness.

Of course, Abby made the dress.

Ward Sister

They toasted Georgia in gin.

She took a gulp, spat out the vile liquid, coughing and gasping for air. The background was one of laughter, forming a circle of English around her, enclosing and enveloping her. Then Mark stepped forward and banged her hard on the back, thumping air into her, calming the panic.

"Thank you, Mark," she gasped. She put her glass down on the medicine cabinet in the corner, wanting to forget it existed. She would never drink gin again.

"You've gone quite red, Georgia," Barbara said, taking another slug of the evil liquid.

"I'm not used to gin … Miss Barbara. I prefer schnapps," she lied, having never been allowed any spirits, only an occasional glass of champagne.

"We could probably rustle up some schnapps from somewhere," Margaret said, joining in the fun.

"No, that's quite alright … I've got things to do. I must get on."

"Georgia, wait a moment," Janet Fisher spoke up. "I wanted to suggest something to you." Janet came to the middle of the circle, to where Georgia was standing awkwardly, beginning to expect another scene to this little play. Janet placed her chapped, scrubbed hands on Georgia's shoulders. "You have done so well, Georgia. Not just with the medical supplies but with the care here in our hospital."

"Hear, hear!" That was Barbara, stretching around the doctor to shake Georgia's hand warmly. "You have been an inspiration to us and to all the patients."

"It was nothing…"

But it was something and they meant to follow up on it.

"Georgia, we want you to take charge of a shift."

"What?"

"Take charge of a shift."

"You mean … just like Barbara, I mean Miss Barbara?"

"Exactly like Barbara. She and Margaret are too stretched.

With you taking a shift it will ease them quite a bit."

"But..." The smile was spreading. She was to have her own shift.

"Of course, I will do my rounds and always be available," Janet continued. "And if a new shipment of wounded arrive, it will be all hands on deck. But if you could take charge of the evening shift that would be a great help. I know your training has been scanty but so has Barbara's and Margaret's and the fact is, you are ready and we need you."

Georgia accepted, then broke up the circle by pretending she heard a cry from a patient. She moved across the ward with an extra spring in her heels. She had been promoted and endorsed by her new friends.

Moreover, when Mark had banged her on the back she had felt again the thrill of his presence.

The phone call came at exactly the scheduled time. The superintendent took it in the commandeered inspector's office, hand cupped over the mouthpiece, earpiece pressed tightly against his ear.

He had been warned it was not a conversation to be shared.

It took one minute and forty seconds. One minute and forty seconds of treason. There could be no other word for it.

Frau Nullgeben was moved by fury. And she did not care that it undermined her husband.

"Superintendent, can I count on you to do something very brave?" she opened the call. He blustered in reply, too clever to commit too early. Her anger drove her on. "It would be a chance to make your name." He sat up at that. She had hit the right note.

"How might that be, Frau Nullgeben?"

"I want you to rescue my daughter."

"That's what I am trying to do, plus catch the perpetrators of her kidnapping."

"But I know precisely how you can do it." Now he was standing up, foot drumming on the linoleum, smiling at himself in the mirror on the back of the office door. "It involves some nifty footwork. I won't describe it on the telephone. We need to meet. Come to Rizio's Coffee House on Piccadilly at 10am tomorrow morning. Don't be late."

He, like the phone call, was dead on time.

Georgia's idea first came to her when she heard over lunch one day that there was a seamstress in residence called Abby Ryder. Her husband was staying in the hospital with both legs missing from a landmine. She sat with him most of the day, although that same mine had blown his mind, such that he did not recognise her. Instead he kept mumbling, "Back to bloody bed again" but when Georgia led him to his bed he broke down and wept, crying, "No, no, not there, please no."

"This is the type of thing we are not equipped for," Georgia said after a particularly unpleasant morning when he had tried to get into any bed he could but still panicked when led to his own. "We just don't have the capability for psychiatric injuries."

"You won't send him away, will you?" Abby asked, pale, the tension twisting her pretty features.

"Not if I have any say in it," Georgia replied. The relief on Abby's face was obvious, devotion replacing anxiety. Barbara, sitting at the same table, noted that Abby, like so many of the others, seemed to look naturally to Georgia for guidance and leadership. After Janet, Georgia was next port of call.

"I can earn my keep. I am a really good seamstress. We just need a roof, somewhere safe and warm. I'll do anything."

"Come and see me this afternoon," Georgia said. "We'll sort something out."

"Thank you, Fraulein."

Georgia's idea started as a small one. Her clothes were threadbare. She needed replacements, something practical for working in the hospital.

"Can you do this for me?" she asked Abby.

"Of course, let me just take some measurements, Fraulein."

"You don't need to call me Fraulein, Abby, Georgia will do fine. I'm just one of you now."

"Yes, Fraulein." The girl seemed happier that way so Georgia left it.

Three days later, Abby asked if she could meet Georgia in her bedroom. "For a trial fitting," she added shyly.

Abby had done wonders in those three days, cobbling together an approximation of a nurse's uniform from cast-offs. It was far from perfect but had an element of style and was practical, too.

"I look quite the part!" Georgia cried, twirling in front of the mirror on the wardrobe door.

It needed a little adjustment but Abby promised to have it ready for her main shift that evening.

"No, I have a better idea," Georgia replied. "Do one for Miss Barbara and Miss Margaret and then we will all be the same. Also, we could do something for Dr Fisher. Let me see…"

Another three days passed with the grind of routine on the wards. There were two deaths during those three days. One was a young factory worker who had come in with a hole in his chest pumping blood like an oil well. They had not expected him to live and it was no surprise when he died. Georgia had held his hand for hours as he slipped from pain to a blessed slumber and then on to the next world, only there was no next world. But the other death was a huge colonel with a broken arm and a loud voice that Georgia recognised. He had come to their summer camp the previous year and given a lecture on leadership by example. Georgia remembered thinking why did he not lead by example and slim down a bit? But now he was loud no more, a sheet lay across his body, awaiting burial.

Janet informed the staff that he had died of a massive heart attack in the middle of the night. His broken arm had nothing to do with it. It was sad, but not as sad as the young factory worker.

During these three days, Georgia and Abby were seen whispering from time to time but everybody was too busy to speculate as to the reason.

But at the end of her evening shift on the third day, just as Barbara came on duty, Georgia announced with a smile that Abby and she had a surprise for them. She led Barbara, Margaret and Janet to her room, where hangers held clothes lined up on the wardrobe door.

"Fitting time!" she explained.

Ten minutes later, all of them were in fits of laughter as they paraded in their new outfits. Abby had run out of suitable material, so the uniforms for Barbara and Margaret were cut from an old army greatcoat.

"It was the big colonel's," she explained. "He doesn't need it anymore."

She had stitched large red crosses back and front, using curtains from the dining room. The linen lining of those curtains had been turned into quaint caps, peaked with cardboard sewn in.

But chief amongst her new outfit for Georgia was the badge made of cardboard, upon which was written in beautifully neat letters:

Georgia Nullgeben: Ward Sister

She read it over and over again.

Today was her eighteenth birthday and she could not imagine a more wanted gift than the badge that Abby had made for her.

The superintendent was nervous. He reasoned who would not be, discussing clandestine matters with the first lady of the sector to which he was assigned. He looked across the table at her while the waiter fiddled with the cakes and poured rich coffee from a tall silver pot with a crest embossed on the upper half like lichen clinging to a shiny rock. Frau Nullgeben outshone that elegant coffee pot and was the centre of any world she entered.

"Superintendent, please give me an update on efforts to find my beloved daughter," she said in a loud voice that rang across the coffee house, causing heads to turn. He obliged, raising his voice as he gathered what she was doing.

"Frau Nullgeben, we are certain she is being held captive in R1. We are searching from village to village in the area we control but the southern section is held by the rebels. We control as far down as Tunbridge Wells and across to Canterbury but there is a wild country in between that we need to recapture. I am confident that when we do so we will find her."

All this was known to Carla but gaining an update on Georgia was not her objective in seeking this visit.

"Be so kind, Superintendent, as to return to my town house with me and show me on a map of R1. I find it hard to visualise the places you mention. The female sex is not known for its skill in geography!"

That produced a ripple of controlled amusement across the room, even the stiff English waiters smiling politely at the joke. But it served its purpose. Now the superintendent had a perfectly acceptable invitation to visit the Nullgeben home in Old London where they could discuss matters with total privacy.

He needed a dozen trusted men. He told Frau Nullgeben they would be his disciples, only there had not been any disciples.

"With my twelve men, I can do as you require," he had said, further explaining, "with four teams of three each, we can follow anybody. With radio contact, if one team is thrown off they can be brought back in."

"I do not need or want to hear the details, Superintendent. I just need to know that you are on it and it is the most important item on your busy desk."

"By a long way, Frau Nullgeben, by a long way."

"Report back to me weekly at least. Telephone this number." She handed him a folded piece of headed paper with the town address and phone number on it. "Say you are Bloomsbury Florist calling concerning my special order."

"Yes, Frau Nullgeben. And if you are not in residence in Old London?"

"The phone is diverted to the mansion. Understand, I do not want details of your plan, just confirmation that it is on track for delivery, not flowers but my daughter."

"I understand."

"Now, let's discuss your reward. I assume you would like a posting, a promotion, back to the homeland. This can be arranged through my contacts."

"Thank you, Frau Nullgeben. That is exactly what I would like. You are very kind." If he could make chief superintendent by next year, he would be leapfrogging ahead of his colleagues and in pole position for commissioner inside a half-dozen years.

Wounds to be Healed

They brought Mark in on a torn stretcher at ten to six on the last Monday of October. Georgia was just preparing herself to go back on duty. Since the second truce had expired on Friday, there had been hellish fighting and a steady stream of wounded through the doors of Betherington Manor. Shift timings had gone, replaced with eighteen-hour days, often just snatching a few hours' sleep before exhaustion caused a major accident on the wards. They had been close a few times. Georgia had woken from a two-hour nap on her sofa cushions and had taken a quick bath. Dressed in the now tired but spotlessly clean uniform Abby had made for her, she tied her hair back with a sigh. The laughter with which they had tried their new clothes on seemed long, long ago now.

For some reason, she went down the main stairs. Usually, she would go the back way. But she seemed guided by something that evening, confirmed when she came to the first-floor landing and saw the body lying there.

"Mark," she cried, rushing to him. But Mark was unconscious, a great and ugly wound across the side of his head, blood swelling like an underground stream breaking to the surface. His face was paler than the moon, flecked with camouflage and grime, as if stamped into his flesh by a giant printing machine.

"Quick, get him on the ward," Georgia shrieked, but nobody moved. It was like a surreal comedy film. Nobody heard her. Everyone seemed determinedly set on other purposes, anything other than to help Mark. The panic rose in her.

"You oafs, get here and help Mark."

But still nobody responded. She wondered if she was dreaming. Maybe this was all a sick nightmare. She sat back to pinch herself into reality, to get from her dream world into the one inhabited by all her colleagues, the world where Mark was not lying wounded, bloody and pale, on the torn stretcher on the first-floor landing of Betherington Manor Hospital.

She did not pinch herself, for another contact got there first.

Janet Fisher pulled her away, hugging her shoulders and turning her in a neat move, so she did not face Mark on the stretcher.

"It's Mark."

"Yes, it is," Janet said. Now the two worlds were firmly one. There was only the here and now world.

But this world was agony.

"It's Mark," she said again, as if the English could not understand her.

"I know, but Georgia, we have a strict triage system as you know. You set it up for us and it has saved many lives." It was true. Georgia had seen how they treated every patient in the order they had come in. She had seen youngsters dying before they could receive treatment. She had thought there must be a better way. She remembered the triage system being explained to her when her mother had opened a new hospital in Doncaster. She had introduced it here in her own hospital and it had worked well.

But not now, surely?

"But it's Mark."

"Yes, but he is a Stage Three patient. First, we must deal with the priorities and the urgent cases. That was the system you set up, Georgia. We must follow it every time. Now, Mark is comfortable and his life is not in danger. Here we have a young soldier who is in critical need. This is your job now."

It was twenty past midnight before they got on to Stage Three patients. Georgia had treated ten, making decisions as to what to do herself and when to call Janet Fisher. She reset broken bones, bandaged viscous wounds to the body and head, held hands and spoke soft words to those she could not help, thus helping them after all.

"Two died, six are satisfactory, and two remain critical," she reported to Dr Fisher at 12.20. "One in particular I am concerned about. You amputated the leg but he lost a lot of blood."

"I'll watch him," Janet replied. "You go and see to Mark."

Mark woke to late October sunshine. It slanted through the long bank of leaded light windows forming squares on the hardwood floors, the counterpanes, pillows and patients, not discriminating against what it framed with its brown-at-the-edges light. Autumn was come now, its shades so hard to reproduce; yellow, brown and red, some green still, dancing and mixing across the canvas, producing multitudes of sub-colours. They could not claim primacy; some were little more than shades, but they gave depth to straight lines, vibrancy to blocks and patches, insight into the slow death of the world.

Perhaps a hospital in autumn is all wrong. As the earth settles down to death outside the hospital walls, everyone inside is scrambling for hope, for life saved, for success in their purpose. Perhaps a hospital sits better in the springtime.

But it has to get through autumn and winter to be there for spring. Death before life.

"Georgia."

"Mark. You're awake?" But not fully, not ready for conversation.

"My head, it is like..."

She gave him morphine and he slept again. She sat there, watching his face, half covered in a white bandage tinged with red, knowing she would have to change it soon. She knew she should call Dr Fisher to look at the wound, but also knew she was sleeping after thirty-six hours on the wards.

"You need to get some rest," Barbara said, walking in a sideways swing, the baby now massive on her tummy.

"You, too," Georgia replied with a smile. "I'll go if you go. Deal?" She smiled and rose from her stool, wobbled with exhaustion, her hand slipping on the bedstead. She landed heavily back on the stool.

"See what I mean?" Barbara said, holding out one hand to help Georgia, the other perpetually rubbing her back. "I'm like a great big anchor in the sea with this monster inside me! You can grab onto me." Georgia's second attempt was successful, buoyed by the anchor and the humour.

"Eric, keep an eye on Mark Smith for me. Wake me immediately if there is any change or if he wakes."

"Of course, Georgie P." Many working on the wards had called her Georgia for a short while, but the name had started evolving almost as soon as they started using it. Georgia could not understand why anyone would spend precious moments playing with names, competing for the most ridiculous derivative, not realising that they only did it with those they looked up to.

"Miss Barbara, may I ask you a question?"

"On one condition."

"What is that?" Georgia imagined rubbing the back of this redhead who she had worked with day in and day out for three solid months now.

"You drop the 'Miss'."

"OK, if you're sure Baba?"

The jump from formal to her sister's term of endearment for Barbara was enormous. But it worked, breaking down any reserve still between them. They smiled with their eyes, did not laugh; too solemn suddenly for laughter, almost like a friendship ceremony dreamed up long ago to forge lifetime bonds between young girls.

They were still holding hands when Georgia asked her question.

"Miss … I mean Baba, who is the father of your child?"

And they were still holding hands as Barbara answered truthfully and absolutely, as friends do.

Mark's stroke caught everyone by surprise. He slept throughout Tuesday, waking on Wednesday and sitting up in his hospital bed, smiling and eating scrambled eggs and toast. He spoke about getting back into action.

"We suffered a big setback on Monday. The authorities are really stepping up their counter attacks. How many wounded came in here with me?"

"84 British and 32 others," Dr Fisher replied. "Four of the others were civilians caught in the crossfire. I've heard that other hospitals in Kent have had similar numbers."

Grey and Sandy came to see him later on Wednesday, planning the next moves, trying to keep the rebellion alive with so little support from HQ. Sandy had a note from Jo Macclesfield which she read out. It expressed similar frustration.

"They just don't seem to understand that, unless they support the rebellion, it is doomed to fail."

"I don't think they have the slightest idea of what to do," Grey replied. "Mark, are you okay? Nurse, nurse, quickly." Georgia had deliberately left them to their tactical discussions but was back there in an instant.

"Go and get Dr Fisher, now!" Mark had slipped from his propped-up position, slumped sideways and in obvious discomfort. He tried to talk but only managed a slurred noise, like a drunken man. Georgia took his limp hand and squeezed it.

"It's okay Mark, we're all here." But no response, fright in his eyes. "Where's Dr Fisher?" she yelled, unable to keep panic from her voice.

"I'm here, I'm here." Georgia backed away so that Janet could examine him. She kept hold of his hand, stretching under the doctor to reach it, but it was not recognised by Mark.

"He's had a stroke," Janet stated. Georgia had already suspected a stroke. "But it's not a massive one," Janet continued.

"What do we do?"

"There is not much we can do: rest, plenty of aspirin for the pain. I've heard that aspirin helps prevent heart conditions so it may also help prevent a reoccurrence."

"Nothing else?" Georgia was dismayed.

"Only physiotherapy, massage and repeated speech therapy."

"I'll get that organised."

And she did. A lot she did herself, but also cajoled, ordered and begged others to do what they could.

She would bring Mark back to health if it were the last thing she did.

Georgia felt very alone that night and the next. Any time not on duty she spent at Mark's side, talking to him as he slept and woke, easing things for him. She told him not to try and talk, just to rest.

"You're in good hands," she said, then wondering if he was. She was no expert. Dr Fisher was stretched beyond belief.

Linda and Thomas came by on Thursday, fresh from battle. Linda insisted on sitting with Mark while Georgia got some sleep.

"You're being foolish my love," Linda had a way of being familiar with everyone. "You need to rest a bit so you can help him."

Georgia agreed, but on condition that Thomas go to the nearest town and seek out a library.

"It will be closed because of the rebellion but find a way in and get me any books on strokes you can find."

"Will do, Fraulein." As a servant, he still used the formal address. He kissed Linda on the mouth and went, leaving Georgia alone with Linda and the sleeping Mark.

"So how is married life?"

"One word – fantastic."

"Did you mind me sending him out to the library? It's just that…"

"Not at all, Porgie. If it helps you understand what has happened to Mark and what to do about it, I would be happy for him to go to Timbuktu!"

"Thank you, Linda. I am sort of fond of Mark, like you are with Thomas I mean." Suddenly, Georgia was all-thumbs with her speech. She was not used to expressing herself, more to command. Trying to reach out to Linda she went a step further. "You know he blames himself for the treatment you received at the hands of the authorities."

"He told me that he talked to the bastards. I told him stuff and nonsense." That was Linda all over. "I talked too, everyone does. I told him who was really to blame."

"Who?"

"Your father, of course. The vile policeman who tortured me told me it was strictly on your father's instructions. He ordered it."

"No, he never would! Mother maybe, but never Father. You don't understand. I mean…"

Linda turned through 90 degrees to look directly at Georgia, looked from the same height into her eyes, saw indignation but sensed it was righteous. She also saw fear, plus flashes of pride like thunderbolts in the clear blue sky, but mostly the wispy, insubstantial clouds of fear. Something told her that Georgia was no longer the enemy, no longer the authority; just a girl with an odd past and a great deal on her shoulders right now. Linda instinctively built a bridge in that sky.

"Fraulein, I suppose the policeman could have been lying. I heard about the other guard, Ernst Horer. He was executed without trial and I can't imagine your father would do that in a million years, not ignoring the justice process." It was a magnificent bridge with girders deep in the earth and towering into the sky; yet, for all its substance, it seemed to float. It seemed a bridge to another world; yet there were no other worlds, no heaven or hell to shuffle off to.

Georgia looked at Linda a long moment, then reached across the bed and picked up her hand, turned it over and saw again the long, thin burn scars crossing the young palm like spaghetti carelessly heaped on a plate. Electricity had made those scars.

"Thank you," she said, the clear blue sky-like eyes brimming with new rain.

Georgia did not want to leave the bedside but did. A part of her recognised that sleep was vital to function and be there for Mark and everyone else who needed her.

She lay on her cushions on the floor, closed her eyes and thought of Mark. Then she thought of Linda looking over him; how relieved she had been to find out that she was dating Thomas, not Mark. And how generous she had been about blame and her father. She felt like Linda had stretched out to her, despite the fact that all Georgia had done was to treat her as just another English. Why were some English so warm and full of joy and kindness? Why did they not know about command and order? Or perhaps they did know but chose deliberately to ignore it? The English were so strange.

This took her thoughts to Barbara and the incredible news she had spoken of. She knew something of her father's affair, but never imagined that the girl would be an English. By rights, she should hate Barbara but instead she was excessively fond of the redhead.

"And now I am to have a little brother or sister," she muttered to herself. That gave a glow to her thoughts that sent her soundly to sleep.

The next thing she knew, was someone shaking her.

"Wake up, Georgia." It was Dr Fisher. "We left you as long as possible."

"Mark?"

"He's sleeping. I need you, Georgia, I'm all in. I need you to take over."

Ten minutes later, after washing in the sink in her bedroom, Georgia was back on duty. She found no time to check on Mark during a long and difficult shift in which she saw much blood, taking sole charge while Dr Fisher slept. Towards the end, with a new day starting with grey fog like an old miser's fingers, creeping over the crevices to seek out riches, she found a little time. With a guilty start, she realised she had not seen Mark for almost sixteen hours. She found Linda slumped over the bed, Thomas standing over her, rubbing her neck with his large hands. On the bedside table was a stack of books on the management of strokes.

"I broke in, Fraulein," Thomas grinned. "I had about sixty seconds until I heard the police sirens. I hope they are okay."

"They are perfect, Thomas, thank you. Now it is my turn to send Linda to bed!"

Mark was still sleeping so Georgia took Linda's chair and settled down with the books. A little while later, Abby came around with a cup of hot, steaming coffee and a plate of biscuits. Georgia thanked her briefly with a smile and turned back to *The Modern Management of Strokes and Cardio Diseases*.

The Witch Hunt

Old Strife got his vengeful way.

Edmund faithfully reported Strifer's concerns the next time he saw his father. Things began to move speedily; perhaps too fast even for an old fighter pilot. Of course, nothing moved that fast, really. Forms had to be filled in, procedures followed. But this was fast for the bureaucracy.

The first Strifer heard about it was a summons to the principal's office. There was no indication of why, just a command to be there at 11.20am the next day.

Strifer arranged cover for his history class and was waiting outside the office at 11.05. He stood feet slightly apart, arms behind his back. Bracing, perhaps?

"Ah, Strifer." The principal, a gaunt and yellowing figure scruffily dressed in grey suit with mortar board and gown, looked up from his paperwork. "How are you today?"

"Very well, sir. And you?"

"Tolerable, Strifer, tolerable. My back aches a great deal." *That is because you bend over your paperwork, old man,* thought Strifer. "And trouble with the gout." *That will be the port you consume,* Strifer said silently.

"I'm sorry to hear it, sir. My father always used to eat raw cabbage for gout. He swore it worked wonders."

"I will try it, thank you indeed." The principal picked up a heavy pen and wrote 'Raw Cabbage' in the large, loopy letters that the children knew so well from their end-of-term reports.

"Now, what can I do you for, Strifer?"

"You asked to see me, sir."

"Did I? Did I indeed?" He removed his mortarboard, rubbed his bald patch and replaced the board, now at an angle like the deck of an aircraft carrier. "Now, what do you suppose that was about?"

Strifer despised this man. He despised the bumble, the bluster and the inefficiency. He longed to take over the school, to have a chance to run it how it should be run.

As he had run his squadron.

Eventually, the principal found the memo.

"You should read this." He tossed it across his desk so that it took off and floated like a glider through the dust of his study to land precisely at Strifer's feet. "Sit down, man." Strifer had to move a pile of homework to free up a chair. "Latin, Class Three," the principal explained, as if it excused the musty mess.

Strifer would have preferred to stand at attention, as befitted reporting to one's senior officer, but he sat on the edge of the chair and read the memo from the commissioner of security to the principal.

"They want to see me immediately," he said. It was a call to arms, a return to the days of old.

You are commanded to attend upon the Office of the Security Commission forthwith.

"I must go."

"But your classes?"

"My classes be damned…sir…my country needs me."

"Strifer, I understand you have information regarding clandestine activities."

Strifer was standing again, this time not offered a seat, but he did not care. He felt suddenly important, a significant cog.

"I voiced my suspicions, sir." His interviewer could not be more different from the principal of the school. It was a different league he moved in now; no more dowdiness, no longer on the fringes. This was real power he was rubbing alongside. The man sitting at the desk was ramrod-backed, fitting neatly into a police commissioner uniform. His office was spacious and modern. There were performance charts on the wall and a bank of windows overlooking the Thames far below. There was a single silver photograph frame on the desk but facing away from Strifer so he could not see what the commissioner's wife looked like. But he imagined her with long blonde hair, well-cut suits and expensive handbags, equally able to make conversation with the top echelons and the newest recruit. To get really high you needed a wife like that; like the Nullgebens, for instance.

The commissioner was a 10:90 man. In any given hour he would allocate up to 10%, six minutes, for niceties, never any more. It was not that he was rude or abrupt or arrogant, just that he was efficient.

With Strifer, it was easy. The commissioner spent four minutes reliving Strifer's fighter pilot past, adding a few compliments about those great days, then he was free to move onto business.

"I need you to write down everything about your suspicions so that we can follow it up thoroughly." He said 'thoroughly' but meant 'ruthlessly'. "No, not here. In a moment, you will go with one of my deputies. You obviously appreciate that with this rebel activity in R1 and R4, RUDD are under enormous pressure. It is vital that we root out any underhand moves to embarrass or damage RUDD in its exercise of supreme power."

"Yes, sir, I appreciate that fully, sir." Things were looking up for Old Strife. He heard the whine of aircraft engines, the chatter of gunfire high in the sky. He was young again, as it should be.

Things were an awful lot better still when Strifer opened the next communication from the security commission; a branch of the central police force under RUDD. He had spent a tedious day elaborating on his suspicions, going over countless details; some genuine, quite a few invented. The deputy was satisfied. He had a thick file already: what better way of marking his efficiency?

The order was much longer than the first one, going into a lot of detail, but Old Strife's heart beat a merry tune when he read the key words:

You are required to change occupation with immediate effect. We instruct you to attach yourself to the command of Superintendent Counter-Revolutionary Forces and assist him in rooting out all anti-RUDD elements.

These words sat so well, but even they were superseded when he had his second personal chat with the commissioner of security. This time he was invited to sit, but not across the desk. Instead, the ramrod commissioner rose from his seat and crossed the spacious office to a set of low chairs with a coffee table between. He pulled the chair back for Old Strife. His secretary brought in coffee. She poured it from a heavy dull metallic coffee pot into beautiful white bone china cups embossed with the RUDD emblem.

"We need you, Strifer. The superintendent is doing a first-class job but is weighed down with work. We need someone to be his right-hand man. We need someone with a military background and a high level of intelligence. Will you divert from your teaching career long enough to assist us with this task of vital importance?"

"Yes, sir, of course, sir." Old Strife was in Heaven, only there was no heaven.

'Good, now down to details." The commissioner opened a file. The 10:90 man was spent on his ten percent.

They arrested von Schnappmann and three other teachers the next day. They handled the arrests with practised style, swooping in in their big black cars.

Afterwards, they played the recording of the arrests for Old Strife. They asked him to confirm there were no other suspects in the school. Strifer was uncomfortable with the note of panic in the voices of the arrested, especially von Schnappmann, who seemed more terrified than the others. It was easier, he reflected, to shoot down planes in the sky than to hear the fear bursting out of the celluloid.

Strifer was allocated a small office without a window or a visitor chair. He sat there alone, realising it was not much larger than a cockpit. He adjusted the flaps, checked the instruments, increased throttle and pulled the stick back. All afternoon, he flew the skies, making ever more intricate kills, remembering the old tricks.

The next morning, as he walked into the security headquarters from his room in the Police Club, he was met by a young lady; tall and thin, with elegant glasses in front of lovely grey eyes.

"Mr Strifer, I'm your new secretary. My name is Gisela." She had thick fair hair, cut short at the back. He kept looking at her neck as she led him to his new office. "Here we are, sir. I'll just bring in the coffee."

His new office was a corner one on the ninth floor, only five floors below the commissioner and three below the superintendent. It had a desk bigger than his old office, a sofa, coffee table, bookcases, paintings of aeroplanes on the walls and, best of all, two long and high windows looking onto Old London.

And the coffee was served in white bone china cups with the RUDD emblem embossed on the side.

"Sir, the superintendent would very much like to see you at 10am in the twelfth-floor conference room. Do you know where that is, sir?"

"I'll find it, Gisela, not to worry."

"I'll just smarten you up a bit, sir." She pulled a small leather pouch from the drawer of a cabinet against one wall. Inside were a clothes brush, shoe polish and a comb. In a few minutes, she had her boss ready for the day.

While he found the close contact with her exactly what he needed for his spirits.

Strifer was surprised to find the conference room almost bursting with security agents and police officers.

"Ah Strifer, there you are." The superintendent clapped him on the back and led him across to a group of senior officers. "Come and meet the crowd."

When the commissioner arrived, they all settled down.

"Carry on, Super."

"Yes, sir. Now, some of you may be wondering why we have called you together. You are the leaders in the security world; that is without doubt. We convened this meeting in order to (a) introduce Special Agent Strifer and (b) to congratulate him on his remarkable coup." Old Strife still did not have a clue what this was about but decided to keep quiet. He would listen and learn rather than expose his ignorance.

Gradually, over the following hour, he discovered that von

Schnappmann was not a leisurely aristocrat taken to teaching in order to do his bit. His name was not von Schnappmann at all, nor was he an aristocrat from the homeland. His real name was Adok Lisowski, a Polish dissident. Worse still, he was a communist and wanted for several atrocious murders and other terrorist attacks.

"Single-handedly, Strifer has brought us one of the top five most wanted terrorists on our list. And this on his first day in the job!" Everyone applauded politely, thinking back to their own first day, the paperwork they had pushed around, the errands they had run. Here was a shrewd operator they had better keep an eye on. "So please welcome Detective Chief Inspector Strifer. I'm sure you'll all do your best to make him feel welcome and to settle in. Great start, Strifer!"

"Welcome, sir," called the more junior officers.

"Glad to have you aboard, Strifer," lied the more senior ones.

Later, the commissioner took Strifer to one side and asked him what he was earning as a teacher.

"Your salary as a DCI is four times that, Strifer. Welcome to the world of success."

"Thank you, sir."

Afterwards, when the meeting had broken up and everyone gone back to their jobs and their routines, Gisela had a special message for her boss.

"I'm single, sir, in case you were wondering."

And he had been.

Day one saw four arrests, von Schnappmann the key prize. There was a lull on day two, followed by just two arrests on day three. Perhaps, everyone wondered, this was just a flash in the pan. But they had not allowed for the questioning time. By day four, the first results were coming in. There were four arrests again that day, including a police officer.

From then on, it spread. Day five saw nine taken into custody, that number doubling over the next two days.

By the last day of October there were 212 detainees. By mid-November it had topped a thousand.

And the beauty of it was that the rumour started by Old Strife out of spite led to the arrest and eventual execution of 264 known terrorists, plus several thousand others caught in the crossfire.

On 18th November, early in the morning, Herr Nullgeben sought out Strifer. He said a few words of praise, then moved on to the superintendent to talk about Georgia, not knowing the police chief was working secretly for his wife. But if the address from Herr Nullgeben was fleeting, that of Frau Nullgeben was fulsome; sufficient to mend any wound to Strifer's ego.

"I hear you are in line for promotion when the superintendent goes back to the Homeland." That was an excellent way to start any conversation but Strifer, though puffed with pride, had to play his part.

"I know nothing of that, Frau Nullgeben, but thank you for your kind words of support."

"You would make an excellent superintendent, I believe. We need men like you; the backbone of empire. Now tell me, Strifer, were you working undercover at my children's school?" It was easy to imply such, without actually telling a lie. Carla Nullgeben could not believe such talent was laid fallow for so long. She wanted to hear that it was all by some great design, some master plan. "You must come to dinner and tell me all about your war record. I hear it is quite spectacular." He would be of some use to her, she felt sure.

"You are too kind, Frau Nullgeben, but I accept your invitation with the greatest pleasure."

"You must come on Friday next. I will have my personal secretary issue an invitation. Please bring Frau Strifer, also."

He did not mention that there was no Frau Strifer. Instead, he resolved to bring Gisela. Her long legs would win many a male heart but she was his, all his.

He would parade her like he was carrying the cup on a victory lap.

The Nativity

Georgia and Barbara were sharing a rare break together, huddled by the dining room fire, sipping hot chocolate. Then Barbara's waters broke.

"Oh my God!" she cried, only there was no god.

Georgia had no experience of childbirth, did not see the signs.

"What is it, Baba?"

"You oaf! The baby! It's coming."

Georgia straightened her tired cardboard cap, stood up and took command.

"Can you walk?"

"I can crawl." She was doubled over in agony.

"Stretcher bearers to the dining room."

There followed five minutes of order clashing with disorder, clarity with muddle. Georgia won through and Barbara was installed in a single room annex to the main ward.

"This will be our first delivery," Janet said, washing her hands, checking over the scant equipment.

Georgia loved it. Here they were, one old medical degree amongst them, bringing forth new life like the first article off a new production line.

Georgia loved it, except when she looked down to Barbara and saw the pain on her wretched face. Normally, it shone with beauty and character. But not now. The birth was long and difficult, stretching their knowledge to the limit. Janet Fisher frequently wiped her forehead of sweat, wondered what to try next, for the baby would not come out; not into this world, not at this time.

But the baby did come. It burst out when they all thought they could not do any more. It seemed healthy and strong.

Nobody had any energy left so Georgia took the baby, cleaned it by instinct, cut the cord and carried it carefully back to the mother, wondering how there could be no god when this beautiful creation was here and the same in every birthing room across the empire.

"It's a boy," she said, passing the bundle to Barbara.

"My Werner." Barbara looked at Georgia through a dense mist of weariness.

"Your Werner," Georgia replied, her clear sky-blue eyes raining with tears, as much of joy for the new-born as worry for the state of the mother. She turned to where Janet Fisher was slumped on the floor, seeing for the first time a tired old lady. She must be well into her seventies, Georgia thought, as she knelt beside her with a cup of water and a flannel.

"Someone needs to stay up with Baba. I can take first watch if you like."

"Can you, Georgia? I'm just all in."

"I'll do three hours, then Maggot can take over. That will give you time for a rest. Go now, Janet, I mean Dr…"

"Janet is fine."

"You know I will call you if there is a problem. Go now and get the rest you have earned … Janet." The name used shyly, responded to with a squeeze of the hand as Georgia helped her mentor up from the floor and guided her out of the birthing room.

Much later that day, Georgia lay down for her rest. As she closed her eyes she thought, today I brought a baby into this world. Yesterday, I saved the life of a seventeen-year-old. The day before, I closed the eyes of a young female rebel shot to pieces by a machine gun. It could have been Linda but it was not. I am here at the beginning and at the end. In between, I help wherever I can. Some situations work out well and some do not. But I choose this life wholeheartedly.

This last thought was not conscious; more a glow around her whole body as she snuggled in amongst her blankets on her makeshift bed on the floor of her bedroom, now shared with Margaret and Dr Fisher to make more room for patients. She was alone in that room right now but did not feel alone. She was a part of a great thing.

As her mind grew quiet for sleep, just one thing bothered her. It would have to wait for the morning. She was too tired for complex thinking.

Down in the basement, in the old servants' hall, Sandy was cleaning a machine gun that kept jamming. It was a powerful weapon but she was tempted to dispose of it as a danger to life. That very morning, it had let her down. She had been leading an attack on Portsmouth, trying desperately to spread the rebellion further west along the coast. They had crept through the streets in the November dark, darting from one house to another, edging towards the dockyards. There had been over 400 of them, dressed like dockyard workers and mechanics; weapons concealed under coats like gangsters in an old movie.

Fewer than 200 had made it back to Betherington and the other bases deep in Kent. She had almost been one of those killed or captured. *Probably better to be killed,* she reflected grimly.

And it had been her fault.

Well, fault can always be expanded up or contracted down like great bellows firing up an oven.

She was at fault but she could blame her machine gun. It had never worked properly since she had captured it three weeks ago, the same raid that had seen Mark wounded in the head, followed by his stroke. It had jammed at the moment she needed it. She had walked out of a shop doorway opposite the main gates, as if buying a newspaper to read in the tea breaks; another worker getting ready for her shift. Her move was timed to perfection. 300-plus rebels in position ready to follow her, one company in reserve and allocated to sharp shooting from the upper windows of surrounding buildings.

"Wait for the signal," she had said "I'll fire three short bursts from my Henkle with its distinctive sound. Then everyone opens fire and we rush the gates."

But the Henkle had jammed, no signal had been given, and a massacre had occurred.

So, she could contract it down to the machine gun, but she should have known not to rely on the unreliable.

Next, she tried expanding fault, moving it up the chain. She was under intense pressure. It was not surprising that she made mistakes from time to time. That pressure was caused primarily by HQ's indecision. They were at fault. In her anger, she saw herself taking the machine gun and slamming it down on the table in front of their leaders, shouting, "This is the instrument of failure but it is you who are ultimately responsible. You are murderers through hopeless indecision. Your lack of backbone is why my men suffered a massacre today."

But, in her heart, she knew it was her fault.

Made a thousand times worse because Thomas had gone missing during the attack.

And Linda had defied orders and gone off to look for him. Both had now disappeared. And when Mark next wakened, it was down to her to tell him.

A little later, she found why the Henkle was not working. A tiny bit of cleaning rag was stuck under the firing pin. With the gun vertical, so the muzzle looked up into the sky, the mechanism was not jammed, but brought back to the horizontal, ready to use, it stuck fast.

So over 200 good men and women had been killed or captured because of a careless cleaning job by the original owner.

Sandy no longer wanted to get rid of the high-powered weapon.

But it did not make her feel any better.

Later still, Sandy could not sleep. With Mark in the hospital and Grey gone one last time to plead their case with HQ, she was in sole charge of operations and not finding it easy. She had sent scouts to look for Linda, Thomas, any stray rebels they could find, and now waited for them to report back. She had received one sketchy radio message concerning a group of twenty or so struggling to get their wounded back. She had immediately radioed everyone still in the field but received no more news of them.

In despair, she wandered around the wards, telling herself she was checking up; another pair of eyes, but those eyes were seeking not faults and problems to solve but a young girl with long blonde hair and clear blue eyes; a girl who would be a doctor.

She found her in the very early hours, on her sixth restless tour of the network of wards and operating rooms and storerooms that Betherington Manor had become. Georgia looked relaxed after three hours sleep; neat in all regards, hair tied below her cap, which was clean but tatty now.

She had a shine to her that made the world seem more possible, more hopeful.

And it spilled over to Sandy. Who needed something to grab hold of.

"How's Mark?" she asked, suddenly needing a reason to be seeking out Georgia who was so busy.

"The therapy is working well," Georgia reported. "Yesterday he spoke clearly for the first time."

"What did he say?"

"Oh, nothing much, I can't remember now." Georgia was no good at lying. He had looked at her and said as clearly as day, "I love you."

"Have you heard about Baba and the baby?" This was a clumsy attempt to divert Sandy but it worked.

Sandy had not heard. She had been too closed in the kitchen basement, fighting her personal war against the machine gun. Now she spent a happy hour with mother and baby, before the need for sleep sent her to bed.

She slept soundly, the first time in weeks.

Little Werner, born into uncertain times, had good health in abundance. It became obvious that this came as part of a package that included good humour, such that he smiled and laughed easily and liked to hold out his tiny pink fingers for anybody who would grab them and make appropriate noises in his direction. He quickly built up a fan club of patients and staff alike, so that Alf Turner offered to sell tickets but Barbara politely turned him down.

"We could make our fortunes, miss."

"I already have two fortunes, Alf." She indicated Werner and then, for the second fortune, opened her arms in a panoramic gesture to encompass her new home, turned into a hospital the week after she had moved in.

"What? This pile? I'd sooner have one of those penthouse flats they're building in the old brewery in Maidstone. I've heard they even give you a barrel of premium ale as a moving-in present."

"Well, we've got half a harvest of the best hops in the country. One day we'll have premium ale coming out of the taps!"

"That's the ticket, miss. I could live with that."

There was only one thing that bothered Barbara about her baby. Janet told her not to worry; in fact, worrying might make it worse. There was every chance it would sort itself out in time, as long as she rested and kept calm.

But she could not rest while her baby would not take milk from her.

There were things they could do. Alf made an ingenious pump so she could express her milk and keep the pain of swollen breasts at bay. Margaret spent hours teasing Werner with a makeshift teat so he might take to her milk indirectly at first. Sandy took a section of rebels out and obtained eight tins of powdered baby milk.

"Better that he does not go hungry," she explained, stacking the tins by her bedside. "I'll see Georgia about setting up a sterilising unit, but it is dead easy to make up the formula."

But all their kindness did not console Barbara, who wept quietly whenever she was left alone. Her tears soaked her sheets, making Janet worry that she was sweating badly and must have a fever, which would also explain her moroseness.

But Barbara just wanted her little Werner to take her milk. Nothing more and nothing less.

The Story of Linda and Thomas Part Two

Linda looked back and saw the bullet hit Thomas in the arm. He spun around in a circle, mouth wide open, then shifted his machine gun to his left arm and continued to dart forward.

Portsmouth was a mass of terraced houses, long lines winding through the flatland that led to the dockyard. Real workers moved in gatherings, swapping newspapers and cigarettes, pausing on street corners for colleagues to catch up. As they turned west they put their coat collars up against the wind, cigarette ends glowing like lighted buoys in the Solent, marking tricky waters and safe passages through.

Linda led her team. They were behind, needed to catch up, and now Thomas was wounded.

"Thomas, are you okay?"

"Don't stop. I'll be fine," he gasped, short of breath.

"Are you sure? I could send someone back with you."

"No, I want to go on. I want to stay with you."

They moved forward. They were twenty rebels in the dark city streets.

But now they were in position: breathless, waiting, nerve ends sending sensations against their skin. In a moment, Sandy would give the signal and they would advance at a mad run.

"Get your breath back, all of you," Linda whispered. "Any moment now for the signal." She turned back to Thomas, whose white teeth seemed golden under the orange lamplight. She could not tell how pale he might be in that distorted light. But he squeezed her arm with his good hand as they waited.

They waited some more. They saw a dark shape move across the road. It seemed to point to the sky, then come down to the level.

"That's Sandy."

But no signal, no flashes and stabs to rip into the silence and start the battle. The dark shape stopped walking, turned back, then forward again. Despite the dark, the indecision was written large in the air, as if lit up by the first rays of the new day.

There was a shout. It was a challenge from the gatehouse.

Then everything moved so fast. A searchlight swept the scene, then more clicked in. Cries of alarm became orders, boots on hard surfaces, weapons thumbed off safety.

For one brief moment, Sandy was spotlighted centre-stage. Linda expected a speech, maybe a famous soliloquy.

But the only voice that night was a choir of machine guns singing their death song.

It brought death to those that had hoped to deliver death themselves.

And it brought panic to those that had hoped to create their own.

Linda thought faster than most. She saw the hopelessness of advancing towards the growing weaponry. But if they moved quickly they might save Sandy, pinned now against the row of houses facing the dockyard gate. With the growing light, Sandy and her company would be sitting ducks.

"Advance," she shouted, then screamed. Her section moved immediately, another forty from the adjacent sections followed their lead.

They had sixty men and women to save 100 pinned under the guns of maybe 500.

Their only advantage was that nobody would expect anybody to be so foolish as to advance into the face of death.

Which is exactly what Linda's plan was.

Nobody was sure afterwards, during the endless debriefs, whether Thomas or Linda was hit first. They were certain that both took bullets but they argued whether they were fatal or not.

Linda and her sixty had put up a barrage of fire, augmented by grenades and a team with a homemade bazooka. Sandy and her company scrambled to safety then provided covering fire for Linda's retreat.

But all the time the authorities were advancing; moving

relentlessly forward, shooting any wounded.

Linda's section fell back steadily, using whatever cover they could find. Sandy, recovered from her shock, deployed people in the upstairs windows of houses. Linda looked sideways and saw Thomas, grim with concentration, firing one-handed. She loved him all over again in that street as night left and day arrived, with murder all around.

It looked like they might make it. They were retreating down the street. The narrowness was their friend for it meant no more than twenty soldiers could face them at any one time. So far, the authorities had not thought to rush down side streets and get behind them. Or perhaps their attack had been successful in part and the other streets were blocked? It just mattered that they could give bullet for bullet as they stepped backwards.

They might make it.

In fact, many did.

But not Thomas or Linda.

In actual fact, Thomas fell first. He was hit a second time. Linda, fifteen yards behind, seeking a route out, saw him stumble into the gutter like a drunk unable to find his way home.

"Thomas!"

She forgot everything else. Suddenly there was nothing else; no gunfire, no agony of dying people, not even the sun moving up behind the houses. There was nothing but her and her beloved lying in the gutter fifteen yards ahead.

She ran for him.

And as she ran, the bullet left the handgun of Leutnant Doppelkreuz and made its way straight for the scurrying figure of Linda Burton. God, only there was no god, would have slowed down time to see His sunlight dancing on the bright brass shell as it revolved forwards. He might have taken pity and deflected it, sending it instead to chip against the bricks or, perhaps, to wedge into a wooden doorway. Long afterwards, the woman of the house would tell stories of how her husband was just opening the door when the bullet jammed into the frame, inches from his face.

"He almost came a cropper that morning."

But there was no god, not in this world at any rate. The bullet was guided by science, not by divine act. The gun was kept spotlessly clean. The aim was good. And there was no slowing down of time; it just seemed that way to observers.

The bullet went on its way at normal speed and it hit its target.

Leutnant Doppelkreuz was an average shot, not a marksman. He aimed for the heart of a moving target. He hit her left leg, shattering the thighbone.

The *leutnant* had over-compensated for kick. He cursed, then lost sight of the target as it sank to street level.

Linda had reached Thomas but both were unconscious. The authorities were up to them now, passing over and moving on, their bodies just obstacles.

Sandy organised the rest of the retreat, regrouped two hours later in Horndean, then, after quizzing everybody about the fate of Linda, Thomas and the others who were missing, gave the reluctant order to disperse and make their way back to Betherington.

Linda and Thomas lay with dozens of others in the street, rain pattering down all around, making puddles in the uneven road. A drain at Linda's feet was blocked and washed up again, spreading more water over them. The authorities, flushed with success, did not bother to go out in the rain to check bodies. Instead, they ordered the police to gather up any survivors and make lists of their names, their condition, their age, their equipment; anything that could be listed. The dead were to be put in a common grave, dug with a shiny yellow mechanical digger that pushed the earth back over them afterwards. There was no need for lists for them.

Tactical Planning

"It's easy, sir," Strifer said with growing confidence. Why had he ever gone into teaching? He could have done so much more with the second half of his life. "Just about anything you ever do or want to do can be improved with a modicum of planning. "

He had spent last night with Gisela. And the night before; in fact, every night for a month now. At work, he sat in his plush swivel chair and thought of the central problem facing the superintendent. Gisela would bring in coffee at 10.30, then remind him of a lunch appointment at 12.45.

The lunches were fantastic. The superintendent had explained that Strifer, as a senior officer, had a generous expense allowance.

"You don't need to know what the limit is, Strifer my man. Suffice it to say that in fifteen years as a senior officer I have spent their money without a second thought and never once been questioned about it. Of course, your limit is not as big as mine, but I was a chief inspector once, you know."

A typical lunch was like the one yesterday. He had not known the man who had invited him so, as they sat down to their schnapps, questions about Strifer's past started the conversation rolling. Strifer had no problem in talking about his glory days, no problem either in hinting that they had continued just as gloriously over the last decade; the lost decade, as he was coming to think of it. But there was no need to allude to that in public. He did not hide the fact that he had been a teacher but allowed the suggestion to settle that it was an elaborate cover while he sought out the rebels.

"And your patience paid off, Chief Inspector, for you had a remarkable coup with your first arrest."

"Yes, Operation Bushel has been a great success. We have 349 known terrorists in custody now and the list is growing all the time. After a few days in the cells, they are ready to incriminate all their colleagues. We've got twenty-four teachers in custody, seventeen engineers, thirty-nine police; the list just goes on and on."

Old Strife's lunch partner that day was a top-level journalist, writing for the RUDD magazine, the *RUDDER*. He was ever on the look-out for new stories and this had the sound of a good one.

Over caviar and champagne, the journalist quizzed Strifer on his flying career, scribbling notes in a tiny leather notebook. When they moved on to fried trout with blackcurrant source, the conversation became more substantial. The journalist wanted to know more of Strifer's techniques. He gulped his Puligny-Montrachet 1948 and made something up. He was good at that, at blurring the line between fact and fiction, at living half in another world.

"So, tell me, Chief Inspector, what made you suspect Schnappmann, or should I say Lisowski?"

"Observation, man, pure observation."

"You mean around the school?"

"Exactly."

"But I thought you went to the school because you suspected dissidents?"

"Exactly." Strifer had to think fast. "Exactly, I suspected dissidents and went there to observe and came to the conclusion that Lisowski was the ringleader. You asked me how I came to suspect Lisowski to be the ringleader. I did that by pure observation."

The difficulty passed, for the head waiter brought out pork steaks and cabbage surrounded, at precisely spaced intervals on the shiny-white plates, by perfectly round boiled potatoes with pats of butter sliding down like pitiful skiers doing it all wrong. Strifer made a joke about boiling a few English heads. Afterwards, he could not remember the punch line, but it sufficed. It turned the conversation nicely.

The wine with the main course was a delicious Rothschild 1954, something to savour slowly. Strifer enjoyed the company, relished the food, and loved the wine.

But now was work time. He was in the superintendent's office and his boss was badly in need of a little military discipline. Luckily, Old Strife was the man to give it.

"Sir, with a little planning and foresight it is remarkable what can be achieved. I have been thinking about this little problem and it seems we must do a few things. Shall I explain?"

"Yes, Strifer, in a moment. Let's get coffee and I'll send my secretary away for the day. Confidentiality is all important here."

"Exactly, sir."

They started ten minutes later. It was half past five, the time of day when junior staff wonder when their bosses might leave so they can go home. There was a restlessness about the office, drawers being closed firmly, watches checked frequently. Beatrice was delighted to be sent home by the superintendent. She had a new boyfriend and did not want to be coaxed onto the office rug by her boss again, flattery and veiled threats mixing like dancers going in and out with their complicated patterns.

"Over to you, Strifer." So Strifer took centre-stage.

"It seems to me, sir, that you don't know exactly where the Fraulein is."

"That's obvious."

"Yes, sir, but the trick is to exploit their weakness to find this information out." Strifer paused a second, saw the impatience on the superintendent's face, continued quickly. "Their weakness is their need for medical supplies."

"That's why they called the truce in the first place; to get their grubby hands on the medical supplies."

"So, we follow their trucks and find out where this hospital is."

"But part of the truce is that we don't follow them."

Strifer fought down a sigh; it would not do to show exasperation when senior officers failed to pick up his ideas. He had to keep his boss on his side or he might be sent back to the school in disgrace. His rise had been meteoric. He knew that a fall could match that pace.

"Sir, we just don't let them know. We don't let either side know. We follow discretely and find out where the Fraulein is operating this precious hospital. Then we infiltrate it with someone we can trust and our inside man gets the whole layout back to us. From there it is a simple step to come up with a plan to raid the place and snatch the Fraulein back."

"Brilliant, Strifer, brilliant. I knew I was doing the right thing bringing you on board."

That's how it works, thought Old Strife, *let credit flow upwards, defying gravity, so long as I rise with it.*

"If it works, sir, you will be a hero. My role is to give it the best chance of success and I'm ready to start."

"Lead on, man, lead on."

Georgia waited patiently for Janet Fisher. While waiting, she looked at herself in the mirror on the first-floor landing.

But someone else looked back. Someone with dark-rimmed eyes, hair bundled into a makeshift net under a cap that was torn on one side. The dress this girl wore was spattered with faded bloodstains, patched in several places where scrubbing those bloodstains had worn through the paper-thin cloth. Her cardigan had no buttons. Instead, it was tied with bits of string and an old hair ribbon. This was not Fraulein Georgia Nullgeben looking back at her. It was someone with an interest in Georgia but it was not her. Georgia could see the puzzled expression on the reflected face, as if saying to the real Georgia, *Well who on earth are you come to this old house-turned-hospital?*

"Hi, Pie," that was the latest variant of her name. Georgia had evolved to Georgie, then following some silly nursery rhyme it became Porgie. Porgie was the name of a pig in a popular children's book, hence Porky and finally Pie. It seemed to Georgia that the English were forever playing with names, evolving them with tiny witty steps that built collectively into a mass of distortion, playing on word associations, teasing endlessly. Margaret became Maggot and Barbara changed to Baba. It made no sense to Georgia to waste precious time playing name games. It did not improve their efficiency in any way.

"I'm sorry I'm late. I got involved with that sad soldier who came in last night." Janet opened the door to her tiny office and stood back to let Georgia go in first.

"You mean Leutnant Doppelkreuz? What is wrong with

him? There are no signs of serious injuries, really just scratches, but he is behaving so strangely."

"He has severe concussion. He has just enough English and just enough sense to tell me the story. A mortar bomb exploded in his lorry. He was blown clear by the blast by some fluke, but the others were all blown to smithereens."

"How sad." Georgia thought again of the waste.

"We are not equipped for his type of injury. We need to care for him right now but get him back to the authorities as soon as possible. We just cannot handle cases like this."

"Maybe we can arrange another truce and hand over those injured we cannot care for?" Georgia asked.

"It will mean starring in another movie," Janet joked. "But this is not what you wanted to talk about, is it?"

Georgia had wanted to talk to Janet about how to get on, how to accelerate her learning. Her joy of working as a nurse, of her promotion to ward sister, of her remarkably early responsibility and her lead role in running the hospital; all that was fading because she could not study medicine properly.

"I've read the books on strokes and cardiac diseases that Thomas brought from the library for me several times. I need more books but can't risk someone going out again. That would be folly with the... the authorities closing in."

When Janet looked at Georgia, with her torn but scrubbed dress, she saw a fine mind combined with a passion to learn. She yearned to help her; to be a small part of her future. But she also followed Georgia's logic concerning trips out for books.

"I agree it is too risky to get more books." She stopped a moment and looked carefully at her protégé. What would they have done without her and her extraordinary organisational capabilities? The truce idea added up to more than the combined efforts of all other members of staff.

She did not want to say what she said next but said it regardless.

"Perhaps, Georgia, you should think of leaving us now..."

"No way. I'm not going to leave."

"But to go somewhere to start your medical studies? That would be such a positive thing."

"I am needed here and will stay until you look me in the eye and say I am not required anymore. Can you say that now?"

Janet could not.

But the end of their hospital was coming sooner than they imagined. Like a year in the calendar it had grown up, changed, become something else, and now, in its very success, it was sowing the seeds of its own destruction.

"I tell you what I will do," Janet said, sudden inspiration coming to her. "Each day I will write a small section of a text book on medicine. You will study it and the next day, when I hand you the next section, I will test you on the first one."

"Will you really do that for me, Dr Fisher?"

"If you would do my rounds for me, Trainee Doctor Nullgeben, I will start right now."

Georgia, forgetting what was proper, sprang up and kissed Janet warmly.

"Thank you, Dr Fisher!" she said. "I'll start the rounds right now."

She lingered just a few minutes longer than necessary at Mark's bed. He was sitting up against his pillows. There was a light in his eyes as he slurred out, "Hi Fraulein."

"You should really call me 'sister'," she said in mock disapproval.

"Hel ... lo sister," he struggled over the words, his grin making his face look like a floppy fish. She leant over the bed and whispered that now she would be the naughty one and gave him a long kiss.

Mark was improving daily; hourly, even. The speech therapy and the other practices Georgia had introduced were working well.

"Fighting soon," he said, another floppy-fish grin. "Come back soon see me." She felt warm as she closed the door, warm against the chill of the brittle winter days. She would get Mark fit again. She hoped he would not need to fight; maybe this silly crossness between the authorities and the English would be resolved soon and everyone could go back to doing what they normally did.

But would Mark go back to prison? Perhaps she could talk to her father. Yes, she could persuade him, not Mother, to put all charges aside, especially if they were man and … no, she must not think of that. It would be so strange, of course, to marry an English with all their funny ways. When she thought of the English she thought of Alf Turner or Linda; Thomas, even, with his fanatical hatred of all who hurt his beloved. But Mark did not come to mind as an English. He was special, different; like a resident of a grey misty country somewhere in between the divisions she had grown up with.

Gosh, it was all too much to think about. She was exhausted and had too much to worry about with the hospital and the patients and the supplies.

Georgia's next port of call was directly below Mark's room. She knocked on the door before entering.

"Can I come in, Baba?"

"Of course! I'm just trying to feed Werner." She was having no success. Georgia immediately noticed the wet tissues on her bedside table. Barbara had been crying. Now Werner was crying. Georgia kissed Barbara and picked up Werner to comfort him. "I can't do anything right," Barbara cried.

"Nonsense, Baba. Whoever said caring for a baby was easy? But you can rely on one fact."

"What's that?"

"Millions have been there before you!" That brought a smile to Barbara's face. They laughed long and hard, both releasing tension.

Her final visit was to the special ward where Leutnant Doppelkreuz had a cubicle arrangement, giving him semi-privacy. When she had attended him earlier in the day he had been confused, not making much sense. Now he seemed calmer; in fact, was lucid.

"So, you are the actual person behind the myth?" he started when she introduced herself.

"What do you mean?"

"The myth of the Teenage Angel Doctor! It is all around the

camps. You are famous, Fraulein."

"I'm not a doctor at all, not one bit of it. I'm just a trainee nurse."

"Well, Dr Fraulein, your reputation goes before you."

"You are very kind, Leutnant." He was handsome; perhaps too handsome. She did not like him. "Now I have to go."

"Just a minute, Fraulein." As he spoke, he gripped her arm. It hurt. He was very strong, with large hands, short stubby fingernails. His skin was pale sandstone.

"Please let me go. You're hurting me."

"I'm so sorry, Fraulein." But his eyes told a different story. He was enjoying the discomfort he inflicted. "Where are we? I just need to get my bearings." He eased off the pressure slightly but did not release her arm.

"You're in a hospital."

"In R1 somewhere?"

"I can't say. We're not allowed to talk about it. Now, please let me go. I have things to do."

"Things to do, places to go to." He released his grip and moved his voice up half an octave to a more light-hearted place. "I need to get out of bed. I need to go … to the boys' room."

"It's at the end of the corridor." She felt a coldness taking over as she let the curtain swing back, just as Leutnant Doppelkreuz pulled back the covers to rise from the bed.

She was glad to get away, involved with her rounds, then studying Dr Fisher's newly written notes on the sections of the heart so that the unpleasant episode with the young *leutnant* went to the back of her mind.

Until the alarm was raised the next morning.

"He's gone!"

They searched the manor, the grounds, sent parties out across the countryside. They saw the motorbike tyre tracks and guessed the rest. Several people reported him asking odd questions, mainly about their location and the forces stationed at the hospital.

"It's only a matter of time now, Pie," Alf Turner said in a surprisingly sombre tone.

"You are free to go at any time, Alf," Georgia replied, feeling again the *leutnant*'s grip on her arm, seeing the piercing eyes that seemed to emanate with evil.

"No way, Fraulein, you're not getting rid of me that easily. You ain't even given me a kiss yet." He danced in front of her, offered his lips up then shot back in surprise when she stood on her toes and kissed him fully on the mouth.

"Now you can leave," she said.

But he did not. He never would while Georgia was there.

Raid and Retribution

They shot Alf Turner in cold blood. Afterwards, they said he had threatened them. But Georgia had witnessed the murder from a first storey window.

Leutnant Doppelkreuz was one of them. He was in the lead car, speeding up the drive at 3.45pm on a grey leaden Tuesday in December. Doppelkreuz had won the debate as to when to attack.

"It would be best when they sit down for their cups of tea," he had said firmly.

"What about while they are all sleeping before dawn?"

But Doppelkreuz had argued that the darkest hours were when the troops arrived back.

"They will be tired, yes, but armed and angry, especially if we have routed them again. They sit around for a few hours complaining and smoking while the hospital staff wake up for the day, then they turn in. Far better would be to get them at their teatime when the oafs can't resist a 'cuppa' and a gossip."

The weather was on their side. By 3.45pm the grey day was several shades darker, slipping by degrees into night. It was spitting with rain. The wind tried to blow the leaves but lacked the strength to lift the sodden masses. There was nothing to draw attention to the outside, no one to see the advancing raiders, creeping silently before a headlong rush.

They had slipped through the outer ring of guards twenty-four hours earlier. In a remarkably successful dress rehearsal they had penetrated several layers of the English without detection. It was as if the English were drunk on their semi-independence and existed in a world where they could not be harmed. Furthermore, they had waited the balance of the day in the woods just three miles from Betherington with no one discovering them, before their final strike at 3.45pm on that cold Tuesday in December that saw the hospital at Betherington closed for ever.

Strifer was in the fourth vehicle to charge up the drive, not sabres rattling but machine guns chattering. There were rams to batter the doors and boots aplenty to kick over operating tables, medicine trolleys and everything else.

Alf Turner was the first to die. He had been running around the garden, trying to catch a brace of pheasant that he claimed had invited themselves to be the main course. He had been bragging, as he would, about his mother's game stew when the bullet entered his skull from behind, leaving a neat entry hole but a massive exit wound, blowing off the front of his head and making his face crumple like a landslide.

As he died, his cheeky smile was dying also, replaced with shock and terror.

After Alf, they blazed through a knot of orderlies and rebels, caring nothing for whether they were armed or not. They were extremely efficient and totally impartial.

Grey, just back from HQ, hobbled together some resistance, but it lasted only minutes. He fell, a bullet in his leg, then was run over by Strifer's staff car. He choked out his life in solitary agony in the mud and leaves of Betherington Manor, the house they thought they would turn into a hospital. The rain spattered down, washing the grime, the mud, the blood into a mire of death. But the authorities rolled on, efficiency glistening like a lizard's skin in the rain.

Inside, they brought havoc down, breaking what lay in their way. They burst into every room they found, demanding to know where the Fraulein was.

She was in the bathroom. She had been bathing little Werner and playing games with him but stopped as the cars screeched up the drive. She rushed to the window to witness Alf Turner laughing and running in crazy circles then crumpling to the ground, as if he was no more than a suit of clothes, all backbone and muscles dissolved in the rain and the hatred. She knew immediately what was going on but stood motionless at the window, unable to accept the truth and the awfulness of it all. From her vantage point she saw Grey's resistance, then watched him fall to the ground. She knew the car would kill him as it crunched his bones. Still, she stayed transfixed, only brought back to reality when Werner started crying. She went back to him and dressed him quickly. At least she could save her brother.

Through the open door from the bathroom to Barbara's room she heard first the banging on the door, the clatter of boots, and then the siphoned silence of a single bullet; no ricochet to sustain the noise of death. Looking, while holding Werner close to her, a natural instinct, she saw first the growing bloodstains on the sheets of Barbara's bed through the doorway, then the body of her friend twitching her life away.

"She's not in here."

"Hang on, there is another door."

They did not recognise Georgia when they found her crouching in the bath, covering the baby boy with her body for frail protection.

"Here's another English oaf, in fact two including a baby," someone cried. Then Doppelkreuz barged his way in.

"That's her," he said. "That's the Fraulein. We've got her. Take her to the chief inspector's car."

"What shall we do with the baby?"

"Kill it."

"No!" Everyone stared at Georgia, one soldier frozen with rifle raised, safety catch off. Georgia thought wildly. How could she save Werner?

"It's my child," she cried.

"I did not hear of you being a mother during my stay in this pleasant residence," Doppelkreuz replied. "Someone would have mentioned it, I am sure."

"Do you want to take that chance, Leutnant?" she deliberately challenged him. "Think of the transfer to the coal mines that awaits you. A lifetime of checking grimy initials in the attendance register, day in and day out."

"I only remember one child. That was born to this woman." He turned back to Barbara, waving his arm in the direction of her lifeless body half-tipped over the side of the bed. She had died trying to get to her son. "Another English. We don't need to worry about them."

"Look!" Georgia thrust forward the baby's foot, showing the

name tag attached to his ankle; an idea of hers even though there had been only one pregnancy, one birth, in their hospital. The order and preciseness had appealed to her. "Would an English have called her son after the commander, my father?" For the first time in her life, Georgia was pleading with the authorities rather than issuing orders.

But it worked. It sowed enough doubt.

"Leutnant, it must be hers. You must have been mistaken. There must have been two babies," a sergeant said with assurance.

"Her baby died. The English baby, I mean," Georgia lied, then took a big risk. "I can take you to the grave if you like. It was buried yesterday."

"No need", the *leutnant* said then, sideshow over, addressed the main purpose. "We have the Fraulein; mission accomplished. Now we just need to make sure this place stays closed. We continue the sweep through to eliminate all subversive elements."

Georgia, thinking very, very fast, had to do something to save as many of her colleagues as she could. She had to get the confidence of the authorities. She knew only one way, had been taught since birth to command.

"It's about time you arrived to save me, you bunch of tortoises." Get them on the back foot. They were expecting gratitude so give them derision. "Now my baby and I will accompany you on a tour of the hospital to show you the key players. One of them is lying dead on the bed there." She indicated towards Barbara, hardly believing that she was dead. But, she reasoned, the dead bodies might as well be the subversive ones so the living could have a chance. "Come along, I haven't got all day."

The tour took two hours. Georgia was determined to take her time, keep them to her pace so as to keep the advantage. She started by dismissing the juniors, other than two heavily armed soldiers to guard the senior officers. Even within the leaders, she kept a strict regime of seniority, demanding that the chief inspector attend upon her immediately. She would not deal with a mere *leutnant*.

"You?" she gasped on being introduced to Old Strife. "What are you doing here?" she asked of her old history teacher.

"Promotion. I am now a chief inspector of the Sector 8 Armed Police." As if to demonstrate this fact he tapped his shoulder pistol so that Georgia could see the bulk against his jacket.

She thought fast, something she was good at. Was it instinct rather than thought? There was not enough time to analyse what it was. She had to act.

"I always knew you were more than a teacher," she flattered. "You had something about you."

"You are very kind, Fraulein. Now, shall we move on?" There was a danger he would grasp control from her.

"In a moment, sir." That was a clever move. Nobody would expect the commander's daughter to address a chief inspector with reverence, but this chief inspector was a massive cloud of insecurity waiting to burst. She would keep the storm at bay. "First, I need to explain the layout as I have come to understand it. Also, I would like to explain that there are many non-combatants here in the hospital. They will need to be treated with delicacy. There is little to be gained from aggravating an already tense situation, as I am sure you agree, sir."

"Agreed, Fraulein. Please start your briefing." The chief inspector was delighted by the attention. It was very like the old days, only with no aeroplanes to take up in the sky.

Fifteen love to the Fraulein.

"This ward is entirely occupied by civilians," Georgia lied, indicating the ward that Mark's private room led off from.

"Let me see."

"Yes, sir." Georgia opened the door. She hoped the interior did not give a military impression; young men with combat jackets draped over the bed. She tried to picture what it looked like.

It was a picture of a civilian ward. Someone had got there before her. Most of the beds seemed occupied by older men, a few women. There were no signs of the military anywhere.

"It seems okay," Strifer said, turning around in the doorway.

But Doppelkreuz was a head taller, he could see over Strifer. "What about the door over there?" That was Mark's door.

"Well spotted, Leutnant, check it for me."

Doppelkreuz and one of the guards crossed the room, their boots clicking on the hardwood floors. Patients shrank away from them, as if contact could set their recoveries back.

They did not knock on the door. The *leutnant* just flung it open and stepped back while the guard covered the open doorway with his machine gun. Georgia did not dare to look so closed her eyes tightly, trying to shut out the expected stab of pistol or machine gun and the cry as Mark gave up on life.

"Empty, let's move on."

Thirty love, looking good.

That was when Georgia served an ace, making it forty love. She took them up the back stairs to the top floor and tried their patience searching the staff bedrooms. There was nobody to wake, of course; all those not on duty had been alerted by then.

"Are you trying to waste our time, Fraulein?" Doppelkreuz asked when the seventh dormitory revealed nothing but crumpled bedding and spare clothes on the floor.

"Leutnant, hold your tongue," Strifer replied, before Georgia could give an answer. "Think of who you are talking to, man."

"Sir."

"But we do need to move on, Fraulein, and get you to safety," Strifer said.

"Sir, if you will allow me I believe it is necessary to make a thorough search. We are through most of it now, sir." She could turn him with the odd 'sir'. He had always been a weak one, so seeking self-importance.

The final point of the game to love came with an extended tour of the enemy wards. She reflected on the irony that she had insisted on separation when she had first become involved with the hospital. She had been concerned that her soldiers would be contaminated by too much contact with the English. Now it seemed her quirky response would save quite a few of the English, allowing them to disappear or hide while Georgia led the authorities on a wild goose chase.

The game was won. Georgia was escorted to Strifer's car and driven off for delivery to the superintendent. The escort was impressive with armoured cars, troop carriers and motorcyclists; sidecars with heavy machine guns ready for use. The motorcyclists sped ahead to check out the likely ambush spots, working in pairs to relay information on safety back to the main group. As the cavalcade went down the darkened drive she wondered anxiously what had become of Mark and all her other patients. Were they hiding in the woods? Or had they got away to the other hospitals in the area? Every few minutes, gunfire came to her ears; sometimes close, sometimes further away. They were flushing out the woods and fields of that corner of R1, reclaiming what they had claimed twenty-five years ago.

"Sir, we got the Fraulein but no sign of Smith, perhaps he was never there. Grey is dead, along with a dozen others. We're just going through ID checks now. I've left young Doppelkreuz in charge." Strifer was reporting in on the radio. "Yes, sir, we should be with you in a couple of hours. No, I won't inform anyone else. I thought you might want to do that, sir. Thank you, sir."

Similar radio conversations dotted their journey, Strifer at his most important. The messages comforted Georgia because there was no mention of capturing Mark. But he was mentioned often. They were certainly looking for him.

Back at Betherington, as Georgia's vehicles sped to the A21 and rapid transit to London, Doppelkreuz lined up two-dozen of the English and had them shot one by one. He personally inspected each body, pulling his pistol twice to finish off the job properly.

Sometimes, if you wanted a job done properly you had to be prepared to do it yourself.

So perhaps Georgia's game to love was not representative of the match as a whole.

Reunion

Events moved rapidly for Georgia. She left Betherington at 6.24pm on a windy, wet and soulless Tuesday night in mid-December. The superintendent was waiting for her as the convoy pulled in at 8.37pm to the central armed police HQ. The escort vehicles sheared off to the left in a neat move that looked well-rehearsed. The superintendent opened her door, could not conceal his smile, contrasting with Georgia's scowl.

Then Georgia shook herself, knowing she had to play the part.

But the superintendent's smile was gone when he saw the baby Georgia was holding.

"Fraulein, I will get a nurse for the baby." Strifer had not mentioned a baby on his frequent and jubilant radio reports. It was an irritant. *I suppose it was understandable given that the Fraulein had been working as some kind of nurse.* The last thing they needed was an attachment to some English brat.

"You will do no such thing, Superintendent," she snapped back.

"But... but..."

"Are you a goat, Superintendent?" He shook his head dumbly. "Then I would take it kindly if you would not butt me." This was Georgia at her most imperious, a fine scene to witness.

The truth was, she was fighting for her baby brother's life.

"However, I will require facilities to change my son. See to it immediately."

"Yes, Fraulein." *Did she say 'her son'?*

Back to the timeline of that dark and depressing Tuesday when any spare thoughts within Georgia were spent on those for whom it was the last day on earth. And, of course, there was no heaven to move on to. Georgia was overwhelmed with misery. In the space of a few hours she had lost several dear friends, did not know of the safety or otherwise of her one-time lover, who may be lost and wondering in the woods, unable to look after himself.

The only emotion stronger than misery is fear. And it was fear that drove her on to the greatest performance of her young life.

At 8.46, she was shown into a public bathroom, quickly vacated by office staff. At 8.54, a flustered janitor brought in some towels and cloths.

"It's all we could find, Fraulein. If we had had some notice…"

"No matter, it will suffice, thank you. Now, be off with you." She smiled at the English janitor, who shuffled backwards, charmed and flattered by her kind words.

Suddenly, it was just Georgia, alone with Barbara's baby. Barbara who was no more, just a body on a slab somewhere, or perhaps being bulldozed into a common grave? And she had seen Alf Turner shot down in cold blood. No more would he dance and jig upon this earth with a joke and a money-earning scheme trotting out each minute. She leaned back against the bathroom wall, the baby in her right arm, looking up at her face and beyond at the world he had been born into. She wept for her losses, for the kindness, the solidarity, the togetherness she had never known before.

She had found love amongst the English; something she would never have deemed possible. They had found a purpose for her; a role. They had found it for her without even trying. Then the authorities she had always thought infallible had ripped that away from her, like a baby snatched from a cradle.

She wept.

But then she remembered herself, who she was. She washed her face at the sink with her left arm then placed Werner down on the counter top and changed him.

By 9.07pm she was job done, the bathroom door closed behind her and ready for whatever she had to face.

"I shall not travel further tonight."

"But Fraulein, your parents?" The superintendent was anxious for glory. Glory would dilute itself by the morning. He would have to inform them on the phone. He had dreamed of delivering her himself, striding up the steps of the mansion, three at a time, pulling the bell cord. Afterwards, the commander would take him into his study. He would offer him a cigar and some schnapps and want to know how he had done it; how he had brought their only daughter back to safety.

"I shall telephone them from my bedroom in the hotel."

"Hotel?"

"Yes, kindly have someone book the Empire Suite at Randle's." It was the only hotel she knew. They had stayed there when they first came to this sector, before the mansion was ready. "I shall require a cot, formula and a bottle. I will also require my clothes to be laundered overnight."

"Fraulein, we will get you some new clothes," the superintendent said, dismayed at the collapse of his dream, looking at her shabby, makeshift clothes.

"You will do no such thing. My clothing is fit for purpose, just requires cleaning. Please see to it."

"Yes, Fraulein."

At 9.38, the superintendent was opening the car door for the Fraulein, then taking Strifer's seat in the front. The escort gathered again and they moved out, slowly and steadily, through the silent streets. It was after curfew for the English; only those working would have transit passes.

At 9.54, Strifer's car drew up outside Randle's in Piccadilly. The superintendent jumped out but was not as fast as the doorman.

"I would like to accompany you in to the hotel, Fraulein."

"Thank you, Superintendent but that is not necessary. Tell me, was this your plan to free me?"

"It was, Fraulein."

"All yours?"

"All mine."

"I will see you have full recognition, Superintendent," but thinking, *You bastard, you are the one behind the slaughter of my new friends and the closure of my hospital.* "Now, thank you for accommodating me so graciously, Superintendent, but I am very tired and I need to settle down Bar… I mean my son. Please come for me at 10am tomorrow morning and we will travel to my home together so that you can report to my father. I suggest you have the list of dead and captured ready for him. He is a stickler for lists. Put women and children first so he can see that it was mostly men."

And that way he will see Barbara Leyland at the top of the list.

"Thank you, Fraulein; for the advice, I mean. I will get straight on to it."

"Goodnight, Superintendent."

"Goodnight, Fraulein."

At 10.39, Georgia switched off the bedside light. Werner had been fractious, guzzling noisily at his bottle, then crying again with that little sheep-like bleat. Rather than put him in the cot, she cuddled him in her bed, needing him as much as he needed her. He was her link to Barbara, to the hospital she had loved, and to her new people; Mark included. As sleep settled on her and she felt the warmth of the baby, its breathing and chuckling noises as vibrations through her body, she remembered she had not called her parents.

It would wait.

"This is too much, Georgia," her father said, running his hand through his hair, walking backwards and forwards across the hearth of the drawing room. "I am … we are … delighted to have you safe. It is the most wonderful thing ever. But you are a mother at eighteen and unmarried?"

"Yes, Father."

"We will have to give it for adoption immediately," Carla broke into the conversation. "It is essential that this does not get out."

"Mother, it is my child. I intend to keep it. I will look after it either here or somewhere else, but I will not be parted from my little Werner." Her father smiled at the choice of name. "Now I have to see to my son." With a confidence that staggered even her, Georgia rose and left the room, calling to a maid to bring her a bottle and to run a bath for her baby.

"This is preposterous! I bet the baby is not even hers," Carla spoke as Mr Fairway closed the door silently. Georgia could not hear from upstairs, but the door to Werner's study, where the superintendent waited patiently, was wide open.

"I know little of such things, but I believe it is possible to run a check? A blood test, perhaps? But right now, I need to interview the superintendent and thank him for bringing our daughter back."

"I'll see him as well," Carla replied. "I would like to thank him too." *And give him his reward,* she added to herself.

"He's waiting now, Carla."

The superintendent had slept well, dreaming of his future, while his juniors stayed up to put together the lists Georgia had spoken about. He looked at them now for the first time while waiting in the commander's study. Outside, the December sun played hide and seek, slanting low through the east-facing window, disappearing behind the great clouds that seemed to boil up in every quadrant of the sky. There was a change coming in the weather; even the superintendent, a city man, could sense it. But perhaps he would be gone before the dirty winter settled in with its depressing British rain and wind that turned each downpour horizontal, defeating the best coats and scarves. He did not know how quickly his promotion might come. Did Carla Nullgeben have the power to make it happen immediately? Did she just pick up the phone and it happened? Or did she work her influence behind the scenes; quiet words here and there, gently pushing until she achieved her objective and the superintendent could pack his scant belongings and pick up his first-class plane ticket, specially delivered to his secretary.

He looked again at the reports. There had been forty-eight deaths, including two women and a child. The top report listed the names with notes by the non-combatants. All said 'killed in crossfire' in Doppelkreuz' neat and clinical handwriting.

The second report was more detailed. It covered a brief medial synopsis of the wounded that had been liberated. He was surprised to see that there were only twelve, but then considered that with the monthly truce and transfer of the wounded, that was not surprising. There was no mention of the English wounded, other than a note that fifty-four rebel wounded had been transferred to a field hospital in Canterbury; four had died during the transfer, fifteen were not expected to live long.

The third report was tedious, listing the supplies and equipment captured and intended disposition of each article. Surely the commander was not interested in this information? But it bulked out the folder.

The final report was a layout and condition of Betherington Manor. It concluded that it was too dilapidated to be of use to the authorities and recommended no further action. A sub note said as the owner had died in the raid it would pass to her sister: Leyland, Margaret, Miss. She would be informed by the regional office for the English. She had not been found on site and it was assumed she had no part in the illegal hospital.

That reminded the superintendent that they had not found their second objective, Mark Smith. There was no report detailing this failure.

"Superintendent, we are so delighted..." Both Werner and Carla were talking together, so Werner made way for his wife.

"Superintendent, we are so delighted that you have been so successful in getting our beloved daughter back to us and saving her from that terrible world she was captured into."

"I was just doing my job, Frau Nullgeben."

"Well, you clearly did your job very well and are clearly capable of much more. Would you not say so, my dear?" She turned to her husband for confirmation. The superintendent thought this must be how she works, how she repays the debt. It was starting.

"Excellent work, no doubt. Thank you for delivering the Fraulein safely to us. It is a great relief to us to have her back under our roof. Are these the reports on the operation?" The superintendent confirmed and passed them over. Things were going well. Only one hurdle to get over: any questions about the baby.

"Tell me, Superintendent, what do you know about the baby?" Carla could not make herself refer to it as Georgia's baby.

The superintendent told what he knew, which was not much. It had been a surprise to him. The Fraulein claimed it was hers but he wondered whether she was protecting it for someone else.

"Captivity does strange things for one," he pronounced, not realising how pompous he sounded. "Perhaps it has distorted the Fraulein's sense of loyalty. You never know."

"I'm sure, Superintendent, we can count on your absolute discretion in this regard?" Carla was anxious to stop gossip.

"Of course, Frau Nullgeben, my lips are sealed." His grin made the commander look away in distaste. He thought his wife too friendly with this policeman who, he was sure, would work every angle for his own advantage.

"Now, Superintendent, we are remiss in our duties as hosts. We have offered you no refreshments. You will stay for lunch? We have some interesting people coming and it will be our delight to have one more distinguished guest," Carla said. "Come with me and have some coffee while the commander reads your reports."

The superintendent held the door open for Carla. Werner watched them go, sensing an ounce too much familiarity between them. He could not put words to it. Sighing, he sat back down at his desk and opened the first report.

An hour later, when the gong went for lunch, he was still on the first page. In fact, he had not got beyond the first four lines. At the top of the list was 'Leyland, Barbara, Miss', described as a red head English in her mid-thirties.

His lover was dead.

Testing Times

"Who is the father, Georgia? Is it some...?" Carla had not given up over the last few days, questioning Georgia relentlessly, hoping for some evidence that the baby was not hers.

"You mean English, Mother? Can you not say the word?"

"Who is the father, Georgia? You cannot hide this from us. We can check easily enough. I have looked into this."

"What do you mean?"

"Blood tests, Georgia."

"They will just say what blood group the baby is. That cannot prove parenthood."

"Except for your father's condition." There was an air of triumph on Carla as she said these words, her hand revealed at last. It shook Georgia. Was there something she had not thought of?

"What condition?"

"He is a hemochromatosis carrier..."

"You mean the...?"

"Yes, the iron storage disease. He is just a carrier, as are you and Edmund. Because of his condition, we had you checked as babies. You cannot suffer from the disease. But it will be in any children of yours or Edmund's."

"Oh."

"So, who are the parents of this brat?"

But Georgia had stormed out, slammed the door, stamped upstairs. She hated her mother, flung herself on her bed, wept, then started to think it through again; start at the beginning.

She was interrupted by a knock on the door.

"Enter." She dried her eyes, got up from the bed and went to sit on the window seat, then thought better, for the weather outside was atrocious.

Her new maid came in. She was Daisy or Dizzie or something like that. Her old maid had been let go after the kidnapping.

"Ah, the baby is asleep so I am going to have a bath and then sleep myself. Please wash my clothes by hand. I want them back to wear this evening."

"Yes, Fraulein," but Daisy had other instructions. She ran the bath, poured in the luxurious bubble bath, gathered up the clothes as Georgia stripped. "Fraulein, surely you don't want all these old clothes back again? You have a wardrobe full of beautiful things."

"Just do as I say, eh..."

"It is Daisy, Fraulein."

"Yes, I know that," Georgia lied.

"Fraulein, you will be awake for the doctor, won't you?"

Georgia had not scheduled a visit from the doctor but thought it reasonable to have a check-up after what she had been through the last few months.

"Wake me twenty minutes before he arrives," Georgia replied, thinking all contact with medical staff was beneficial. She might learn something. She sunk back in the bath, dismissed Daisy with a wave and closed her eyes.

It was a struggle to get out of the bath fifteen minutes later but then glorious to sink into her own luxurious bed. She went into a deep sleep, the baby obliging her by sleeping soundly. As long as he was fed regularly, Werner was little trouble, seeming to accept routine like a soldier. Thinking of soldiers made her think of Mark. He was not a natural fighter but had a brilliant tactical mind. She knew that the English rebels had not had the backing of their central organisation but, in her view, the decline in their fortunes started with Mark's stroke. Before that, they were doing well enough to survive without central support. After Mark's stroke, they were on a slippery slope.

Where was Mark now? Was he safe somewhere, being cared for? She had made good progress with his recovery through sheer determination; pressing everyone to do the simple exercises and drills she had read about. Was that all gone to waste now? How would a stroke victim cope without that constant support? She wanted, suddenly, to pray for him, only prayer was forbidden because there was no god; no one to pray to. There was, likewise, nowhere to go on to when your time came in this world. Everyone knew that, everyone knew the law.

Baba and Alf and all those others were gone forever. It was so final, scary, cold, hopeless.

"Fraulein, wake up please," Daisy whispered urgently, shaking her on the shoulder. "You told me to wake you before the doctor came. He is on his way upstairs now."

"What? My clothes, where are they?"

"I chose a dress for you from your wardrobe."

"I said to bring back my nurse's clothes. Where are they?"

Her mother came to the doorway, Daisy stood back.

"I told her to dispose of those old rags."

"What? They were special."

"Georgia, I won't have a child of mine dressing like a vagabond. You are not camping out in some derelict slum any more. You are the daughter of the commander. Daisy, help the Fraulein get dressed quickly. Do her hair in braids, just like in the picture over there." She pointed to a photograph of Georgia and Edmund at school several years earlier. "I'll go and talk to the doctor. I'll bring him up in ten minutes."

Georgia knew she was beaten. She did not object as Daisy dressed her in a yellow dress, white socks and shiny flat shoes, nor when she did her hair up in braids and pinned them against the sides of her head, consulting the photograph to get it just right.

When the doctor entered after exactly ten minutes, Carla was pleased to see her daughter sitting neatly on the window seat, reading a book. Outside there was a gale blowing, slapping bare branches against the window, the wind rising in confidence as it strode out across the grounds, turning over most things in its path.

"Frau Nullgeben, I will call you when I have finished," the rosy-cheeked, squat doctor said, placing his bag on the bedside table.

Only when the door was closed behind Carla and Daisy did the doctor speak again.

"Good evening, Fraulein. My name is Dr Hamilton."

"You're an English?"

"No, far from it!" There was a twinkle in his eyes, matching the dimples in his cheeks. He looked like a tubby favourite uncle. "I am a Scot."

"Ah, from the north."

"But in your eyes, no doubt, I am just another English."

"No, Dr Hamilton, far from it! Anyway, I like the English very much indeed." She looked to Dr Hamilton like any young and privileged girl of the upper class, but he knew something of this girl, something that set her apart. "And the Scots as well of course!" she added. "Although you are the first one I have ever met."

They laughed at this, laughed against the rising wind and thrashing rain, laughing in spite of the vengeful weather that tried to get in through any crack and soak and blow indoors as well as out.

Dr Hamilton was thorough and efficient. Within ten minutes he had finished an examination and drawn blood for a test.

"Well, Fraulein, the only thing left to do is to take the baby's blood. I am in no hurry so can wait for *your* baby to wake up."

Georgia was thrown. Why the emphasis on the possessive? Did he know something about her? Did he know the truth? It also threw her because he sat down heavily on the end of her bed, smiled and stroked his greying beard. It seemed he was settling down.

What would they talk about?

But talking was not a problem.

"I trained under a remarkable doctor at Cambridge. It was before the occupation."

"Oh."

"You might recall that female doctors were permitted before the occupation."

"Yes, like Dr Fisher..." Then it came to her, the direction of this conversation. "You mean...?"

"I mean exactly that, my dear. Janet Fisher was my tutor. She has a remarkable medical brain and an even more remarkable character. I would walk over hot coals for that lady. I am informed that she has your acquaintance?"

Suddenly the heat rose in her bedroom, from politely cool to something close to boiling. Animation came to Georgia's face; a glow to put a bonfire to shame.

And it would only get better.

"I saw her recently," the doctor continued, patting her leg as if her uncle.

"When, where?" Georgia jumped up, springing on the bed like a puppy where a puppy should not be.

"Do you really want to know?" Dr Hamilton had abandoned most of his caution, leaving just a little in reserve. "Tell me your story first."

So as Werner slept on, Georgia related her story, trying to explain what she thought of Dr Fisher, what she had done for Georgia, letting a little slip also about what Georgia had done for the hospital.

But Dr Hamilton knew it already. Dr Fisher had briefed him only that morning.

"Is she close?" Georgia asked, when Dr Hamilton told her he had spoken to his old tutor that morning.

"She is very close, Fraulein, but I won't tell you where, in case they worm it out of you. But I can take you there tomorrow if you can get away."

They arranged to meet on the playing fields at 10am the next morning.

"I have another surprise for you tomorrow but I will say no more at present. Now I'll have to wake the baby or they will get suspicious downstairs."

Five minutes later, he was gone, two blood samples in his bag. Georgia stayed in her bedroom. Werner was awake now so she rang for a bottle of milk and took the baby to the window seat to feed him against a backdrop of coursing rain and wind.

Edmund came back from his interview that night, full of his trip to the homeland.

"The trains run on time, Father! And the streets are so clean."

"Quite!" his mother interposed, timeliness and cleanliness being the two principal ingredients of civilisation. "Soon, you will be back there all the time."

"How can you be so sure, Mother?"

"Because, my wonderful son, I received a phone call this afternoon while you were on the aeroplane."

She teased her son a little longer, before letting on that the president of the *Statenthrump* had phoned her shortly after the committee had met.

"You have a place, Edmund, starting next month. The president said you espoused everything that was important about the values of future leaders. It helped that you had a glowing recommendation from the RUDD President. You clearly made a great impression on him."

"Did I too have a recommendation?" Georgia asked; a little of the old Georgia was still in her. Carla did not answer immediately, so her father spoke up.

"Georgia, you received an equally glowing report and your place has been held open for you. You are to start with Edmund. He will be in the main school and you will be in the senior academy. I must say your adventures this summer have helped in a strange way. Usually, you have to accept within seven days to secure your place but you have been granted an open enrolment. The president is looking forward to you giving a talk on dealing with captivity at the hands of the English as soon as you are ready to do so."

That little bit of the old Georgia felt a glow inside.

Later, after supper, Edmund came into Georgia's room as she was feeding Werner.

"It's not really yours, is it?" he asked, wrinkling his nose at the baby. "I mean, you didn't really give birth?"

"I did," she lied, looking straight into his eyes. Edmund's eyes were even bluer and clearer than Georgia's, the brightest of summer skies come into the depth of winter with its grey spatterings all around. It was like clean laundry and the water it was washed in.

"Did you really kill that English?" she asked.

In reply he went white, sat down on her bed uninvited, head in hands.

"Yes." That was it, all he said.

"Why, Edmund?"

"Because I couldn't help myself. I was crazed with the injustice of being held captive against my will. "

"Every English is held by us against their will." Georgia surprised herself with her answer. Did she really think that?

"But we are better than them." But the strength was not in his voice. Instead, it wallowed and wavered in indecision.

"No, Edmund, we are different to them, not always better than them. I know, I've lived with them. They are just so different."

Edmund did not speak. If he had, Georgia would not have heard him. She was back on her wards, commanding respect, issuing orders, making practical suggestions. She was needed.

She was part of a team.

But she was the leader.

Later that night, Edmund broke a confidence.

His mother came to visit him as he lay restless in bed, sweating, seeing Elisa Houndsworthy's pretty face cast in terror as the implication of the plunging scissors dawned on her. "No!" she had cried, but it was done, no going back. Actions are momentary, with a lifetime to spend in regret. He had justified his actions a thousand times; woke screaming from terrible dreams.

"My dearest boy," Carla started, "I hope you will not dream badly tonight. You have done so well, my treasure. You are the future of our family."

"And Georgia, Mother!"

"Only if she can have some sense talked into her. We need to sort out this baby situation." This last bit was said as if it was a blocked sink or a pernicious weed that would not give up.

"It is her baby, Mother. She told me so."

"But who is the father?"

"It is Mark Smith. It has to be. I saw them, I mean together."

"The English tutor? The rebel leader?" Carla had not expected it. "You mean when he was here with her? In the nursery?" It was the greatest shame of her life that she had housed a rebel leader in her house, posing as a tutor; the irony that he had got her daughter into the *Statenthrump* rubbed at her equally.

But Edmund had remembered his pledge and closed his eyes, pretending to be asleep to avoid more questions.

Dr Hamilton stood in front of Carla, twisting his shabby brown hat, his favourite.

"I examined your daughter, Frau Nullgeben, and it is confirmed that she is not a virgin. It is my opinion that she has not indulged recently, not for at least six months."

"Indulged? Indulged? You oaf, she was clearly raped by some awful English."

"In my opinion, Frau Nullgeben, it was not forced."

"How do you know this?" Carla stood and crossed the room with purpose, putting the doctor under pressure.

But he stuck with what he considered was the truth.

"I spoke with her and she has happy memories; no fear, no shock value."

"So, you are a psychiatrist now as well as a gynaecologist?" Her sarcasm hit him full frontal, but his feet remained slightly sprayed outwards to give him balance.

"No, Frau Nullgeben, but you did call me in for my opinion. And my opinion, taking everything into account, is that she had consensual intercourse at least once; probably more often, but not in the last six months."

"And the blood tests? What did they reveal?" This was her last hope. If they indicated that the baby was not Georgia's it would be on its way to a state orphanage that very day. You did not have influence and not use it.

"The blood test results are quite clear, Frau Nullgeben. The baby has hemochromatosis as a carrier, just like the Fraulein."

"Thank you, doctor. So that means the Fraulein is the mother? What are the chances that the real father is also a carrier?"

"It is a tiny possibility, Frau Nullgeben. If we knew who the father was, we could test his blood. If that was positive, it would throw some doubt on whether the Fraulein is the boy's mother."

"Thank you... eh... Doctor." It was as if she struggled to give him his title, not liking the message he brought. "One final thing before you go, is my daughter healthy?"

"She is fit as a fiddle, Frau Nullgeben."

It took only a quick phone call to the prison, then twenty minutes for the return call. They said they would send written confirmation, but Smith XX1Z2495 was not a carrier of the iron storage disease.

"She was telling the truth, after all," Carla said to herself after replacing the receiver.

She never considered the possibility of another carrier being the parent and certainly not that it was her husband.

But then she had not seen the report listing the dead delivered so punctually by the superintendent.

The Story of Linda and Thomas Part Three

Mr Fairway and Mrs Britain were lovers. They were also senior in the resistance organisation. They left fighting to people like Jo Macclesfield, Grey, and Sandy. Instead, they concentrated on recruitment, movement of people, supplies, communication and safe houses. It was Mrs Britain who found the old army base for the beat kids. She controlled the eight houses they used from time to time in New London and the dozens of other safe refuges across Southern England. Others did it in the north, the west and the east, but from Margate to Weymouth she controlled who went in and out of every safe location.

They heard about the raid on Betherington Manor within twenty minutes of its start. They cursed themselves for not hearing about it earlier. They had infiltrated several command structures but this seemed to be organised outside the normal channels.

Hence no prior warning.

But from the moment they heard, they operated swiftly, saving many lives in the process. From the butler's pantry of the mansion, door double-locked, they issued their instructions by radio, calming the panic and getting people out of the building.

Mrs Britain had insisted on an old bus being kept in the kitchen courtyard. Bonnet open, one wheel jacked up, it looked like it would never move. The soldiers checked it cursorily and moved on to the kitchen and then the main part of the house. They missed the keys in the ignition. They also missed that the jacked-up wheel was fully inflated. The soldiers were in a rush for glory, thus not noticing the side door onto the kitchen courtyard.

Margaret's first thought was for her sister, Barbara. But Margaret was working with Mark when the raid started. She fulfilled her duty, took Mark down the backstairs, and loaded him into the bus.

She never saw Barbara alive again.

Janet went to look for Georgia, not realising that she was helping Barbara and was already captured. She searched the manor, picked up several people, one of whom told her that Georgia had been taken already and that Barbara was shot in her bed. Seeing no point in staying, she bundled her collection into the bus and drove it off the jack and down the back drive to the road. The bonnet was still up, slipped off its catch and banged up and down on the engine casing like a drum roll. It did not matter for they got clear away.

Margaret counted the haul. Besides herself, Janet and Mark, there were five other nurses and nine patients. They had four machine guns, seven grenades and two pistols.

Margaret took the front seat upstairs. From there, although it was dark, she had the best view of headlights in front or behind that might mean danger. She was also responsible for changing the destination by winding the letters on the rolls to display the town on the outside of the bus.

They were bus number 13; lucky for some. They did not change the number but as they reached each town, Margaret stood on tiptoes and dialled the next destination onto the board.

Janet had the good sense to drive north. She had thought first to go west, towards relative safety. But that meant crossing the A21 and that was fraught with difficulty.

"Put Tunbridge Wells up and put on the conductor's uniform," she told Margaret. When they got to Tunbridge Wells, they switched to Sevenoaks, then Orpington, followed by Bromley and Westminster.

They stopped at each bus stop, took on passengers. Margaret made up fares, took the sparse coins and worked out how to use the ticket machine. They rumbled on, never going above thirty-five miles an hour, for the bus could not go faster.

"Are you going to Riverside?" one customer shouted at a stop in Sevenoaks.

"No mate, you need number 65 for Riverside."

"I asked the 65 and they said it was the 13!"

"Did I say 65? I meant 56. It's my mind gets the bleeding numbers round wrong." Janet swung the doors closed and moved off, almost hitting a small car with a giant man in it who honked furiously for five minutes until he turned left.

At one point all traffic was waved to a halt as a stream of cars and motorcycles shot past.

"My goodness, they've come from Betherington." Trying not to stare, they looked as the cars flashed by, trying to glimpse their colleagues. But the biggest car had its windows darkened and they could see nothing.

They never went to Westminster, never intended to. Instead, moments before the curfew started, Janet brought the bus to a stop outside a large house in Shooters Hill. Everybody scrambled off and into the house. Janet left the engine running, for fear it would not start again. A man in black clothes took her seat and the bus moved off into the dark, no lights on now for the curfew was in place. The bus had served its purpose. It was redundant.

Inside, they were made welcome. They settled the patients, then the house leader took Janet to one side.

"Can you look at a wounded girl I have here? She's in a bad way."

It was Linda.

Her right leg was a mess. Thomas stood over her bed, desperate and miserable.

"Can you do something for her, Dr Fisher?"

Gangrene had not taken hold but was close by, hovering. The bone was broken in two places, plus a bullet hole in the calf. Thomas explained that the bullet wound happened during the failed attack on the dockyard. But the broken leg was more recent.

Linda, being Linda, was smiling through the pain, making jokes about Hop Along Cassidy, also what she would do with the crutches when she got better.

Janet and Margaret scrubbed up while others prepared an operating table by taking a door off its hinges and balancing it on two armchairs. Margaret tested it and it seemed sturdy enough.

They worked as a pair into the night. Janet had a little anaesthetic in her bag, sufficient to put Linda out for a couple of hours. First, they washed the bullet wound with plenty of alcohol.

"The bone is not so bad. There is a chance it can be reset." They used splints Thomas fashioned by pulling apart kitchen chairs. Linda was awake now, but drowsy. She screamed as Janet moved the bone ends together, digging her nails into Thomas' face as he leant over her.

Then she slept.

Someone made a large pot of tea and Thomas told his story as they drank, one eye on Linda in the centre of the room.

It started in the rain-washed streets of Portsmouth, two back from the main dockyard entrance. It was mid-morning, rain thundering, overflowing gutters, noisy as a million drops bounced off the street and echoed and amplified down the funnel of terraced houses.

Bodies lay upon the street. Some were propped against lampposts or doorways like dolls placed by a little girl into her play scene. Some held their hands and fingers as if they were firing weapons at the rain. They had once, not long ago, held weapons and fired them in a bitter retreat when they had expected to advance. The police, tasked with clearing up the mess, had coursed through, taking weapons and ammunition. They would come back for the dead when the rain stopped.

But four of the dead were not dead at all, although they gave the appearance of it. One of those four died in silent agony, determined not to alert the dockyard guards less than 100 yards away. That left three: Linda, Thomas and one other. The third spent the morning hours creeping on her stomach from one body to the next, checking for life, then moving on. She held the hand of the dying man, then found Linda and did elementary first aid. Finally, she finished her tour of the dead by discovering Thomas, one bullet in his leg, the other had seared across his forehead, giving him a haircut to wonder at, as Linda later commented. But both were superficial wounds. Thomas would survive and fight again.

"My name is Eva," the girl said in her strange accent.

"I am Thomas."

She checked Thomas over, never minding the livid scar across her cheek, a cheek that flapped in the wind and closed one eye as if barricading oneself in against the storm.

"You're gonna be okay," she said with a grin. "I'm concerned about this other one."

"She is Linda Burton…"

"Not *the* Linda? Caught and tortured then escaped? She is an icon for the resistance!"

"And she is my wife," Thomas said proudly.

"You're a lucky man, Tom!"

Eva was short for Evangeline. She was tiny, rounded with puppy fat and had a grin that went well with her freckles. Yet, to Thomas, she seemed to have the strength of Samson.

Somehow, they got Linda indoors. The occupant of 38, Riggers Street, was not happy to receive them.

"My husband has a good job at the dockyard. I don't want to do anything to jeopardise his position." Tall and thin, wrapped in a neat patterned overall, tied in the middle with a bow, she seemed a shoe-in for a casting director. Her role would be the passer-by who kept on passing-by.

"What's his position?" Eva asked. As she looked up at the woman at the top of the steps leading to the front door, Eva seemed less than half her height.

"He's in security," the housewife could not help bragging. "He gets information about seditious activity. We're only living here temporarily. We're on the waiting list for a detached house with its own garage." She tried to slam the door, but Eva's foot prevented her.

"Quick, in!" she called to Thomas. "Get Linda in." She went in, drawing a knife out of her waistband, stopped the housewife using the phone just in time.

"Let me go, you filthy scum!" she cried butEva gagged her then trussed her up with cord from the curtains.

"I bet your husband betrayed us to the authorities, causing this whole debacle." The way Eva said 'debacle' sounded like a whole storybook on the subject.

Thomas liked her, knew instinctively that Linda would like her, too.

But they were too busy for likes and dislikes. Together, they had to attend to their own wounds and patch up Linda as best they could.

"We need to get out of here quickly," Thomas said.

"We certainly do, Tom. The police counted the bodies in the rain earlier. They will know there are three missing as soon as this rain stops."

Thomas had the brainwave that made their escape possible.

"She said they were waiting for a house with a garage," he cried suddenly.

"So?"

"You only need a garage if you've got a car. Hubby won't drive one street to work so the car must be here."

"Bravo, Tom!"

They found the car in the back alley. It was so tightly parked that Eva had to reverse it out before the others could get in. They also found several maps of southern England in the glove box.

They made sandwiches for lunch, found some beer in the scullery, and left within the hour. Eva made sure she paid generously for the provisions they had taken, leaving three marks spinning on the kitchen table as they left by the back door.

The A3 was far less guarded than the A21, but there were still roadblocks and patrols. They were lucky at first because the car had a R6 zone sticker on the windscreen, meaning they were unlikely to be stopped provided they stayed in Hampshire. So they left the A3 just before Petersfield and worked their way north on small roads slowly.

At half past five, they reached Farnborough.

"Stop the car!" Thomas said. "Over there. Have you got any money?" He went into a shop and came back seven minutes later with two cod and chips. He handed Eva the change. "If Linda wakes up, she can share mine."

It was Eva's first time with fish and chips. She came from a tiny prairie town in Manitoba.

"One school, one library, one restaurant and six churches. We don't waste time on choices, other than for church!"

"What's a church?"

Eva told them about her church, then about God and everything else. She gave a neat précis of the other churches in her hometown. Linda opened her eyes, saw Thomas in the front seat, closed her eyes again and listened enraptured, just like Thomas.

"You mean you can choose to go to this church? And choose what to believe?"

Thomas was amazed. To his mind, his upbringing, the rigid framework of society that surrounded him, god was something used in speech on occasion, often by mistake because the speaker would then look embarrassed and try to say the whole thing again without using the words 'god' or 'prayer' or 'heaven'.

"We have a sort of church," Linda said suddenly. Both turned around, Eva quickly looking back at the twisty road. They were in Knaphill, hoping to bypass the centre of Woking on their way to Old London.

"You're awake!" Thomas was delighted. "Are you okay? How are you feeling?"

Linda was feeling a little better. She was without painkillers but reasoned it was probably not a lot worse than a complicated childbirth. She would cope.

"So, what is your version of church?" Eva asked.

"Assembly, of course. We have to go every Sunday. We sing patriotic songs, listen to a local representative and salute the flag. We have to dress up in our best clothes and be there ten minutes before it starts."

"You say you have to go?"

"Yeah, you get a warning first absence, fine on second and three months on the third occasion."

"Then it is not church. If you have to go then it is not church."

This silenced Linda and Thomas. They found it hard to think of real choice, not realising at the moment that they were making a big choice in fighting.

And that they were fighting for choice in all its forms.

"So how did you end up here and how did Linda break her leg?" Margaret asked as Thomas came to a natural pause. Janet rose to check on Linda. She was sleeping deeply, helped by a little morphine.

"Well, this is Eva's home base, her safe house. That is why she drove here. We wove through a thousand lanes and minor roads that night, often switching off the lights and driving in darkness. We got here about four o'clock in the morning and we've been here ever since. I've been going out on jobs with Eva's lot but Linda hasn't made it out yet; besides, there is a huge price on her head."

"And the broken leg?"

"Do you really want to know?"

They both affirmed, noting the slight smile on Thomas' face.

"She did the high jump over the back fence to prove she was fit to fight! She did it last Sunday. She landed in a drain and snapped her leg. We could all hear it from our side of the fence."

Early next morning, the house leader shook Janet and Margaret awake.

"Quick, girls. We have the perfect transport coming in a few minutes. Just time to wash and have some porridge."

They washed, dressed, checked on Linda. She was awake and told them not to fuss over her so; also, when could she have her gun back?

"You're going with them." The house leader walked into the room. "You, Thomas and Eva, along with the others who came in last night. Now, Linda, I have a serious question for you. Can you pay attention a minute?"

"Sure." She sat up more, using her elbows to lever her splinted leg up the bed.

"Do you think you can play the part of a sick patient for just a few hours? You know; the forlorn, sad, pitiful look. No jokes whatsoever?"

"Of course I can. No, I really can!" Everybody was laughing

now. "Can you tell me what the plan is?"

Eva had stolen some medical movement papers from a local hospital, forged a few signatures. Someone else had created excellent copies of ID documents using real names of people who had died over the last twelve months. The reasoning was that the authorities left non-suspicious deaths to the English to administer. It was highly unlikely that they would think to check the death register.

"You're all going to the Regional R9 Hospital in Reading. It's the old Royal Berks on London Road. And, courtesy of the authorities, the ambulances will be here in ten minutes, each one with a bona fide driver trained by them!"

She explained that Eva would shadow them down and assist in the case of any problems. "It is the only way we can hope to move a body of people, especially the wounded. We wouldn't have a cat's chance of avoiding the endless roadblocks and checks. One person like Eva can make it but not half a busload!"

"But once we are in the hospital we won't find it easy to get out."

"I know, but if we don't get Linda's leg in plaster pronto I can't speak for the likely long-term damage. And then there are several others in critical states. We'll do something to get out but at the moment we have to look after the medical priorities."

There was no more argument; everybody would take their chances.

It was in the back of the first of the three ambulances that Janet told Margaret about Barbara's death.

The driver thought the intense crying from the rear must be something to do with the critical state of one of the patients. He switched on his siren and picked up speed. He would do his bit to get that patient to the care he or she needed.

Hospital Procedures

Regional R9 wore its scaffolding like a chain-mail coat. Builders' lorries took up much of the available parking space, but this was not a problem for the three ambulances, pulling in at the new entrance on Craven Road. The lead driver had radioed ahead and a cohort of smart orderlies, dressed entirely in white with tops that crossed over their chests and buttoned up under their chins, were waiting in a group, ready to disembark the patients.

They waited quietly; no smoking, no idle chatter. They had a job to do.

And they knew that the commissioner's office suite looked directly over the main entrance. He was quite possibly watching.

The commissioner made it a rule to watch, look, listen, and walk about for several hours a day.

"Someone will always take care of the paperwork. I want to run the best hospital in the sector, right here in the commander's back yard."

Another favourite phrase was 'no piece of paper ever made a patient better'.

Yet, for all his favourite sayings, he was a stickler for paperwork and there was, under his watch, a form for every procedure, every activity, every movement across the hospital. Every happening produced a slip of paper that went up the chain, was reviewed by managers, of which there were dozens, then filed by clerks, of which there were hundreds.

And he led the charge of the efficiency brigade. The commissioner worked from 5am to 8pm every weekday and was often seen on site at weekends. He believed in all the right things such as order, discipline, cleanliness and smartness. In his opinion, there was no second chance to make a first impression. And orderliness was efficiency, presentation was professionalism, punctuality was productivity.

And he swore he would bring the lazy, shiftless English up to his standard if it were the last thing he ever did.

Thus, the orderlies were ready and waiting twenty minutes before the ambulances swung through the gates. Inside, a hassled matron was trying to allocate beds before she even saw the injuries she and her team would have to cope with. She called it 'advance planning'. It led to a bewildering half hour in which existing patients were trundled here and trundled there, beds just avoiding beds in long, brightly-lit corridors, expertly guided by more orderlies, each one with an accompanying nurse in charge.

There were no accidents, no clashes of metal ringing out, no dropped notes or drip stands left behind.

Mistakes, like unnecessary chatter, were not tolerated in Regional R9.

Then the commissioner appeared from nowhere, as was his trademark. One minute there was an orderly chaos of beds and gurneys, the next a perfectly groomed gentleman headed an arrow formation, flanked on each side by a doctor, a matron and an orderly, the sevensome piercing their way through casualty, like birds in flight to hotter climes. They swung right into cardio, keeping perfect formation, a slight increase in pace for the outermost left-hand wing, then up the wide stairs – never the lift – to ENT and the children's ward at the end.

"Reports are there are three minors amongst the incoming party."

"Yes, sir. We have space here for three."

"I want every patient to go to Casualty first, then on to the designated wards. Is this understood?"

"Yes, sir." But panicked faces filled the gap left by the arrowhead sweeping through the hospital. Beds and gurneys moved again, more urgency now as the ambulances were reported to have arrived, reversing all the last half hour in a crazy reallocation, a silent slapstick movie run in reverse.

"You can't be a doctor, you're a woman," the commissioner declared, looking at Janet Fisher with incredulity.

Janet thought quickly, mainly about the safety of her charges.

"I'm sorry, sir, I must have been confused after the long journey. I meant to say that the doctor signed the medical movement forms at point of origin and I counter-signed as the senior member on duty.

"So, you are a nurse and not a doctor?"

"Yes, sir." It hurt her pride; all those years of training and practising, but necessity spoke above pride.

"Then why aren't you in uniform? That goes for both of you." He looked across at Margaret in her remnants of the makeshift clothes Abby Ryder had prepared for her in happier times. "I've never seen such a ragamuffin outfit as you lot. You need sorting out." He pressed his buzzer and told his secretary to get the uniform supervisor.

Forty minutes later, Nurses Fisher J. and Leyland M. looked themselves over in the mirror before reporting to the senior hospital matron. They were dressed identically and self-consciously in the standard Regional R9 nurse uniform. Their caps were starched and stood tall and proud, bent to the shape of their heads and tied with ribbons at the back. They stood in the navy-blue cloaks that all nurses wore when not on duty, red straps coming across the standard white-and-blue dress to hold the cloak in place. Black, highly polished shoes and white tights made up the picture, plus a name badge almost as large as a postcard.

The matron looked them over, sighing more from habit than genuine condemnation.

"You'll do, I suppose; at least it is an improvement on how you were before. I don't know anything about you and I don't trust the English qualifications. But we are short staffed." She stopped and watched them as they stood in front of her. Janet thought she had never seen a hospital so well staffed; the corridors full of nurses, orderlies, doctors and clerks; all purpose and order, like troop movements in a railway station. "I welcome you, Fisher and Leyland, to Regional R9. You will be grade one until your superiors deem otherwise." Grade one was the lowest grade of auxiliary. "You will report to Ward Sister Meyer on Casualty." She wrote on tiny slips of paper and handed one to each of the new nurses. "This is to draw bedding for the main nurses' dorm. Next time I see you I will test you on the dorm rules. Thank you for volunteering. Now, run along and make yourselves useful."

"Yes, Matron, thank you, Matron."

"Well of all the cheeky buggers…" Janet started as soon as they were outside the office.

"Silence in the corridors!"

"Come on," whispered Margaret, "at least we'll have some oversight of our charges." She looked white and tired, her eyes surrounded by patchy red puffs from crying for Barbara.

What courage, thought Janet, to carry on with her sister shot like a common criminal. If Maggot could bear up like this, the least she could do was go along with it, for their patients' sake.

"Let's be the best trainee nurses in town," she whispered back, squeezing her friend's hand. "Who knows, we might even get promotion," she giggled.

"No touching between nurses!" Would these English never learn?

However, it was not so funny when they arrived at Casualty, presented themselves for a withering inspection and were set to work with a host of menial tasks, each one announced with more urgency than the last so that none were ever finished.

"I'm exhausted," Janet said when they got thirty minutes for lunch and were standing in line for thin slices of ham, mashed potato, green beans you could make rope out of and 'all the tea you can drink but bear in mind that you won't be allowed to the little girls' room when on duty!'

This advice was given with the cheeriness of someone moving up at last from the bottom rung of the ladder through the arrival of newbies. Earlier, she had told them to stick by her to learn the ropes but then had just delegated all the dirtiest jobs to Janet and Margaret.

"Not quite the giggle I thought it would be, but at least we are close to our patients."

"No talking in the queue."

There was only one way to control the English.

Later that afternoon, when Janet was really feeling her age, a young nurse came up to her.

"Nurse Fisher?"

"Yes, how can I help you?" She was expecting another series of orders to countermand the last set.

"I'm Staff Nurse Willow. I was just going through the admissions records for the patients you brought in today and I'm puzzled by something." She had a beautiful Welsh lilt, the spoken word almost singing. She was tall and thin, just like a willow branch, thought Janet.

"What is it, dear … I mean, Staff Nurse?"

"You have a patient here," she thrust a record card towards Janet, "called Frederick Arthur Willow." The surname did not click with Janet immediately, but then came to her.

"That's right." Janet and Margaret had gone through the records quickly in the back of the ambulance in order to familiarise themselves.

"Born on 19th March 1937 to Mabel and Arthur Willow of 32 Cherry Field Lane, Taplow."

"I believe so, yes. Is there a problem with that?" Now Janet stopped scrubbing the bedpans and looked at the staff nurse. There were tears in her eyes. She appeared flustered, her pale Welsh skin reddening at the difficulty of the task facing her.

"That is my husband. He died five months ago. I don't understand." Now those tears had broken the dam, were ready to course down and overflow the banks.

"Oh my god!" Janet spoke too loudly. Luckily, nobody else was in the utility room where she had been working. "They assured me this would not happen. I'm so sorry." By instinct, she touched Nurse Willow's face with the tips of her fingers, an expression of tenderness that Nurse Willow seemed to need. "I'll explain everything to you as soon as we're off duty. Can you keep quiet until then?" Fred Willow was Mark's alias. If she blew his cover he would be executed without doubt.

"If you could explain, please. I know, meet me in the dorm at 6.15. They moved me back in when Fred died. We are allowed out until 9pm, curfew time, so we'll go to a pub I know."

"There'll be one other with me; Nurse Leyland. Is that

okay?"

"Your colleague, yes," then she thought again and asked, "you're not going to hurt me, are you?"

"Of course not, not in the slightest."

They met at 6.15 in the dorm; a long, low building of bunk beds and lockers, with bathrooms and laundry rooms cut into it at intervals. Janet was in Section Four on a top bunk, while Margaret had a bottom bunk in Section Six.

"Goodness me, you can't go out like that." Nurse Willow exclaimed when she saw Janet and Margaret were in their own clothes. "You need to get changed back straight away or they won't let you out of the main gate. We won't have much time if you're not quick. The pub is half an hour of fast walking from here."

"Can we get a bus?" Janet was exhausted. "Or maybe a taxi?"

"I suppose so but I always walk to save money." She looked down in embarrassment. "The wages are not that great and then we have to pay for the dorm and our meals. I keep everything I can for my parents."

"The taxi is on me," Janet was quick to make the suggestion.

Twenty-five minutes later, three off-duty nurses, cloaks wrapped around them against the winter cold, walked into the salon bar at the Shirker on Caversham Bridge.

Long ago, it had been the Crown, but young Albert Heffernott had shuddered at any reference, however slight, to royalty. Instead, he had selected a name he was told would celebrate the English worker.

He had hoped to inspire them.

Janet organised drinks while the others found a table in the corner of the room. They took a sip each then Janet thought, *Hang this,* and downed her gin in one. With the fire of the gin inside her, Margaret getting a second one in, she told the young staff nurse almost everything.

"I'm really sorry about the name. They promised me there would be no clash with people from around here. They've really messed up that one!"

"Do they all have false names? And you are part of the resistance?"

"Yes, and we are desperately trying to save some of our brave wounded fighters. I won't tell you their real names because you don't need to know them, but every last one of them is a hero."

The staff nurse went very quiet, drained her second gin and said in a small voice that bounced from high to low, "Fred was in the resistance. That is how he died."

"Goodness me!" Margaret was first to reply. "Do you want to talk about it? What is your name, by the way? We can't keep calling you Staff Nurse Willow."

"My name is Gwenda Willow, but I was born Gwenda Gofalu in the back streets of Swansea. My father lost his job as an engineer when the occupation began and the worry of caring for Mother and the two of us babies drove him sick. I used to care for him. It seemed natural to do it. One day my older sister said to me, 'Gwen, you should be a nurse, you care so well for the ill and needy.' So, I became a nurse and then one day, just as I finished my training, I got a ZA in the post. You know, a *Zuordnung Auftrag*? It sent me here but would not let my parents come with me. They seemed to have it in for my father. He is a brilliant man, by all accounts. He worked on the aeroplanes but they kept delaying the projects and then when the invasion came, that was it. He has never worked again, at least not as an engineer. When his health is a little better he gets work unloading lorries at the aircraft factory where he used to be chief designer."

Gwenda had come to Reading on her own, a nervous twenty-one-year-old. She had never left Wales before. Then she had fallen in love with Fred Willow and they had married two years ago.

"He had a job as an orderly at the hospital but his heart was with the resistance. He worked for Jo Macclesfield. I heard him say the name. He was a sector leader under her. But he was shot dead when they did an attack on the communications centre in Didcot. I had to identify the body. And..." She stopped a moment, not sure whether to go on.

"And?" Janet prompted her.

"And he did not even have a proper funeral, just a mass grave. I was not allowed any time off. I was given extra duties at the weekend, like cleaning the bathrooms, and made to move back into the dorm. They started taking deductions from my pay also so I cannot send so much back to my parents. They called it compensation. I really do not like them."

When Janet heard this last sentence, she thought that here was a person who could not hate. The furthest she could go down that road was to really not like them. She took Gwen's hand in hers.

But Margaret went a step further and stood up and hugged her, causing large tears to run down and smudge her new uniform.

Janet went to the bar and ordered three more gins.

With the third gin nearing the end, Janet made a decision.

"What time is it?"

"Almost eight o'clock," the others replied at once, both having looked down at the watch hanging upside down next to their name badges.

"Let's go," Janet said. "We'll walk back and see if we can get something to eat on the way."

"Fred used to bring me to that pub. He always called it by its real name, the Crown." They were walking over the bridge. It was cold with a dry, light wind and a sky full of speckled stars. "Sometimes I think we become stars when we die so Fred is one of those stars looking out for me."

"We met someone yesterday who believes there is a god. She is Canadian, fighting over here. You would like her."

"Gosh, I've heard of those people. That seems so strange. I heard that they believe there is another world after this world."

"I remember," Janet said; "your parents will, too. Before the invasion there were churches here and people could believe if they wanted to. We had a chapel – that is a little church – in the Cavern for a while but the youngsters were so brainwashed that there was no god. In the end there was no point and we turned it into an audio-visual room where they could enjoy cine films of American bands."

"What is the Cavern?" Gwen asked. In response, all the way to the centre of town and out to Southampton Street towards the hospital, Janet spoke about her time in the Cavern. Gwen listened with wide eyes, sometimes saying, "I would like that," and, "What fun it sounds!"

They could not find a café open so bought fish and chips on the corner of Southampton Street and London Road. Then Janet gave her chips to Gwen.

"Hold these a second, take some if you like. I've had enough." She could see how hungry Gwen was. "I need to make a phone call." She went into a phone box and was lost to view for there were notices on all the glass reminding people of the 9pm curfew and of what happened to drunks and the rowdy; also one notice asking for workers at the hospital as they were still so short-staffed.

"We offer accommodation and meals and a great career," Margaret read from the notice.

"Sure," Gwen spoke up, "but you work every hour of the day and pay for the meals and for your dorm space! But at least it is a worthwhile job, isn't it, Margaret?" It was as close as Gwen came to bitterness. But Margaret also saw how vulnerable and youthful she was, like a kitten finding its way around its new home, wide-eyed and trembling.

The way nurses were woken in the dorm was efficiency itself. First, at 4.40am, the lights went on. To help the nurses dress promptly there were bright strip lights glaring like the cheeky grins of young boys. About thirty of the 104 nurses in Janet's section got up with the lights. They were the first into the bathrooms and the first to hoist on their underwear and prepare for a new day. They were, Janet supposed, the ones hoping and planning for promotion.

Then the bell rang. At first, it was a low buzz, almost harmonious with the rhythm of sleep. But it inched up in scale and volume, making a step every fifteen-seconds. Another dozen got up the moment the bell first sounded, hurrying into the bathroom for the bell did not sound in there. These, she reasoned, were those recently promoted, who could relax a little as their next promotion would be years away.

As the bell wound itself on and up, most of the remaining nurses rose from their bed, some with hands on ears, one or two with their dressing gowns over their heads – elementary dampening.

But there were always a few laggards who could not seem to rise. Stage three was the duty orderly with his baton.

Janet rose with the threat of the baton. Her tired bones ached enough. She did not want to add to that ache.

Daily Assembly was at 5.20. It lasted eight minutes and forty-five seconds, never varying because breakfast was at half-past. They reported to their wards at 5.45, ready to start the new day.

Routine, everyone knew, was good for the soul; only there was no soul, and no afterlife for it to go on to. But it worked as a figure of speech. Routine was especially good for the English. It drummed obedience into a disobedient race.

This morning was no different.

At least, not until 10.15. For at 10.15, Generalleutnant Erich von Keinunsinn's car drove up to the hospital entrance. His driver rushed to open the door, beating the orderly by several seconds.

Generalleutnant Keinunsinn was a great slab of a man with a granite face that spoke no nonsense.

"I want to see the commissioner."

"I'll see if he is available, sir."

'You don't understand me, eh, English? I said I want to see the commissioner and that means right now." The man scurried off. Keinunsinn strode around the reception, slapping his large gloves against his leg, muttering about inefficiency.

"Call this a hospital?" he cried suddenly. "I've been waiting six minutes. What if I was wounded?"

"Generalleutnant, it is a pleasure to meet you. I am the commissioner." He offered a hand but was met with, "About time, where can we talk privately?"

"In my office, if you would follow me, please. I was in the army once." The commissioner tried to make conversation.

"What rank and corps?"

"*Leutnant* in the Medical Corps, sir."

"So, the army paid for your education?"

"If you put it that way, yes."

"I do put it that way. Now." As they entered the commissioner's spacious office, the *generalleutnant* took the seat behind the desk without the slightest hesitation, breaking etiquette and leaving the commissioner standing before his own desk, "I have two reasons for visiting you. First, I have a bone to pick with you." The *generalleutnant* gave a thorough blasting about the treatment of his men as patients in the hospital, a blistering attack.

It was well rehearsed for the whole plan was to wither this commissioner, bombard him with anger, then steal away what they needed.

It took fifteen minutes to reduce the commissioner to a ready state. Fifteen minutes in which his secretary started wondering why she had never heard of Generalleutnant Keinunsinn before. She heard the blasting through the office door and considered why, if he led the local forces, he was unknown at the hospital.

She made a few phone calls. That meant she was occupied on the phone when the *generalleutnant* gave his second instruction.

"Commissioner, you won't know it but three of your residents are actually enemy agents. They were brought in here just yesterday amongst a consignment of genuine patients. I need to take them for questioning, along with the two nurses who brought them in."

"But sir…"

"Really, to think the English can be so stupid as to believe they could get away with this. We have, of course, been tracking their every move. I thank you for their care over twenty-four hours, but now I need to claim them back."

"Who are these villains, sir?" The commissioner tried to use robust language to meet the robust, but from his lips it sounded false, like an actor reading someone else's part in dress rehearsal.

"You know them as Willow, Frant and Williams. The nurses in question are Leyland and Fisher."

"What are their real names, Generalleutnant?"

"If I told you that I would have to arrest you as well!" Generalleutnant Keinunsinn tried the oldest joke in the world on the slow commissioner. "Please tell me where the five are and I promise to extract them from your hospital with the minimum of fuss."

The commissioner was beaten. It had not been much of a contest. Perhaps if he had looked at the *generalleutnant* a little more closely he would have seen the sweat glistening on his face, noticed the fingers drumming against his legs. But he was impressed with the authority and the arguments.

He pressed his buzzer and asked his secretary to come in. She had just finished with the office of the commander on the phone.

"Ah, Wissler," he started, "be so kind as to check which ward these patients are in."

"Sir, could I have a word?"

"Yes, go on."

"In private, sir?" She looked imploringly at him.

But it was time for him to reassert his authority.

"Not now, Wissler. Jump to it and I'll see to your personal issue later today."

"Sir, please…"

"Wissler, go and do as I say."

"Yes, sir."

"I also require the drugs they are on, sufficient for say three weeks. I doubt they will need longer than that," the *generalleutnant* added as the secretary hurried out.

"I don't need an ambulance, Commissioner but thank you for offering."

"Then, I'll say goodbye, sir. It was a pleasure to meet you and to be of service."

"A pleasure also, Commissioner." The generalleutnant replaced his hat and gloves and strode from the reception.

"Bring the five out. Sergeant, bring up the lorry and load them in. Guard them carefully and follow my car."

"Yes, sir," said the surprisingly youthful sergeant, also not able completely to hide his English accent. There were a few sergeants amongst the English but not many. It registered with the commissioner as out of the ordinary. But exploded in his mind when he got back to his office.

"Sir, I must talk with you. As a precaution, I called the commander's office. There is no Generalleutnant Keinunsinn on the staff in this sector. I suspect he is a fake, sir."

"I knew it!" the commissioner lied. "Quick, we have to stop them." He rushed down the corridor. His secretary went to the phone and called reception.

"Is the *generalleutnant* still there?" she asked of reception.

"Yes, Frau Liesen, they are taking the patients to the lorry right now."

"Stop them." But she lacked authority on her own.

"I can't do that," said the receptionist, a friend of Fred Willow's. "It's more than my life is worth to stop a real-life general!"

"He's not a general at all. Call security. The commissioner is coming down right now."

"Well, I'll act on the commissioner's orders of course, but I can't stop a senior army officer on the say-so of even a grade nine secretary."

The commissioner made a fateful decision that morning, hurrying down the corridor at 11.05am. He decided to use the lift to save time. He never usually used the lift.

At the last moment as he was pressing 'ground floor', a cheerful English technician got in and started to push a lot of different buttons.

"Morning sir," he pronounced, "been having a spot of bother with these here lifts today, sir."

The lorry containing Mark, Linda, Thomas and the handcuffed Margaret and Janet rolled out of the main hospital exit and headed north, led by the *generalleutnant*'s car. After much twisting and turning, they pulled up at Harry Bootle's house.

Eddie the English jumped out of the lorry and made a mock salute to Harry.

"Any more orders, Generalleutnant?" he said.

"No, sergeant," Harry replied, "that will be all, except get me a glass of gin. I need it!" He smiled much more often these days.

The commissioner was finally freed from his metal box prison, suspended midway between Floors Four and Three, at a little after noon. Pete, Mark's childhood friend, was glad, too. He had exhausted his bank of banal jokes.

Winners and Losers

"I think you'll agree it is good news, Superintendent," Carla spoke but with an undercurrent that denied her conviction. "I'll tell you now if you like, but my husband will tell you formally tomorrow and it would be best to feign surprise."

"Of course, Frau Nullgeben." What did her tone mean? He did not know her well enough to be sure, but her words sounded ominous. He shifted in his seat, sipped his coffee, dreamed briefly of the homeland and his life there. Would he be able to swing it to take his latest boy back with him? He was an English so it depended on the level of promotion.

"You're being made up to sector commander," Carla came out with it, knowing it would cause astonishment, but knowing also that disappointment would be right behind; a bitter-sweet zigzag of emotion ahead. It was a tremendous leap, eight grades up from his current level, but it meant no immediate return to the homeland. But perhaps after a few years he would be catapulted to the very highest office and could return home in style.

It was up to him, of course; what he could make of the opportunity.

"At least you won't have to go to the trouble of moving." This statement from Carla was unfair. She knew how much he wanted to leave.

"You mean?"

"Precisely, Superintendent! I have managed to secure for you my husband's position as commander of sector eight. Congratulations, my dear man, I am so pleased for you."

"Thank you." But his mind was in turmoil.

"And you will have all your current friends to support you, especially as you are unmarried." This was said with a sideways, sharp look. Did she know about his 'friends'?

She did, and it disgusted her. But most of all, she wanted this interview over. She had fought long and hard with her husband who, for some strange reason, had taken against the superintendent with vehemence. When she raised the subject of promotion as his reward for delivering Georgia back to them, he had taken the opposite view, wanted to send him away in disgrace, had even mentioned demotion in the heated argument that followed.

But he never would say what caused his anger. Carla had tried everything to get Werner to approve a posting back home, but he was adamant.

It was puzzling and she did not like puzzles unless she posed them.

She had had to go over his head to RUDD HQ. With Werner unwilling to counter-sign the promotion, it was the best she could do.

And it was still an incredible promotion.

"Might I ask, Frau Nullgeben, what you are doing next?"

"Yes, Superintendent, or should I say Commander?" The joke was received with the thinnest of smiles. "We are returning to the homeland where my husband is taking a senior position."

"How interesting. I congratulate you, Frau Nullgeben. You have done very well." The subtext was anything but congratulatory. "Might I enquire what position your husband has secured?" He thought he knew but was not sure.

"You may enquire, Superintendent, but I am not at liberty to disclose. All will become clear tomorrow. Now, if there is nothing else?" She rose to exclude any other questions. The superintendent rose, as was polite, but thought what a bastard she was. He had been used. He would not forget it.

Carla was oblivious. She had little interest in the concerns of the professional classes. But it burned inside her to know why Werner had turned so strongly against this hideous man. She had never liked him but he had worked with her to get Georgia back and deserved some reward, rather than the sting of enduring another posting in this hellhole of a sector.

But, more than anything, she needed to understand why her husband had so steadfastly refused to disclose his reasons.

If she had known, she would have mixed rage with jubilation, triumphalism with relief; something distasteful with lovely red hair cut forever from her husband's life.

But she was not to know, at least not from her husband's lips.

Leutnant Doppelkreuz also queued up for promotion; it was hoped and expected. When it did not come, he went to see the superintendent, the commander-to-be.

"Sir, I would have expected some recognition. I put myself at great risk, infiltrating the enemy and working out the plan of attack." He meant that the superintendent would not be the commander-in-waiting without his assistance.

"My dear fellow, I had not forgotten you." They both knew that was a lie. "I was waiting for the dust to settle." The superintendent was thinking quickly now. "What would you consider suitable?" He hoped it was not much, maybe leapfrogging two rungs to lord it over some of his colleagues from the police academy. Or maybe something even cheaper, such as an award? It would be minimal cost to have a small ceremony and present him with a good pair of binoculars or perhaps a field camping kit, engraved with some sincere words of gratitude. Words were free, provided they were lies.

It was only the truth that cost.

"Sir, I believe I am ready for a senior role in this sector's government. Would you not agree?"

Damn, thought the superintendent, *he has gone for the kill.*

Two days after the announcement of the superintendent's promotion to commander, effective April 1st 1966, the commander's office issued a series of appointments to take effect from the same day. Strifer was made up to chief of staff, while Doppelkreuz became his deputy, number three in the power game in sector eight.

It was a huge promotion.

Happiness can be defined as being reasonably content, neither ecstatic nor distraught; the bitter-sweet zigzag of emotion mentioned before. Most people in the equation; those that mattered, at least, could count themselves happy. Whenever a big cheese moves on, there is opportunity in abundance.

But let us dwell a minute on those that were not happy. First amongst these were the departing commander and his wife. Werner was obvious; lost in regret, anger, bitterness. Never mind that he had given Barbara up. She had still been snatched from him; emotion is perverse in its distortion of reality.

Carla was far from content; driven by the intense irritation born of something elusive, something outside her knowledge, hence control; not a position she liked to be in. As a result, both were sombre, wistful, fragile as they made their final rounds of sector eight.

The good English people, like the Scots and the Welsh and Irish alongside them, forgetting the troubles of summer, imagined the commander's family was upset to be shortly leaving this lovely land.

In that respect, perhaps the leaders of the resistance movement had been right after all. For all Mark's brilliant tactical touch, for all Jo's and Pete's and Sandy's and Grey's grit and determination, perhaps the people were not ready for revolt that summer. Perhaps the memories of the clampdown of '59 were just that bit too fresh in the collective mind.

But that determination did not dissolve in the next cup of tea, swimming and swirling before sinking below the surface. Grey was gone; many good and devoted people were dead or captured, but the fighters remained committed, backed by the non-combatants. In every region of the sector there were the likes of Mrs Britain and Mr Fairway. True, not in every region were they sharing a bed, planning and scheming through the early hours when sleep evaded their determined minds, but every region had a backbone.

And like the granite ranges that crossed the land, up the spine and out into the limbs, this backbone would remain, immovable and permanent, until woken to rumble in anger again.

Room for the Cat

"Lordy me!" laughed Harry's mother. "There's no room in here to swing a cat!" The kitchen seemed spacious under normal occupation but cramped beyond belief the morning Harry brought the five back from the hospital in Reading. Eddie the English was still there, eating the buns Harry's mother had made and pouring tea for all the others.

"Well, the main guests are still to arrive," Harry said, bun in one hand and a large glass of gin in the other.

"Who are they?" Mark asked. Speech to Mark seemed easier every day. He struggled still to find particular phrases and tried to talk around the words. Linda had turned it into a game she called 'Wordo'. She would time how long it took Mark to find the word he was searching for. Then, she started throwing false clues, turning them this way and that and giggling, "Hotter, hotter; no - colder now," as the others tried to guess. She was the chief player, the arbiter and the rule-maker. That was the way she approached life.

Janet had wondered whether she should stop Linda as she developed the game in the back of the lorry, swinging around the corners of the lanes on their way to Cheerwell. She was concerned that it might damage his confidence, like a child with a stammer taunted in the schoolyard. But then she noticed that Mark seemed to talk more with Linda playing her game, his smile broader all the time. And his mouth was better controlled; the floppy fishiness almost entirely gone.

Nobody, she concluded, could ever take offence at Linda and her antics.

The lorry had stopped a mile outside Reading, pulling into a layby. Those in the back thought the worst; they had been captured after fifteen minutes of glorious freedom. The back cover was thrown open. They expected machine guns and curt orders to get out.

But instead, Harry Bootle jumped up into the back to take the handcuffs off Margaret and Janet.

"I will have no one tied when I can do something about it."
He was another one smiling much more often now.

"Wait and see who the guest of honour is," was the response
Harry gave Mark with a slurp of gin. But Mark knew; had
guessed it was Georgia because of their teasing.

As if following exact stage directions in a comedy play, there
was a sharp rap on the door at that very moment.

"Sounds very authoritative," Linda said with a large wink of
her one good eye. She stood up to answer the door, wobbling
on her new crutches, with 'Sector Eight Government Property'
burned down each side. "Don't you dare take my chair when
I'm gone!"

A half-minute later, Linda was back with Georgia and a
pram, trailed by Dr Hamilton. But Mark only saw Georgia. She
was wearing a red knee-length skirt with short white socks
almost covered by fashionable tan walking boots. As she took
off her thick brown coat and removed her hat, Mark saw the
young girl of the nursery again, sitting at her desk, feet
drumming with desire, wanting to move around the room,
careless of what others thought of her, prim in her righteous
confidence. She was thinner. The wide belt around her middle
gave evidence of that, as did her stick-arms poking out of the
white mid-sleeved blouse that he noted was buttoned up to her
chin. Her hair was neatly braided, as it always had been; pulled
back to display her face, proud features standing like a
landscape.

But then he saw her eyes. He knew then that she was a
woman, not a girl.

And she was looking directly at him.

Then she turned, said, "I'll leave the pram in the hall. As you
English say, there's not room in here for swinging a cat. Why
are you laughing so? It was not that funny."

Then, when Harry's mother's identical observation was
referenced, she smiled and Mark felt that smile deep inside him.

"Well, aren't you going to do the introductions, then?"
Georgia said. "I know most people in this cubbyhole but not
everyone. This is Dr Hamilton. He brought me here. He must

be part of your poxy underground organisation! But Bootle, you too?"

Linda did the introductions. She stood by the dresser and gave exactly two sentences on each person.

"Meet the Fraulein," she said. "Confidently in charge, competently in control, completely in love." That made Georgia blush so furiously she had to go to the hall to sort out something with little Werner.

When she introduced Mark she said, "In my short acquaintance, Mark Smith has risen from his prison cell origins to being a leader of men and women. He is the stuff of heroes and we wish them well together."

"What do you mean, 'well together'?" Georgia felt her world hit by a sledgehammer. Who could be together with Mark?

"Why you of course, dear Pudding Pie!" They were playing evolving names again; always changing with the shifty English. Names should be anchor points, references to be relied on like map co-ordinates. Yet they moved constantly with the English. You never knew where you stood. "Anyone can see that you two were made for each other!" Relief flowed in Georgia, followed by the deep heat of embarrassment.

"Who is the redder?" Margaret asked to general laughter.

It was hard to tell, although Georgia had further to travel, being so fair to start with.

But Georgia did not laugh; the reference to red made her think of her redhead friend, the mother of her baby brother.

"Time to get down to business," Mark spoke through the petering-out laughter, not needing another embarrassment. "What's on the menu?" Understanding he meant 'agenda' but could not find the word, they all turned to Mr Fairway and Mrs Britain, sitting quietly on a couple of stools in the corner to the left of the dresser.

"We need to plan for the future." It was Mrs Britain who spoke first. After all, she had been in just such a place before. She had seen her world blown open. She had lived through a day when death had surrounded her; taken her beloveds from her, put them in the ground. Yet, she had lived to fight on. She had buried Mike Jazz and their son, Steve, in the same grave.

She had not gone back to their lodgings that evening. Instead, she had drunk a glass of gin with her friends and asked about joining the resistance.

"The only thing that matters is that we who are alive fight on. We have to put the dead behind us."

"Eternal rest grant them, O Lord. May perpetual light shine upon them and may they rest in peace." Harry's mother crossed herself, looked up at the crucifix above the heads of Mrs Britain and Mr Fairway. All followed her eyes, the younger ones wondering at the strange words; Georgia included.

But not Eva, standing at the back by the stove. Her Canadian accent rang across the hushed room.

"Amen," she said. "I am not a Catholic; far from it, but I am a Christian and I know that the departed are gone to a better place."

This was intensely puzzling to Georgia, and equally to Linda, Thomas and Eddie the English. They knew there was nothing to this religion stuff and nonsense. Yet why did the words produce such calm? Not only was the room calm, but deep inside they were as well.

For Mark and some of the others it was something vague from the past. Mark suddenly remembered going to church as a youngster, before the invasion, before the declarations.

It was Linda who broke the intense stillness of that room in the cottage in the hamlet of Cheerwell, or Cheerful as the locals called it.

"Any tea in that pot, Chalky? I'm gasping for a cuppa!" Chalky was another nickname Linda had dreamed up, reflecting Georgia's intensely fair skin.

Mrs Britain quickly established order. She instructed each person in turn to state what they considered to be important and what they intended to do about it.

"We've got to keep the structure and organisation of the resistance going," Mr Fairway spoke first. "We've hit bad times before but have been able to fall back on the fundamentals. It is essential to keep that going. I hope that Mrs Britain will remain with me in this region to (a) keep the regional organisation going and (b) as a beacon for the other regions, particularly Kent which has been hit so hard. So, in summary, it's back to basics like we did in '59. I'm in it for the long-haul."

"Agreed, Mr Fairway," said Sandy, speaking up for the first time. "But I think we should bypass HQ. They let us down very badly from their comfortable base far away from the fighting. It was more than that, though, for they were so indecisive. I say we branch out on our own and set up our own movement."

Mrs Britain and Mr Fairway spoke against it, but there had been too much dithering, too many lives lost to indecision; great opportunities passed up as if they had been a trip to the cinema.

They discussed it for half an hour, employing arguments such as solidarity and there being no need to reinvent the wheel. Jo Macclesfield was the most voluble voice for splitting. "They've done nothing for us, not one iota of assistance. They sat back and let us die." The vote was twenty-one for separation, with just Mrs Britain and Mr Fairway choosing to stay.

Linda was busy counting heads. "Actually, there are twenty-four of us," she said. "Someone didn't vote."

"I did not think it appropriate," Georgia said. "I am not an English."

"Nor am I," that was Eva. "But I still voted."

"Pie Squared, you are not an English but you have shown yourself to be every bit one of us. You have been an inspiration to us all. You are a leader and a dear colleague. I want a vote that Porky Pie here be accepted as an honorary English with immediate effect."

This vote was unanimous. It left Georgia with rain in her eyes again, great drops moving slowly down her cheeks like the creation of a stalactite.

It took Werner, waking up in his pram and crying for milk, to break the spell.

Georgia had the only armchair in the room, vacated by Harry Bootle who stood by her right shoulder, as if still responsible for her security. There was a pause in the discussion while Georgia settled back in the chair, passing the prepared bottle round the table along a chain of hands, to Mrs Britain who placed it in a jug of boiling water. Only when Werner was slurping at the teat, with Georgia expertly patting her for wind every few minutes, did the talk start again.

"We need a leader," Linda said. "We're officially separate now so we need to vote on a leader."

It was the third time they voted in ten minutes. Georgia did not understand why they did so; thinking it like the schoolyard, when they voted on what game to play next. Grown-ups either gave orders or obeyed them. That was the proper order of things.

But the proper order seemed dispersed on the gentle wind, washed by the dry, brittle sunshine of that December day when the year gives its last gasps and the new one is waiting to inherit.

This election was done with scraps of paper, each person writing the name of who should be leader. Linda, ever the master of ceremonies, collected in twenty-four slips and managed to make a drama out of the count.

"Come on, Linda," Sandy said. "We haven't got all day."

"You have to do these things properly. There, now I've finished. I'll read out the top three in reverse order. Numbers four and below were limited to one vote each."

In third place was Mark with three votes, narrowly beaten by Mr Fairway, who had five to his name.

"But the clear leader, with thirteen votes; a majority of the twenty-four votes cast – and thank you to the Pudding for actually voting this time – is…" She paused for effect, Thomas did a mock drum roll on the table top, "… the winner and our new leader is Mrs Britain!"

And so it was that the lover of the first ever resistance leader, shot in the dockyard by accident, became leader in her own right.

To the calls of "Speech, speech," Mrs Britain said, "No speech today. We have business to attend to, decisions to be made, and actions to take. Today is the first day of the New Resistance. I accept leadership, am overwhelmed by your selection, and proud as shiny buttons. I will serve you dutifully and diligently all my waking moments from now on. Did I say no speech? There, it seems like you have elected an old woman with quite a strain of verbal diarrhoea! Back to business now!"

Georgia listened to the English woman, her cook, with amazement. Here was someone elected, not appointed, and the first thing she had said was she would serve her followers. It made no sense. Followers were to follow, leaders to lead. Where was the order, the structure, the hierarchy in all this?

Next it was Janet's turn to speak. Her purpose was firm and clear. "I need someone to get me to Wiltshire."

"Why Wiltshire?" Sandy asked.

"The beat kids are there. They need me and I intend to go to them."

"That can be easily arranged," Mr Fairway said.

The meeting broke up after Mrs Britain gave a hurried shuffle of top positions, asking Mr Fairway to be her deputy and Jo Macclesfield to be chief of operations with Harry Bootle as Jo's deputy.

"Jo, will you come with me to explain our decision to the old command structure? Sandy, I would like you to go back to Kent with Margaret and take over that region. We will be expanding to other regions in the next few months, approaching each region and asking them to join us. One final word; I did not want this and Mr Fairway and I voted against it, but it is done now and Mr Fairway and I will give our all to make it a success. Have no doubt about that!" As she spoke, Mr Fairway's hand found hers. "We'll meet here again in two weeks. Go carefully and take minimal risks. At the moment, we are about conserving what we have. Later, we will grow again and become stronger."

"Mark, can I have a word?"

"Of course, Georgia." She had noticed that Mark never played with her name. It was as if he held it sacred. "I'll walk partway back with you, but only through the woods. I don't need to get caught again. But what about the baby?"

"Let me help." Dr Hamilton had overheard their conversation. "Let me take your son back in his pram. The walk will do me good!" He patted his belly, as if it added to his argument. "I'll say goodbye now, Fraulein. Call this number if you need me." He handed her a gold embossed card.

Mark and Georgia walked up the hill out of Cheerwell. They turned right at the junction, as if going on up to Hennington, but then turned right again onto a footpath through the woods that surrounded Cheerwell, making it seem a medieval village in a tiny clearing in the forest.

At the start of the footpath, Mark held back so that Georgia could go on the narrow way first. But instead she insisted they walk side-by-side and took the slightly higher ground, rutted with tree roots, to give Mark the main path and easier footing.

"I've got my boots on," she laughed. "I'll be alright."

But she clearly had something on her mind. Something she edged around; several conversations starting and halting awkwardly or changing direction. She asked after his health, was told he was much better, thanks to her care.

She glowed at this. "I was just doing my duty."

Suddenly, Mark stopped walking. They were so close together on the path that Georgia stumbled with the change of pace. Righting herself, turning towards him. She was suddenly face-to-face with Mark.

"Will you marry me?" he asked into the stillness of the December woods. Above, there was double chequering. First, the sky was half-covered in patches of white cloud, like countries on an inverted map, sun shining through where it could. Those rays that made it through the cloud block then had to filter through the bare tree branches before making it to earth. Hence there were patches of deep shade, some blocks of pure sunshine, others of flickering, changing light; a million fluctuating stars somehow visible in a blue and white sky.

Georgia's face was in shadow so he could not see her expression, could not read her thoughts. There was a long silence. He felt compelled to fill it but could not think of anything to say. He had, after all, just asked the most momentous question of his life. He was yet to be answered.

Maybe one day, long in the future when their two bodies and souls were entwined like the ivy which wound its way along the branches of the trees above, maybe then she would declare the panic that hit her at that moment, on hearing those celebrated words.

Could she marry an English?

She had to answer him soon.

But right now, she could not think at all.

What does one do when thinking fails? Rely on instinct, as Jo Macclesfield had done at Betherington Manor, facing the disaster that Heffernott was no longer there? Depend not on reason but on the feeling in your gut, as Mark had done when passing on information to Linda Burton during his tutoring days? As Georgia herself had done in the old nursery, if she only admitted it, when she had approached Mark to first touch him then to lie down with him? But it was so alien to who she was.

But maybe not to the person she had become.

Suddenly, a block of sunlight landed on her slightly upturned face. It felt warm, like spring come early. She felt it in her bones. She suddenly knew her future.

"No," she said, but flatly. "I mean … I want to, nothing would be better, but I can't, not right now."

"Why?" He sensed the struggle within.

"Because when I am single I have a chance of becoming a doctor. I know it is a slim chance but I have to give it everything. I might be able to persuade the authorities that I am an unusual case, especially as Father has had a major promotion. But if I married I would belong to my husband." She did not mention that her family's influence would be lost to her if she married an English, especially one sought by the authorities for treason. "All I know is that I have to become a doctor. It is like a great urge within me. There is nobody I would like to marry more; nobody I could ever love like you, but I would be denying who I am, what my mission is, if I married now."

Most people would have argued long and hard, sensing the terrible dilemma she faced; wanting her for themselves.

But Mark loved her too deeply. He accepted this reason, argument and counter-argument running across his face like racing dogs, before coming to his inevitable conclusion. It blocked out the sun for him, but it was what she wanted. It had to be right.

They started walking again, then talking again, but not with any weight to their words; nothing that would burden the other too much. They forced a laugh about Linda and her playful games. Mark commented on the early snowdrops and how mild and wet the winter had been. They held hands, after a while, Mark using one finger to tickle her palm. She smiled in return, looked across at him, smiled more.

Then they were at the edge of the wood, where the playground started. It was the end of the walk for Mark and Georgia. To their left was the gate to Georgia's and Edmund's old school.

"Edmund is going to the *Statenthrump*," she said, not wanting to part. "I got a place too, but I want to study for a medical degree."

"That's good for Edmund, I suppose." He was thinking of the girl Edmund had killed to escape from the Cavern. Mark had heard the story from Janet.

"He's not all bad, you know."

"Really?" he replied, then said, "Let's not talk about Edmund. We have to part now. It's too risky to be out in the open. I love you, Georgia." They kissed while the wind, free of the sheltering trees, rustled at their coats, strong gusts rising in an attempt to bowl them along together.

Like it should have been.

Something of a Solution

"Where did you go, Georgia?"
"Just for a walk."
"I followed you."
"What? How dare you!"
"I wanted to see where you were going. You've changed since you went away to that hospital place."

Edmund had tracked her and Dr Hamilton from the playing fields all the way by the lanes to Cheerwell, staying just out of sight like he had been taught in surveillance class in camp.

"You were careless, way too careless."

"What do you know, bro?" There was something about the way Georgia asked that question that made Edmund stop his teasing and enquiring. He felt like he had just seen her for the first time.

"I won't tell anyone," he said, but it sounded limp, like he suddenly wanted to be on her side, to have a soulmate.

And for all Georgia's faults, her imperiousness, her arrogance, she recognised something in her brother. Instead of talking, she reached out her fingers and touched him on the cheek. Then she kissed him and said, "You're my brother," but it meant so much more.

And then there was no anger, no rivalry, no jealousy between them. They were left and right, boat and sail, horse and saddle, brother and sister.

And she told him everything. On instinct.

And, in answer, he did not swear to secrecy on the honour of the family name.

There was no need to ask for it, for she trusted him.

"What will you do?" he asked when he had heard everything.

"All I know is that I need to become a doctor. Nothing else will do. I can't marry Mark because then I will lose any chance of persuading Father and Mother to allow me to study medicine."

Georgia was acting on instinct but it took the logic of

Edmund to make a plan.

It did not start well.

"Stuff and nonsense," he said.

"What?" For a moment the new tie between them was stretched unbearably. Georgia wondered whether this was all a ruse and the spiteful, teasing boy was back in the fore.

"I'll explain," he said, without a tint of how he had been. "You've got to be realistic. Mother wants you to go to the *Statenthrump* with me." His chest rose a little with pride; it could not be helped. "There is no way she is ever going to let you go off to study medicine. Firstly, it is against all convention and secondly, she wants you where she can control you." How could a fifteen-year-old boy have such understanding? Georgia wondered.

"But Father…"

"Father be stuffed! No, I mean no disrespect but Georgia, you have to ask yourself, who is in charge in our family? That's right, it is Mother. If she does not want you to go to medical school you will not be going any place that she has any control over."

"So what am I to do?"

"Easy! You go somewhere where she has no control."

"What, I mean where?" It was too much for Georgia to take in. "You don't mean America? We've been told what an awful place that is."

"Well, the beat kids certainly like it. They were full of the place!"

"Yes, but the stories…"

"It doesn't have to be America," Edmund interrupted her again. "It could be anywhere where Mother's influence does not extend. For instance, Australia, New Zealand, Barbados, South Africa…"

"Or Canada?"

"Yes, or Canada."

"There was a girl there today from Canada. I could ask her when I see her again."

"So now you have a plan, sis! Can you help me to pack in return?"

"Yes, Eddie, as soon as I've fed Werner." Had she caught the English name disease or was it just a way to express the fondness she had found for her brother?

But all Edmund heard was the Eddie of the football fields, carefree and easy-going. His heart skipped another beat.

"Georgia, it is so nice to see you dressed respectably. I am sure you agree that those dirty old clothes were best burned." Georgia had been dismayed to lose the clothes Abby had stitched together for her, but then reasoned that they were only material. It did not diminish her experience or her conviction. Clothes do not make people.

Thus, she had gone to the expensive boutiques and dressmakers in Old London, accompanied by her mother. She came away with a new wardrobe of things that were beautiful, exquisite, but held no value for her.

Her mother was talking. She would soon expect an answer. She would have to listen.

"Georgia, my dear, as I have been saying we have to know your intentions with regard to the *Statenthrump*. Edmund left on Monday and I received a phone call from the commandant yesterday saying he was settling in well. I am sure the same would apply to you too if you just got there." Her mother poured coffee from the elegant silver pot into her cup and another for her daughter. She drank hers black but prepared Georgia's with plenty of warmed milk. Georgia felt like asking for tea but knew it would not go down well. Tea was for the English.

"Mother, I'm trying to decide. I need a little time after what I've been through." Georgia was desperate to hold out to the next resistance meeting. That was planned in Harry Bootle's cottage for a week tomorrow. But she was being pressed daily for a decision. Her fear was that her mother would make that decision for her before she could enlist the assistance of her father who was away introducing the new commander to his duties.

"They won't keep it open forever, my girl."

"I know, Mother. Please get them to keep it open a little longer." She knew what would come next; relentless questions about little Werner, his parentage. This would be followed by good, practical suggestions about what to do with the child.

"Mother, please excuse me." She offered no reason, waited for no response; just rose from her chair and left the room, closing the door firmly behind her.

"Georgia…" But it was too late. She was gone. She went upstairs, found Werner almost awake so woke him, changed him, fed him and carried him back down.

"Stephens, where is the pram?" she asked of the first domestic she saw.

"In the back hall, Fraulein." The girl curtsied. "Would you like me to bring it around to the front?"

"No, I will leave by the back door. Fetch my coat and gloves. I will go for a walk with my baby."

"Yes Fraulein."

Twenty minutes later she was on the playing fields, pushing the pram over the lumpy grass, avoiding the tarmac path because it led to the school gates. For a few minutes she watched some boys playing football on a muddy pitch. The goal net had a huge hole in it and the ball kept flying through the net and down into the woods behind. The boys argued all the time about who should go and fetch it. Georgia could not understand why someone was not in charge. Then they could select ball boys who would know to fetch the ball each time without complaint or delay. Better still, she reflected, why not mend the net?

Either way, they would get far more football in.

"The English are impossible," she said.

"At least we have something to distinguish ourselves." Georgia swung around to the direction of the voice, but the sunlight was playing games again, making vision at the edge of the woods difficult.

"Who's there?"

Harry Bootle realised she was frightened and stepped out of the shadows. The protective instinct was hard to kill.

"It's only me."

She had not recognised his voice because it was two shades lighter, rid of much stress.

"Oh Beetle, I mean Bootle, it's just you."

"Yes, it is the Hairy Beetle, Fraulein. Are you all right? You look unwell."

She tried to pass it off; something about being fine, nothing to worry about, just a little tired from pushing the pram over the rough ground. But she failed at the first hurdle; tears broke her vision and made a haze of the world around her.

"Oh Bootle," was all that she could say.

Harry moved right out of the tree cover and took Georgia in his arms. He held her in silence as she sobbed. He knew that words were nothing. He just held her in the dead quiet of the early January day; stillness, frostiness all around.

Much later he asked if she wanted to walk in the woods with him. "I know a way that can take the pram." She nodded, dried her eyes on his handkerchief, checked Werner and made off after Harry.

"I know they call you all sorts of names back there," he indicated his cottage, referring to the resistance meeting, "but to me you will always be Fraulein."

"And you will always be the Hairy Beetle!" she laughed. He laughed, too.

"Tell me about what is worrying you, Fraulein."

And so, for the second time that week, Georgia told the whole story without exception or deception; no twists or turns, just as it came.

They stopped only when Werner needed changing. Georgia placed him on a bed of pine needles and did it quickly and efficiently, taking care to keep a large mat between the needles and Werner. Then they sat with their backs against two giant pines, talking as she fed the baby with a bottle she had kept warm inside her coat.

Harry was an intelligent man, a fine engineer although rusty with disuse in recent years; a capable manager, an efficient administrator. But he could have kicked himself that he did not see the connection that was so obvious. He had read Mark's file when Linda had first sprung him on the household as Georgia's tutor. He had seen, immediately, that Mark was innocent. Mark had been caught up in the raid on the nightclub in '59, was pressed to go in the first place. Harry had liked Mark immediately, never thought of him as a criminal.

But at that present moment, as Georgia, Harry and Werner made stately passage on the old track around the back of the school, he did not have an answer to Georgia's problems.

"Edmund's advice is sound," he said, "although I hate to think of you going to a distant country." That prompted a question from her as to why he cared for her so much.

"I always treated you with disdain," she said.

"Yes, you did. And to be honest the 'Hairy Beetle' thing was, at the time, a step too far. I was incensed. I thought I hated you and your brother. But then I remembered my own son, Jake. He is autistic, you know." She had not known; in fact, had known nothing about the big, slab-like security manager. It had never entered her head to consider any personal aspects. He could have been a cardboard cut-out for all she had cared.

"You mean you have a disabled boy? Does he live with you?"

"Yes and yes." It was a measure of the new relationship that, in return for her honesty, he gave back the same. Both were living with enormous risk. "We care for him at home secretly."

He told Georgia then about the fake death and burial, the tiny coffin weighed down with stones. "At one point the coffin tipped and the stones inside made a terrible racket as they rolled down the length. I thought someone was bound to guess. And if enough people guess then one will surely betray us."

"Did they?"

"Guess? Yes. Betray? No. That was a lesson I learned from this. There is something honourable that binds most humans together. They will give and give for each other; not all humans, but most." His words made Georgia think of the hospital. Had she become bound to the English with all their foolishness? Why tie yourself to chaos? Yet disorder marched the road as any other form of organization would; just with arms swinging erratically, comically.

And pace uneven and unsure.

Like the hospital.

But thoughts of the hospital reminded her of those new friends she had lost. Tears came again, so often these days. She needed to brighten the moment.

"Well, Hairy Fairy, I think that amounts to more words than you have ever said throughout the last five years of our acquaintance!" She stood up, laughing fighting crying. "Come, or we'll never get there."

"Where are we going, Fraulein?" He rose, less agile than her.

"Why, to see your son, of course!"

It was Linda who came up with the solution.

And it happened a lot earlier than Georgia could hope for.

They arrived at Harry's cottage in the late morning. She remembered Harry pointing out the sun close to its zenith. All the greyness and gloom of November and early December had crystallised during the last days of 1965 into sharp days of frost and crunchiness underfoot; like a butterfly from a caterpillar. The sun was a bright hard ball, rising and sinking in the distant southern sky as if away visiting relatives in another world. Hence there was very little heat to warm the still and dry air that sat upon them without pressure; a dab of a paint brush rather than a block of colour.

It seemed a time for making plans, a hopeful time, a time for new life poking through.

And Linda was superb at making plans.

But first Georgia went straight upstairs to meet Jake. He was standing at the desk in his room, bent over a project of his. His father introduced Georgia.

"Have you ever been in an aeroplane?"

"I have not," she replied.

"Would you like to go in mine? Only when I have finished it, of course."

"I would like that a lot. But first I would have to inspect it, to make sure it was capable of flying safely. I would not want your aeroplane to crash."

"The chances are we would all be dead."

"Yes, I agree," Georgia replied, liking Jake instinctively,

although he would clearly be useless in a proper functioning society where everyone had a distinct purpose. "What is the wingspan? And the weight? How do you propose to power it?"

In reply, he offered his papers to her, stepping back slightly from the desk so that she could find space there. They were a mass of detailed drawings and calculations, very neat with tiny writing. He launched into a monologue covering every aspect. Every couple of minutes he would pause, hit himself hard on the side of his head and say, "Focus, focus," then come back to one of the questions Georgia had asked.

Eventually he stopped, dropped onto his bed and curled up.

"This is very impressive, Jake." But he was not listening, humming to himself, as if winding down a great spring inside him.

"The beauty of it," Harry said, coming into the room from his station by the door, "is that it all makes sense. If he were able to build this aeroplane it would fly."

"How do you know?"

"Because I am, or was, an aeronautical design engineer."

"But … you were always … why?"

"It was before the invasion. I was a young designer then, just starting out. Then after the invasion it was not permitted so I became a security guard. Twenty years later your father appointed me head of personal security and five years after that he fired me."

That was the history of the Hairy Beetle. It was a history that Georgia had never asked about, despite daily contact with this big, silent man.

It had never crossed her mind to ask, but she wished now that she had.

They returned downstairs, where the kitchen was not so packed as the meeting but still fairly full, with people coming and going. Harry's mother was boiling water for tea.

"It's like a bloody café in here," she said, "only we don't get tips! Would you like a cuppa?"

Before Georgia could reply that she would like a cup of tea to warm her, Linda barged in on her crutches shouting, "Did I hear talk of a brew? Put me down for a big mug, I'm parched. Oh, hello there, Stalk. All well with you?"

"Stalk?" Georgia looked puzzled. "I can't work that one out."

"Pork Stalk, it rhymes. And you've got super long legs too, like a stalk."

"Yes, but they have bumps all over them. Look." She pulled up the skirt of her dress a few inches, pushed down her socks to reveal her white skin with a series of tiny pale pink mole hills spoiling her otherwise smooth legs.

'Take a look at mine, then!" Linda replied, pulling up her skirt also to reveal the plaster on one leg and a nasty bullet scar on the other.

Georgia was drawn to examine her. It was instinct, not reason. She was on the mend but Georgia could not help but approach it from a medical perspective.

"How is the plaster? Is it itching? I see the bullet wound is mending well. I think you will always have a scar there but maybe it will look quite dashing. It is much fainter than last time I saw it."

"I'm sorry, Fraulein, I was showing off. You've dressed that wound a hundred times. You know exactly what it is like. I shouldn't have…" Linda was without words for once.

"You called me Fraulein?"

"Yes, I suppose I did."

"I prefer Porkie, or Pie, or even Stalk."

"What brings you here, Georgie?" Janet asked. "Did you come to say goodbye to me?"

"Are you going? To the beat kids?" Georgia remembered, but it still shook her, not wanting to lose her friend to others. "I don't know what brought me here. I just walked aimlessly for a while and then followed Beetle, I mean Bootle … Harry, I mean." Her voice petered out as she tottered between the two worlds she knew; the secure and ordered one and the wild and impetuous one. She plunged from security into adventure and then frantically backpedalled for safety again.

"Yes, I'm going today, back to the beat kids. It's where I

belong, Pork." The last comment was added because Janet could see the stress on Georgia. "You know we did not speak about your future at the last meeting," she added.

"I have a place at the *Statenthrump*." It was intended with pride but came out with a sigh of resignation."

"Is that what you want?"

"It is a great honour." That was Georgia's second attempt at salvaging something of the past, of reasserting some order in the chaos that lapped at her, threatening to topple her into the ocean.

"Stuff and nonsense!" As Linda spoke, she raised her crutch and pointed the end at Georgia's chest, pinning her in a skewering type motion.

'What on earth..?" Janet started, but Linda interrupted her.

"It is clear as anything, our young Porkie Pie here needs to become a doctor."

"But I can't. The authorities won't allow it. I'd have to go some other part of the world where they have no say. And there is no way I will get an exit visa even if I could get permission to study."

"Where would you go? No, don't say you can't go, just imagine a mo, where you would go if you could."

It was too hard a question for Georgia. She saw rapid pictures in her mind, like the old silent movies, flicking from one to the other with the little she knew of the outside world. Hence there were kangaroos and koalas on the beach in one scene, cowboys chasing Red Indians in another. Then she thought of what she had heard about these places; they were raw, violent, full of corruption. The pictures faded as blood spilled over them, from outside inwards; seeping like floodwaters over the plain. The pictures were gone. She had no answer. She closed her eyes, hoping to rid herself of the visions; to think with clarity and logic like she had been taught.

Taught since her earliest days.

But when she opened them again there was nothing but light, as if her head was buried in the deep folds of a pure-white wedding dress. There were little movements, blurs around the expanse of white. She forced herself to focus on one, centre-right. It formed slowly into a person, features emerging like a figure approaching in a gun sight. It was a young face with eyes that were hard and soft at the same time, reflecting hardness out and softness in. Her hair was tied up but looked like it would fall in abundance past her shoulders if only it were freed. She was small. It was Eva. She could see that now.

"Canada," she said. "I would go to Canada."

"My country," said Eva, her smile breaking, releasing tension in Georgia.

"Yes, your country. If your people will have me."

"I am sure they will, Porkie. We can help you get to the embassy."

"Stuff and nonsense!" repeated Linda, evidently the saying of the moment.

"What do you mean?"

"I mean, she doesn't need to apply for a visa and all that stuff and nonsense! All she needs to do is marry Mark."

"But … how … why?"

"Don't you know? I read Mark's prison file inside out. His father is Canadian. He came across on a teacher exchange years ago, married Mark's mother and stayed. Mark is a Canadian citizen. Mark's wife can go anywhere she pleases with him … as long as it is Canada, of course!"

Thirty minutes later, Georgia was pushing the pram back along the path that skirted her old school. Werner, having been fed again, was gurgling and spluttering, looking up at his adoptive mother.

Beside her walked Mark. He had come to the kitchen as Georgia was leaving, hugging Janet and telling each other they would meet again soon. There was a brightness in their tears that Mark could not understand. But it matched the day for the wind had tempered and warmed, more akin to a spring breeze. It seemed to Mark like a light day, one with nothing much to do except plan the future. Yet it sat so incongruously with the fact that Georgia was going away, either to the *Statenthrump* or, if she was lucky, a medical school somewhere that could be persuaded to take her. He was not a part of that future.

On this walk it was Georgia's turn to stop suddenly. The path was wide enough and even enough that Mark did not stumble.

"Marky, remember that question you asked me last time?"

"I could never forget." The answer had been slow to come but a definite no.

"Ask me again."

"Georgia, will you…"

"No!"

"They why ask me to ask again?"

"I meant no, don't ask me again like that. Do it like a gentleman should."

He knelt down on one knee, took her hand in his and asked her again to marry him.

"Yes," she said, her clear blue eyes reflecting the winter sky high above their heads.

2024: A History of the Future

Brexit is dead. Long live Brexit.

George Unwin-Smith is from the establishment; educated, enlightened, wearing privilege as if it were his skin. Yet he joins a ragbag of resistance fighters, the Spiders, seemingly forever on the back foot.

Maybe because of Gerry Matthews, equally well-educated, from across the Atlantic. She believes every person has a destiny, a path to follow; they just have to find it.

George is not a natural fighter. His habitat is not the battlefield or skirmishes amongst rocks and bushes, rifle and radio in hand.

Yet, somehow, he has to find a way through this impossible barrier that is the United States of Europe. He has to abandon childish images and learn that heroes are those that persevere and confide in their colleagues, pooling strengths and weaknesses as a true team.

The authorities will do anything to stop the rebels, including breaking the law; their law. It becomes a desperate struggle to turn the tide and stand up for liberty.

Far from his comfort zone, surrounded by foes and with just a handful of close friends to help him, it falls to George to lead his country to a new beginning.

18 Acres of England

Ben Franklin has a mind-numbing job as a White House security guard. Dakota Jamieson is one quarter into a forty-year sentence for a crime she didn't commit. The link is Dakota's mother who is Ben's landlady in DC.

Ben stumbles upon a secret so incredible it threatens to turn the western world in on itself, setting friendly nations against each other; undermining the foundations of the first world.

The question is: Did America get its independence or is it still a vassal of the British Empire?

Dakota has slaved her way through a history degree from her prison cell. Now, for her master's thesis she must uncover what went on a quarter of a millennium ago, when America and Britain were sworn enemies. She has to call upon her scant resources and, surprisingly, Ben is chief amongst them.

Richard Sutherland was long dead to Ben and Dakota. Centuries had passed but it was their mission to bring out his legacy from the depths of history.

Both Ben and Dakota fight the system and must pull on every fibre, flexing their personalities in an attempt at the truth. And they find the most unexpected friendships along the way.

Through love, determination, and long forgotten documents they will unravel the life changing mystery that lay upon American soil.